Alice au Pays des Merveilles

A French to English Bilingual Book with French to English Dictionary

Learn French Fast and Easy with Dual Language Parallel Text Books

Originally written by Lewis Carroll. Translation by Henri Bué.

Edited by MostUsedWords
Dictionary by MostUsedWords

3rd edition. First Printing, May 2019

MostUsedWords
10685-B Hazelhurst Dr. # 22933
HOUSTON, TX 77043
United States

www.MostUsedWords.com

Table of Contents

Table of Contents 3
Preface 4
On Bilingual Books 5
1. Down the Rabbit Hole 7
1. Au Fond du Terrier 7
2. The Pool of Tears 13
2. La Mare aux Larmes 13
3. A Caucas Race and a Long Tail 19
3. La Course Cocasse 19
4. The Rabbit Sends in a Little Bill 24
4. l'Habitation du Lapin Blanc 24
5. Advice from a Caterpillar 31
5. Conseils d'une Chenille 31
6. Pig and Pepper 38
6. Porc et Poivre 38
7. A Mad Tea Party 46
7. Un Thé de Fous 46
8. The Queen's Croquet Ground 53
8. Le Croquet de la Reine 53
9. The Mock Turtle's Story 61
9. Histoire de la Fausse-Tortue 61
10. The Lobster's Quadrille 68
10. Le Quadrille de Homards 68
11. Who Stole the Tarts? 74
11. Qui a Volé les Tartes? 74
12. Alice's Evidence 80
12. Déposition d'Alice 80
How To Use This Dictionary 87
French-English Frequency Dictionary 88
French-English Dictionary 109
Contact, Further Reading & Resources 133

Preface

Hello. Thank you for your purchase! We at MostUsedWords value each and every customer.

You probably already know the value of reading when it comes to expanding your vocabulary in a language you're learning. If not, we give you some short pointers in the next chapter.

We made this book to help you improve your French. This is Lewis Carroll's original version of the story, aligned with its official translation by Henri Bué.

It´s a great book for beginner to intermediate students. But ultimately, everyone can enjoy this wonderful story.

As you can see from the numbers below, this book only contains 2032 different lemmas. A lemma is the dictionary form of a word.

Lexical Information (French version)	
Number of characters (including spaces) :	154162
Number of characters (without spaces) :	117499
Number of words :	30278
Number of lemmas:	2032
Lexical density :	11.5827
Number of sentences :	1752
Number of syllables :	41798

We hope this book brings you much value and helps you on your journey of learning French.

If you have read this book, please let us know your feedback by leaving us a review on Amazon or any other online retailer, our website store.mostusedwords.com or you can send an e-mail to contact@mostusedwords.com.

Customer feedback helps us to improve our products. We can find out about our strengths and discover where we can do better.

Thank you in advance and enjoy this book!

On Bilingual Books

A tried and tested method, bilingual books, also known as parallel text books or dual language books, have been used to assist language learning for hundreds of years.

There are several benefits to be gained by reading bilingual books.

You will naturally broaden your vocabulary.

The best-known benefit of reading is that you broaden your vocabulary quickly. We know that a single exposure to a word does not let you learn that piece of vocabulary. Experts in language learning believe that you need to encounter a word or phrase in different contexts between 15 and 20 times to have a high possibility of remembering the word or phrase.

You will become a better reader

The more language students read, the better readers they become. A big part of this is learning new vocabulary. But several studies have shown that reading also significantly helps to increase other crucial language skills.

You will improve your writing skills

If you spend a lot of time reading French texts, your proficiency in written French will improve. (Elley and Mangubhai 1981, and Hafiz and Tudor 1989). This is probably because as you encounter more language, more frequently, through extensive reading, your language acquisition mechanism is ready to reproduce what you learned by reading in writing.

You will become better at listening and speaking

Research shows that if you read a lot, you improve your listening and speaking skills. For example, Cho and Krashen (1994) reported that their four adult ESL learners increased competence in both listening and speaking abilities through reading extensively. Extensive reading benefits all language skills, not only reading and writing.

You will be more motivated to read.

The one-to-one sentence correspondence will save you from reaching for the dictionary to look up the meaning of a word. You can read a more complex text without feeling lost in translation.

You can also discover how the grammar rules of your target language compare with your own, thanks to this layout. You'll be able to take advantage of the similarities, and be aware of the differences between English and French.

Learn anytime, anywhere, on your own schedule.

Language students can read anywhere and at any time. Reading helps them become more independent learners. You should decide what, when, where and how often you read. By sitting down and reading, you're going to get yourself farther, faster. Invest in yourself now, and get this book.

1. Down the Rabbit Hole

Alice was beginning to get very tired of sitting by her sister on the bank, and of having nothing to do: once or twice she had peeped into the book her sister was reading, but it had no pictures or conversations in it:

and what is the use of a book,' thought Alice 'without pictures or conversation?'

So she was considering in her own mind (as well as she could, for the hot day made her feel very sleepy and stupid), whether the pleasure of making a daisy-chain would be worth the trouble of getting up and picking the daisies, when suddenly a White Rabbit with pink eyes ran close by her.

There was nothing so very remarkable in that; nor did Alice think it so very much out of the way to hear the Rabbit say to itself,

Oh dear! Oh dear! I shall be late!'

(when she thought it over afterwards, it occurred to her that she ought to have wondered at this, but at the time it all seemed quite natural);

but when the Rabbit actually took a watch out of its waistcoat-pocket, and looked at it, and then hurried on, Alice started to her feet, for it flashed across her mind that she had never before seen a rabbit with either a waistcoat-pocket, or a watch to take out of it, and burning with curiosity, she ran across the field after it, and fortunately was just in time to see it pop down a large rabbit-hole under the hedge.

In another moment down went Alice after it, never once considering how in the world she was to get out again.

The rabbit-hole went straight on like a tunnel for some way, and then dipped suddenly down, so suddenly that Alice had not a moment to think about stopping herself before she found herself falling down a very deep well.

Either the well was very deep, or she fell very slowly, for she had plenty of time as she went down to look about her and to wonder what was going to happen next.

First, she tried to look down and make out what she was coming to, but it was too dark to see anything; then she

1. Au Fond du Terrier

Alice, assise auprès de sa sœur sur le gazon, commençait à s'ennuyer de rester là à ne rien faire; une ou deux fois elle avait jeté les yeux sur le livre que lisait sa sœur; mais quoi! pas d'images, pas de dialogues!

"La belle avance," pensait Alice, "qu'un livre sans images, sans causeries!"

Elle s'était mise à réfléchir, (tant bien que mal, car la chaleur du jour l'endormait et la rendait lourde,) se demandant si le plaisir de faire une couronne de marguerites valait bien la peine de se lever et de cueillir les fleurs, quand tout à coup un lapin blanc aux yeux roses passa près d'elle.

Il n'y avait rien là de bien étonnant, et Alice ne trouva même pas très-extraordinaire d'entendre parler le Lapin qui se disait:

"Ah! j'arriverai trop tard!"

(En y songeant après, il lui sembla bien qu'elle aurait dû s'en étonner, mais sur le moment cela lui avait paru tout naturel.)

Cependant, quand le Lapin vint à tirer une montre de son gousset, la regarda, puis se prit à courir de plus belle, Alice sauta sur ses pieds, frappée de cette idée que jamais elle n'avait vu de lapin avec un gousset et une montre. Entraînée par la curiosité elle s'élança sur ses traces à travers le champ, et arriva tout juste à temps pour le voir disparaître dans un large trou au pied d'une haie.

Un instant après, Alice était à la poursuite du Lapin dans le terrier, sans songer comment elle en sortirait.

Pendant un bout de chemin le trou allait tout droit comme un tunnel, puis tout à coup il plongeait perpendiculairement d'une façon si brusque qu'Alice se sentit tomber comme dans un puits d'une grande profondeur, avant même d'avoir pensé à se retenir.

De deux choses l'une, ou le puits était vraiment bien profond, ou elle tombait bien doucement; car elle eut tout le loisir, dans sa chute, de regarder autour d'elle et de se demander avec étonnement ce qu'elle allait devenir.

D'abord elle regarda dans le fond du trou pour savoir où elle allait; mais il y faisait bien trop sombre pour y rien voir.

looked at the sides of the well, and noticed that they were filled with cupboards and book-shelves; here and there she saw maps and pictures hung upon pegs.

Ensuite elle porta les yeux sur les parois du puits, et s'aperçut qu'elles étaient garnies d'armoires et d'étagères; çà et là, elle vit pendues à des clous des cartes géographiques et des images.

She took down a jar from one of the shelves as she passed; it was labelled 'ORANGE MARMALADE', but to her great disappointment it was empty:

En passant elle prit sur un rayon un pot de confiture portant cette étiquette, “MARMELADE D'ORANGES.” Mais, à son grand regret, le pot était vide:

she did not like to drop the jar for fear of killing somebody, so managed to put it into one of the cupboards as she fell past it.

elle n'osait le laisser tomber dans la crainte de tuer quelqu'un; aussi s'arrangea-t-elle de manière à le déposer en passant dans une des armoires.

Well!' thought Alice to herself: 'after such a fall as this, I shall think nothing of tumbling down stairs! How brave they'll all think me at home! Why, I wouldn't say anything about it, even if I fell off the top of the house!' (Which was very likely true.)

“Certes,” dit Alice, “après une chute pareille je ne me moquerai pas mal de dégringoler l'escalier! Comme ils vont me trouver brave chez nous! Je tomberais du haut des toits que je ne ferais pas entendre une plainte.” (Ce qui était bien probable.)

Down, down, down. Would the fall never come to an end! 'I wonder how many miles I've fallen by this time?' she said aloud. 'I must be getting somewhere near the centre of the earth. Let me see: that would be four thousand miles down, I think—'

Tombe, tombe, tombe! “Cette chute n'en finira donc pas! Je suis curieuse de savoir combien de milles j'ai déjà faits,” dit-elle tout haut. “Je dois être bien près du centre de la terre. Voyons donc, cela serait à quatre mille milles de profondeur, il me semble.”

(for, you see, Alice had learnt several things of this sort in her lessons in the schoolroom, and though this was not a very good opportunity for showing off her knowledge, as there was no one to listen to her, still it was good practice to say it over)

(Comme vous voyez, Alice avait appris pas mal de choses dans ses leçons; et bien que ce ne fût pas là une très-bonne occasion de faire parade de son savoir, vu qu'il n'y avait point d'auditeur, cependant c'était un bon exercice que de répéter sa leçon.)

'—yes, that's about the right distance—but then I wonder what Latitude or Longitude I've got to?' (Alice had no idea what Latitude was, or Longitude either, but thought they were nice grand words to say.)

“Oui, c'est bien à peu près cela; mais alors à quel degré de latitude ou de longitude est-ce que je me trouve?” (Alice n'avait pas la moindre idée de ce que voulait dire latitude ou longitude, mais ces grands mots lui paraissaient beaux et sonores.)

Presently she began again. 'I wonder if I shall fall right through the earth! How funny it'll seem to come out among the people that walk with their heads downward! The Antipathies, I think—'

Bientôt elle reprit: “Si j'allais traverser complétement la terre? Comme ça serait drôle de se trouver au milieu de gens qui marchent la tête en bas. Aux Antipathies, je crois.”

(she was rather glad there was no one listening, this time, as it didn't sound at all the right word)

(Elle n'était pas fâchée cette fois qu'il n'y eût personne là pour l'entendre, car ce mot ne lui faisait pas l'effet d'être bien juste.)

'—but I shall have to ask them what the name of the country is, you know. Please, Ma'am, is this New Zealand or Australia?'

“Eh mais, j'aurai à leur demander le nom du pays. — Pardon, Madame, est-ce ici la Nouvelle-Zemble ou l'Australie?” —

(and she tried to curtsey as she spoke—fancy curtseying as you're falling through the air! Do you think you could manage it?)

En même temps elle essaya de faire la révérence. (Quelle idée! Faire la révérence en l'air! Dites-moi un peu, comment vous y prendriez-vous?)

'And what an ignorant little girl she'll think me for asking! No, it'll never do to ask: perhaps I shall see it written up somewhere.'

“Quelle petite ignorante! pensera la dame quand je lui ferai cette question. Non, il ne faut pas demander cela; peut-être le verrai-je écrit quelque part.”

Down, down, down. There was nothing else to do, so Alice soon began talking again. 'Dinah'll miss me very much to-night, I should think!' (Dinah was the cat.)

Tombe, tombe, tombe! — Donc Alice, faute d'avoir rien de mieux à faire, se remit à se parler: “Dinah remarquera mon absence ce soir, bien sûr.” (Dinah c'était son chat.)

'I hope they'll remember her saucer of milk at tea-time. Dinah my dear! I wish you were down here with me! There are no mice in the air, I'm afraid, but you might catch a bat, and that's very like a mouse, you know.

“Pourvu qu'on n'oublie pas de lui donner sa jatte de lait à l'heure du thé. Dinah, ma minette, que n'es-tu ici avec moi? Il n'y a pas de souris dans les airs, j'en ai bien peur; mais tu pourrais attraper une chauve-souris, et cela ressemble beaucoup à une souris, tu sais.

But do cats eat bats, I wonder?' And here Alice began to get rather sleepy, and went on saying to herself, in a dreamy sort of way,

Mais les chats mangent-ils les chauves-souris?” Ici le sommeil commença à gagner Alice. Elle répétait, à moitié endormie:

'Do cats eat bats? Do cats eat bats?' and sometimes: 'Do bats eat cats?' for, you see, as she couldn't answer either question, it didn't much matter which way she put it.

“Les chats mangent-ils les chauves-souris? Les chats mangent-ils les chauves-souris?” Et quelquefois: “Les chauves-souris mangent-elles les chats?” Car vous comprenez bien que, puisqu'elle ne pouvait répondre ni à l'une ni à l'autre de ces questions, peu importait la manière de les poser.

She felt that she was dozing off, and had just begun to dream that she was walking hand in hand with Dinah, and saying to her very earnestly,

Elle s'assoupissait et commençait à rêver qu'elle se promenait tenant Dinah par la main, lui disant très-sérieusement :

'Now, Dinah, tell me the truth: did you ever eat a bat?' when suddenly, thump! thump! down she came upon a heap of sticks and dry leaves, and the fall was over.

“Voyons, Dinah, dis-moi la vérité, as-tu jamais mangé des chauves-souris?” Quand tout à coup, pouf! la voilà étendue sur un tas de fagots et de feuilles sèches, — et elle a fini de tomber.

Alice was not a bit hurt, and she jumped up on to her feet in a moment: she looked up, but it was all dark overhead; before her was another long passage, and the White Rabbit was still in sight, hurrying down it.

Alice ne s'était pas fait le moindre mal. Vite elle se remet sur ses pieds et regarde en l'air; mais tout est noir là-haut. Elle voit devant elle un long passage et le Lapin Blanc qui court à toutes jambes.

There was not a moment to be lost: away went Alice like the wind, and was just in time to hear it say, as it turned a corner: 'Oh my ears and whiskers, how late it's getting!'

Il n'y a pas un instant à perdre; Alice part comme le vent et arrive tout juste à temps pour entendre le Lapin dire, tandis qu'il tourne le coin: “Par ma moustache et mes oreilles, comme il se fait tard!”

She was close behind it when she turned the corner, but the Rabbit was no longer to be seen: she found herself in a long, low hall, which was lit up by a row of lamps hanging from the roof.

Elle n'en était plus qu'à deux pas: mais le coin tourné, le Lapin avait disparu. Elle se trouva alors dans une salle longue et basse, éclairée par une rangée de lampes pendues au plafond.

There were doors all round the hall, but they were all locked; and when Alice had been all the way down one side and up the other, trying every door, she walked sadly down the middle, wondering how she was ever to get out again.

Il y avait des portes tout autour de la salle: ces portes étaient toutes fermées, et, après avoir vainement tenté d'ouvrir celles du côté droit, puis celles du côté gauche, Alice se promena tristement au beau milieu de cette salle, se demandant comment elle en sortirait.

Suddenly she came upon a little three-legged table, all made of solid glass; there was nothing on it except a tiny golden key, and Alice's first thought was that it might belong to one of the doors of the hall; but, alas! either the locks were too large, or the key was too small, but at any rate it would not open any of them.

However, on the second time round, she came upon a low curtain she had not noticed before, and behind it was a little door about fifteen inches high: she tried the little golden key in the lock, and to her great delight it fitted!

Alice opened the door and found that it led into a small passage, not much larger than a rat-hole: she knelt down and looked along the passage into the loveliest garden you ever saw.

How she longed to get out of that dark hall, and wander about among those beds of bright flowers and those cool fountains, but she could not even get her head though the doorway;

and even if my head would go through,' thought poor Alice: 'it would be of very little use without my shoulders. Oh, how I wish I could shut up like a telescope! I think I could, if I only know how to begin.' For, you see, so many out-of-the-way things had happened lately, that Alice had begun to think that very few things indeed were really impossible. There seemed to be no use in waiting by the little door, so she went back to the table, half hoping she might find another key on it, or at any rate a book of rules for shutting people up like telescopes: this time she found a little bottle on it, ('which certainly was not here before,' said Alice,) and round the neck of the bottle was a paper label, with the words 'DRINK ME' beautifully printed on it in large letters.

It was all very well to say 'Drink me,' but the wise little Alice was not going to do that in a hurry.

'No, I'll look first,' she said: 'and see whether it's marked "poison" or not'; for she had read several nice little histories about children who had got burnt, and eaten up by wild beasts and other unpleasant things, all because they would not remember the simple rules their friends had taught them:

such as, that a red-hot poker will burn you if you hold it too long; and that if you cut your finger very deeply with a knife, it usually bleeds; and she had never forgotten that, if you drink much from a bottle marked 'poison,' it is almost certain to disagree with you, sooner or later.

Tout à coup elle rencontra sur son passage une petite table à trois pieds, en verre massif, et rien dessus qu'une toute petite clef d'or. Alice pensa aussitôt que ce pouvait être celle d'une des portes; mais hélas! soit que les serrures fussent trop grandes, soit que la clef fût trop petite, elle ne put toujours en ouvrir aucune.

Cependant, ayant fait un second tour, elle aperçut un rideau placé très-bas et qu'elle n'avait pas vu d'abord; par derrière se trouvait encore une petite porte à peu près quinze pouces de haut; elle essaya la petite clef d'or à la serrure, et, à sa grande joie, il se trouva qu'elle y allait à merveille.

Alice ouvrit la porte, et vit qu'elle conduisait dans un étroit passage à peine plus large qu'un trou à rat. Elle s'agenouilla, et, jetant les yeux le long du passage, découvrit le plus ravissant jardin du monde.

Oh! Qu'il lui tardait de sortir de cette salle ténébreuse et d'errer au milieu de ces carrés de fleurs brillantes, de ces fraîches fontaines! Mais sa tête ne pouvait même pas passer par la porte.

"Et quand même ma tête y passerait," pensait Alice, "à quoi cela servirait-il sans mes épaules? Oh! que je voudrais donc avoir la faculté de me fermer comme un télescope! Ça se pourrait peut-être, si je savais comment m'y prendre." Il lui était déjà arrivé tant de choses extraordinaires, qu'Alice commençait à croire qu'il n'y en avait guère d'impossibles. Comme cela n'avançait à rien de passer son temps à attendre à la petite porte, elle retourna vers la table, espérant presque y trouver une autre clef, ou tout au moins quelque grimoire donnant les règles à suivre pour se fermer comme un télescope. Cette fois elle trouva sur la table une petite bouteille (qui certes n'était pas là tout à l'heure). Au cou de cette petite bouteille était attachée une étiquette en papier, avec ces mots "BUVEZ-MOI" admirablement imprimés en grosses lettres.

C'est bien facile à dire "Buvez-moi," mais Alice était trop fine pour obéir à l'aveuglette.

"Examinons d'abord," dit-elle, "et voyons s'il y a écrit dessus "Poison" ou non." Car elle avait lu dans de jolis petits contes, que des enfants avaient été brûlés, dévorés par des bêtes féroces, et qu'il leur était arrivé d'autres choses très-désagréables, tout cela pour ne s'être pas souvenus des instructions bien simples que leur donnaient leurs parents:

par exemple, que le tisonnier chauffé à blanc brûle les mains qui le tiennent trop longtemps; que si on se fait au doigt une coupure profonde, il saigne d'ordinaire; et elle n'avait point oublié que si l'on boit immodérément d'une bouteille marquée "Poison" cela ne manque pas de brouiller le cœur tôt ou tard.

However, this bottle was not marked 'poison,' so Alice ventured to taste it, and finding it very nice,

Cependant, comme cette bouteille n'était pas marquée "Poison," Alice se hasarda à en goûter le contenu, et le trouvant fort bon,

(it had, in fact, a sort of mixed flavour of cherry-tart, custard, pine-apple, roast turkey, toffee, and hot buttered toast,) she very soon finished it off.

(au fait c'était comme un mélange de tarte aux cerises, de crême, d'ananas, de dinde truffée, de nougat, et de rôties au beurre,) elle eut bientôt tout avalé.

'What a curious feeling!' said Alice; 'I must be shutting up like a telescope.'

"Je me sens toute drôle," dit Alice, "on dirait que je rentre en moi-même et que je me ferme comme un télescope."

And so it was indeed: she was now only ten inches high, and her face brightened up at the thought that she was now the right size for going through the little door into that lovely garden.

C'est bien ce qui arrivait en effet. Elle n'avait plus que dix pouces de haut, et un éclair de joie passa sur son visage à la pensée qu'elle était maintenant de la grandeur voulue pour pénétrer par la petite porte dans ce beau jardin.

First, however, she waited for a few minutes to see if she was going to shrink any further: she felt a little nervous about this; 'for it might end, you know,' said Alice to herself: 'in my going out altogether, like a candle. I wonder what I should be like then?'

Elle attendit pourtant quelques minutes, pour voir si elle allait rapetisser encore. Cela lui faisait bien un peu peur. "Songez donc," se disait Alice, "je pourrais bien finir par m'éteindre comme une chandelle. Que deviendrais-je alors?"

And she tried to fancy what the flame of a candle is like after the candle is blown out, for she could not remember ever having seen such a thing.

Et elle cherchait à s'imaginer l'air que pouvait avoir la flamme d'une chandelle éteinte, car elle ne se rappelait pas avoir jamais rien vu de la sorte.

After a while, finding that nothing more happened, she decided on going into the garden at once;

Un moment après, voyant qu'il ne se passait plus rien, elle se décida à aller de suite au jardin;

but, alas for poor Alice, when she got to the door, she found she had forgotten the little golden key, and when she went back to the table for it, she found she could not possibly reach it:

mais hélas, pauvre Alice! en arrivant à la porte, elle s'aperçut qu'elle avait oublié la petite clef d'or. Elle revint sur ses pas pour la prendre sur la table. Bah! impossible d'atteindre à la clef qu'elle voyait bien clairement à travers le verre.

she could see it quite plainly through the glass, and she tried her best to climb up one of the legs of the table, but it was too slippery; and when she had tired herself out with trying, the poor little thing sat down and cried.

Elle fit alors tout son possible pour grimper le long d'un des pieds de la table, mais il était trop glissant; et enfin, épuisée de fatigue, la pauvre enfant s'assit et pleura.

Come, there's no use in crying like that!' said Alice to herself, rather sharply; 'I advise you to leave off this minute!'

"Allons, à quoi bon pleurer ainsi," se dit Alice vivement. "Je vous conseille, Mademoiselle, de cesser tout de suite!"

She generally gave herself very good advice, (though she very seldom followed it), and sometimes she scolded herself so severely as to bring tears into her eyes;

Elle avait pour habitude de se donner de très-bons conseils (bien qu'elle les suivît rarement), et quelquefois elle se grondait si fort que les larmes lui en venaient aux yeux;

and once she remembered trying to box her own ears for having cheated herself in a game of croquet she was playing against herself, for this curious child was very fond of pretending to be two people.

une fois même elle s'était donné des tapes pour avoir triché dans une partie de croquet qu'elle jouait toute seule; car cette étrange enfant aimait beaucoup à faire deux personnages.

'But it's no use now,' thought poor Alice: 'to pretend to be two people! Why, there's hardly enough of me left to make one respectable person!'

"Mais," pensa la pauvre Alice, "il n'y a plus moyen de faire deux personnages, à présent qu'il me reste à peine de quoi en faire un."

Soon her eye fell on a little glass box that was lying under the table: she opened it, and found in it a very small cake, on which the words 'EAT ME' were beautifully marked in currants.

Well, I'll eat it,' said Alice: 'and if it makes me grow larger, I can reach the key; and if it makes me grow smaller, I can creep under the door; so either way I'll get into the garden, and I don't care which happens!'

She ate a little bit, and said anxiously to herself: 'Which way? Which way?', holding her hand on the top of her head to feel which way it was growing, and she was quite surprised to find that she remained the same size:

to be sure, this generally happens when one eats cake, but Alice had got so much into the way of expecting nothing but out-of-the-way things to happen, that it seemed quite dull and stupid for life to go on in the common way.

So she set to work, and very soon finished off the cake.

Elle aperçut alors une petite boîte en verre qui était sous la table, l'ouvrit et y trouva un tout petit gâteau sur lequel les mots "MANGEZ-MOI" étaient admirablement tracés avec des raisins de Corinthe.

"Tiens, je vais le manger," dit Alice: "si cela me fait grandir, je pourrai atteindre à la clef; si cela me fait rapetisser, je pourrai ramper sous la porte; d'une façon ou de l'autre, je pénétrerai dans le jardin, et alors, arrive que pourra!"

Elle mangea donc un petit morceau du gâteau, et, portant sa main sur sa tête, elle se dit tout inquiète: "Lequel est-ce? Lequel est-ce?" Elle voulait savoir si elle grandissait ou rapetissait, et fut tout étonnée de rester la même;

franchement, c'est ce qui arrive le plus souvent lorsqu'on mange du gâteau; mais Alice avait tellement pris l'habitude de s'attendre à des choses extraordinaires, que cela lui paraissait ennuyeux et stupide de vivre comme tout le monde.

Aussi elle se remit à l'œuvre, et eut bien vite fait disparaître le gâteau.

2. The Pool of Tears

Curiouser and curiouser!' cried Alice (she was so much surprised, that for the moment she quite forgot how to speak good English);

'now I'm opening out like the largest telescope that ever was! Good-bye, feet!' (for when she looked down at her feet, they seemed to be almost out of sight, they were getting so far off).

'Oh, my poor little feet, I wonder who will put on your shoes and stockings for you now, dears? I'm sure I shan't be able! I shall be a great deal too far off to trouble myself about you: you must manage the best way you can;

—but I must be kind to them,' thought Alice: 'or perhaps they won't walk the way I want to go! Let me see: I'll give them a new pair of boots every Christmas.'

And she went on planning to herself how she would manage it. 'They must go by the carrier,' she thought; 'and how funny it'll seem, sending presents to one's own feet! And how odd the directions will look!

ALICE'S RIGHT FOOT, ESQ.

HEARTHRUG,

NEAR THE FENDER,

(WITH ALICE'S LOVE).

Oh dear, what nonsense I'm talking!'

Just then her head struck against the roof of the hall: in fact she was now more than nine feet high, and she at once took up the little golden key and hurried off to the garden door.

Poor Alice! It was as much as she could do, lying down on one side, to look through into the garden with one eye; but to get through was more hopeless than ever: she sat down and began to cry again.

You ought to be ashamed of yourself,' said Alice: 'a great girl like you,' (she might well say this): 'to go on crying in this way! Stop this moment, I tell you!'

2. La Mare aux Larmes

“De plus très-curieux en plus très-curieux!” s'écria Alice (sa surprise était si grande qu'elle ne pouvait s'exprimer correctement):

“Voilà que je m'allonge comme le plus grand télescope qui fût jamais! Adieu mes pieds!” (Elle venait de baisser les yeux, et ses pieds lui semblaient s'éloigner à perte de vue.)

“Oh! mes pauvres petits pieds! Qui vous mettra vos bas et vos souliers maintenant, mes mignons? Quant à moi, je ne le pourrai certainement pas! Je serai bien trop loin pour m'occuper de vous: arrangez-vous du mieux que vous pourrez.

— Il faut cependant que je sois bonne pour eux,” pensa Alice, “sans cela ils refuseront peut-être d'aller du côté que je voudrai. Ah! je sais ce que je ferai: je leur donnerai une belle paire de bottines à Noël.”

Puis elle chercha dans son esprit comment elle s'y prendrait. “Il faudra les envoyer par le messager,” pensa-t-elle; “quelle étrange chose d'envoyer des présents à ses pieds! Et l'adresse donc! C'est cela qui sera drôle.

À Monsieur Lepiédroit d'Alice,

Tapis du foyer,

Près le garde-feu.

(De la part de Mlle Alice.)

Oh! que d'enfantillages je dis là!”

Au même instant, sa tête heurta contre le plafond de la salle: c'est qu'elle avait alors un peu plus de neuf pieds de haut. Vite elle saisit la petite clef d'or et courut à la porte du jardin.

Pauvre Alice! C'est tout ce qu'elle put faire, après s'être étendue de tout son long sur le côté, que de regarder du coin de l'œil dans le jardin. Quant à traverser le passage, il n'y fallait plus songer. Elle s'assit donc, et se remit à pleurer.

“Quelle honte!” dit Alice. “Une grande fille comme vous” (“grande” était bien le mot) “pleurer de la sorte! Allons, finissez, vous dis-je!”

But she went on all the same, shedding gallons of tears, until there was a large pool all round her, about four inches deep and reaching half down the hall.

Mais elle continua de pleurer, versant des torrents de larmes, si bien qu'elle se vit à la fin entourée d'une grande mare, profonde d'environ quatre pouces et s'étendant jusqu'au milieu de la salle.

After a time she heard a little pattering of feet in the distance, and she hastily dried her eyes to see what was coming.

Quelque temps après, elle entendit un petit bruit de pas dans le lointain; vite, elle s'essuya les yeux pour voir ce que c'était.

It was the White Rabbit returning, splendidly dressed, with a pair of white kid gloves in one hand and a large fan in the other: he came trotting along in a great hurry, muttering to himself as he came,

C'était le Lapin Blanc, en grande toilette, tenant d'une main une paire de gants paille, et de l'autre un large éventail. Il accourait tout affairé, marmottant entre ses dents:

'Oh! the Duchess, the Duchess! Oh! won't she be savage if I've kept her waiting!' Alice felt so desperate that she was ready to ask help of any one; so, when the Rabbit came near her, she began, in a low, timid voice,

"Oh! la Duchesse, la Duchesse! Elle sera dans une belle colère si je l'ai fait attendre!" trouvait si malheureuse, qu'elle était disposée à demander secours au premier venu; ainsi, quand le Lapin fut près d'elle, elle lui dit d'une voix humble et timide,

'If you please, sir—' The Rabbit started violently, dropped the white kid gloves and the fan, and skurried away into the darkness as hard as he could go.

"Je vous en prie, Monsieur —" Le Lapin tressaillit d'épouvante, laissa tomber les gants et l'éventail, se mit à courir à toutes jambes et disparut dans les ténèbres.

Alice took up the fan and gloves, and, as the hall was very hot, she kept fanning herself all the time she went on talking:

Alice ramassa les gants et l'éventail, et, comme il faisait très-chaud dans cette salle, elle s'éventa tout en se faisant la conversation:

'Dear, dear! How queer everything is to-day! And yesterday things went on just as usual. I wonder if I've been changed in the night? Let me think: was I the same when I got up this morning? I almost think I can remember feeling a little different. But if I'm not the same, the next question is, Who in the world am I? Ah, that's the great puzzle!' And she began thinking over all the children she knew that were of the same age as herself, to see if she could have been changed for any of them.

"Que tout est étrange, aujourd'hui! Hier les choses se passaient comme à l'ordinaire. Peut-être m'a-t-on changée cette nuit! Voyons, étais-je la même petite fille ce matin en me levant? — Je crois bien me rappeler que je me suis trouvée un peu différente. — Mais si je ne suis pas la même, qui suis-je donc, je vous prie? Voilà l'embarras." Elle se mit à passer en revue dans son esprit toutes les petites filles de son âge qu'elle connaissait, pour voir si elle avait été transformée en l'une d'elles.

I'm sure I'm not Ada,' she said: 'for her hair goes in such long ringlets, and mine doesn't go in ringlets at all; and I'm sure I can't be Mabel, for I know all sorts of things, and she, oh! she knows such a very little!

"Bien sûr, je ne suis pas Ada," dit-elle. "Elle a de longs cheveux bouclés et les miens ne frisent pas du tout. — Assurément je ne suis pas Mabel, car je sais tout plein de choses et Mabel ne sait presque rien;

Besides, she's she, and I'm I, and—oh dear, how puzzling it all is! I'll try if I know all the things I used to know. Let me see: four times five is twelve, and four times six is thirteen, and four times seven is—oh dear! I shall never get to twenty at that rate!

et puis, du reste, Mabel, c'est Mabel; Alice c'est Alice! — Oh! mais quelle énigme que cela! — Voyons si je me souviendrai de tout ce que je savais: quatre fois cinq font douze, quatre fois six font treize, quatre fois sept font — je n'arriverai jamais à vingt de ce train-là.

However, the Multiplication Table doesn't signify: let's try Geography. London is the capital of Paris, and Paris is the capital of Rome, and Rome—no, that's all wrong, I'm certain! I must have been changed for Mabel!

Mais peu importe la table de multiplication. Essayons de la Géographie: Londres est la capitale de Paris, Paris la capitale de Rome, et Rome la capitale de — Mais non, ce n'est pas cela, j'en suis bien sûre! Je dois être changée en Mabel!

I'll try and say "How doth the little—"' and she crossed her hands on her lap as if she were saying lessons, and

— Je vais tâcher de réciter Maître Corbeau." Elle croisa les mains sur ses genoux comme quand elle disait ses leçons, et

began to repeat it, but her voice sounded hoarse and strange, and the words did not come the same as they used to do:—

'How doth the little crocodile

Improve his shining tail,

And pour the waters of the Nile

On every golden scale!

'How cheerfully he seems to grin,

How neatly spread his claws,

And welcome little fishes in

With gently smiling jaws!'

I'm sure those are not the right words,' said poor Alice, and her eyes filled with tears again as she went on,

'I must be Mabel after all, and I shall have to go and live in that poky little house, and have next to no toys to play with, and oh! ever so many lessons to learn!

No, I've made up my mind about it; if I'm Mabel, I'll stay down here! It'll be no use their putting their heads down and saying "Come up again, dear!"

I shall only look up and say "Who am I then? Tell me that first, and then, if I like being that person, I'll come up: if not, I'll stay down here till I'm somebody else"

—but, oh dear!' cried Alice, with a sudden burst of tears: 'I do wish they would put their heads down! I am so very tired of being all alone here!'

As she said this she looked down at her hands, and was surprised to see that she had put on one of the Rabbit's little white kid gloves while she was talking.

How can I have done that?' she thought. 'I must be growing small again.' She got up and went to the table to measure herself by it, and found that, as nearly as she could guess, she was now about two feet high, and was going on shrinking rapidly:

she soon found out that the cause of this was the fan she was holding, and she dropped it hastily, just in time to avoid shrinking away altogether.

se mit à répéter la fable, d'une voix rauque et étrange, et les mots ne se présentaient plus comme autrefois: "Maître Corbeau sur un arbre perché,

Faisait son nid entre des branches;

Il avait relevé ses manches,

Car il était très-affairé.

Maître Renard, par là passant,

Lui dit: "Descendez donc, compère;

Venez embrasser votre frère."

Le Corbeau, le reconnaissant,

Lui répondit en son ramage: "Fromage.""

"Je suis bien sûre que ce n'est pas ça du tout," s'écria la pauvre Alice, et ses yeux se remplirent de larmes.

"Ah! je le vois bien, je ne suis plus Alice, je suis Mabel, et il me faudra aller vivre dans cette vilaine petite maison, où je n'aurai presque pas de jouets pour m'amuser. — Oh! que de leçons on me fera apprendre! —

Oui, certes, j'y suis bien résolue, si je suis Mabel je resterai ici. Ils auront beau passer la tête là-haut et me crier, "Reviens auprès de nous, ma chérie!"

Je me contenterai de regarder en l'air et de dire, "Dites-moi d'abord qui je suis, et, s'il me plaît d'être cette personne-là, j'irai vous trouver; sinon, je resterai ici jusqu'à ce que je devienne une autre petite fille."

— Et pourtant," dit Alice en fondant en larmes, "je donnerais tout au monde pour les voir montrer la tête là-haut! Je m'ennuie tant d'être ici toute seule."

Comme elle disait ces mots, elle fut bien surprise de voir que tout en parlant elle avait mis un des petits gants du Lapin.

"Comment ai-je pu mettre ce gant?" pensa-t-elle. "Je rapetisse donc de nouveau?" Elle se leva, alla près de la table pour se mesurer, et jugea, autant qu'elle pouvait s'en rendre compte, qu'elle avait environ deux pieds de haut, et continuait de raccourcir rapidement.

Bientôt elle s'aperçut que l'éventail qu'elle avait à la main en était la cause; vite elle le lâcha, tout juste à temps pour s'empêcher de disparaître tout à fait.

That was a narrow escape!' said Alice, a good deal frightened at the sudden change, but very glad to find herself still in existence;

'and now for the garden!' and she ran with all speed back to the little door: but, alas! the little door was shut again, and the little golden key was lying on the glass table as before,

and things are worse than ever,' thought the poor child: 'for I never was so small as this before, never! And I declare it's too bad, that it is!'

As she said these words her foot slipped, and in another moment, splash! she was up to her chin in salt water.

Her first idea was that she had somehow fallen into the sea: 'and in that case I can go back by railway,' she said to herself.

(Alice had been to the seaside once in her life, and had come to the general conclusion, that wherever you go to on the English coast you find a number of bathing machines in the sea, some children digging in the sand with wooden spades, then a row of lodging houses, and behind them a railway station.)

However, she soon made out that she was in the pool of tears which she had wept when she was nine feet high.

I wish I hadn't cried so much!' said Alice, as she swam about, trying to find her way out.

'I shall be punished for it now, I suppose, by being drowned in my own tears! That will be a queer thing, to be sure! However, everything is queer to-day.'

Just then she heard something splashing about in the pool a little way off, and she swam nearer to make out what it was:

at first she thought it must be a walrus or hippopotamus, but then she remembered how small she was now, and she soon made out that it was only a mouse that had slipped in like herself.

Would it be of any use, now,' thought Alice: 'to speak to this mouse? Everything is so out-of-the-way down here, that I should think very likely it can talk: at any rate, there's no harm in trying.'

So she began: 'O Mouse, do you know the way out of this pool? I am very tired of swimming about here, O Mouse!'

"Je viens de l'échapper belle," dit Alice, tout émue de ce brusque changement, mais bien aise de voir qu'elle existait encore.

"Maintenant, vite au jardin!" — Elle se hâta de courir vers la petite porte; mais hélas! elle s'était refermée et la petite clef d'or se trouvait sur la table de verre, comme tout à l'heure.

"Les choses vont de mal en pis," pensa la pauvre enfant. "Jamais je ne me suis vue si petite, jamais! Et c'est vraiment par trop fort!"

À ces mots son pied glissa, et flac! La voilà dans l'eau salée jusqu'au menton.

Elle se crut d'abord tombée dans la mer. "Dans ce cas je retournerai chez nous en chemin de fer," se dit-elle.

(Alice avait été au bord de la mer une fois en sa vie, et se figurait que sur n'importe quel point des côtes se trouvent un grand nombre de cabines pour les baigneurs, des enfants qui font des trous dans le sable avec des pelles en bois, une longue ligne de maisons garnies, et derrière ces maisons une gare de chemin de fer.)

Mais elle comprit bientôt qu'elle était dans une mare formée des larmes qu'elle avait pleurées, quand elle avait neuf pieds de haut.

"Je voudrais bien n'avoir pas tant pleuré," dit Alice tout en nageant de côté et d'autre pour tâcher de sortir de là.

"Je vais en être punie sans doute, en me noyant dans mes propres larmes. C'est cela qui sera drôle! Du reste, tout est drôle aujourd'hui."

Au même instant elle entendit patauger dans la mare à quelques pas de là, et elle nagea de ce côté pour voir ce que c'était.

Elle pensa d'abord que ce devait être un cheval marin ou hippopotame; puis elle se rappela combien elle était petite maintenant, et découvrit bientôt que c'était tout simplement une souris qui, comme elle, avait glissé dans la mare.

"Si j'adressais la parole à cette souris? Tout est si extraordinaire ici qu'il se pourrait bien qu'elle sût parler: dans tous les cas, il n'y a pas de mal à essayer."

Elle commença donc: "Ô Souris, savez-vous comment on pourrait sortir de cette mare? Je suis bien fatiguée de nager, Ô Souris!"

(Alice thought this must be the right way of speaking to a mouse: she had never done such a thing before, but she remembered having seen in her brother's Latin Grammar: 'A mouse—of a mouse—to a mouse—a mouse—O mouse!')

(Alice pensait que c'était là la bonne manière d'interpeller une souris. Pareille chose ne lui était jamais arrivée, mais elle se souvenait d'avoir vu dans la grammaire latine de son frère: — "La souris, de la souris, à la souris, ô souris.")

The Mouse looked at her rather inquisitively, and seemed to her to wink with one of its little eyes, but it said nothing.

La Souris la regarda d'un air inquisiteur; Alice crut même la voir cligner un de ses petits yeux, mais elle ne dit mot.

Perhaps it doesn't understand English,' thought Alice; 'I daresay it's a French mouse, come over with William the Conqueror.'

"Peut-être ne comprend-elle pas cette langue," dit Alice; "c'est sans doute une souris étrangère nouvellement débarquée.

(For, with all her knowledge of history, Alice had no very clear notion how long ago anything had happened.)

(text not in original translation)

So she began again: 'Ou est ma chatte?' which was the first sentence in her French lesson-book. The Mouse gave a sudden leap out of the water, and seemed to quiver all over with fright.

Je vais essayer de lui parler italien: "Dove è il mio gatto?"" C'étaient là les premiers mots de son livre de dialogues. La Souris fit un bond hors de l'eau, et parut trembler de tous ses membres.

Oh, I beg your pardon!' cried Alice hastily, afraid that she had hurt the poor animal's feelings. 'I quite forgot you didn't like cats.'

"Oh! mille pardons!" s'écria vivement Alice, qui craignait d'avoir fait de la peine au pauvre animal. "J'oubliais que vous n'aimez pas les chats."

'Not like cats!' cried the Mouse, in a shrill, passionate voice. 'Would you like cats if you were me?'

"Aimer les chats!" cria la Souris d'une voix perçante et colère. "Et vous, les aimeriez-vous si vous étiez à ma place?"

Well, perhaps not,' said Alice in a soothing tone: 'don't be angry about it. And yet I wish I could show you our cat Dinah: I think you'd take a fancy to cats if you could only see her. She is such a dear quiet thing,'

"Non, sans doute," dit Alice d'une voix caressante, pour l'apaiser. "Ne vous fâchez pas. Pourtant je voudrais bien vous montrer Dinah, notre chatte. Oh! si vous la voyiez, je suis sûre que vous prendriez de l'affection pour les chats. Dinah est si douce et si gentille."

Alice went on, half to herself, as she swam lazily about in the pool: 'and she sits purring so nicely by the fire, licking her paws and washing her face—and she is such a nice soft thing to nurse—and she's such a capital one for catching mice—oh, I beg your pardon!'

Tout en nageant nonchalamment dans la mare et parlant moitié à part soi, moitié à la Souris, Alice continua: "Elle se tient si gentiment auprès du feu à faire son rouet, à se lécher les pattes, et à se débarbouiller; son poil est si doux à caresser; et comme elle attrape bien les souris! — Oh! pardon!"

cried Alice again, for this time the Mouse was bristling all over, and she felt certain it must be really offended. 'We won't talk about her any more if you'd rather not.'

dit encore Alice, car cette fois le poil de la Souris s'était tout hérissé, et on voyait bien qu'elle était fâchée tout de bon. "Nous n'en parlerons plus si cela vous fait de la peine."

We indeed!' cried the Mouse, who was trembling down to the end of his tail. 'As if I would talk on such a subject!

"Nous! dites-vous," s'écria la Souris, en tremblant de la tête à la queue. "Comme si moi je parlais jamais de pareilles choses!

Our family always hated cats: nasty, low, vulgar things! Don't let me hear the name again!'

Dans notre famille on a toujours détesté les chats, viles créatures sans foi ni loi. Que je ne vous en entende plus parler!"

I won't indeed!' said Alice, in a great hurry to change the subject of conversation. 'Are you—are you fond—of—of dogs?'

"Eh bien non," dit Alice, qui avait hâte de changer la conversation. "Est-ce que — est-ce que vous aimez les chiens?"

The Mouse did not answer, so Alice went on eagerly: 'There is such a nice little dog near our house I should like to show you!

La Souris ne répondit pas, et Alice dit vivement: "Il y a tout près de chez nous un petit chien bien mignon que je voudrais vous montrer!

A little bright-eyed terrier, you know, with oh, such long curly brown hair! And it'll fetch things when you throw them, and it'll sit up and beg for its dinner, and all sorts of things—I can't remember half of them—and it belongs to a farmer, you know, and he says it's so useful, it's worth a hundred pounds!

C'est un petit terrier aux yeux vifs, avec de longs poils bruns frisés! Il rapporte très-bien; il se tient sur ses deux pattes de derrière, et fait le beau pour avoir à manger. Enfin il fait tant de tours que j'en oublie plus de la moitié! Il appartient à un fermier qui ne le donnerait pas pour mille francs, tant il lui est utile;

He says it kills all the rats and—oh dear!' cried Alice in a sorrowful tone: 'I'm afraid I've offended it again!' For the Mouse was swimming away from her as hard as it could go, and making quite a commotion in the pool as it went.

il tue tous les rats et aussi — Oh!" reprit Alice d'un ton chagrin, "voilà que je vous ai encore offensée!" En effet, la Souris s'éloignait en nageant de toutes ses forces, si bien que l'eau de la mare en était tout agitée.

So she called softly after it: 'Mouse dear! Do come back again, and we won't talk about cats or dogs either, if you don't like them!'

Alice la rappela doucement: "Ma petite Souris! Revenez, je vous en prie, nous ne parlerons plus ni de chien ni de chat, puisque vous ne les aimez pas!"

When the Mouse heard this, it turned round and swam slowly back to her: its face was quite pale (with passion, Alice thought), and it said in a low trembling voice,

À ces mots la Souris fit volte-face, et se rapprocha tout doucement; elle était toute pâle (de colère, pensait Alice). La Souris dit d'une voix basse et tremblante:

'Let us get to the shore, and then I'll tell you my history, and you'll understand why it is I hate cats and dogs.'

"Gagnons la rive, je vous conterai mon histoire, et vous verrez pourquoi je hais les chats et les chiens."

It was high time to go, for the pool was getting quite crowded with the birds and animals that had fallen into it:

Il était grand temps de s'en aller, car la mare se couvrait d'oiseaux et de toutes sortes d'animaux qui y étaient tombés.

there were a Duck and a Dodo, a Lory and an Eaglet, and several other curious creatures. Alice led the way, and the whole party swam to the shore.

Il y avait un canard, un dodo, un lory, un aiglon, et d'autres bêtes extraordinaires. Alice prit les devants, et toute la troupe nagea vers la rive.

3. A Caucas Race and a Long Tail

They were indeed a queer-looking party that assembled on the bank—the birds with draggled feathers, the animals with their fur clinging close to them, and all dripping wet, cross, and uncomfortable.

The first question of course was, how to get dry again: they had a consultation about this, and after a few minutes it seemed quite natural to Alice to find herself talking familiarly with them, as if she had known them all her life.

Indeed, she had quite a long argument with the Lory, who at last turned sulky, and would only say: 'I am older than you, and must know better';

and this Alice would not allow without knowing how old it was, and, as the Lory positively refused to tell its age, there was no more to be said.

At last the Mouse, who seemed to be a person of authority among them, called out: 'Sit down, all of you, and listen to me! I'll soon make you dry enough!'

They all sat down at once, in a large ring, with the Mouse in the middle. Alice kept her eyes anxiously fixed on it, for she felt sure she would catch a bad cold if she did not get dry very soon.

Ahem!' said the Mouse with an important air: 'are you all ready? This is the driest thing I know. Silence all round, if you please!

William the Conqueror, whose cause was favoured by the pope, was soon submitted to by the English, who wanted leaders, and had been of late much accustomed to usurpation and conquest. Edwin and Morcar, the earls of Mercia and Northumbria—'

'Ugh!' said the Lory, with a shiver.

'I beg your pardon!' said the Mouse, frowning, but very politely: 'Did you speak?'

'Not I!' said the Lory hastily.

I thought you did,' said the Mouse. '—I proceed. "Edwin and Morcar, the earls of Mercia and Northumbria,

3. La Course Cocasse

Ils formaient une assemblée bien grotesque ces êtres singuliers réunis sur le bord de la mare; les uns avaient leurs plumes tout en désordre, les autres le poil plaqué contre le corps. Tous étaient trempés, de mauvaise humeur, et fort mal à l'aise.

"Comment faire pour nous sécher?" ce fut la première question, cela va sans dire. Au bout de quelques instants, il sembla tout naturel à Alice de causer familièrement avec ces animaux, comme si elle les connaissait depuis son berceau.

Elle eut même une longue discussion avec le Lory, qui, à la fin, lui fit la mine et lui dit d'un air boudeur: "Je suis plus âgé que vous, et je dois par conséquent en savoir plus long."

Alice ne voulut pas accepter cette conclusion avant de savoir l'âge du Lory, et comme celui-ci refusa tout net de le lui dire, cela mit un terme au débat.

Enfin la Souris, qui paraissait avoir un certain ascendant sur les autres, leur cria: "Asseyez-vous tous, et écoutez-moi! Je vais bientôt vous faire sécher, je vous en réponds!"

Vite, tout le monde s'assit en rond autour de la Souris, sur qui Alice tenait les yeux fixés avec inquiétude, car elle se disait: "Je vais attraper un vilain rhume si je ne sèche pas bientôt."

"Hum!" fit la Souris d'un air d'importance; "êtes-vous prêts? Je ne sais rien de plus sec que ceci. Silence dans le cercle, je vous prie.

"Guillaume le Conquérant, dont le pape avait embrassé le parti, soumit bientôt les Anglais, qui manquaient de chefs, et commençaient à s'accoutumer aux usurpations et aux conquêtes des étrangers. Edwin et Morcar, comtes de Mercie et de Northumbrie —"“

"Brrr," fit le Lory, qui grelottait.

"Pardon," demanda la Souris en fronçant le sourcil, mais fort poliment, "qu'avez-vous dit?"

"Moi! rien," répliqua vivement le Lory.

"Ah! je croyais," dit la Souris. "Je continue. "Edwin et Morcar, comtes de Mercie et de Northumbrie, se déclarèrent

declared for him: and even Stigand, the patriotic archbishop of Canterbury, found it

advisable—""Found what?' said the Duck.

'Found it,' the Mouse replied rather crossly: 'of course you know what "it" means.'

'I know what "it" means well enough, when I find a thing,' said the Duck: 'it's generally a frog or a worm. The question is, what did the archbishop find?'

The Mouse did not notice this question, but hurriedly went on,

"—found it advisable to go with Edgar Atheling to meet William and offer him the crown. William's conduct at first was moderate. But the insolence of his Normans—

How are you getting on now, my dear?' it continued, turning to Alice as it spoke.

'As wet as ever,' said Alice in a melancholy tone: 'it doesn't seem to dry me at all.'

In that case,' said the Dodo solemnly, rising to its feet: 'I move that the meeting adjourn, for the immediate adoption of more energetic remedies—'

Speak English!' said the Eaglet. 'I don't know the meaning of half those long words, and, what's more, I don't believe you do either!'

And the Eaglet bent down its head to hide a smile: some of the other birds tittered audibly.

What I was going to say,' said the Dodo in an offended tone: 'was, that the best thing to get us dry would be a Caucus-race.'

'What is a Caucus-race?' said Alice; not that she wanted much to know, but the Dodo had paused as if it thought that somebody ought to speak, and no one else seemed inclined to say anything.

Why,' said the Dodo: 'the best way to explain it is to do it.' (And, as you might like to try the thing yourself, some winter day, I will tell you how the Dodo managed it.)

First it marked out a race-course, in a sort of circle, ('the exact shape doesn't matter,' it said,) and then all the party were placed along the course, here and there.

en sa faveur, et Stigand, l'archevêque patriote de Cantorbery, trouva cela —"“

“Trouva quoi?” dit le Canard.

“Il trouva cela,” répondit la Souris avec impatience. “Assurément vous savez ce que “cela” veut dire.”

“Je sais parfaitement ce que “cela” veut dire; par exemple: quand moi j'ai trouvé cela bon; “cela” veut dire un ver ou une grenouille,” ajouta le Canard. “Mais il s'agit de savoir ce que l'archevêque trouva.”

La Souris, sans prendre garde à cette question, se hâta de continuer.

"“L'archevêque trouva cela de bonne politique d'aller avec Edgar Atheling à la rencontre de Guillaume, pour lui offrir la couronne. Guillaume, d'abord, fut bon prince; mais l'insolence des vassaux normands —

» Eh bien, comment cela va-t-il, mon enfant?” ajouta-t-elle en se tournant vers Alice.

“Toujours aussi mouillée,” dit Alice tristement. “Je ne sèche que d'ennui.”

“Dans ce cas,” dit le Dodo avec emphase, se dressant sur ses pattes, “je propose l'ajournement, et l'adoption immédiate de mesures énergiques.”

“Parlez français,” dit l'Aiglon; “je ne comprends pas la moitié de ces grands mots, et, qui plus est, je ne crois pas que vous les compreniez vous-même.”

L'Aiglon baissa la tête pour cacher un sourire, et quelques-uns des autres oiseaux ricanèrent tout haut.

“J'allais proposer,” dit le Dodo d'un ton vexé, “une course cocasse; c'est ce que nous pouvons faire de mieux pour nous sécher.”

“Qu'est-ce qu'une course cocasse?” demanda Alice; non qu'elle tînt beaucoup à le savoir, mais le Dodo avait fait une pause comme s'il s'attendait à être questionné par quelqu'un, et personne ne semblait disposé à prendre la parole.

“La meilleure manière de l'expliquer,” dit le Dodo, “c'est de le faire.” (Et comme vous pourriez bien, un de ces jours d'hiver, avoir envie de l'essayer, je vais vous dire comment le Dodo s'y prit.)

D'abord il traça un terrain de course, une espèce de cercle (“Du reste,” disait-il, “la forme n'y fait rien”), et les coureurs furent placés indifféremment çà et là sur le terrain.

There was no 'One, two, three, and away,' but they began running when they liked, and left off when they liked, so that it was not easy to know when the race was over.

However, when they had been running half an hour or so, and were quite dry again, the Dodo suddenly called out 'The race is over!' and they all crowded round it, panting, and asking: 'But who has won?'

This question the Dodo could not answer without a great deal of thought, and it sat for a long time with one finger pressed upon its forehead (the position in which you usually see Shakespeare, in the pictures of him), while the rest waited in silence.

At last the Dodo said: 'everybody has won, and all must have prizes.'

But who is to give the prizes?' quite a chorus of voices asked. 'Why, she, of course,' said the Dodo, pointing to Alice with one finger; and the whole party at once crowded round her, calling out in a confused way: 'Prizes! Prizes!'

Alice had no idea what to do, and in despair she put her hand in her pocket, and pulled out a box of comfits, (luckily the salt water had not got into it), and handed them round as prizes.

There was exactly one a-piece all round. 'But she must have a prize herself, you know,' said the Mouse.

'Of course,' the Dodo replied very gravely. 'What else have you got in your pocket?' he went on, turning to Alice.

'Only a thimble,' said Alice sadly.

'Hand it over here,' said the Dodo.

Then they all crowded round her once more, while the Dodo solemnly presented the thimble, saying:

'We beg your acceptance of this elegant thimble'; and, when it had finished this short speech, they all cheered.

Alice thought the whole thing very absurd, but they all looked so grave that she did not dare to laugh; and, as she could not think of anything to say, she simply bowed, and took the thimble, looking as solemn as she could.

The next thing was to eat the comfits: this caused some noise and confusion, as the large birds complained that they could not taste theirs, and the small ones choked and had to be patted on the back.

Personne ne cria, “Un, deux, trois, en avant!” mais chacun partit et s’arrêta quand il voulut, de sorte qu’il n’était pas aisé de savoir quand la course finirait.

Cependant, au bout d’une demi-heure, tout le monde étant sec, le Dodo cria tout à coup: “La course est finie!” et les voilà tous haletants qui entourent le Dodo et lui demandent: “Qui a gagné?”

Cette question donna bien à réfléchir au Dodo; il resta longtemps assis, un doigt appuyé sur le front (pose ordinaire de Shakespeare dans ses portraits); tandis que les autres attendaient en silence.

Enfin le Dodo dit: “Tout le monde a gagné, et tout le monde aura un prix.”

“Mais qui donnera les prix?” demandèrent-ils tous à la fois. “Elle, cela va sans dire,” répondit le Dodo, en montrant Alice du doigt, et toute la troupe l’entoura aussitôt en criant confusément: “Les prix! Les prix!”

Alice ne savait que faire; pour sortir d’embarras elle mit la main dans sa poche et en tira une boîte de dragées (heureusement l’eau salée n’y avait pas pénétré); puis en donna une en prix à chacun;

il y en eut juste assez pour faire le tour. “Mais il faut aussi qu’elle ait un prix, elle,” dit la Souris.

“Comme de raison,” reprit le Dodo gravement. “Avez-vous encore quelque chose dans votre poche?” continua-t-il en se tournant vers Alice.

“Un dé; pas autre chose,” dit Alice d’un ton chagrin.

“Faites passer,” dit le Dodo.

Tous se groupèrent de nouveau autour d’Alice, tandis que le Dodo lui présentait solennellement le dé en disant:

“Nous vous prions d’accepter ce superbe dé.” Lorsqu’il eut fini ce petit discours, tout le monde cria “Hourra!”

Alice trouvait tout cela bien ridicule, mais les autres avaient l’air si grave, qu’elle n’osait pas rire; aucune réponse ne lui venant à l’esprit, elle se contenta de faire la révérence, et prit le dé de son air le plus sérieux.

Il n’y avait plus maintenant qu’à manger les dragées; ce qui ne se fit pas sans un peu de bruit et de désordre, car les gros oiseaux se plaignirent de n’y trouver aucun goût, et il fallut taper dans le dos des petits qui étranglaient.

However, it was over at last, and they sat down again in a ring, and begged the Mouse to tell them something more.

You promised to tell me your history, you know,' said Alice: 'and why it is you hate—C and D,' she added in a whisper, half afraid that it would be offended again.

'Mine is a long and a sad tale!' said the Mouse, turning to Alice, and sighing.

It is a long tail, certainly,' said Alice, looking down with wonder at the Mouse's tail; 'but why do you call it sad?'

And she kept on puzzling about it while the Mouse was speaking, so that her idea of the tale was something like this:

— 'Fury said to a mouse, that he met in the house, "Let us both go to law: I will prosecute you. —Come, I'll take no denial; We must have a trial: For really this morning I've nothing to do." Said the mouse to the cur, "Such a trial, dear Sir, With no jury or judge, would be wasting our breath." "I'll be judge, I'll be jury," said cunning old Fury: "I'll try the whole cause, and condemn you to death."'

'You are not attending!' said the Mouse to Alice severely. 'What are you thinking of?'

'I beg your pardon,' said Alice very humbly: 'you had got to the fifth bend, I think?'

'I had not!' cried the Mouse, sharply and very angrily.

A knot!' said Alice, always ready to make herself useful, and looking anxiously about her. 'Oh, do let me help to undo it!'

'I shall do nothing of the sort,' said the Mouse, getting up and walking away. 'You insult me by talking such nonsense!'

I didn't mean it!' pleaded poor Alice. 'But you're so easily offended, you know!' The Mouse only growled in reply.

Please come back and finish your story!' Alice called after it; and the others all joined in chorus: 'Yes, please do!' but the Mouse only shook its head impatiently, and walked a little quicker.

Enfin tout rentra dans le calme. On s'assit en rond autour de la Souris, et on la pria de raconter encore quelque chose.

"Vous m'avez promis de me raconter votre histoire," dit Alice, "et de m'expliquer pourquoi vous détestez — les chats et les chiens," ajouta-t-elle tout bas, craignant encore de déplaire.

La Souris, se tournant vers Alice, soupira et lui dit: "Mon histoire sera longue et traînante."

"Tiens! tout comme votre queue," dit Alice, frappée de la ressemblance, et regardant avec étonnement la queue de la Souris tandis que celle-ci parlait.

Les idées d'histoire et de queue longue et traînante se brouillaient dans l'esprit d'Alice à peu près de cette façon:

— "Canichon dit à la Souris, Qu'il rencontra dans le logis: "Je crois le moment fort propice De te faire aller en justice. Je ne doute pas du succès Que doit avoir notre procès. Vite, allons, commençons l'affaire. Ce matin je n'ai rien à faire." La Souris dit à Canichon: "Sans juge et sans jurés, mon bon!" Mais Canichon plein de malice Dit: "C'est moi qui suis la justice, Et, que tu aies raison ou tort, Je vais te condamner à mort."

"Vous ne m'écoutez pas," dit la Souris à Alice d'un air sévère. "À quoi pensez-vous donc?"

"Pardon," dit Alice humblement. "Vous en étiez au cinquième détour."

"Détour!" dit la Souris d'un ton sec. "Croyez-vous donc que je manque de véracité?"

"Des vers à citer? oh! je puis vous en fournir quelques-uns!" dit Alice, toujours prête à rendre service.

"On n'a pas besoin de vous," dit la Souris. "C'est m'insulter que de dire de pareilles sottises." Puis elle se leva pour s'en aller.

"Je n'avais pas l'intention de vous offenser," dit Alice d'une voix conciliante. "Mais franchement vous êtes bien susceptible." La Souris grommela quelque chose entre ses dents et s'éloigna.

"Revenez, je vous en prie, finissez votre histoire," lui cria Alice; et tous les autres dirent en chœur: "Oui, nous vous en supplions." Mais la Souris secouant la tête ne s'en alla que plus vite.

What a pity it wouldn't stay!' sighed the Lory, as soon as it was quite out of sight; and an old Crab took the opportunity of saying to her daughter 'Ah, my dear! Let this be a lesson to you never to lose your temper!'

"Quel dommage qu'elle ne soit pas restée!" dit en soupirant le Lory, sitôt que la Souris eut disparu. Un vieux crabe, profitant de l'occasion, dit à son fils: "Mon enfant, que cela vous serve de leçon, et vous apprenne à ne vous emporter jamais!"

'Hold your tongue, Ma!' said the young Crab, a little snappishly. 'You're enough to try the patience of an oyster!'

"Taisez-vous donc, papa," dit le jeune crabe d'un ton aigre. "Vous feriez perdre patience à une huître."

'I wish I had our Dinah here, I know I do!' said Alice aloud, addressing nobody in particular. 'She'd soon fetch it back!'

"Ah! si Dinah était ici," dit Alice tout haut sans s'adresser à personne. "C'est elle qui l'aurait bientôt ramenée."

'And who is Dinah, if I might venture to ask the question?' said the Lory.

"Et qui est Dinah, s'il n'y a pas d'indiscrétion à le demander?" dit le Lory.

Alice replied eagerly, for she was always ready to talk about her pet:

Alice répondit avec empressement, car elle était toujours prête à parler de sa favorite:

'Dinah's our cat. And she's such a capital one for catching mice you can't think! And oh, I wish you could see her after the birds! Why, she'll eat a little bird as soon as look at it!'

"Dinah, c'est notre chatte. Si vous saviez comme elle attrape bien les souris! Et si vous la voyiez courir après les oiseaux; aussitôt vus, aussitôt croqués."

This speech caused a remarkable sensation among the party. Some of the birds hurried off at once:

Ces paroles produisirent un effet singulier sur l'assemblée. Quelques oiseaux s'enfuirent aussitôt;

one old Magpie began wrapping itself up very carefully, remarking: 'I really must be getting home; the night-air doesn't suit my throat!' and a Canary called out in a trembling voice to its children:

une vieille pie s'enveloppant avec soin murmura: "Il faut vraiment que je rentre chez moi, l'air du soir ne vaut rien pour ma gorge!" Et un canari cria à ses petits d'une voix tremblante:

Come away, my dears! It's high time you were all in bed!' On various pretexts they all moved off, and Alice was soon left alone.

"Venez, mes enfants; il est grand temps que vous vous mettiez au lit!" Enfin, sous un prétexte ou sous un autre, chacun s'esquiva, et Alice se trouva bientôt seule.

I wish I hadn't mentioned Dinah!' she said to herself in a melancholy tone.

"Je voudrais bien n'avoir pas parlé de Dinah," se dit-elle tristement.

'Nobody seems to like her, down here, and I'm sure she's the best cat in the world! Oh, my dear Dinah! I wonder if I shall ever see you any more!'

"Personne ne l'aime ici, et pourtant c'est la meilleure chatte du monde! Oh! chère Dinah, te reverrai-je jamais?"

And here poor Alice began to cry again, for she felt very lonely and low-spirited.

Ici la pauvre Alice se reprit à pleurer; elle se sentait seule, triste, et abattue.

In a little while, however, she again heard a little pattering of footsteps in the distance, and she looked up eagerly, half hoping that the Mouse had changed his mind, and was coming back to finish his story.

Au bout de quelque temps elle entendit au loin un petit bruit de pas; elle s'empressa de regarder, espérant que la Souris avait changé d'idée et revenait finir son histoire.

4. The Rabbit Sends in a Little Bill

It was the White Rabbit, trotting slowly back again, and looking anxiously about as it went, as if it had lost something; and she heard it muttering to itself

'The Duchess! The Duchess! Oh my dear paws! Oh my fur and whiskers! She'll get me executed, as sure as ferrets are ferrets! Where can I have dropped them, I wonder?'

Alice guessed in a moment that it was looking for the fan and the pair of white kid gloves, and she very good-naturedly began hunting about for them, but they were nowhere to be seen.

Everything seemed to have changed since her swim in the pool, and the great hall, with the glass table and the little door, had vanished completely.

Very soon the Rabbit noticed Alice, as she went hunting about, and called out to her in an angry tone:

'Why, Mary Ann, what are you doing out here? Run home this moment, and fetch me a pair of gloves and a fan! Quick, now!'

And Alice was so much frightened that she ran off at once in the direction it pointed to, without trying to explain the mistake it had made.

He took me for his housemaid,' she said to herself as she ran. 'How surprised he'll be when he finds out who I am! But I'd better take him his fan and gloves—that is, if I can find them.'

As she said this, she came upon a neat little house, on the door of which was a bright brass plate with the name 'W. RABBIT' engraved upon it.

She went in without knocking, and hurried upstairs, in great fear lest she should meet the real Mary Ann, and be turned out of the house before she had found the fan and gloves.

How queer it seems,' Alice said to herself: 'to be going messages for a rabbit! I suppose Dinah'll be sending me on messages next!'

4. l'Habitation du Lapin Blanc

C'était le Lapin Blanc qui revenait en trottinant, et qui cherchait de tous côtés, d'un air inquiet, comme s'il avait perdu quelque chose; Alice l'entendit qui marmottait:

"La Duchesse! La Duchesse! Oh! mes pauvres pattes; oh! ma robe et mes moustaches! Elle me fera guillotiner aussi vrai que des furets sont des furets! Où pourrais-je bien les avoir perdus?"

Alice devina tout de suite qu'il cherchait l'éventail et la paire de gants paille, et, comme elle avait bon cœur, elle se mit à les chercher aussi; mais pas moyen de les trouver.

Du reste, depuis son bain dans la mare aux larmes, tout était changé: la salle, la table de verre, et la petite porte avaient complétement disparu.

Bientôt le Lapin aperçut Alice qui furetait; il lui cria d'un ton d'impatience:

"Eh bien! Marianne, que faites-vous ici? Courez vite à la maison me chercher une paire de gants et un éventail! Allons, dépêchons-nous."

Alice eut si grand' peur qu'elle se mit aussitôt à courir dans la direction qu'il indiquait, sans chercher à lui expliquer qu'il se trompait.

"Il m'a pris pour sa bonne," se disait-elle en courant. "Comme il sera étonné quand il saura qui je suis! Mais je ferai bien de lui porter ses gants et son éventail; c'est-à-dire, si je les trouve."

Ce disant, elle arriva en face d'une petite maison, et vit sur la porte une plaque en cuivre avec ces mots, "JEAN LAPIN."

Elle monta l'escalier, entra sans frapper, tout en tremblant de rencontrer la vraie Marianne, et d'être mise à la porte avant d'avoir trouvé les gants et l'éventail.

"Que c'est drôle," se dit Alice, "de faire des commissions pour un lapin! Bientôt ce sera Dinah qui m'enverra en commission."

And she began fancying the sort of thing that would happen: "'Miss Alice! Come here directly, and get ready for your walk!"

Coming in a minute, nurse! But I've got to see that the mouse doesn't get out. Only I don't think,' Alice went on: 'that they'd let Dinah stop in the house if it began ordering people about like that!'

By this time she had found her way into a tidy little room with a table in the window, and on it (as she had hoped) a fan and two or three pairs of tiny white kid gloves:

she took up the fan and a pair of the gloves, and was just going to leave the room, when her eye fell upon a little bottle that stood near the looking- glass.

There was no label this time with the words 'DRINK ME,' but nevertheless she uncorked it and put it to her lips. 'I know something interesting is sure to happen,' she said to herself:

'whenever I eat or drink anything; so I'll just see what this bottle does. I do hope it'll make me grow large again, for really I'm quite tired of being such a tiny little thing!'

It did so indeed, and much sooner than she had expected: before she had drunk half the bottle, she found her head pressing against the ceiling, and had to stoop to save her neck from being broken.

She hastily put down the bottle, saying to herself 'That's quite enough—I hope I shan't grow any more—As it is, I can't get out at the door—I do wish I hadn't drunk quite so much!'

Alas! it was too late to wish that! She went on growing, and growing, and very soon had to kneel down on the floor:

in another minute there was not even room for this, and she tried the effect of lying down with one elbow against the door, and the other arm curled round her head.

Still she went on growing, and, as a last resource, she put one arm out of the window, and one foot up the chimney, and said to herself 'Now I can do no more, whatever happens. What will become of me?'

Luckily for Alice, the little magic bottle had now had its full effect, and she grew no larger:

Elle se prit alors à imaginer comment les choses se passeraient. — ""Mademoiselle Alice, venez ici tout de suite vous apprêter pour la promenade."

"Dans l'instant, ma bonne! Il faut d'abord que je veille sur ce trou jusqu'à ce que Dinah revienne, pour empêcher que la souris ne sorte." Mais je ne pense pas," continua Alice, "qu'on garderait Dinah à la maison si elle se mettait dans la tête de commander comme cela aux gens."

Tout en causant ainsi, Alice était entrée dans une petite chambre bien rangée, et, comme elle s'y attendait, sur une petite table dans l'embrasure de la fenêtre, elle vit un éventail et deux ou trois paires de gants de chevreau tout petits.

Elle en prit une paire, ainsi que l'éventail, et allait quitter la chambre lorsqu'elle aperçut, près du miroir, une petite bouteille.

Cette fois il n'y avait pas l'inscription BUVEZ-MOI — ce qui n'empêcha pas Alice de la déboucher et de la porter à ses lèvres. "Il m'arrive toujours quelque chose d'intéressant," se dit-elle,

"lorsque je mange ou que je bois. Je vais voir un peu l'effet de cette bouteille. J'espère bien qu'elle me fera regrandir, car je suis vraiment fatiguée de n'être qu'une petite nabote!"

C'est ce qui arriva en effet, et bien plus tôt qu'elle ne s'y attendait. Elle n'avait pas bu la moitié de la bouteille, que sa tête touchait au plafond et qu'elle fut forcée de se baisser pour ne pas se casser le cou.

Elle remit bien vite la bouteille sur la table en se disant: "En voilà assez; j'espère ne pas grandir davantage. Je ne puis déjà plus passer par la porte. Oh! je voudrais bien n'avoir pas tant bu!"

Hélas! il était trop tard; elle grandissait, grandissait, et eut bientôt à se mettre à genoux sur le plancher.

Mais un instant après, il n'y avait même plus assez de place pour rester dans cette position, et elle essaya de se tenir étendue par terre, un coude contre la porte et l'autre bras passé autour de sa tête.

Cependant, comme elle grandissait toujours, elle fut obligée, comme dernière ressource, de laisser pendre un de ses bras par la fenêtre et d'enfoncer un pied dans la cheminée en disant: "À présent c'est tout ce que je peux faire, quoi qu'il arrive. Que vais-je devenir?"

Heureusement pour Alice, la petite bouteille magique avait alors produit tout son effet, et elle cessa de grandir.

still it was very uncomfortable, and, as there seemed to be no sort of chance of her ever getting out of the room again, no wonder she felt unhappy.

It was much pleasanter at home,' thought poor Alice: 'when one wasn't always growing larger and smaller, and being ordered about by mice and rabbits.

I almost wish I hadn't gone down that rabbit-hole—and yet—and yet—it's rather curious, you know, this sort of life! I do wonder what can have happened to me!

When I used to read fairy-tales, I fancied that kind of thing never happened, and now here I am in the middle of one! There ought to be a book written about me, that there ought!

And when I grow up, I'll write one—but I'm grown up now,' she added in a sorrowful tone; 'at least there's no room to grow up any more here.''But then,' thought Alice: 'shall I never get any older than I am now?

That'll be a comfort, one way—never to be an old woman— but then—always to have lessons to learn! Oh, I shouldn't like that!''Oh, you foolish Alice!' she answered herself.

'How can you learn lessons in here? Why, there's hardly room for you, and no room at all for any lesson-books!'

And so she went on, taking first one side and then the other, and making quite a conversation of it altogether; but after a few minutes she heard a voice outside, and stopped to listen.

Mary Ann! Mary Ann!' said the voice. 'Fetch me my gloves this moment!' Then came a little pattering of feet on the stairs.

Alice knew it was the Rabbit coming to look for her, and she trembled till she shook the house, quite forgetting that she was now about a thousand times as large as the Rabbit, and had no reason to be afraid of it.

Presently the Rabbit came up to the door, and tried to open it; but, as the door opened inwards, and Alice's elbow was pressed hard against it, that attempt proved a failure.

Alice heard it say to itself 'Then I'll go round and get in at the window.'

Cependant sa position était bien gênante, et comme il ne semblait pas y avoir la moindre chance qu'elle pût jamais sortir de cette chambre, il n'y a pas à s'étonner qu'elle se trouvât bien malheureuse.

"C'était bien plus agréable chez nous," pensa la pauvre enfant. "Là du moins je ne passais pas mon temps à grandir et à rapetisser, et je n'étais pas la domestique des lapins et des souris.

Je voudrais bien n'être jamais descendue dans ce terrier; et pourtant c'est assez drôle cette manière de vivre! Je suis curieuse de savoir ce que c'est qui m'est arrivé.

Autrefois, quand je lisais des contes de fées, je m'imaginais que rien de tout cela ne pouvait être, et maintenant me voilà en pleine féerie. On devrait faire un livre sur mes aventures; il y aurait de quoi!

Quand je serai grande j'en ferai un, moi. — Mais je suis déjà bien grande!" dit-elle tristement. "Dans tous les cas, il n'y a plus de place ici pour grandir davantage." "Mais alors," pensa Alice, "ne serai-je donc jamais plus vieille que je ne le suis maintenant?

D'un côté cela aura ses avantages, ne jamais être une vieille femme. Mais alors avoir toujours des leçons à apprendre! Oh, je n'aimerais pas cela du tout." "Oh! Alice, petite folle," se répondit-elle.

"Comment pourriez-vous apprendre des leçons ici? Il y a à peine de la place pour vous, et il n'y en a pas du tout pour vos livres de leçons."

Et elle continua ainsi, faisant tantôt les demandes et tantôt les réponses, et établissant sur ce sujet toute une conversation; mais au bout de quelques instants elle entendit une voix au dehors, et s'arrêta pour écouter.

"Marianne! Marianne!" criait la voix; "allez chercher mes gants bien vite!" Puis Alice entendit des piétinements dans l'escalier.

Elle savait que c'était le Lapin qui la cherchait; elle trembla si fort qu'elle en ébranla la maison, oubliant que maintenant elle était mille fois plus grande que le Lapin, et n'avait rien à craindre de lui.

Le Lapin, arrivé à la porte, essaya de l'ouvrir; mais, comme elle s'ouvrait en dedans et que le coude d'Alice était fortement appuyé contre la porte, la tentative fut vaine.

Alice entendit le Lapin qui murmurait: "C'est bon, je vais faire le tour et j'entrerai par la fenêtre."

That you won't' thought Alice, and, after waiting till she fancied she heard the Rabbit just under the window, she suddenly spread out her hand, and made a snatch in the air.

She did not get hold of anything, but she heard a little shriek and a fall, and a crash of broken glass, from which she concluded that it was just possible it had fallen into a cucumber-frame, or something of the sort.

Next came an angry voice—the Rabbit's—'Pat! Pat! Where are you?' And then a voice she had never heard before: 'Sure then I'm here! Digging for apples, yer honour!'

'Digging for apples, indeed!' said the Rabbit angrily. 'Here! Come and help me out of this!' (Sounds of more broken glass.)

'Now tell me, Pat, what's that in the window?'

'Sure, it's an arm, yer honour!' (He pronounced it 'arrum.')

'An arm, you goose! Who ever saw one that size? Why, it fills the whole window!'

'Sure, it does, yer honour: but it's an arm for all that.'

'Well, it's got no business there, at any rate: go and take it away!'

There was a long silence after this, and Alice could only hear whispers now and then; such as:

Sure, I don't like it, yer honour, at all, at all!' 'Do as I tell you, you coward!' and at last she spread out her hand again, and made another snatch in the air. This time there were two little shrieks, and more sounds of broken glass.

'What a number of cucumber-frames there must be!' thought Alice. 'I wonder what they'll do next! As for pulling me out of the window, I only wish they could! I'm sure I don't want to stay in here any longer!'

She waited for some time without hearing anything more: at last came a rumbling of little cartwheels, and the sound of a good many voices all talking together: she made out the words: 'Where's the other ladder?

—Why, I hadn't to bring but one; Bill's got the other—Bill! fetch it here, lad!—Here, put 'em up at this corner—No, tie 'em together first—they don't reach half high enough yet—Oh! they'll do well enough; don't be particular…

"Je t'en défie!" pensa Alice. Elle attendit un peu; puis, quand elle crut que le Lapin était sous la fenêtre, elle étendit le bras tout à coup pour le saisir; elle ne prit que du vent.

Mais elle entendit un petit cri, puis le bruit d'une chute et de vitres cassées (ce qui lui fit penser que le Lapin était tombé sur les châssis de quelque serre à concombre),

puis une voix colère, celle du Lapin: "Patrice! Patrice! où es-tu?" Une voix qu'elle ne connaissait pas répondit: "Me v'là, not' maître! J'bêchons la terre pour trouver des pommes!"

"Pour trouver des pommes!" dit le Lapin furieux. "Viens m'aider à me tirer d'ici." (Nouveau bruit de vitres cassées.)

"Dis-moi un peu, Patrice, qu'est-ce qu'il y a là à la fenêtre?"

"Ça, not' maître, c'est un bras."

"Un bras, imbécile! Qui a jamais vu un bras de cette dimension? Ça bouche toute la fenêtre."

"Bien sûr, not' maître, mais c'est un bras tout de même."

"Dans tous les cas il n'a rien à faire ici. Enlève-moi ça bien vite."

Il se fit un long silence, et Alice n'entendait plus que des chuchotements de temps à autre, comme:

"Maître, j'osons point." — "Fais ce que je te dis, capon!" Alice étendit le bras de nouveau comme pour agripper quelque chose; cette fois il y eut deux petits cris et encore un bruit de vitres cassées. "Que de châssis il doit y avoir là!" pensa Alice.

"Je me demande ce qu'ils vont faire à présent. Quant à me retirer par la fenêtre, je le souhaite de tout mon cœur, car je n'ai pas la moindre envie de rester ici plus longtemps!"

Il se fit quelques instants de silence. À la fin, Alice entendit un bruit de petites roues, puis le son d'un grand nombre de voix; elle distingua ces mots: "Où est l'autre échelle?

— Je n'avais point qu'à en apporter une; c'est Jacques qui a l'autre. — Allons, Jacques, apporte ici, mon garçon! — Dressez-les là au coin. — Non, attachez-les d'abord l'une au bout de l'autre. — Elles ne vont pas encore moitié assez haut. — Ça fera l'affaire; ne soyez pas si difficile.

—Here, Bill! catch hold of this rope—Will the roof bear?—Mind that loose slate—Oh, it's coming down! Heads below!' (a loud crash)—'Now, who did that?

—It was Bill, I fancy—Who's to go down the chimney?—Nay, I shan't! you do it!—That I won't, then!—Bill's to go down—Here, Bill! the master says you're to go down the chimney!'

'Oh! So Bill's got to come down the chimney, has he?' said Alice to herself. 'Shy, they seem to put everything upon Bill! I wouldn't be in Bill's place for a good deal: this fireplace is narrow, to be sure; but I think I can kick a little!'

She drew her foot as far down the chimney as she could, and waited till she heard a little animal (she couldn't guess of what sort it was) scratching and scrambling about in the chimney close above her: then, saying to herself 'This is Bill,' she gave one sharp kick, and waited to see what would happen next.

The first thing she heard was a general chorus of 'There goes Bill!' then the Rabbit's voice along—'Catch him, you by the hedge!' then silence, and then another confusion of voices—

'Hold up his head—Brandy now—Don't choke him—How was it, old fellow? What happened to you? Tell us all about it!'

Last came a little feeble, squeaking voice, ('That's Bill,' thought Alice,) 'Well, I hardly know—No more, thank ye; I'm better now—but I'm a deal too flustered to tell you—all I know is, something comes at me like a Jack-in-the-box, and up I goes like a sky-rocket!'

'So you did, old fellow!' said the others.

We must burn the house down!' said the Rabbit's voice; and Alice called out as loud as she could: 'If you do. I'll set Dinah at you!'

There was a dead silence instantly, and Alice thought to herself: 'I wonder what they will do next! If they had any sense, they'd take the roof off.' After a minute or two, they began moving about again, and Alice heard the Rabbit say: 'A barrowful will do, to begin with.'

A barrowful of what?' thought Alice; but she had not long to doubt, for the next moment a shower of little pebbles came rattling in at the window, and some of them hit her in the face.

— Tiens, Jacques, attrape ce bout de corde. — Le toit portera-t-il bien? — Attention à cette tuile qui ne tient pas. — Bon! la voilà qui dégringole. Gare les têtes!” (Il se fit un grand fracas.) “Qui a fait cela?

— Je crois bien que c’est Jacques. — Qui est-ce qui va descendre par la cheminée? — Pas moi, bien sûr! Allez-y, vous. — Non pas, vraiment. — C’est à vous, Jacques, à descendre. — Hohé, Jacques, not’ maître dit qu’il faut que tu descendes par la cheminée!”

“Ah!” se dit Alice, “c’est donc Jacques qui va descendre. Il paraît qu’on met tout sur le dos de Jacques. Je ne voudrais pas pour beaucoup être Jacques. Ce foyer est étroit certainement, mais je crois bien que je pourrai tout de même lui lancer un coup de pied.”

Elle retira son pied aussi bas que possible, et ne bougea plus jusqu’à ce qu’elle entendît le bruit d’un petit animal (elle ne pouvait deviner de quelle espèce) qui grattait et cherchait à descendre dans la cheminée, juste au-dessus d’elle; alors se disant: “Voilà Jacques sans doute,” elle lança un bon coup de pied, et attendit pour voir ce qui allait arriver.

La première chose qu’elle entendit fut un cri général de: “Tiens, voilà Jacques en l’air!” Puis la voix du Lapin, qui criait: “Attrapez-le, vous là-bas, près de la haie!” Puis un long silence; ensuite un mélange confus de voix:

“Soutenez-lui la tête. — De l’eau-de-vie maintenant. — Ne le faites pas engouer. — Qu’est-ce donc, vieux camarade? — Que t’est-il arrivé? Raconte-nous ça!”

Enfin une petite voix faible et flûtée se fit entendre. (“C’est la voix de Jacques,” pensa Alice.) “Je n’en sais vraiment rien. Merci, c’est assez; je me sens mieux maintenant; mais je suis encore trop bouleversé pour vous conter la chose. Tout ce que je sais, c’est que j’ai été poussé comme par un ressort, et que je suis parti en l’air comme une fusée.”

“Ça, c’est vrai, vieux camarade,” disaient les autres.

“Il faut mettre le feu à la maison,” dit le Lapin.Alors Alice cria de toutes ses forces: “Si vous osez faire cela, j’envoie Dinah à votre poursuite.”

Il se fit tout à coup un silence de mort. “Que vont-ils faire à présent?” pensa Alice. “S’ils avaient un peu d’esprit, ils enlèveraient le toit.” Quelques minutes après, les allées et venues recommencèrent, et Alice entendit le Lapin, qui disait: “Une brouettée d’abord, ça suffira.”

“Une brouettée de quoi?” pensa Alice. Il ne lui resta bientôt plus de doute, car, un instant après, une grêle de petits cailloux vint battre contre la fenêtre, et quelques-uns même l’atteignirent au visage.

'I'll put a stop to this,' she said to herself, and shouted out: 'You'd better not do that again!' which produced another dead silence.

Alice noticed with some surprise that the pebbles were all turning into little cakes as they lay on the floor, and a bright idea came into her head.

'If I eat one of these cakes,' she thought: 'it's sure to make some change in my size; and as it can't possibly make me larger, it must make me smaller, I suppose.'

So she swallowed one of the cakes, and was delighted to find that she began shrinking directly.

As soon as she was small enough to get through the door, she ran out of the house, and found quite a crowd of little animals and birds waiting outside.

The poor little Lizard, Bill, was in the middle, being held up by two guinea-pigs, who were giving it something out of a bottle.

They all made a rush at Alice the moment she appeared; but she ran off as hard as she could, and soon found herself safe in a thick wood.

The first thing I've got to do,' said Alice to herself, as she wandered about in the wood: 'is to grow to my right size again; and the second thing is to find my way into that lovely garden. I think that will be the best plan.'

It sounded an excellent plan, no doubt, and very neatly and simply arranged; the only difficulty was, that she had not the smallest idea how to set about it;

and while she was peering about anxiously among the trees, a little sharp bark just over her head made her look up in a great hurry.

An enormous puppy was looking down at her with large round eyes, and feebly stretching out one paw, trying to touch her.

'Poor little thing!' said Alice, in a coaxing tone, and she tried hard to whistle to it; but she was terribly frightened all the time at the thought that it might be hungry, in which case it would be very likely to eat her up in spite of all her coaxing.

Hardly knowing what she did, she picked up a little bit of stick, and held it out to the puppy; whereupon the puppy jumped into the air off all its feet at once, with a yelp of delight, and rushed at the stick, and made believe to worry it.

“Je vais bientôt mettre fin à cela,” se dit-elle; puis elle cria: “Vous ferez bien de ne pas recommencer.” Ce qui produisit encore un profond silence.

Alice remarqua, avec quelque surprise, qu’en tombant sur le plancher les cailloux se changeaient en petits gâteaux, et une brillante idée lui traversa l’esprit.

“Si je mange un de ces gâteaux,” pensa-t-elle, “cela ne manquera pas de me faire ou grandir ou rapetisser; or, je ne puis plus grandir, c’est impossible, donc je rapetisserai!”

Elle avala un des gâteaux, et s’aperçut avec joie qu’elle diminuait rapidement.

Aussitôt qu’elle fut assez petite pour passer par la porte, elle s’échappa de la maison, et trouva toute une foule d’oiseaux et d’autres petits animaux qui attendaient dehors.

Le pauvre petit lézard, Jacques, était au milieu d’eux, soutenu par des cochons d’Inde, qui le faisaient boire à une bouteille.

Tous se précipitèrent sur Alice aussitôt qu’elle parut; mais elle se mit à courir de toutes ses forces, et se trouva bientôt en sûreté dans un bois touffu.

“La première chose que j’aie à faire,” dit Alice en errant çà et là dans les bois, “c’est de revenir à ma première grandeur; la seconde, de chercher un chemin qui me conduise dans ce ravissant jardin. C’est là, je crois, ce que j’ai de mieux à faire!”

En effet c’était un plan de campagne excellent, très-simple et très-habilement combiné. Toute la difficulté était de savoir comment s’y prendre pour l’exécuter.

Tandis qu’elle regardait en tapinois et avec précaution à travers les arbres, un petit aboiement sec, juste au-dessus de sa tête, lui fit tout à coup lever les yeux.

Un jeune chien (qui lui parut énorme) la regardait avec de grands yeux ronds, et étendait légèrement la patte pour tâcher de la toucher.

“Pauvre petit!” dit Alice d’une voix caressante et essayant de siffler. Elle avait une peur terrible cependant, car elle pensait qu’il pouvait bien avoir faim, et que dans ce cas il était probable qu’il la mangerait, en dépit de toutes ses câlineries.

Sans trop savoir ce qu’elle faisait, elle ramassa une petite baguette et la présenta au petit chien qui bondit des quatre pattes à la fois, aboyant de joie, et se jeta sur le bâton comme pour jouer avec.

Then Alice dodged behind a great thistle, to keep herself from being run over; and the moment she appeared on the other side, the puppy made another rush at the stick, and tumbled head over heels in its hurry to get hold of it.

Alice passa de l'autre côté d'un gros chardon pour n'être pas foulée aux pieds. Sitôt qu'elle reparut, le petit chien se précipita de nouveau sur le bâton, et, dans son empressement de le saisir, butta et fit une cabriole.

Then Alice, thinking it was very like having a game of play with a cart-horse, and expecting every moment to be trampled under its feet, ran round the thistle again.

Mais Alice, trouvant que cela ressemblait beaucoup à une partie qu'elle ferait avec un cheval de charrette, et craignant à chaque instant d'être écrasée par le chien, se remit à tourner autour du chardon.

Then the puppy began a series of short charges at the stick, running a very little way forwards each time and a long way back, and barking hoarsely all the while, till at last it sat down a good way off, panting, with its tongue hanging out of its mouth, and its great eyes half shut.

Alors le petit chien fit une série de charges contre le bâton. Il avançait un peu chaque fois, puis reculait bien loin en faisant des aboiements rauques; puis enfin il se coucha à une grande distance de là, tout haletant, la langue pendante, et ses grands yeux à moitié fermés.

This seemed to Alice a good opportunity for making her escape; so she set off at once, and ran till she was quite tired and out of breath, and till the puppy's bark sounded quite faint in the distance.

Alice jugea que le moment était venu de s'échapper. Elle prit sa course aussitôt, et ne s'arrêta que lorsqu'elle se sentit fatiguée et hors d'haleine, et qu'elle n'entendit plus que faiblement dans le lointain les aboiements du petit chien.

And yet what a dear little puppy it was!' said Alice, as she leant against a buttercup to rest herself, and fanned herself with one of the leaves:

"C'était pourtant un bien joli petit chien," dit Alice, en s'appuyant sur un bouton d'or pour se reposer, et en s'éventant avec une des feuilles de la plante.

'I should have liked teaching it tricks very much, if—if I'd only been the right size to do it! Oh dear! I'd nearly forgotten that I've got to grow up again!

"Je lui aurais volontiers enseigné tout plein de jolis tours si — si j'avais été assez grande pour cela! Oh! mais j'oubliais que j'avais encore à grandir!

Let me see—how is it to be managed? I suppose I ought to eat or drink something or other; but the great question is, what?'

Voyons. Comment faire? Je devrais sans doute boire ou manger quelque chose; mais quoi? Voilà la grande question."

The great question certainly was, what? Alice looked all round her at the flowers and the blades of grass, but she did not see anything that looked like the right thing to eat or drink under the circumstances.

En effet, la grande question était bien de savoir quoi? Alice regarda tout autour d'elle les fleurs et les brins d'herbes; mais elle ne vit rien qui lui parût bon à boire ou à manger dans les circonstances présentes.

There was a large mushroom growing near her, about the same height as herself; and when she had looked under it, and on both sides of it, and behind it, it occurred to her that she might as well look and see what was on the top of it.

Près d'elle poussait un large champignon, à peu près haut comme elle. Lorsqu'elle l'eut examiné par-dessous, d'un côté et de l'autre, par-devant et par-derrière, l'idée lui vint qu'elle ferait bien de regarder ce qu'il y avait dessus.

She stretched herself up on tiptoe, and peeped over the edge of the mushroom, and her eyes immediately met those of a large caterpillar, that was sitting on the top with its arms folded, quietly smoking a long hookah, and taking not the smallest notice of her or of anything else.

Elle se dressa sur la pointe des pieds, et, glissant les yeux par-dessus le bord du champignon, ses regards rencontrèrent ceux d'une grosse chenille bleue assise au sommet, les bras croisés, fumant tranquillement une longue pipe turque sans faire la moindre attention à elle ni à quoi que ce fût.

5. Advice from a Caterpillar

The Caterpillar and Alice looked at each other for some time in silence: at last the Caterpillar took the hookah out of its mouth, and addressed her in a languid, sleepy voice.

'Who are you?' said the Caterpillar.

This was not an encouraging opening for a conversation. Alice replied, rather shyly:

'I—I hardly know, sir, just at present— at least I know who I was when I got up this morning, but I think I must have been changed several times since then.'

'What do you mean by that?' said the Caterpillar sternly. 'Explain yourself!'

I can't explain myself, I'm afraid, sir' said Alice: 'because I'm not myself, you see.'

'I don't see,' said the Caterpillar.

I'm afraid I can't put it more clearly,' Alice replied very politely: 'for I can't understand it myself to begin with; and being so many different sizes in a day is very confusing.'

'It isn't,' said the Caterpillar.

Well, perhaps you haven't found it so yet,' said Alice; 'but when you have to turn into a chrysalis—you will some day, you know—and then after that into a butterfly, I should think you'll feel it a little queer, won't you?'

'Not a bit,' said the Caterpillar.

'Well, perhaps your feelings may be different,' said Alice; 'all I know is, it would feel very queer to me.'

'You!' said the Caterpillar contemptuously. 'Who are you?'

Which brought them back again to the beginning of the conversation. Alice felt a little irritated at the Caterpillar's making such very short remarks, and she drew herself up and said, very gravely: 'I think, you ought to tell me who you are, first.'

'Why?' said the Caterpillar.

5. Conseils d'une Chenille

La Chenille et Alice se considérèrent un instant en silence. Enfin la Chenille sortit le houka de sa bouche, et lui adressa la parole d'une voix endormie et traînante.

"Qui êtes-vous?" dit la Chenille.

Ce n'était pas là une manière encourageante d'entamer la conversation. Alice répondit, un peu confuse:

"Je — je le sais à peine moi-même quant à présent. Je sais bien ce que j'étais en me levant ce matin, mais je crois avoir changé plusieurs fois depuis."

"Qu'entendez-vous par là?" dit la Chenille d'un ton sévère. "Expliquez-vous."

"Je crains bien de ne pouvoir pas m'expliquer," dit Alice, "car, voyez-vous, je ne suis plus moi-même."

"Je ne vois pas du tout," répondit la Chenille.

"J'ai bien peur de ne pouvoir pas dire les choses plus clairement," répliqua Alice fort poliment; "car d'abord je n'y comprends rien moi-même. Grandir et rapetisser si souvent en un seul jour, cela embrouille un peu les idées."

"Pas du tout," dit la Chenille.

"Peut-être ne vous en êtes-vous pas encore aperçue," dit Alice. "Mais quand vous deviendrez chrysalide, car c'est ce qui vous arrivera, sachez-le bien, et ensuite papillon, je crois bien que vous vous sentirez un peu drôle, qu'en dites-vous?"

"Pas du tout," dit la Chenille.

"Vos sensations sont peut-être différentes des miennes," dit Alice. "Tout ce que je sais, c'est que cela me semblerait bien drôle à moi."

"À vous!" dit la Chenille d'un ton de mépris. "Qui êtes-vous?"

Cette question les ramena au commencement de la conversation. Alice, un peu irritée du parler bref de la Chenille, se redressa de toute sa hauteur et répondit bien gravement: "Il me semble que vous devriez d'abord me dire qui vous êtes vous-même."

"Pourquoi?" dit la Chenille.

Here was another puzzling question; and as Alice could not think of any good reason, and as the Caterpillar seemed to be in a very unpleasant state of mind, she turned away.

'Come back!' the Caterpillar called after her. 'I've something important to say!'

This sounded promising, certainly: Alice turned and came back again.

'Keep your temper,' said the Caterpillar.

'Is that all?' said Alice, swallowing down her anger as well as she could.

'No,' said the Caterpillar.

Alice thought she might as well wait, as she had nothing else to do, and perhaps after all it might tell her something worth hearing.

For some minutes it puffed away without speaking, but at last it unfolded its arms, took the hookah out of its mouth again, and said: 'So you think you're changed, do you?'

I'm afraid I am, sir,' said Alice; 'I can't remember things as I used—and I don't keep the same size for ten minutes together!'

'Can't remember what things?' said the Caterpillar.

'Well, I've tried to say "How doth the little busy bee," but it all came different!' Alice replied in a very melancholy voice.

'Repeat, "you are old, Father William,"' said the Caterpillar.

Alice folded her hands, and began:—

'You are old, Father William,' the young man said,

'And your hair has become very white;

And yet you incessantly stand on your head — Do you think, at your age, it is right?'

'In my youth,' Father William replied to his son,

'I feared it might injure the brain;

But, now that I'm perfectly sure I have none,

Why, I do it again and again.'

C'était encore là une question bien embarrassante; et comme Alice ne trouvait pas de bonne raison à donner, et que la Chenille avait l'air de très-mauvaise humeur, Alice lui tourna le dos et s'éloigna.

"Revenez," lui cria la Chenille. "J'ai quelque chose d'important à vous dire!"

L'invitation était engageante assurément; Alice revint sur ses pas.

"Ne vous emportez pas," dit la Chenille.

"Est-ce tout?" dit Alice, cherchant à retenir sa colère.

"Non," répondit la Chenille.

Alice pensa qu'elle ferait tout aussi bien d'attendre, et qu'après tout la Chenille lui dirait peut-être quelque chose de bon à savoir.

La Chenille continua de fumer pendant quelques minutes sans rien dire. Puis, retirant enfin la pipe de sa bouche, elle se croisa les bras et dit: "Ainsi vous vous figurez que vous êtes changée, hein?"

"Je le crains bien," dit Alice. "Je ne peux plus me souvenir des choses comme autrefois, et je ne reste pas dix minutes de suite de la même grandeur!"

"De quoi est-ce que vous ne pouvez pas vous souvenir?" dit la Chenille.

"J'ai essayé de réciter la fable de Maître Corbeau, mais ce n'était plus la même chose," répondit Alice d'un ton chagrin.

"Récitez: "Vous êtes vieux, Père Guillaume,"" dit la Chenille.

Alice croisa les mains et commença:

"Vous êtes vieux, Père Guillaume.

Vous avez des cheveux tout gris…

La tête en bas! Père Guillaume; À votre âge, c'est peu permis!

— Étant jeune, pour ma cervelle

Je craignais fort, mon cher enfant;

Je n'en ai plus une parcelle,

J'en suis bien certain maintenant.

You are old,' said the youth: 'as I mentioned before,

And have grown most uncommonly fat;

Yet you turned a back-somersault in at the door—

Pray, what is the reason of that?'

'In my youth,' said the sage, as he shook his grey locks,

'I kept all my limbs very supple

By the use of this ointment—one shilling the box-

Allow me to sell you a couple?'

You are old,' said the youth: 'and your jaws are too weak

For anything tougher than suet;

Yet you finished the goose, with the bones and the beak—

Pray how did you manage to do it?'

In my youth,' said his father: 'I took to the law,

And argued each case with my wife;

And the muscular strength, which it gave to my jaw,

Has lasted the rest of my life.'

You are old,' said the youth: 'one would hardly suppose

That your eye was as steady as ever;

Yet you balanced an eel on the end of your nose—

What made you so awfully clever?'

'I have answered three questions, and that is enough,' Said his father; 'don't give yourself airs! Do you think I can listen all day to such stuff?

Be off, or I'll kick you down stairs!'

'That is not said right,' said the Caterpillar.

'Not quite right, I'm afraid,' said Alice, timidly; 'some of the words have got altered.'

'It is wrong from beginning to end,' said the Caterpillar decidedly, and there was silence for some minutes.

The Caterpillar was the first to speak.

— Vous êtes vieux, je vous l'ai dit,

Mais comment donc par cette porte,

Vous, dont la taille est comme un muid!

Cabriolez-vous de la sorte?

— Étant jeune, mon cher enfant,

J'avais chaque jointure bonne;

Je me frottais de cet onguent;

Si vous payez je vous en donne.

— Vous êtes vieux, et vous mangez

Les os comme de la bouillie;

Et jamais rien ne me laissez.

Comment faites-vous, je vous prie?

— Étant jeune, je disputais

Tous les jours avec votre mère;

C'est ainsi que je me suis fait

Un si puissant os maxillaire.

— Vous êtes vieux, par quelle adresse Tenez-vous debout sur le nez

Une anguille qui se redresse

Droit comme un I quand vous sifflez?

— Cette question est trop sotte!

Cessez de babiller ainsi, Ou je vais, du bout de ma botte,

Vous envoyer bien loin d'ici."

"Ce n'est pas cela," dit la Chenille.

"Pas tout à fait, je le crains bien," dit Alice timidement. "Tous les mots ne sont pas les mêmes."

"C'est tout de travers d'un bout à l'autre," dit la Chenille d'un ton décidé; et il se fit un silence de quelques minutes.

La Chenille fut la première à reprendre la parole.

'What size do you want to be?' it asked.

'Oh, I'm not particular as to size,' Alice hastily replied; 'only one doesn't like changing so often, you know.'

'I don't know,' said the Caterpillar.

Alice said nothing: she had never been so much contradicted in her life before, and she felt that she was losing her temper.

'Are you content now?' said the Caterpillar.

'Well, I should like to be a little larger, sir, if you wouldn't mind,' said Alice: 'three inches is such a wretched height to be.'

'It is a very good height indeed!' said the Caterpillar angrily, rearing itself upright as it spoke (it was exactly three inches high).

But I'm not used to it!' pleaded poor Alice in a piteous tone. And she thought of herself: 'I wish the creatures wouldn't be so easily offended!'

'You'll get used to it in time,' said the Caterpillar; and it put the hookah into its mouth and began smoking again.

This time Alice waited patiently until it chose to speak again. In a minute or two the Caterpillar took the hookah out of its mouth and yawned once or twice, and shook itself.

Then it got down off the mushroom, and crawled away in the grass, merely remarking as it went: 'One side will make you grow taller, and the other side will make you grow shorter.'

'One side of what? The other side of what?' thought Alice to herself.

'Of the mushroom,' said the Caterpillar, just as if she had asked it aloud; and in another moment it was out of sight.

Alice remained looking thoughtfully at the mushroom for a minute, trying to make out which were the two sides of it; and as it was perfectly round, she found this a very difficult question.

However, at last she stretched her arms round it as far as they would go, and broke off a bit of the edge with each hand.

'And now which is which?' she said to herself, and nibbled a little of the right-hand bit to try the effect: the next

"De quelle grandeur voulez-vous être?" demanda-t-elle.

"Oh! je ne suis pas difficile, quant à la taille," reprit vivement Alice. "Mais vous comprenez bien qu'on n'aime pas à en changer si souvent."

"Je ne comprends pas du tout," dit la Chenille.

Alice se tut; elle n'avait jamais de sa vie été si souvent contredite, et elle sentait qu'elle allait perdre patience.

"Êtes-vous satisfaite maintenant?" dit la Chenille.

"J'aimerais bien à être un petit peu plus grande, si cela vous était égal," dit Alice. "Trois pouces de haut, c'est si peu!"

"C'est une très-belle taille," dit la Chenille en colère, se dressant de toute sa hauteur. (Elle avait tout juste trois pouces de haut.)

"Mais je n'y suis pas habituée," répliqua Alice d'un ton piteux, et elle fit cette réflexion: "Je voudrais bien que ces gens-là ne fussent pas si susceptibles."

"Vous finirez par vous y habituer," dit la Chenille. Elle remit la pipe à sa bouche, et fuma de plus belle.

Cette fois Alice attendit patiemment qu'elle se décidât à parler. Au bout de deux ou trois minutes la Chenille sortit le houka de sa bouche, bâilla une ou deux fois et se secoua;

puis elle descendit de dessus le champignon, glissa dans le gazon, et dit tout simplement en s'en allant: "Un côté vous fera grandir, et l'autre vous fera rapetisser."

"Un côté de quoi, l'autre côté de quoi?" pensa Alice.

"Du champignon," dit la Chenille, comme si Alice avait parlé tout haut; et un moment après la Chenille avait disparu.

Alice contempla le champignon d'un air pensif pendant un instant, essayant de deviner quels en étaient les côtés; et comme le champignon était tout rond, elle trouva la question fort embarrassante.

Enfin elle étendit ses bras tout autour, en les allongeant autant que possible, et, de chaque main, enleva une petite partie du bord du champignon.

"Maintenant, lequel des deux?" se dit-elle, et elle grignota un peu du morceau de la main droite pour voir quel effet il

moment she felt a violent blow underneath her chin: it had struck her foot!

produirait. Presque aussitôt elle reçut un coup violent sous le menton; il venait de frapper contre son pied.

She was a good deal frightened by this very sudden change, but she felt that there was no time to be lost, as she was shrinking rapidly; so she set to work at once to eat some of the other bit.

Ce brusque changement lui fit grand' peur, mais elle comprit qu'il n'y avait pas de temps à perdre, car elle diminuait rapidement. Elle se mit donc bien vite à manger un peu de l'autre morceau.

Her chin was pressed so closely against her foot, that there was hardly room to open her mouth; but she did it at last, and managed to swallow a morsel of the lefthand bit.

Son menton était si rapproché de son pied qu'il y avait à peine assez de place pour qu'elle pût ouvrir la bouche. Elle y réussit enfin, et parvint à avaler une partie du morceau de la main gauche.

Come, my head's free at last!' said Alice in a tone of delight, which changed into alarm in another moment, when she found that her shoulders were nowhere to be found:

"Voilà enfin ma tête libre," dit Alice d'un ton joyeux qui se changea bientôt en cris d'épouvante, quand elle s'aperçut de l'absence de ses épaules.

all she could see, when she looked down, was an immense length of neck, which seemed to rise like a stalk out of a sea of green leaves that lay far below her.

Tout ce qu'elle pouvait voir en regardant en bas, c'était un cou long à n'en plus finir qui semblait se dresser comme une tige, du milieu d'un océan de verdure s'étendant bien loin au-dessous d'elle,

What can all that green stuff be?' said Alice. 'And where have my shoulders got to? And oh, my poor hands, how is it I can't see you?'

"Qu'est-ce que c'est que toute cette verdure?" dit Alice. "Et où donc sont mes épaules? Oh! mes pauvres mains! Comment se fait-il que je ne puis vous voir?"

She was moving them about as she spoke, but no result seemed to follow, except a little shaking among the distant green leaves.

Tout en parlant elle agitait les mains, mais il n'en résulta qu'un petit mouvement au loin parmi les feuilles vertes.

As there seemed to be no chance of getting her hands up to her head, she tried to get her head down to them, and was delighted to find that her neck would bend about easily in any direction, like a serpent.

Comme elle ne trouvait pas le moyen de porter ses mains à sa tête, elle tâcha de porter sa tête à ses mains, et s'aperçut avec joie que son cou se repliait avec aisance de tous côtés comme un serpent.

She had just succeeded in curving it down into a graceful zigzag, and was going to dive in among the leaves, which she found to be nothing but the tops of the trees under which she had been wandering, when a sharp hiss made her draw back in a hurry:

Elle venait de réussir à le plier en un gracieux zigzag, et allait plonger parmi les feuilles, qui étaient tout simplement le haut des arbres sous lesquels elle avait erré, quand un sifflement aigu la força de reculer promptement;

a large pigeon had flown into her face, and was beating her violently with its wings.

un gros pigeon venait de lui voler à la figure, et lui donnait de grands coups d'ailes.

'Serpent!' screamed the Pigeon.

"Serpent!" criait le Pigeon.

'I'm not a serpent!' said Alice indignantly. 'Let me alone!'

"Je ne suis pas un serpent," dit Alice, avec indignation. "Laissez-moi tranquille."

Serpent, I say again!' repeated the Pigeon, but in a more subdued tone, and added with a kind of sob: 'I've tried every way, and nothing seems to suit them!'

"Serpent! Je le répète," dit le Pigeon, mais d'un ton plus doux; puis il continua avec une espèce de sanglot: "J'ai essayé de toutes les façons, rien ne semble les satisfaire."

'I haven't the least idea what you're talking about,' said Alice.

"Je n'ai pas la moindre idée de ce que vous voulez dire," répondit Alice.

'I've tried the roots of trees, and I've tried banks, and I've tried hedges,' the Pigeon went on, without attending to her; 'but those serpents! There's no pleasing them!'

Alice was more and more puzzled, but she thought there was no use in saying anything more till the Pigeon had finished.

'As if it wasn't trouble enough hatching the eggs,' said the Pigeon; 'but I must be on the look-out for serpents night and day! Why, I haven't had a wink of sleep these three weeks!'

'I'm very sorry you've been annoyed,' said Alice, who was beginning to see its meaning.

And just as I'd taken the highest tree in the wood,' continued the Pigeon, raising its voice to a shriek:

'and just as I was thinking I should be free of them at last, they must needs come wriggling down from the sky! Ugh, Serpent!'

But I'm not a serpent, I tell you!' said Alice. 'I'm a—I'm a—'

'Well! what are you?' said the Pigeon. 'I can see you're trying to invent something!'

I—I'm a little girl,' said Alice, rather doubtfully, as she remembered the number of changes she had gone through that day.

A likely story indeed!' said the Pigeon in a tone of the deepest contempt.

'I've seen a good many little girls in my time, but never one with such a neck as that! No, no! You're a serpent; and there's no use denying it. I suppose you'll be telling me next that you never tasted an egg!'

'I have tasted eggs, certainly,' said Alice, who was a very truthful child; 'but little girls eat eggs quite as much as serpents do, you know.'

'I don't believe it,' said the Pigeon; 'but if they do, why then they're a kind of serpent, that's all I can say.'

This was such a new idea to Alice, that she was quite silent for a minute or two, which gave the Pigeon the opportunity of adding:

'You're looking for eggs, I know that well enough; and what does it matter to me whether you're a little girl or a serpent?'

"J'ai essayé des racines d'arbres; j'ai essayé des talus; j'ai essayé des haies," continua le Pigeon sans faire attention à elle. "Mais ces serpents! il n'y a pas moyen de les satisfaire."

Alice était de plus en plus intriguée, mais elle pensa que ce n'était pas la peine de rien dire avant que le Pigeon eût fini de parler.

"Je n'ai donc pas assez de mal à couver mes œufs," dit le Pigeon. "Il faut encore que je guette les serpents nuit et jour. Je n'ai pas fermé l'œil depuis trois semaines!"

"Je suis fâchée que vous ayez été tourmenté," dit Alice, qui commençait à comprendre.

"Au moment ou je venais de choisir l'arbre le plus haut de la forêt," continua le Pigeon en élevant la voix jusqu'à crier, —

"au moment où je me figurais que j'allais en être enfin débarrassé, les voilà qui tombent du ciel "en replis tortueux." Oh! le vilain serpent!"

"Mais je ne suis pas un serpent," dit Alice. "Je suis une — Je suis —"

"Eh bien! qu'êtes-vous!" dit le Pigeon "Je vois que vous cherchez à inventer quelque chose."

"Je — je suis une petite fille," répondit Alice avec quelque hésitation, car elle se rappelait combien de changements elle avait éprouvés ce jour-là.

"Voilà une histoire bien vraisemblable!" dit le Pigeon d'un air de profond mépris.

"J'ai vu bien des petites filles dans mon temps, mais je n'en ai jamais vu avec un cou comme cela. Non, non; vous êtes un serpent; il est inutile de le nier. Vous allez sans doute me dire que vous n'avez jamais mangé d'œufs."

"Si fait, j'ai mangé des œufs," dit Alice, qui ne savait pas mentir; "mais vous savez que les petites filles mangent des œufs aussi bien que les serpents."

"Je n'en crois rien," dit le Pigeon, "mais s'il en est ainsi, elles sont une espèce de serpent; c'est tout ce que j'ai à vous dire."

Cette idée était si nouvelle pour Alice qu'elle resta muette pendant une ou deux minutes, ce qui donna au Pigeon le temps d'ajouter:

"Vous cherchez des œufs, ça j'en suis bien sûr, et alors que m'importe que vous soyez une petite fille ou un serpent?"

'It matters a good deal to me,' said Alice hastily; 'but I'm not looking for eggs, as it happens; and if I was, I shouldn't want yours: I don't like them raw.'

"Cela m'importe beaucoup à moi," dit Alice vivement; "mais je ne cherche pas d'œufs justement, et quand même j'en chercherais je ne voudrais pas des vôtres; je ne les aime pas crus."

Well, be off, then!' said the Pigeon in a sulky tone, as it settled down again into its nest.

"Eh bien! allez-vous-en alors," dit le Pigeon d'un ton boudeur en se remettant dans son nid.

Alice crouched down among the trees as well as she could, for her neck kept getting entangled among the branches, and every now and then she had to stop and untwist it.

Alice se glissa parmi les arbres du mieux qu'elle put en se baissant, car son cou s'entortillait dans les branches, et à chaque instant il lui fallait s'arrêter et le désentortiller.

After a while she remembered that she still held the pieces of mushroom in her hands, and she set to work very carefully, nibbling first at one and then at the other, and growing sometimes taller and sometimes shorter, until she had succeeded in bringing herself down to her usual height.

Au bout de quelque temps, elle se rappela qu'elle tenait encore dans ses mains les morceaux de champignon, et elle se mit à l'œuvre avec grand soin, grignotant tantôt l'un, tantôt l'autre, et tantôt grandissant, tantôt rapetissant, jusqu'à ce qu'enfin elle parvint à se ramener à sa grandeur naturelle.

It was so long since she had been anything near the right size, that it felt quite strange at first; but she got used to it in a few minutes, and began talking to herself, as usual.

Il y avait si longtemps qu'elle n'avait été d'une taille raisonnable que cela lui parut d'abord tout drôle, mais elle finit par s'y accoutumer, et commença à se parler à elle-même, comme d'habitude.

'Come, there's half my plan done now! How puzzling all these changes are! I'm never sure what I'm going to be, from one minute to another!

"Allons, voilà maintenant la moitié de mon projet exécuté. Comme tous ces changements sont embarrassants! Je ne suis jamais sûre de ce que je vais devenir d'une minute à l'autre.

However, I've got back to my right size: the next thing is, to get into that beautiful garden—how is that to be done, I wonder?'

Toutefois, je suis redevenue de la bonne grandeur; il me reste maintenant à pénétrer dans ce magnifique jardin. Comment faire?"

As she said this, she came suddenly upon an open place, with a little house in it about four feet high.

En disant ces mots elle arriva tout à coup à une clairière, où se trouvait une maison d'environ quatre pieds de haut.

'Whoever lives there,' thought Alice: 'it'll never do to come upon them this size: why, I should frighten them out of their wits!'

"Quels que soient les gens qui demeurent là," pensa Alice, "il ne serait pas raisonnable de se présenter à eux grande comme je suis. Ils deviendraient fous de frayeur."

So she began nibbling at the righthand bit again, and did not venture to go near the house till she had brought herself down to nine inches high.

Elle se mit de nouveau à grignoter le morceau qu'elle tenait dans sa main droite, et ne s'aventura pas près de la maison avant d'avoir réduit sa taille à neuf pouces.

6. Pig and Pepper

For a minute or two she stood looking at the house, and wondering what to do next, when suddenly a footman in livery came running out of the wood—

(she considered him to be a footman because he was in livery: otherwise, judging by his face only, she would have called him a fish) — and rapped loudly at the door with his knuckles.

It was opened by another footman in livery, with a round face, and large eyes like a frog; and both footmen, Alice noticed, had powdered hair that curled all over their heads.

She felt very curious to know what it was all about, and crept a little way out of the wood to listen.

The Fish-Footman began by producing from under his arm a great letter, nearly as large as himself, and this he handed over to the other, saying, in a solemn tone:

'For the Duchess. An invitation from the Queen to play croquet.' The Frog-Footman repeated, in the same solemn tone, only changing the order of the words a little: 'From the Queen. An invitation for the Duchess to play croquet.'

Then they both bowed low, and their curls got entangled together.

Alice laughed so much at this, that she had to run back into the wood for fear of their hearing her; and when she next peeped out the Fish-Footman was gone, and the other was sitting on the ground near the door, staring stupidly up into the sky.

Alice went timidly up to the door, and knocked.

There's no sort of use in knocking,' said the Footman: 'and that for two reasons. First, because I'm on the same side of the door as you are; secondly, because they're making such a noise inside, no one could possibly hear you.'

And certainly there was a most extraordinary noise going on within—a constant howling and sneezing, and every now and then a great crash, as if a dish or kettle had been broken to pieces.

6. Porc et Poivre

Alice resta une ou deux minutes à regarder à la porte; elle se demandait ce qu'il fallait faire, quand tout à coup un laquais en livrée sortit du bois en courant.

(Elle le prit pour un laquais à cause de sa livrée; sans cela, à n'en juger que par la figure, elle l'aurait pris pour un poisson.) Il frappa fortement avec son doigt à la porte.

Elle fut ouverte par un autre laquais en livrée qui avait la face toute ronde et de gros yeux comme une grenouille. Alice remarqua que les deux laquais avaient les cheveux poudrés et tout frisés.

Elle se sentit piquée de curiosité, et, voulant savoir ce que tout cela signifiait, elle se glissa un peu en dehors du bois afin d'écouter.

Le Laquais-Poisson prit de dessous son bras une lettre énorme, presque aussi grande que lui, et la présenta au Laquais-Grenouille en disant d'un ton solennel:

"Pour Madame la Duchesse, une invitation de la Reine à une partie de croquet." Le Laquais-Grenouille répéta sur le même ton solennel, en changeant un peu l'ordre des mots: "De la part de la Reine une invitation pour Madame la Duchesse à une partie de croquet;"

puis tous deux se firent un profond salut et les boucles de leurs chevelures s'entremêlèrent.

Cela fit tellement rire Alice qu'elle eut à rentrer bien vite dans le bois de peur d'être entendue; et quand elle avança la tête pour regarder de nouveau, le Laquais-Poisson était parti, et l'autre était assis par terre près de la route, regardant niaisement en l'air.

Alice s'approcha timidement de la porte et frappa.

"Cela ne sert à rien du tout de frapper," dit le Laquais, "et cela pour deux raisons: premièrement, parce que je suis du même côté de la porte que vous; deuxièmement, parce qu'on fait là-dedans un tel bruit que personne ne peut vous entendre."

En effet, il se faisait dans l'intérieur un bruit extraordinaire, des hurlements et des éternuements continuels, et de temps à autre un grand fracas comme si on brisait de la vaisselle.

Please, then,' said Alice: 'how am I to get in?'

"Eh bien! comment puis-je entrer, s'il vous plaît?" demanda Alice.

There might be some sense in your knocking,' the Footman went on without attending to her: 'if we had the door between us. For instance, if you were inside, you might knock, and I could let you out, you know.'

"Il y aurait quelque bon sens à frapper à cette porte," continua le Laquais sans l'écouter, "si nous avions la porte entre nous deux. Par exemple, si vous étiez à l'intérieur vous pourriez frapper et je pourrais vous laisser sortir."

He was looking up into the sky all the time he was speaking, and this Alice thought decidedly uncivil.

Il regardait en l'air tout le temps qu'il parlait, et Alice trouvait cela très-impoli.

'But perhaps he can't help it,' she said to herself; 'his eyes are so very nearly at the top of his head. But at any rate he might answer questions.—How am I to get in?' she repeated, aloud.

"Mais peut-être ne peut-il pas s'en empêcher," dit-elle; "il a les yeux presque sur le sommet de la tête. Dans tous les cas il pourrait bien répondre à mes questions. — Comment faire pour entrer?" répéta-t-elle tout haut.

I shall sit here,' the Footman remarked: 'till tomorrow—'

"Je vais rester assis ici," dit le Laquais, "jusqu'à demain —"

At this moment the door of the house opened, and a large plate came skimming out, straight at the Footman's head: it just grazed his nose, and broke to pieces against one of the trees behind him.

Au même instant la porte de la maison s'ouvrit, et une grande assiette vola tout droit dans la direction de la tête du Laquais; elle lui effleura le nez, et alla se briser contre un arbre derrière lui.

—or next day, maybe,' the Footman continued in the same tone, exactly as if nothing had happened.

"— ou le jour suivant peut-être," continua le Laquais sur le même ton, tout comme si rien n'était arrivé.

'How am I to get in?' asked Alice again, in a louder tone.

"Comment faire pour entrer?" redemanda Alice en élevant la voix.

'Are you to get in at all?' said the Footman. 'That's the first question, you know.'

"Mais devriez-vous entrer?" dit le Laquais. "C'est ce qu'il faut se demander, n'est-ce pas?"

It was, no doubt: only Alice did not like to be told so. 'It's really dreadful,' she muttered to herself: 'the way all the creatures argue. It's enough to drive one crazy!'

Bien certainement, mais Alice trouva mauvais qu'on le lui dît. "C'est vraiment terrible," murmura-t-elle, "de voir la manière dont ces gens-là discutent, il y a de quoi rendre fou."

The Footman seemed to think this a good opportunity for repeating his remark, with variations. 'I shall sit here,' he said: 'on and off, for days and days.'

Le Laquais trouva l'occasion bonne pour répéter son observation avec des variantes. "Je resterai assis ici," dit-il, "l'un dans l'autre, pendant des jours et des jours!"

'But what am I to do?' said Alice.

"Mais que faut-il que je fasse?" dit Alice.

'Anything you like,' said the Footman, and began whistling.

"Tout ce que vous voudrez," dit le Laquais; et il se mit à siffler.

'Oh, there's no use in talking to him,' said Alice desperately: 'he's perfectly idiotic!' And she opened the door and went in.

"Oh! ce n'est pas la peine de lui parler," dit Alice, désespérée; "c'est un parfait idiot." Puis elle ouvrit la porte et entra.

The door led right into a large kitchen, which was full of smoke from one end to the other:

La porte donnait sur une grande cuisine qui était pleine de fumée d'un bout à l'autre.

the Duchess was sitting on a three-legged stool in the middle, nursing a baby; the cook was leaning over the fire, stirring a large cauldron which seemed to be full of soup.

La Duchesse était assise sur un tabouret à trois pieds, au milieu de la cuisine, et dorlotait un bébé; la cuisinière, penchée sur le feu, brassait quelque chose dans un grand chaudron qui paraissait rempli de soupe.

'There's certainly too much pepper in that soup!' Alice said to herself, as well as she could for sneezing.

"Bien sûr, il y a trop de poivre dans la soupe," se dit Alice, tout empêchée par les éternuements.

There was certainly too much of it in the air. Even the Duchess sneezed occasionally; and as for the baby, it was sneezing and howling alternately without a moment's pause.

Il y en avait certainement trop dans l'air. La Duchesse elle-même éternuait de temps en temps, et quant au bébé il éternuait et hurlait alternativement sans aucune interruption.

The only things in the kitchen that did not sneeze, were the cook, and a large cat which was sitting on the hearth and grinning from ear to ear.

Les deux seules créatures qui n'éternuassent pas, étaient la cuisinière et un gros chat assis sur l'âtre et dont la bouche grimaçante était fendue d'une oreille à l'autre.

Please would you tell me,' said Alice, a little timidly, for she was not quite sure whether it was good manners for her to speak first: 'why your cat grins like that?'

"Pourriez-vous m'apprendre," dit Alice un peu timidement, car elle ne savait pas s'il était bien convenable qu'elle parlât la première, "pourquoi votre chat grimace ainsi?"

It's a Cheshire cat,' said the Duchess: 'and that's why. Pig!'

"C'est un Grimaçon," dit la Duchesse; "voilà pourquoi. — Porc!"

She said the last word with such sudden violence that Alice quite jumped; but she saw in another moment that it was addressed to the baby, and not to her, so she took courage, and went on again:—

Elle prononça ce dernier mot si fort et si subitement qu'Alice en frémit. Mais elle comprit bientôt que cela s'adressait au bébé et non pas à elle; elle reprit donc courage et continua:

'I didn't know that Cheshire cats always grinned; in fact, I didn't know that cats could grin.'

"J'ignorais qu'il y eût des chats de cette espèce. Au fait j'ignorais qu'un chat pût grimacer."

'They all can,' said the Duchess; 'and most of 'em do.'

"Ils le peuvent tous," dit la Duchesse; "et la plupart le font."

'I don't know of any that do,' Alice said very politely, feeling quite pleased to have got into a conversation.

"Je n'en connais pas un qui grimace," dit Alice poliment, bien contente d'être entrée en conversation.

'You don't know much,' said the Duchess; 'and that's a fact.'

"Le fait est que vous ne savez pas grand'chose," dit la Duchesse.

Alice did not at all like the tone of this remark, and thought it would be as well to introduce some other subject of conversation.

Le ton sur lequel fut faite cette observation ne plut pas du tout à Alice, et elle pensa qu'il serait bon de changer la conversation.

While she was trying to fix on one, the cook took the cauldron of soup off the fire, and at once set to work throwing everything within her reach at the Duchess and the baby —the fire-irons came first; then followed a shower of saucepans, plates, and dishes.

Tandis qu'elle cherchait un autre sujet, la cuisinière retira de dessus le feu le chaudron plein de soupe, et se mit aussitôt à jeter tout ce qui lui tomba sous la main à la Duchesse et au bébé — la pelle et les pincettes d'abord, à leur suite vint une pluie de casseroles, d'assiettes et de plats.

The Duchess took no notice of them even when they hit her; and the baby was howling so much already, that it was quite impossible to say whether the blows hurt it or not.

La Duchesse n'y faisait pas la moindre attention, même quand elle en était atteinte, et l'enfant hurlait déjà si fort auparavant qu'il était impossible de savoir si les coups lui faisaient mal ou non.

'Oh, please mind what you're doing!' cried Alice, jumping up and down in an agony of terror. 'Oh, there goes his precious nose'; as an unusually large saucepan flew close by it, and very nearly carried it off.

"Oh! je vous en prie, prenez garde à ce que vous faites," criait Alice, sautant ça et là et en proie à la terreur. "Oh! son cher petit nez!" Une casserole d'une grandeur peu ordinaire venait de voler tout près du bébé, et avait failli lui emporter le nez.

If everybody minded their own business,' the Duchess said in a hoarse growl: 'the world would go round a deal faster than it does.'

"Si chacun s'occupait de ses affaires," dit la Duchesse avec un grognement rauque, "le monde n'en irait que mieux."

Which would not be an advantage,' said Alice, who felt very glad to get an opportunity of showing off a little of her knowledge.

"Ce qui ne serait guère avantageux," dit Alice, enchantée qu'il se présentât une occasion de montrer un peu de son savoir.

'Just think of what work it would make with the day and night! You see the earth takes twenty-four hours to turn round on its axis—'

"Songez à ce que deviendraient le jour et la nuit; vous voyez bien, la terre met vingt-quatre heures à faire sa révolution."

Talking of axes,' said the Duchess: 'chop off her head!'

"Ah! vous parlez de faire des révolutions!" dit la Duchesse. "Qu'on lui coupe la tête!"

Alice glanced rather anxiously at the cook, to see if she meant to take the hint; but the cook was busily stirring the soup, and seemed not to be listening, so she went on again: 'Twenty-four hours, I think; or is it twelve? I—'

Alice jeta un regard inquiet sur la cuisinière pour voir si elle allait obéir; mais la cuisinière était tout occupée à brasser la soupe et paraissait ne pas écouter. Alice continua donc: "Vingt-quatre heures, je crois, ou bien douze? Je pense —"

'Oh, don't bother me,' said the Duchess; 'I never could abide figures!' And with that she began nursing her child again, singing a sort of lullaby to it as she did so, and giving it a violent shake at the end of every line:

"Oh! laissez-moi la paix," dit la Duchesse, "je n'ai jamais pu souffrir les chiffres." Et là-dessus elle recommença à dorloter son enfant, lui chantant une espèce de chanson pour l'endormir et lui donnant une forte secousse au bout de chaque vers.

'Speak roughly to your little boy,

And beat him when he sneezes:

He only does it to annoy,

Because he knows it teases.'

"Grondez-moi ce vilain garçon!

Battez-le quand il éternue;

À vous taquiner, sans façon

Le méchant enfant s'évertue."

CHORUS

Refrain

(In which the cook and the baby joined):— 'Wow! wow! wow!'

(que reprirent en chœur la cuisinière et le bébé). "Brou, Brou, Brou!" (bis.)

While the Duchess sang the second verse of the song, she kept tossing the baby violently up and down, and the poor little thing howled so, that Alice could hardly hear the words:—

En chantant le second couplet de la chanson la Duchesse faisait sauter le bébé et le secouait violemment, si bien que le pauvre petit être hurlait au point qu'Alice put à peine entendre ces mots:

'I speak severely to my boy,

I beat him when he sneezes;

For he can thoroughly enjoy

The pepper when he pleases!'

"Oui, oui, je m'en vais le gronder,

Et le battre, s'il éternue;

Car bientôt à savoir poivrer,

Je veux que l'enfant s'habitue."

CHORUS

Refrain.

'Wow! wow! wow!'

"Brou, Brou, Brou!" (bis.)

Here! you may nurse it a bit, if you like!' the Duchess said to Alice, flinging the baby at her as she spoke.

'I must go and get ready to play croquet with the Queen,' and she hurried out of the room. The cook threw a frying-pan after her as she went out, but it just missed her.

Alice caught the baby with some difficulty, as it was a queer- shaped little creature, and held out its arms and legs in all directions: 'just like a star-fish,' thought Alice.

The poor little thing was snorting like a steam-engine when she caught it, and kept doubling itself up and straightening itself out again, so that altogether, for the first minute or two, it was as much as she could do to hold it.

As soon as she had made out the proper way of nursing it, (which was to twist it up into a sort of knot, and then keep tight hold of its right ear and left foot, so as to prevent its undoing itself,) she carried it out into the open air.

'If I don't take this child away with me,' thought Alice: 'they're sure to kill it in a day or two: wouldn't it be murder to leave it behind?'

She said the last words out loud, and the little thing grunted in reply (it had left off sneezing by this time). 'Don't grunt,' said Alice; 'that's not at all a proper way of expressing yourself.'

The baby grunted again, and Alice looked very anxiously into its face to see what was the matter with it.

There could be no doubt that it had a very turn-up nose, much more like a snout than a real nose; also its eyes were getting extremely small for a baby:

altogether Alice did not like the look of the thing at all. 'But perhaps it was only sobbing,' she thought, and looked into its eyes again, to see if there were any tears.

No, there were no tears. 'If you're going to turn into a pig, my dear,' said Alice, seriously: 'I'll have nothing more to do with you. Mind now!'

The poor little thing sobbed again (or grunted, it was impossible to say which), and they went on for some while in silence.

Alice was just beginning to think to herself: 'Now, what am I to do with this creature when I get it home?' when it

"Tenez, vous pouvez le dorloter si vous voulez!" dit la Duchesse à Alice: et à ces mots elle lui jeta le bébé.

"Il faut que j'aille m'apprêter pour aller jouer au croquet avec la Reine."Et elle se précipita hors de la chambre. La cuisinière lui lança une poêle comme elle s'en allait, mais elle la manqua tout juste.

Alice eut de la peine à attraper le bébé. C'était un petit être d'une forme étrange qui tenait ses bras et ses jambes étendus dans toutes les directions; "Tout comme une étoile de mer," pensait Alice.

La pauvre petite créature ronflait comme une machine à vapeur lorsqu'elle l'attrapa, et ne cessait de se plier en deux, puis de s'étendre tout droit, de sorte qu'avec tout cela, pendant les premiers instants, c'est tout ce qu'elle pouvait faire que de le tenir.

Sitôt qu'elle eut trouvé le bon moyen de le bercer, (qui était d'en faire une espèce de nœud, et puis de le tenir fermement par l'oreille droite et le pied gauche afin de l'empêcher de se dénouer,) elle le porta dehors en plein air.

"Si je n'emporte pas cet enfant avec moi," pensa Alice, "ils le tueront bien sûr un de ces jours. Ne serait-ce pas un meurtre de l'abandonner?"

Elle dit ces derniers mots à haute voix, et la petite créature répondit en grognant (elle avait cessé d'éternuer alors). "Ne grogne pas ainsi," dit Alice; "ce n'est pas là du tout une bonne manière de s'exprimer."

Le bébé grogna de nouveau. Alice le regarda au visage avec inquiétude pour voir ce qu'il avait.

Sans contredit son nez était très-retroussé, et ressemblait bien plutôt à un groin qu'à un vrai nez. Ses yeux aussi devenaient très-petits pour un bébé.

Enfin Alice ne trouva pas du tout de son goût l'aspect de ce petit être. "Mais peut-être sanglotait-il tout simplement," pensa-t-elle, et elle regarda de nouveau les yeux du bébé pour voir s'il n'y avait pas de larmes.

"Si tu vas te changer en porc," dit Alice très-sérieusement, "je ne veux plus rien avoir à faire avec toi. Fais-y bien attention!"

La pauvre petite créature sanglota de nouveau, ou grogna (il était impossible de savoir lequel des deux), et ils continuèrent leur chemin un instant en silence.

Alice commençait à dire en elle-même, "Mais, que faire de cette créature quand je l'aurai portée à la maison?" lorsqu'il

grunted again, so violently, that she looked down into its face in some alarm.

grogna de nouveau si fort qu'elle regarda sa figure avec quelque inquiétude.

This time there could be no mistake about it: it was neither more nor less than a pig, and she felt that it would be quite absurd for her to carry it further.

Cette fois il n'y avait pas à s'y tromper, c'était un porc, ni plus ni moins, et elle comprit qu'il serait ridicule de le porter plus loin.

So she set the little creature down, and felt quite relieved to see it trot away quietly into the wood.

Elle déposa donc par terre le petit animal, et se sentit toute soulagée de le voir trotter tranquillement vers le bois.

'If it had grown up,' she said to herself: 'it would have made a dreadfully ugly child: but it makes rather a handsome pig, I think.'

"S'il avait grandi," se dit-elle, "il serait devenu un bien vilain enfant; tandis qu'il fait un assez joli petit porc, il me semble."

And she began thinking over other children she knew, who might do very well as pigs, and was just saying to herself:

Alors elle se mit à penser à d'autres enfants qu'elle connaissait et qui feraient d'assez jolis porcs,

'if one only knew the right way to change them—' when she was a little startled by seeing the Cheshire Cat sitting on a bough of a tree a few yards off.

si seulement on savait la manière de s'y prendre pour les métamorphoser. Elle était en train de faire ces réflexions, lorsqu'elle tressaillit en voyant tout à coup le Chat assis à quelques pas de là sur la branche d'un arbre.

The Cat only grinned when it saw Alice. It looked good-natured, she thought: still it had very long claws and a great many teeth, so she felt that it ought to be treated with respect.

Le Chat grimaça en apercevant Alice. Elle trouva qu'il avait l'air bon enfant, et cependant il avait de très-longues griffes et une grande rangée de dents; aussi comprit-elle qu'il fallait le traiter avec respect.

Cheshire Puss,' she began, rather timidly, as she did not at all know whether it would like the name:

"Grimaçon!" commença-t-elle un peu timidement, ne sachant pas du tout si cette familiarité lui serait agréable;

however, it only grinned a little wider. 'Come, it's pleased so far,' thought Alice, and she went on. 'Would you tell me, please, which way I ought to go from here?'

toutefois il ne fit qu'allonger sa grimace. "Allons, il est content jusqu'à présent," pensa Alice, et elle continua: "Dites-moi, je vous prie, de quel côté faut-il me diriger?"

'That depends a good deal on where you want to get to,' said the Cat.

"Cela dépend beaucoup de l'endroit où vous voulez aller," dit le Chat.

I don't much care where—' said Alice.

"Cela m'est assez indifférent," dit Alice.

'Then it doesn't matter which way you go,' said the Cat.

"Alors peu importe de quel côté vous irez," dit le Chat.

—so long as I get somewhere,' Alice added as an explanation.

"Pourvu que j'arrive quelque part," ajouta Alice en explication.

Oh, you're sure to do that,' said the Cat: 'if you only walk long enough.'

"Cela ne peut manquer, pourvu que vous marchiez assez longtemps."

Alice felt that this could not be denied, so she tried another question. 'What sort of people live about here?'

Alice comprit que cela était incontestable; elle essaya donc d'une autre question: "Quels sont les gens qui demeurent par ici?"

In that direction,' the Cat said, waving its right paw round: 'lives a Hatter: and in that direction,' waving the other paw: 'lives a March Hare. Visit either you like: they're both mad.'

"De ce côté-ci," dit le Chat, décrivant un cercle avec sa patte droite, "demeure un chapelier; de ce côté-là," faisant de même avec sa patte gauche, "demeure un lièvre. Allez voir celui que vous voudrez, tous deux sont fous."

'But I don't want to go among mad people,' Alice remarked.

"Mais je ne veux pas fréquenter des fous," fit observer Alice.

'Oh, you can't help that,' said the Cat: 'we're all mad here. I'm mad. You're mad.'

"Vous ne pouvez pas vous en défendre, tout le monde est fou ici. Je suis fou, vous êtes folle."

'How do you know I'm mad?' said Alice.

"Comment savez-vous que je suis folle?" dit Alice.

You must be,' said the Cat: 'or you wouldn't have come here.'

"Vous devez l'être," dit le Chat, "sans cela ne seriez pas venue ici."

Alice didn't think that proved it at all; however, she went on 'And how do you know that you're mad?'

Alice pensa que cela ne prouvait rien. Toutefois elle continua: "Et comment savez-vous que vous êtes fou?"

To begin with,' said the Cat: 'a dog's not mad. You grant that?'

"D'abord," dit le Chat, "un chien n'est pas fou; vous convenez de cela."

'I suppose so,' said Alice.

"Je le suppose," dit Alice.

Well, then,' the Cat went on: 'you see, a dog growls when it's angry, and wags its tail when it's pleased. Now I growl when I'm pleased, and wag my tail when I'm angry. Therefore I'm mad.'

"Eh bien!" continua le Chat, "un chien grogne quand il se fâche, et remue la queue lorsqu'il est content. Or, moi, je grogne quand je suis content, et je remue la queue quand je me fâche. Donc je suis fou."

'I call it purring, not growling,' said Alice.

"J'appelle cela faire le rouet, et non pas grogner," dit Alice.

'Call it what you like,' said the Cat. 'Do you play croquet with the Queen to-day?'

"Appelez cela comme vous voudrez," dit le Chat. "Jouez-vous au croquet avec la Reine aujourd'hui?"

I should like it very much,' said Alice: 'but I haven't been invited yet.'

"Cela me ferait grand plaisir," dit Alice, "mais je n'ai pas été invitée."

'You'll see me there,' said the Cat, and vanished.

"Vous m'y verrez," dit le Chat; et il disparut.

Alice was not much surprised at this, she was getting so used to queer things happening. While she was looking at the place where it had been, it suddenly appeared again.

Alice ne fut pas très-étonnée, tant elle commençait à s'habituer aux événements extraordinaires. Tandis qu'elle regardait encore l'endroit que le Chat venait de quitter, il reparut tout à coup.

'By-the-bye, what became of the baby?' said the Cat. 'I'd nearly forgotten to ask.'

"À propos, qu'est devenu le bébé? J'allais oublier de le demander."

'It turned into a pig,' Alice quietly said, just as if it had come back in a natural way.

"Il a été changé en porc," dit tranquillement Alice, comme si le Chat était revenu d'une manière naturelle.

'I thought it would,' said the Cat, and vanished again.

"Je m'en doutais," dit le Chat; et il disparut de nouveau.

Alice waited a little, half expecting to see it again, but it did not appear, and after a minute or two she walked on in the direction in which the March Hare was said to live.

Alice attendit quelques instants, espérant presque le revoir, mais il ne reparut pas; et une ou deux minutes après, elle continua son chemin dans la direction où on lui avait dit que demeurait le Lièvre.

I've seen hatters before,' she said to herself; 'the March Hare will be much the most interesting.

"J'ai déjà vu des chapeliers," se dit-elle; "le Lièvre sera de beaucoup le plus intéressant."

As she said this, she looked up, and there was the Cat again, sitting on a branch of a tree.

'Did you say pig, or fig?' said the Cat.

'I said pig,' replied Alice; 'and I wish you wouldn't keep appearing and vanishing so suddenly: you make one quite giddy.'

'All right,' said the Cat; and this time it vanished quite slowly, beginning with the end of the tail, and ending with the grin, which remained some time after the rest of it had gone.

'Well! I've often seen a cat without a grin,' thought Alice; 'but a grin without a cat! It's the most curious thing I ever saw in my life!'

She had not gone much farther before she came in sight of the house of the March Hare: she thought it must be the right house, because the chimneys were shaped like ears and the roof was thatched with fur.

It was so large a house, that she did not like to go nearer till she had nibbled some more of the lefthand bit of mushroom, and raised herself to about two feet high:

even then she walked up towards it rather timidly, saying to herself 'Suppose it should be raving mad after all! I almost wish I'd gone to see the Hatter instead!'

À ces mots elle leva les yeux, et voilà que le Chat était encore là assis sur une branche d'arbre.

"M'avez-vous dit porc, ou porte?" demanda le Chat.

"J'ai dit porc," répéta Alice. "Ne vous amusez donc pas à paraître et à disparaître si subitement, vous faites tourner la tête aux gens."

"C'est bon," dit le Chat, et cette fois il s'évanouit tout doucement à commencer par le bout de la queue, et finissant par sa grimace qui demeura quelque temps après que le reste fut disparu.

"Certes," pensa Alice, "j'ai souvent vu un chat sans grimace, mais une grimace sans chat, je n'ai jamais de ma vie rien vu de si drôle."

Elle ne fit pas beaucoup de chemin avant d'arriver devant la maison du Lièvre. Elle pensa que ce devait bien être là la maison, car les cheminées étaient en forme d'oreilles et le toit était couvert de fourrure.

La maison était si grande qu'elle n'osa s'approcher avant d'avoir grignoté encore un peu du morceau de champignon qu'elle avait dans la main gauche, et d'avoir atteint la taille de deux pieds environ;

et même alors elle avança timidement en se disant: "Si après tout il était fou furieux! Je voudrais presque avoir été faire visite au Chapelier plutôt que d'être venue ici."

7. A Mad Tea Party

There was a table set out under a tree in front of the house, and the March Hare and the Hatter were having tea at it.

A Dormouse was sitting between them, fast asleep, and the other two were using it as a cushion, resting their elbows on it, and talking over its head.

'Very uncomfortable for the Dormouse,' thought Alice; 'only, as it's asleep, I suppose it doesn't mind.'

The table was a large one, but the three were all crowded together at one corner of it: 'No room! No room!' they cried out when they saw Alice coming.

'There's plenty of room!' said Alice indignantly, and she sat down in a large arm-chair at one end of the table.

'Have some wine,' the March Hare said in an encouraging tone.

Alice looked all round the table, but there was nothing on it but tea. 'I don't see any wine,' she remarked.

'There isn't any,' said the March Hare.

'Then it wasn't very civil of you to offer it,' said Alice angrily.

'It wasn't very civil of you to sit down without being invited,' said the March Hare.

'I didn't know it was your table,' said Alice; 'it's laid for a great many more than three.'

'Your hair wants cutting,' said the Hatter. He had been looking at Alice for some time with great curiosity, and this was his first speech.

'You should learn not to make personal remarks,' Alice said with some severity; 'it's very rude.'

The Hatter opened his eyes very wide on hearing this; but all he said was: 'Why is a raven like a writing-desk?'

Come, we shall have some fun now!' thought Alice. 'I'm glad they've begun asking riddles.—I believe I can guess that,' she added aloud.

7. Un Thé de Fous

Il y avait une table servie sous un arbre devant la maison, et le Lièvre y prenait le thé avec le Chapelier.

Un Loir profondément endormi était assis entre les deux autres qui s'en servaient comme d'un coussin, le coude appuyé sur lui et causant par-dessus sa tête.

"Bien gênant pour le Loir," pensa Alice. "Mais comme il est endormi je suppose que cela lui est égal."

Bien que la table fût très-grande, ils étaient tous trois serrés l'un contre l'autre à un des coins. "Il n'y a pas de place! Il n'y a pas de place!" crièrent-ils en voyant Alice.

"Il y a abondance de place," dit Alice indignée, et elle s'assit dans un large fauteuil à l'un des bouts de la table.

"Prenez donc du vin," dit le Lièvre d'un ton engageant.

Alice regarda tout autour de la table, mais il n'y avait que du thé. "Je ne vois pas de vin," fit-elle observer.

"Il n'y en a pas," dit le Lièvre.

"En ce cas il n'était pas très-poli de votre part de m'en offrir," dit Alice d'un ton fâché.

"Il n'était pas non plus très-poli de votre part de vous mettre à table avant d'y être invitée," dit le Lièvre.

"J'ignorais que ce fût votre table," dit Alice. "Il y a des couverts pour bien plus de trois convives."

"Vos cheveux ont besoin d'être coupés," dit le Chapelier. Il avait considéré Alice pendant quelque temps avec beaucoup de curiosité, et ce fut la première parole qu'il lui adressa.

"Vous devriez apprendre à ne pas faire de remarques sur les gens; c'est très-grossier," dit Alice d'un ton sévère.

À ces mots le Chapelier ouvrit de grands yeux; mais il se contenta de dire: "Pourquoi une pie ressemble-t-elle à un pupitre?"

"Bon! nous allons nous amuser," pensa Alice. "Je suis bien aise qu'ils se mettent à demander des énigmes. Je crois pouvoir deviner cela," ajouta-t-elle tout haut.

'Do you mean that you think you can find out the answer to it?' said the March Hare.

"Voulez-vous dire que vous croyez pouvoir trouver la réponse?" dit le Lièvre.

'Exactly so,' said Alice.

"Précisément," répondit Alice.

'Then you should say what you mean,' the March Hare went on.

"Alors vous devriez dire ce que vous voulez dire," continua le Lièvre.

I do,' Alice hastily replied; 'at least—at least I mean what I say—that's the same thing, you know.'

"C'est ce que je fais," répliqua vivement Alice. "Du moins — je veux dire ce que je dis; c'est la même chose, n'est-ce pas?"

'Not the same thing a bit!' said the Hatter. 'You might just as well say that "I see what I eat" is the same thing as "I eat what I see"!'

"Ce n'est pas du tout la même chose," dit le Chapelier. "Vous pourriez alors dire tout aussi bien que: "Je vois ce que je mange," est la même chose que: "Je mange ce que je vois.""

You might just as well say,' added the March Hare: 'that "I like what I get" is the same thing as "I get what I like"!'

"Vous pourriez alors dire tout aussi bien," ajouta le Lièvre, "que: "J'aime ce qu'on me donne," est la même chose que: "On me donne ce que j'aime.""

You might just as well say,' added the Dormouse, who seemed to be talking in his sleep: 'that "I breathe when I sleep" is the same thing as "I sleep when I breathe"!'

"Vous pourriez dire tout aussi bien," ajouta le Loir, qui paraissait parler tout endormi, "que: "Je respire quand je dors," est la même chose que: "Je dors quand je respire.""

'It is the same thing with you,' said the Hatter, and here the conversation dropped, and the party sat silent for a minute, while Alice thought over all she could remember about ravens and writing-desks, which wasn't much.

"C'est en effet tout un pour vous," dit le Chapelier. Sur ce, la conversation tomba et il se fit un silence de quelques minutes. Pendant ce temps, Alice repassa dans son esprit tout ce qu'elle savait au sujet des pies et des pupitres; ce qui n'était pas grand'chose.

The Hatter was the first to break the silence. 'What day of the month is it?' he said, turning to Alice: he had taken his watch out of his pocket, and was looking at it uneasily, shaking it every now and then, and holding it to his ear.

Le Chapelier rompit le silence le premier. "Quel quantième du mois sommes-nous?" dit-il en se tournant vers Alice. Il avait tiré sa montre de sa poche et la regardait d'un air inquiet, la secouant de temps à autre et l'approchant de son oreille. Alice réfléchit un instant et répondit: "Le quatre."

Alice considered a little, and then said 'The fourth.''Two days wrong!' sighed the Hatter. 'I told you butter wouldn't suit the works!' he added looking angrily at the March Hare.

"Elle est de deux jours en retard," dit le Chapelier avec un soupir. "Je vous disais bien que le beurre ne vaudrait rien au mouvement!" ajouta-t-il en regardant le Lièvre avec colère.

'It was the best butter,' the March Hare meekly replied.

"C'était tout ce qu'il y avait de plus fin en beurre," dit le Lièvre humblement.

'Yes, but some crumbs must have got in as well,' the Hatter grumbled: 'you shouldn't have put it in with the bread-knife.'

"Oui, mais il faut qu'il y soit entré des miettes de pain," grommela le Chapelier. "Vous n'auriez pas dû vous servir du couteau au pain pour mettre le beurre."

The March Hare took the watch and looked at it gloomily: then he dipped it into his cup of tea, and looked at it again:

Le Lièvre prit la montre, et la contempla tristement, puis la trempa dans sa tasse, la contempla de nouveau,

but he could think of nothing better to say than his first remark: 'It was the best butter, you know.'

et pourtant ne trouva rien de mieux à faire que de répéter sa première observation: "C'était tout ce qu'il y avait de plus fin en beurre."

Alice had been looking over his shoulder with some curiosity. 'What a funny watch!' she remarked. 'It tells the day of the month, and doesn't tell what o'clock it is!'

Alice avait regardé par-dessus son épaule avec curiosité: "Quelle singulière montre!" dit-elle. "Elle marque le quantième du mois, et ne marque pas l'heure qu'il est!"

'Why should it?' muttered the Hatter. 'Does your watch tell you what year it is?'

"Et pourquoi marquerait-elle l'heure?" murmura le Chapelier. "Votre montre marque-t-elle dans quelle année vous êtes?"

'Of course not,' Alice replied very readily: 'but that's because it stays the same year for such a long time together.'

"Non, assurément!" répliqua Alice sans hésiter. "Mais c'est parce qu'elle reste à la même année pendant si longtemps."

'Which is just the case with mine,' said the Hatter.

"Tout comme la mienne," dit le Chapelier.

Alice felt dreadfully puzzled. The Hatter's remark seemed to have no sort of meaning in it, and yet it was certainly English.

Alice se trouva fort embarrassée. L'observation du Chapelier lui paraissait n'avoir aucun sens; et cependant la phrase était parfaitement correcte.

'I don't quite understand you,' she said, as politely as she could.

"Je ne vous comprends pas bien," dit-elle, aussi poliment que possible.

'The Dormouse is asleep again,' said the Hatter, and he poured a little hot tea upon its nose.

"Le Loir est rendormi," dit le Chapelier; et il lui versa un peu de thé chaud sur le nez.

The Dormouse shook its head impatiently, and said, without opening its eyes: 'Of course, of course; just what I was going to remark myself.'

Le Loir secoua la tête avec impatience, et dit, sans ouvrir les yeux: "Sans doute, sans doute, c'est justement ce que j'allais dire."

'Have you guessed the riddle yet?' the Hatter said, turning to Alice again.

"Avez-vous deviné l'énigme?" dit le Chapelier, se tournant de nouveau vers Alice.

'No, I give it up,' Alice replied: 'what's the answer?'

"Non, j'y renonce," répondit Alice; "quelle est la réponse?"

'I haven't the slightest idea,' said the Hatter.

"Je n'en ai pas la moindre idée," dit le Chapelier.

'Nor I,' said the March Hare.

"Ni moi non plus," dit le Lièvre.

Alice sighed wearily. 'I think you might do something better with the time,' she said: 'than waste it in asking riddles that have no answers.'

Alice soupira d'ennui. "Il me semble que vous pourriez mieux employer le temps," dit-elle, "et ne pas le gaspiller à proposer des énigmes qui n'ont point de réponses."

If you knew Time as well as I do,' said the Hatter: 'you wouldn't talk about wasting it. It's him.'

"Si vous connaissiez le Temps aussi bien que moi," dit le Chapelier, "vous ne parleriez pas de le gaspiller. On ne gaspille pas quelqu'un."

'I don't know what you mean,' said Alice.

"Je ne vous comprends pas," dit Alice.

'Of course you don't!' the Hatter said, tossing his head contemptuously. 'I dare say you never even spoke to Time!'

"Je le crois bien," répondit le Chapelier, en secouant la tête avec mépris; "je parie que vous n'avez jamais parlé au Temps."

'Perhaps not,' Alice cautiously replied: 'but I know I have to beat time when I learn music.'

"Cela se peut bien," répliqua prudemment Alice, "mais je l'ai souvent mal employé."

Ah! that accounts for it,' said the Hatter. 'He won't stand beating. Now, if you only kept on good terms with him, he'd do almost anything you liked with the clock.

"Ah! voilà donc pourquoi! Il n'aime pas cela," dit le Chapelier. "Mais si seulement vous saviez le ménager, il ferait de la pendule tout ce que vous voudriez.

For instance, suppose it were nine o'clock in the morning, just time to begin lessons: you'd only have to whisper a hint to Time, and round goes the clock in a twinkling!

Par exemple, supposons qu'il soit neuf heures du matin, l'heure de vos leçons, vous n'auriez qu'à dire tout bas un petit mot au Temps, et l'aiguille partirait en un clin d'œil pour marquer

Half-past one, time for dinner!' ('I only wish it was,' the March Hare said to itself in a whisper.)

une heure et demie, l'heure du dîner." ("Je le voudrais bien," dit tout bas le Lièvre.)

That would be grand, certainly,' said Alice thoughtfully: 'but then—I shouldn't be hungry for it, you know.'

"Cela serait très-agréable, certainement," dit Alice d'un air pensif; "mais alors — je n'aurais pas encore faim, comprenez donc."

'Not at first, perhaps,' said the Hatter: 'but you could keep it to half-past one as long as you liked.'

"Peut-être pas d'abord," dit le Chapelier; "mais vous pourriez retenir l'aiguille à une heure et demie aussi longtemps que vous voudriez."

'Is that the way you manage?' Alice asked.

"Est-ce comme cela que vous faites, vous?" demanda Alice.

The Hatter shook his head mournfully. 'Not I!' he replied. 'We quarrelled last March—just before he went mad, you know—' (pointing with his tea spoon at the March Hare,) '—it was at the great concert given by the Queen of Hearts, and I had to sing

Le Chapelier secoua tristement la tête. "Hélas! non," répondit-il, "nous nous sommes querellés au mois de mars dernier, un peu avant qu'il devînt fou." (Il montrait le Lièvre du bout de sa cuiller.) "C'était à un grand concert donné par la Reine de Cœur, et j'eus à chanter:

"Twinkle, twinkle, little bat!

"Ah! vous dirai-je, ma sœur,

How I wonder what you're at!"

Ce qui calme ma douleur!"

You know the song, perhaps?'

"Vous connaissez peut-être cette chanson?"

'I've heard something like it,' said Alice.

"J'ai entendu chanter quelque chose comme ça," dit Alice.

It goes on, you know,' the Hatter continued: 'in this way:—

"Vous savez la suite," dit le Chapelier; et il continua:

"Up above the world you fly,

"C'est que j'avais des dragées,

Like a tea-tray in the sky.

Et que je les ai mangées."

Here the Dormouse shook itself, and began singing in its sleep 'Twinkle, twinkle, twinkle, twinkle—' and went on so long that they had to pinch it to make it stop.

Ici le Loir se secoua et se mit à chanter, tout en dormant: "Et que je les ai mangées, mangées, mangées, mangées, mangées," si longtemps, qu'il fallût le pincer pour le faire taire.

Well, I'd hardly finished the first verse,' said the Hatter: 'when the Queen jumped up and bawled out, "He's murdering the time! Off with his head!"'

"Eh bien, j'avais à peine fini le premier couplet," dit le Chapelier, "que la Reine hurla: "Ah! c'est comme ça que vous tuez le temps! Qu'on lui coupe la tête!""

'How dreadfully savage!' exclaimed Alice.

"Quelle cruauté!" s'écria Alice.

And ever since that,' the Hatter went on in a mournful tone: 'he won't do a thing I ask! It's always six o'clock now.'

"Et, depuis lors," continua le Chapelier avec tristesse, "le Temps ne veut rien faire de ce que je lui demande. Il est toujours six heures maintenant."

A bright idea came into Alice's head. 'Is that the reason so many tea-things are put out here?' she asked.

Une brillante idée traversa l'esprit d'Alice. "Est-ce pour cela qu'il y a tant de tasses à thé ici?" demanda-t-elle.

'Yes, that's it,' said the Hatter with a sigh: 'it's always tea-time, and we've no time to wash the things between whiles.'

"Oui, c'est cela," dit le Chapelier avec un soupir; "il est toujours l'heure du thé, et nous n'avons pas le temps de laver la vaisselle dans l'intervalle."

'Then you keep moving round, I suppose?' said Alice.

"Alors vous faites tout le tour de la table, je suppose?" dit Alice.

'Exactly so,' said the Hatter: 'as the things get used up.'

"Justement," dit le Chapelier, "à mesure que les tasses ont servi."

'But what happens when you come to the beginning again?' Alice ventured to ask.

"Mais, qu'arrive-t-il lorsque vous vous retrouvez au commencement?" se hasarda de dire Alice.

'Suppose we change the subject,' the March Hare interrupted, yawning. 'I'm getting tired of this. I vote the young lady tells us a story.'

"Si nous changions de conversation," interrompit le Lièvre en bâillant; "celle-ci commence à me fatiguer. Je propose que la petite demoiselle nous conte une histoire."

'I'm afraid I don't know one,' said Alice, rather alarmed at the proposal.

"J'ai bien peur de n'en pas savoir," dit Alice, que cette proposition alarmait un peu.

'Then the Dormouse shall!' they both cried. 'Wake up, Dormouse!' And they pinched it on both sides at once.

"Eh bien, le Loir va nous en dire une," crièrent-ils tous deux. "Allons, Loir, réveillez-vous!" et ils le pincèrent des deux côtés à la fois.

The Dormouse slowly opened his eyes. 'I wasn't asleep,' he said in a hoarse, feeble voice: 'I heard every word you fellows were saying.'

Le Loir ouvrit lentement les yeux. "Je ne dormais pas," dit-il d'une voix faible et enrouée. "Je n'ai pas perdu un mot de ce que vous avez dit, vous autres."

'Tell us a story!' said the March Hare.

"Racontez-nous une histoire," dit le Lièvre.

'Yes, please do!' pleaded Alice.

"Ah! Oui, je vous en prie," dit Alice d'un ton suppliant.

And be quick about it,' added the Hatter: 'or you'll be asleep again before it's done.'

"Et faites vite," ajouta le Chapelier, "sans cela vous allez vous rendormir avant de vous mettre en train."

Once upon a time there were three little sisters,' the Dormouse began in a great hurry; 'and their names were Elsie, Lacie, and Tillie; and they lived at the bottom of a well—'

"Il y avait une fois trois petites sœurs," commença bien vite le Loir, "qui s'appelaient Elsie, Lacie, et Tillie, et elles vivaient au fond d'un puits."

'What did they live on?' said Alice, who always took a great interest in questions of eating and drinking.

"De quoi vivaient-elles?" dit Alice, qui s'intéressait toujours aux questions de boire ou de manger.

'They lived on treacle,' said the Dormouse, after thinking a minute or two.

"Elles vivaient de mélasse," dit le Loir, après avoir réfléchi un instant.

'They couldn't have done that, you know,' Alice gently remarked; 'they'd have been ill.'

"Ce n'est pas possible, comprenez donc," fit doucement observer Alice; "cela les aurait rendues malades."

'So they were,' said the Dormouse; 'very ill.'

"Et en effet," dit le Loir, "elles étaient très-malades."

Alice tried to fancy to herself what such an extraordinary ways of living would be like, but it puzzled her too much, so she went on: 'But why did they live at the bottom of a well?'

Alice chercha à se figurer un peu l'effet que produirait sur elle une manière de vivre si extraordinaire, mais cela lui parut trop embarrassant, et elle continua: "Mais pourquoi vivaient-elles au fond d'un puits?"

'Take some more tea,' the March Hare said to Alice, very earnestly.

"Prenez un peu plus de thé," dit le Lièvre à Alice avec empressement.

I've had nothing yet,' Alice replied in an offended tone: 'so I can't take more.'

"Je n'en ai pas pris du tout," répondit Alice d'un air offensé. "Je ne peux donc pas en prendre un peu plus."

'You mean you can't take less,' said the Hatter: 'it's very easy to take more than nothing.'

"Vous voulez dire que vous ne pouvez pas en prendre moins," dit le Chapelier. "Il est très-aisé de prendre un peu plus que pas du tout."

'Nobody asked your opinion,' said Alice.

"On ne vous a pas demandé votre avis, à vous," dit Alice.

'Who's making personal remarks now?' the Hatter asked triumphantly.

"Ah! qui est-ce qui se permet de faire des observations?" demanda le Chapelier d'un air triomphant.

Alice did not quite know what to say to this: so she helped herself to some tea and bread-and-butter, and then turned to the Dormouse, and repeated her question. 'Why did they live at the bottom of a well?'

Alice ne savait pas trop que répondre à cela. Aussi se servit-elle un peu de thé et une tartine de pain et de beurre; puis elle se tourna du côté du Loir, et répéta sa question. "Pourquoi vivaient-elles au fond d'un puits?"

The Dormouse again took a minute or two to think about it, and then said: 'It was a treacle-well.'

Le Loir réfléchit de nouveau pendant quelques instants et dit: "C'était un puits de mélasse."

There's no such thing!' Alice was beginning very angrily, but the Hatter and the March Hare went 'Sh! sh!' and the Dormouse sulkily remarked: 'If you can't be civil, you'd better finish the story for yourself.'

"Il n'en existe pas!" se mit à dire Alice d'un ton courroucé. Mais le Chapelier et le Lièvre firent "Chut! Chut!" et le Loir fit observer d'un ton bourru: "Tâchez d'être polie, ou finissez l'histoire vous-même."

'No, please go on!' Alice said very humbly; 'I won't interrupt again. I dare say there may be one.'

"Non, continuez, je vous prie," dit Alice très-humblement. "Je ne vous interromprai plus; peut-être en existe-t-il un."

One, indeed!' said the Dormouse indignantly. However, he consented to go on. 'And so these three little sisters—they were learning to draw, you know—'

"Un, vraiment!" dit le Loir avec indignation; toutefois il voulut bien continuer. "Donc, ces trois petites sœurs, vous saurez qu'elles faisaient tout ce qu'elles pouvaient pour s'en tirer."

'What did they draw?' said Alice, quite forgetting her promise.

"Comment auraient-elles pu s'en tirer?" dit Alice, oubliant tout à fait sa promesse.

'Treacle,' said the Dormouse, without considering at all this time.

"C'est tout simple —"

'I want a clean cup,' interrupted the Hatter: 'let's all move one place on.'

"Il me faut une tasse propre," interrompit le Chapelier. "Avançons tous d'une place."

He moved on as he spoke, and the Dormouse followed him: the March Hare moved into the Dormouse's place, and Alice rather unwillingly took the place of the March Hare.

Il avançait tout en parlant, et le Loir le suivit; le Lièvre prit la place du Loir, et Alice prit, d'assez mauvaise grâce, celle du Lièvre.

The Hatter was the only one who got any advantage from the change: and Alice was a good deal worse off than before, as the March Hare had just upset the milk-jug into his plate.

Le Chapelier fut le seul qui gagnât au change; Alice se trouva bien plus mal partagée qu'auparavant, car le Lièvre venait de renverser le lait dans son assiette.

Alice did not wish to offend the Dormouse again, so she began very cautiously: 'But I don't understand. Where did they draw the treacle from?'

Alice, craignant d'offenser le Loir, reprit avec circonspection: "Mais je ne comprends pas; comment auraient-elles pu s'en tirer?"

You can draw water out of a water-well,' said the Hatter; 'so I should think you could draw treacle out of a treacle-well—eh, stupid?'

"C'est tout simple," dit le Chapelier. "Quand il y a de l'eau dans un puits, vous savez bien comment on en tire, n'est-ce pas? Eh bien! d'un puits de mélasse on tire de la mélasse, et quand il y a des petites filles dans la mélasse on les tire en même temps; comprenez-vous, petite sotte?"

'But they were in the well,' Alice said to the Dormouse, not choosing to notice this last remark.

"Pas tout à fait," dit Alice, encore plus embarrassée par cette réponse.

'Then you shouldn't talk,' said the Hatter.

"Alors vous feriez bien de vous taire," dit le Chapelier.

This piece of rudeness was more than Alice could bear: she got up in great disgust, and walked off; the Dormouse fell asleep instantly, and neither of the others took the least notice of her going, though she looked back once or twice, half hoping that they would call after her:

Alice trouva cette grossièreté un peu trop forte; elle se leva indignée et s'en alla. Le Loir s'endormit à l'instant même, et les deux autres ne prirent pas garde à son départ, bien qu'elle regardât en arrière deux ou trois fois, espérant presque qu'ils la rappelleraient.

the last time she saw them, they were trying to put the Dormouse into the teapot.

La dernière fois qu'elle les vit, ils cherchaient à mettre le Loir dans la théière.

'At any rate I'll never go there again!' said Alice as she picked her way through the wood. 'It's the stupidest tea-party I ever was at in all my life!'

"À aucun prix je ne voudrais retourner auprès de ces gens-là," dit Alice, en cherchant son chemin à travers le bois. "C'est le thé le plus ridicule auquel j'aie assisté de ma vie!"

Just as she said this, she noticed that one of the trees had a door leading right into it. 'That's very curious!' she thought. 'But everything's curious today. I think I may as well go in at once.' And in she went.

Comme elle disait cela, elle s'aperçut qu'un des arbres avait une porte par laquelle on pouvait pénétrer à l'intérieur. "Voilà qui est curieux," pensa-t-elle. "Mais tout est curieux aujourd'hui. Je crois que je ferai bien d'entrer tout de suite." Elle entra.

Once more she found herself in the long hall, and close to the little glass table. 'Now, I'll manage better this time,' she said to herself, and began by taking the little golden key, and unlocking the door that led into the garden.

Elle se retrouva encore dans la longue salle tout près de la petite table de verre. "Cette fois je m'y prendrai mieux," se dit-elle, et elle commença par saisir la petite clef d'or et par ouvrir la porte qui menait au jardin,

Then she went to work nibbling at the mushroom (she had kept a piece of it in her pocket) till she was about a foot high:

et puis elle se mit à grignoter le morceau de champignon qu'elle avait mis dans sa poche, jusqu'à ce qu'elle fût réduite à environ deux pieds de haut;

then she walked down the little passage: and then—she found herself at last in the beautiful garden, among the bright flower-beds and the cool fountains.

elle prit alors le petit passage; et enfin — elle se trouva dans le superbe jardin au milieu des brillants parterres et des fraîches fontaines.

8. The Queen's Croquet Ground

A large rose-tree stood near the entrance of the garden: the roses growing on it were white, but there were three gardeners at it, busily painting them red.

Alice thought this a very curious thing, and she went nearer to watch them, and just as she came up to them she heard one of them say: 'Look out now, Five! Don't go splashing paint over me like that!'

'I couldn't help it,' said Five, in a sulky tone; 'Seven jogged my elbow.'

On which Seven looked up and said: 'That's right, Five! Always lay the blame on others!'

You'd better not talk!' said Five. 'I heard the Queen say only yesterday you deserved to be beheaded!'

'What for?' said the one who had spoken first.

'That's none of your business, Two!' said Seven.

Yes, it is his business!' said Five: 'and I'll tell him—it was for bringing the cook tulip-roots instead of onions.'

Seven flung down his brush, and had just begun 'Well, of all the unjust things—' when his eye chanced to fall upon Alice, as she stood watching them, and he checked himself suddenly.

The others looked round also, and all of them bowed low.

Would you tell me,' said Alice, a little timidly: 'why you are painting those roses?'

Five and Seven said nothing, but looked at Two. Two began in a low voice:

Why the fact is, you see, Miss, this here ought to have been a red rose-tree, and we put a white one in by mistake; and if the Queen was to find it out, we should all have our heads cut off, you know. So you see, Miss, we're doing our best, afore she comes, to—'

8. Le Croquet de la Reine

Un grand rosier se trouvait à l'entrée du jardin; les roses qu'il portait étaient blanches, mais trois jardiniers étaient en train de les peindre en rouge.

Alice s'avança pour les regarder, et, au moment où elle approchait, elle en entendit un qui disait: "Fais donc attention, Cinq, et ne m'éclabousse pas ainsi avec ta peinture."

"Ce n'est pas de ma faute," dit Cinq d'un ton bourru, "c'est Sept qui m'a poussé le coude."

Là-dessus Sept leva les yeux et dit: "C'est cela, Cinq! Jetez toujours le blâme sur les autres!"

"Vous feriez bien de vous taire, vous," dit Cinq. "J'ai entendu la Reine dire pas plus tard que hier que vous méritiez d'être décapité!"

"Pourquoi donc cela?" dit celui qui avait parlé le premier.

"Cela ne vous regarde pas, Deux," dit Sept.

"Si fait, cela le regarde," dit Cinq; "et je vais le lui dire. C'est pour avoir apporté à la cuisinière des oignons de tulipe au lieu d'oignons à manger."

Sept jeta là son pinceau et s'écriait: "De toutes les injustices —" lorsque ses regards tombèrent par hasard sur Alice, qui restait là à les regarder, et il se retint tout à coup.

Les autres se retournèrent aussi, et tous firent un profond salut.

"Voudriez-vous avoir la bonté de me dire pourquoi vous peignez ces roses?" demanda Alice un peu timidement.

Cinq et Sept ne dirent rien, mais regardèrent Deux. Deux commença à voix basse:

"Le fait est, voyez-vous, mademoiselle, qu'il devrait y avoir ici un rosier à fleurs rouges, et nous en avons mis un à fleurs blanches, par erreur. Si la Reine s'en apercevait nous aurions tous la tête tranchée, vous comprenez. Aussi, mademoiselle, vous voyez que nous faisons de notre mieux avant qu'elle vienne pour —"

At this moment Five, who had been anxiously looking across the garden, called out 'The Queen! The Queen!' and the three gardeners instantly threw themselves flat upon their faces. There was a sound of many footsteps, and Alice looked round, eager to see the Queen.

À ce moment Cinq, qui avait regardé tout le temps avec inquiétude de l'autre côté du jardin, s'écria: "La Reine! La Reine!" et les trois ouvriers se précipitèrent aussitôt la face contre terre. Il se faisait un grand bruit de pas, et Alice se retourna, désireuse de voir la Reine.

First came ten soldiers carrying clubs; these were all shaped like the three gardeners, oblong and flat, with their hands and feet at the corners: next the ten courtiers; these were ornamented all over with diamonds, and walked two and two, as the soldiers did.

D'abord venaient des soldats portant des piques; ils étaient tous faits comme les jardiniers, longs et plats, les mains et les pieds aux coins; ensuite venaient les dix courtisans. Ceux-ci étaient tous parés de carreaux de diamant et marchaient deux à deux comme les soldats.

After these came the royal children; there were ten of them, and the little dears came jumping merrily along hand in hand, in couples: they were all ornamented with hearts.

Derrière eux venaient les enfants de la Reine; il y en avait dix, et les petits chérubins gambadaient joyeusement, se tenant par la main deux à deux; ils étaient tous ornés de cœurs.

Next came the guests, mostly Kings and Queens, and among them Alice recognised the White Rabbit: it was talking in a hurried nervous manner, smiling at everything that was said, and went by without noticing her.

Après eux venaient les invités, des rois et des reines pour la plupart. Dans le nombre, Alice reconnut le Lapin Blanc. Il avait l'air ému et agité en parlant, souriait à tout ce qu'on disait, et passa sans faire attention à elle.

Then followed the Knave of Hearts, carrying the King's crown on a crimson velvet cushion; and, last of all this grand procession, came THE KING AND QUEEN OF HEARTS.

Suivait le Valet de Cœur, portant la couronne sur un coussin de velours; et, fermant cette longue procession, LE ROI ET LA REINE DE CŒUR.

Alice was rather doubtful whether she ought not to lie down on her face like the three gardeners, but she could not remember ever having heard of such a rule at processions;

Alice ne savait pas au juste si elle devait se prosterner comme les trois jardiniers; mais elle ne se rappelait pas avoir jamais entendu parler d'une pareille formalité.

'and besides, what would be the use of a procession,' thought she: 'if people had all to lie down upon their faces, so that they couldn't see it?' So she stood still where she was, and waited.

"Et d'ailleurs à quoi serviraient les processions," pensa-t-elle, "si les gens avaient à se mettre la face contre terre de façon à ne pas les voir?" Elle resta donc debout à sa place et attendit.

When the procession came opposite to Alice, they all stopped and looked at her, and the Queen said severely 'Who is this?' She said it to the Knave of Hearts, who only bowed and smiled in reply.

Quand la procession fut arrivée en face d'Alice, tout le monde s'arrêta pour la regarder, et la Reine dit sévèrement: "Qui est-ce?" Elle s'adressait au Valet de Cœur, qui se contenta de saluer et de sourire pour toute réponse.

Idiot!' said the Queen, tossing her head impatiently; and, turning to Alice, she went on: 'What's your name, child?'

"Idiot!" dit la Reine en rejetant la tête en arrière avec impatience; et, se tournant vers Alice, elle continua: "Votre nom, petite?"

My name is Alice, so please your Majesty,' said Alice very politely; but she added, to herself: 'Why, they're only a pack of cards, after all. I needn't be afraid of them!'

"Je me nomme Alice, s'il plaît à Votre Majesté," dit Alice fort poliment. Mais elle ajouta en elle-même: "Ces gens-là ne sont, après tout, qu'un paquet de cartes. Pourquoi en aurais-je peur?"

'And who are these?' said the Queen, pointing to the three gardeners who were lying round the rosetree; for, you see, as they were lying on their faces, and the pattern on their backs was the same as the rest of the pack, she could not tell whether they were gardeners, or soldiers, or courtiers, or three of her own children.

"Et qui sont ceux-ci?" dit la Reine, montrant du doigt les trois jardiniers étendus autour du rosier. Car vous comprenez que, comme ils avaient la face contre terre et que le dessin qu'ils avaient sur le dos était le même que celui des autres cartes du paquet, elle ne pouvait savoir s'ils étaient des

'How should I know?' said Alice, surprised at her own courage. 'It's no business of mine.'

The Queen turned crimson with fury, and, after glaring at her for a moment like a wild beast, screamed 'Off with her head! Off—'

'Nonsense!' said Alice, very loudly and decidedly, and the Queen was silent.

The King laid his hand upon her arm, and timidly said 'Consider, my dear: she is only a child!'

The Queen turned angrily away from him, and said to the Knave 'Turn them over!'

The Knave did so, very carefully, with one foot.

'Get up!' said the Queen, in a shrill, loud voice, and the three gardeners instantly jumped up, and began bowing to the King, the Queen, the royal children, and everybody else.

Leave off that!' screamed the Queen. 'You make me giddy.' And then, turning to the rose-tree, she went on: 'What have you been doing here?'

May it please your Majesty,' said Two, in a very humble tone, going down on one knee as he spoke: 'we were trying—'

'I see!' said the Queen, who had meanwhile been examining the roses. 'Off with their heads!' and the procession moved on, three of the soldiers remaining behind to execute the unfortunate gardeners, who ran to Alice for protection.

'You shan't be beheaded!' said Alice, and she put them into a large flower-pot that stood near. The three soldiers wandered about for a minute or two, looking for them, and then quietly marched off after the others.

'Are their heads off?' shouted the Queen. 'Their heads are gone, if it please your Majesty!' the soldiers shouted in reply.

'That's right!' shouted the Queen. 'Can you play croquet?'

The soldiers were silent, and looked at Alice, as the question was evidently meant for her.

jardiniers, des soldats, des courtisans, ou bien trois de ses propres enfants.

“Comment voulez-vous que je le sache?” dit Alice avec un courage qui la surprit elle-même. “Cela n’est pas mon affaire à moi.”

La Reine devint pourpre de colère; et après l’avoir considérée un moment avec des yeux flamboyants comme ceux d’une bête fauve, elle se mit à crier: “Qu’on lui coupe la tête!”

“Quelle idée!” dit Alice très-haut et d’un ton décidé. La Reine se tut.

Le Roi lui posa la main sur le bras, et lui dit timidement: “Considérez donc, ma chère amie, que ce n’est qu’une enfant.”

La Reine lui tourna le dos avec colère, et dit au Valet: “Retournez-les!”

Ce que fit le Valet très-soigneusement du bout du pied.

“Debout!” dit la Reine d’une voix forte et stridente. Les trois jardiniers se relevèrent à l’instant et se mirent à saluer le Roi, la Reine, les jeunes princes, et tout le monde.

“Finissez!” cria la Reine. “Vous m’étourdissez.” Alors, se tournant vers le rosier, elle continua: “Qu’est-ce que vous faites donc là?”

“Avec le bon plaisir de Votre Majesté,” dit Deux d’un ton très-humble, mettant un genou en terre, “nous tâchions —”

“Je le vois bien!” dit la Reine, qui avait pendant ce temps examiné les roses. “Qu’on leur coupe la tête!” Et la procession continua sa route, trois des soldats restant en arrière pour exécuter les malheureux jardiniers, qui coururent se mettre sous la protection d’Alice.

“Vous ne serez pas décapités,” dit Alice; et elle les mit dans un grand pot à fleurs qui se trouvait près de là. Les trois soldats errèrent de côté et d’autre, pendant une ou deux minutes, pour les chercher, puis s’en allèrent tranquillement rejoindre les autres.

“Leur a-t-on coupé la tête?” cria la Reine. “Leurs têtes n’y sont plus, s’il plaît à Votre Majesté!” lui crièrent les soldats.

“C’est bien!” cria la Reine. “Savez-vous jouer au croquet?”

Les soldats ne soufflèrent mot, et regardèrent Alice, car, évidemment, c’était à elle que s’adressait la question.

'Yes!' shouted Alice.

'Come on, then!' roared the Queen, and Alice joined the procession, wondering very much what would happen next.

It's—it's a very fine day!' said a timid voice at her side. She was walking by the White Rabbit, who was peeping anxiously into her face.

Very,' said Alice: '—where's the Duchess?'

'Hush! Hush!' said the Rabbit in a low, hurried tone. He looked anxiously over his shoulder as he spoke, and then raised himself upon tiptoe, put his mouth close to her ear, and whispered 'She's under sentence of execution.'

'What for?' said Alice.

'Did you say "What a pity!"?' the Rabbit asked.

'No, I didn't,' said Alice: 'I don't think it's at all a pity. I said "What for?"'

She boxed the Queen's ears—' the Rabbit began. Alice gave a little scream of laughter. 'Oh, hush!' the Rabbit whispered in a frightened tone. 'The Queen will hear you! You see, she came rather late, and the Queen said—'

Get to your places!' shouted the Queen in a voice of thunder, and people began running about in all directions, tumbling up against each other.

However, they got settled down in a minute or two, and the game began.

Alice thought she had never seen such a curious croquet-ground in her life; it was all ridges and furrows; the balls were live hedgehogs, the mallets live flamingoes, and the soldiers had to double themselves up and to stand on their hands and feet, to make the arches.

The chief difficulty Alice found at first was in managing her flamingo.

She succeeded in getting its body tucked away, comfortably enough, under her arm, with its legs hanging down, but generally, just as she had got its neck nicely straightened out, and was going to give the hedgehog a blow with its head, it would twist itself round and look up in her face, with such a puzzled expression that she could not help bursting out laughing:

and when she had got its head down, and was going to begin again, it was very provoking to find that the hedgehog had unrolled itself, and was in the act of crawling away:

“Oui,” cria Alice.

“Eh bien, venez!” hurla la Reine; et Alice se joignit à la procession, fort curieuse de savoir ce qui allait arriver.

“Il fait un bien beau temps aujourd'hui,” dit une voix timide à côté d'elle. Elle marchait auprès du Lapin Blanc, qui la regardait d'un œil inquiet.

“Bien beau,” dit Alice. “Où est la Duchesse?”

“Chut! Chut!” dit vivement le Lapin à voix basse et en regardant avec inquiétude par-dessus son épaule. Puis il se leva sur la pointe des pieds, colla sa bouche à l'oreille d'Alice et lui souffla: “Elle est condamnée à mort”

“Pour quelle raison?” dit Alice.

“Avez-vous dit: “quel dommage?”“ demanda le Lapin.

“Non,” dit Alice. “Je ne pense pas du tout que ce soit dommage. J'ai dit: “pour quelle raison?”“

“Elle a donné des soufflets à la Reine,” commença le Lapin. (Alice fit entendre un petit éclat de rire.) “Oh, chut!” dit tout bas le Lapin d'un ton effrayé. “La Reine va nous entendre! Elle est arrivée un peu tard, voyez-vous, et la Reine a dit —”

“À vos places!” cria la Reine d'une voix de tonnerre, et les gens se mirent à courir dans toutes les directions, trébuchant les uns contre les autres.

Toutefois, au bout de quelques instants chacun fut à sa place et la partie commença.

Alice n'avait de sa vie vu de jeu de croquet aussi curieux que celui-là. Le terrain n'était que billons et sillons; des hérissons vivants servaient de boules, et des flamants de maillets. Les soldats, courbés en deux, avaient à se tenir la tête et les pieds sur le sol pour former des arches.

Ce qui embarrassa le plus Alice au commencement du jeu, ce fut de manier le flamant;

elle parvenait bien à fourrer son corps assez commodément sous son bras, en laissant pendre les pieds; mais, le plus souvent, à peine lui avait-elle allongé le cou bien comme il faut, et allait-elle frapper le hérisson avec la tête, que le flamant se relevait en se tordant, et la regardait d'un air si ébahi qu'elle ne pouvait s'empêcher d'éclater de rire;

et puis, quand elle lui avait fait baisser la tête et allait recommencer, il était bien impatientant de voir que le hérisson s'était déroulé et s'en allait.

besides all this, there was generally a ridge or furrow in the way wherever she wanted to send the hedgehog to, and, as the doubled-up soldiers were always getting up and walking off to other parts of the ground, Alice soon came to the conclusion that it was a very difficult game indeed.

En outre, il se trouvait ordinairement un billon ou un sillon dans son chemin partout où elle voulait envoyer le hérisson, et comme les soldats courbés en deux se relevaient sans cesse pour s'en aller d'un autre côté du terrain, Alice en vint bientôt à cette conclusion: que c'était là un jeu fort difficile, en vérité.

The players all played at once without waiting for turns, quarrelling all the while, and fighting for the hedgehogs;

Les joueurs jouaient tous à la fois, sans attendre leur tour, se querellant tout le temps et se battant à qui aurait les hérissons.

and in a very short time the Queen was in a furious passion, and went stamping about, and shouting 'Off with his head!' or 'Off with her head!' about once in a minute.

La Reine entra bientôt dans une colère furieuse et se mit à trépigner en criant: "Qu'on coupe la tête à celui-ci!" ou bien: "Qu'on coupe la tête à celle-là!" une fois environ par minute.

Alice began to feel very uneasy: to be sure, she had not as yet had any dispute with the Queen, but she knew that it might happen any minute:

Alice commença à se sentir très-mal à l'aise; il est vrai qu'elle ne s'était pas disputée avec la Reine; mais elle savait que cela pouvait lui arriver à tout moment.

'and then,' thought she: 'what would become of me? They're dreadfully fond of beheading people here; the great wonder is, that there's any one left alive!'

"Et alors," pensait-elle, "que deviendrai-je? Ils aiment terriblement à couper la tête aux gens ici. Ce qui m'étonne, c'est qu'il en reste encore de vivants."

She was looking about for some way of escape, and wondering whether she could get away without being seen, when she noticed a curious appearance in the air.

Elle cherchait autour d'elle quelque moyen de s'échapper, et se demandait si elle pourrait se retirer sans être vue; lorsqu'elle aperçut en l'air quelque chose d'étrange;

It puzzled her very much at first, but, after watching it a minute or two, she made it out to be a grin, and she said to herself 'It's the Cheshire Cat: now I shall have somebody to talk to.'

cette apparition l'intrigua beaucoup d'abord, mais, après l'avoir considérée quelques instants, elle découvrit que c'était une grimace, et se dit en elle-même, "C'est le Grimaçon; maintenant j'aurai à qui parler."

'How are you getting on?' said the Cat, as soon as there was mouth enough for it to speak with.

"Comment cela va-t-il?" dit le Chat, quand il y eut assez de sa bouche pour qu'il pût parler.

Alice waited till the eyes appeared, and then nodded. 'It's no use speaking to it,' she thought: 'till its ears have come, or at least one of them.'

Alice attendit que les yeux parussent, et lui fit alors un signe de tête amical. "Il est inutile de lui parler," pensait-elle, "avant que ses oreilles soient venues, l'une d'elle tout au moins."

In another minute the whole head appeared, and then Alice put down her flamingo, and began an account of the game, feeling very glad she had someone to listen to her. The Cat seemed to think that there was enough of it now in sight, and no more of it appeared.

Une minute après, la tête se montra tout entière, et alors Alice posa à terre son flamant et se mit à raconter sa partie de croquet, enchantée d'avoir quelqu'un qui l'écoutât. Le Chat trouva apparemment qu'il s'était assez mis en vue; car sa tête fut tout ce qu'on en aperçut.

I don't think they play at all fairly,' Alice began, in rather a complaining tone:

"Ils ne jouent pas du tout franc jeu," commença Alice d'un ton de mécontentement,

'and they all quarrel so dreadfully one can't hear oneself speak—and they don't seem to have any rules in particular; at least, if there are, nobody attends to them—and you've no idea how confusing it is all the things being alive;

"et ils se querellent tous si fort, qu'on ne peut pas s'entendre parler; et puis on dirait qu'ils n'ont aucune règle précise; du moins, s'il y a des règles, personne ne les suit. Ensuite vous n'avez pas idée comme cela embrouille que tous les instruments du jeu soient vivants;

for instance, there's the arch I've got to go through next walking about at the other end of the ground—and I should have croqueted the Queen's hedgehog just now, only it ran away when it saw mine coming!'

'How do you like the Queen?' said the Cat in a low voice.

Not at all,' said Alice: 'she's so extremely—' Just then she noticed that the Queen was close behind her, listening: so she went on: '—likely to win, that it's hardly worth while finishing the game.'

The Queen smiled and passed on.

'Who are you talking to?' said the King, going up to Alice, and looking at the Cat's head with great curiosity.

It's a friend of mine—a Cheshire Cat,' said Alice: 'allow me to introduce it.'

'I don't like the look of it at all,' said the King: 'however, it may kiss my hand if it likes.'

'I'd rather not,' the Cat remarked.

Don't be impertinent,' said the King: 'and don't look at me like that!' He got behind Alice as he spoke.

'A cat may look at a king,' said Alice. 'I've read that in some book, but I don't remember where.'

Well, it must be removed,' said the King very decidedly, and he called the Queen, who was passing at the moment: 'My dear! I wish you would have this cat removed!'

The Queen had only one way of settling all difficulties, great or small. 'Off with his head!' she said, without even looking round.

'I'll fetch the executioner myself,' said the King eagerly, and he hurried off.

Alice thought she might as well go back, and see how the game was going on, as she heard the Queen's voice in the distance, screaming with passion.

She had already heard her sentence three of the players to be executed for having missed their turns, and she did not like the look of things at all, as the game was in such confusion that she never knew whether it was her turn or not.

So she went in search of her hedgehog.

par exemple, voilà l'arche par laquelle j'ai à passer qui se promène là-bas à l'autre bout du jeu, et j'aurais fait croquet sur le hérisson de la Reine tout à l'heure, s'il ne s'était pas sauvé en voyant venir le mien!"

"Est-ce que vous aimez la Reine?" dit le Chat à voix basse.

"Pas du tout," dit Alice. "Elle est si —" Au même instant elle aperçut la Reine tout près derrière elle, qui écoutait; alors elle continua: "si sûre de gagner, que ce n'est guère la peine de finir la partie."

La Reine sourit et passa.

"Avec qui causez-vous donc là," dit le Roi, s'approchant d'Alice et regardant avec une extrême curiosité la tête du Chat.

"C'est un de mes amis, un Grimaçon," dit Alice: "permettez-moi de vous le présenter."

"Sa mine ne me plaît pas du tout," dit le Roi. "Pourtant il peut me baiser la main, si cela lui fait plaisir."

"Non, grand merci," dit le Chat.

"Ne faites pas l'impertinent," dit le Roi, "et ne me regardez pas ainsi!" Il s'était mis derrière Alice en disant ces mots.

"Un chat peut bien regarder un roi," dit Alice. "J'ai lu quelque chose comme cela dans un livre, mais je ne me rappelle pas où."

"Eh bien, il faut le faire enlever," dit le Roi d'un ton très-décidé; et il cria à la Reine, qui passait en ce moment: "Mon amie, je désirerais que vous fissiez enlever ce chat!"

La Reine n'avait qu'une seule manière de trancher les difficultés, petites ou grandes. "Qu'on lui coupe la tête!" dit-elle sans même se retourner.

"Je vais moi-même chercher le bourreau," dit le Roi avec empressement; et il s'en alla précipitamment.

Alice pensa qu'elle ferait bien de retourner voir où en était la partie, car elle entendait au loin la voix de la Reine qui criait de colère.

Elle l'avait déjà entendue condamner trois des joueurs à avoir la tête coupée, parce qu'ils avaient laissé passer leur tour, et elle n'aimait pas du tout la tournure que prenaient les choses; car le jeu était si embrouillé qu'elle ne savait jamais quand venait son tour.

Elle alla à la recherche de son hérisson.

The hedgehog was engaged in a fight with another hedgehog, which seemed to Alice an excellent opportunity for croqueting one of them with the other:

the only difficulty was, that her flamingo was gone across to the other side of the garden, where Alice could see it trying in a helpless sort of way to fly up into a tree.

By the time she had caught the flamingo and brought it back, the fight was over, and both the hedgehogs were out of sight:

'but it doesn't matter much,' thought Alice: 'as all the arches are gone from this side of the ground.'

So she tucked it away under her arm, that it might not escape again, and went back for a little more conversation with her friend.

When she got back to the Cheshire Cat, she was surprised to find quite a large crowd collected round it: there was a dispute going on between the executioner, the King, and the Queen, who were all talking at once, while all the rest were quite silent, and looked very uncomfortable.

The moment Alice appeared, she was appealed to by all three to settle the question, and they repeated their arguments to her, though, as they all spoke at once, she found it very hard indeed to make out exactly what they said.

The executioner's argument was, that you couldn't cut off a head unless there was a body to cut it off from: that he had never had to do such a thing before, and he wasn't going to begin at his time of life.

The King's argument was, that anything that had a head could be beheaded, and that you weren't to talk nonsense.

The Queen's argument was, that if something wasn't done about it in less than no time she'd have everybody executed, all round. (It was this last remark that had made the whole party look so grave and anxious.)

Alice could think of nothing else to say but 'It belongs to the Duchess: you'd better ask her about it.'

'She's in prison,' the Queen said to the executioner: 'fetch her here.' And the executioner went off like an arrow.

Il était en train de se battre avec un autre hérisson; ce qui parut à Alice une excellente occasion de faire croquet de l'un sur l'autre.

Il n'y avait à cela qu'une difficulté, et c'était que son flamant avait passé de l'autre côté du jardin, où Alice le voyait qui faisait de vains efforts pour s'enlever et se percher sur un arbre.

Quand elle eut rattrapé et ramené le flamant, la bataille était terminée, et les deux hérissons avaient disparu.

"Mais cela ne fait pas grand'chose," pensa Alice, "puisque toutes les arches ont quitté ce côté de la pelouse."

Elle remit donc le flamant sous son bras pour qu'il ne lui échappât plus, et retourna causer un peu avec son ami.

Quand elle revint auprès du Chat, elle fut surprise de trouver une grande foule rassemblée autour de lui. Une discussion avait lieu entre le bourreau, le Roi, et la Reine, qui parlaient tous à la fois, tandis que les autres ne soufflaient mot et semblaient très-mal à l'aise.

Dès que parut Alice, ils en appelèrent à elle tous les trois pour qu'elle décidât la question, et lui répétèrent leurs raisonnements. Comme ils parlaient tous à la fois, elle eut beaucoup de peine à comprendre ce qu'ils disaient. Le raisonnement du bourreau était: qu'on ne pouvait pas trancher une tête, à moins qu'il n'y eût un corps d'où l'on pût la couper; que jamais il n'avait eu pareille chose à faire, et que ce n'était pas à son âge qu'il allait commencer.

Le raisonnement du Roi était: que tout ce qui avait une tête pouvait être décapité, et qu'il ne fallait pas dire des choses qui n'avaient pas de bon sens.

Le raisonnement de la Reine était: que si la question ne se décidait pas en moins de rien, elle ferait trancher la tête à tout le monde à la ronde. (C'était cette dernière observation qui avait donné à toute la compagnie l'air si grave et si inquiet.)

Alice ne trouva rien de mieux à dire que: "Il appartient à la Duchesse; c'est elle que vous feriez bien de consulter à ce sujet."

"Elle est en prison," dit la Reine au bourreau. "Qu'on l'amène ici." Et le bourreau partit comme un trait.

The Cat's head began fading away the moment he was gone, and, by the time he had come back with the Duchess, it had entirely disappeared;

La tête du Chat commença à s'évanouir aussitôt que le bourreau fut parti, et elle avait complétement disparu quand il revint accompagné de la Duchesse;

so the King and the executioner ran wildly up and down looking for it, while the rest of the party went back to the game.

de sorte que le Roi et le bourreau se mirent à courir de côté et d'autre comme des fous pour trouver cette tête, tandis que le reste de la compagnie retournait au jeu.

9. The Mock Turtle's Story

'You can't think how glad I am to see you again, you dear old thing!' said the Duchess, as she tucked her arm affectionately into Alice's, and they walked off together.

Alice was very glad to find her in such a pleasant temper, and thought to herself that perhaps it was only the pepper that had made her so savage when they met in the kitchen.

'When I'm a Duchess,' she said to herself, (not in a very hopeful tone though):

I won't have any pepper in my kitchen at all. Soup does very well without—Maybe it's always pepper that makes people hot-tempered,' she went on, very much pleased at having found out a new kind of rule:

'and vinegar that makes them sour—and camomile that makes them bitter—and—and barley-sugar and such things that make children sweet-tempered. I only wish people knew that: then they wouldn't be so stingy about it, you know—'

She had quite forgotten the Duchess by this time, and was a little startled when she heard her voice close to her ear.

'You're thinking about something, my dear, and that makes you forget to talk. I can't tell you just now what the moral of that is, but I shall remember it in a bit.'

'Perhaps it hasn't one,' Alice ventured to remark.

'Tut, tut, child!' said the Duchess. 'Everything's got a moral, if only you can find it.' And she squeezed herself up closer to Alice's side as she spoke.

Alice did not much like keeping so close to her: first, because the Duchess was very ugly; and secondly, because she was exactly the right height to rest her chin upon Alice's shoulder, and it was an uncomfortably sharp chin.

However, she did not like to be rude, so she bore it as well as she could.

'The game's going on rather better now,' she said, by way of keeping up the conversation a little.

9. Histoire de la Fausse-Tortue

“Vous ne sauriez croire combien je suis heureuse de vous voir, ma bonne vieille fille!” dit la Duchesse, passant amicalement son bras sous celui d'Alice, et elles s'éloignèrent ensemble.

Alice était bien contente de la trouver de si bonne humeur, et pensait en elle-même que c'était peut-être le poivre qui l'avait rendue si méchante, lorsqu'elles se rencontrèrent dans la cuisine.

“Quand je serai Duchesse, moi,” se dit-elle (d'un ton qui exprimait peu d'espérance cependant),

“je n'aurai pas de poivre dans ma cuisine, pas le moindre grain. La soupe peut très-bien s'en passer. Ça pourrait bien être le poivre qui échauffe la bile des gens,” continua-t-elle, enchantée d'avoir fait cette découverte;

“ça pourrait bien être le vinaigre qui les aigrit; la camomille qui les rend amères; et le sucre d'orge et d'autres choses du même genre qui adoucissent le caractère des enfants. Je voudrais bien que tout le monde sût cela; on ne serait pas si chiche de sucreries, voyez-vous.”

Elle avait alors complètement oublié la Duchesse, et tressaillit en entendant sa voix tout près de son oreille.

“Vous pensez à quelque chose, ma chère petite, et cela vous fait oublier de causer. Je ne puis pas vous dire en ce moment quelle est la morale de ce fait, mais je m'en souviendrai tout à l'heure.”

“Peut-être n'y en a-t-il pas,” se hasarda de dire Alice.

“Bah, bah, mon enfant!” dit la Duchesse. “Il y a une morale à tout, si seulement on pouvait la trouver.” Et elle se serra plus près d'Alice en parlant.

Alice n'aimait pas trop qu'elle se tînt si près d'elle; d'abord parce que la Duchesse était très-laide, et ensuite parce qu'elle était juste assez grande pour appuyer son menton sur l'épaule d'Alice, et c'était un menton très-désagréablement pointu.

Pourtant elle ne voulait pas être impolie, et elle supporta cela de son mieux.

“La partie va un peu mieux maintenant,” dit-elle, afin de soutenir la conversation.

'Tis so,' said the Duchess: 'and the moral of that is—"Oh: 'tis love: 'tis love, that makes the world go round!"'

Somebody said,' Alice whispered: 'that it's done by everybody minding their own business!'

Ah, well! It means much the same thing,' said the Duchess, digging her sharp little chin into Alice's shoulder as she added: 'and the moral of that is—"Take care of the sense, and the sounds will take care of themselves."'

'How fond she is of finding morals in things!' Alice thought to herself.

'I dare say you're wondering why I don't put my arm round your waist,' the Duchess said after a pause: 'the reason is, that I'm doubtful about the temper of your flamingo. Shall I try the experiment?'

'He might bite,' Alice cautiously replied, not feeling at all anxious to have the experiment tried.

Very true,' said the Duchess: 'flamingoes and mustard both bite. And the moral of that is—"Birds of a feather flock together."'

'Only mustard isn't a bird,' Alice remarked.

'Right, as usual,' said the Duchess: 'what a clear way you have of putting things!'

'It's a mineral, I think,' said Alice.

Of course it is,' said the Duchess, who seemed ready to agree to everything that Alice said; 'there's a large mustard-mine near here. And the moral of that is—"The more there is of mine, the less there is of yours."'

Oh, I know!' exclaimed Alice, who had not attended to this last remark: 'it's a vegetable. It doesn't look like one, but it is.'

I quite agree with you,' said the Duchess; 'and the moral of that is—"Be what you would seem to be"—or if you'd like it put more simply—

Never imagine yourself not to be otherwise than what it might appear to others that what you were or might have been was not otherwise than what you had been would have appeared to them to be otherwise.'

I think I should understand that better,' Alice said very politely: 'if I had it written down: but I can't quite follow it as you say it.'

"C'est vrai," dit la Duchesse; "et la morale en est: "Oh! c'est l'amour, l'amour qui fait aller le monde à la ronde!""

"Quelqu'un a dit," murmura Alice, "que c'est quand chacun s'occupe de ses affaires que le monde n'en va que mieux."

"Eh bien! Cela signifie presque la même chose," dit la Duchesse, qui enfonça son petit menton pointu dans l'épaule d'Alice, en ajoutant: "Et la morale en est: "Un chien vaut mieux que deux gros rats.""

"Comme elle aime à trouver des morales partout!" pensa Alice.

"Je parie que vous vous demandez pourquoi je ne passe pas mon bras autour de votre taille," dit la Duchesse après une pause: "La raison en est que je ne me fie pas trop à votre flamant. Voulez-vous que j'essaie?"

"Il pourrait mordre," répondit Alice, qui ne se sentait pas la moindre envie de faire l'essai proposé.

"C'est bien vrai," dit la Duchesse; "les flamants et la moutarde mordent tous les deux, et la morale en est: "Qui se ressemble, s'assemble.""

"Seulement la moutarde n'est pas un oiseau," répondit Alice.

"Vous avez raison, comme toujours," dit la Duchesse; "avec quelle clarté, vous présentez les choses!"

"C'est un minéral, je crois," dit Alice.

"Assurément," dit la Duchesse, qui semblait prête à approuver tout ce que disait Alice; "il y a une bonne mine de moutarde près d'ici; la morale en est qu'il faut faire bonne mine à tout le monde!"

"Oh! je sais," s'écria Alice, qui n'avait pas fait attention à cette dernière observation, "c'est un végétal; ça n'en a pas l'air, mais c'en est un."

"Je suis tout à fait de votre avis," dit la Duchesse, "et la morale en est: "Soyez ce que vous voulez paraître;" ou, si vous voulez que je le dise plus simplement:

"Ne vous imaginez jamais de ne pas être autrement que ce qu'il pourrait sembler aux autres que ce que vous étiez ou auriez pu être n'était pas autrement que ce que vous aviez été leur aurait paru être autrement.""

"Il me semble que je comprendrais mieux cela," dit Alice fort poliment, "si je l'avais par écrit: mais je ne peux pas très-bien le suivre comme vous le dites."

'That's nothing to what I could say if I chose,' the Duchess replied, in a pleased tone.

'Pray don't trouble yourself to say it any longer than that,' said Alice.

'Oh, don't talk about trouble!' said the Duchess. 'I make you a present of everything I've said as yet.'

'A cheap sort of present!' thought Alice. 'I'm glad they don't give birthday presents like that!' But she did not venture to say it out loud.

'Thinking again?' the Duchess asked, with another dig of her sharp little chin.

'I've a right to think,' said Alice sharply, for she was beginning to feel a little worried.

Just about as much right,' said the Duchess: 'as pigs have to fly; and the m—'

But here, to Alice's great surprise, the Duchess's voice died away, even in the middle of her favourite word 'moral,' and the arm that was linked into hers began to tremble.

Alice looked up, and there stood the Queen in front of them, with her arms folded, frowning like a thunderstorm.

'A fine day, your Majesty!' the Duchess began in a low, weak voice.

'Now, I give you fair warning,' shouted the Queen, stamping on the ground as she spoke; 'either you or your head must be off, and that in about half no time! Take your choice!'

The Duchess took her choice, and was gone in a moment.

'Let's go on with the game,' the Queen said to Alice; and Alice was too much frightened to say a word, but slowly followed her back to the croquet-ground.

The other guests had taken advantage of the Queen's absence, and were resting in the shade: however, the moment they saw her, they hurried back to the game, the Queen merely remarking that a moment's delay would cost them their lives.

All the time they were playing the Queen never left off quarrelling with the other players, and shouting 'Off with his head!' or 'Off with her head!'

Those whom she sentenced were taken into custody by the soldiers, who of course had to leave off being arches

"Cela n'est rien auprès de ce que je pourrais dire si je voulais," répondit la Duchesse d'un ton satisfait.

"Je vous en prie, ne vous donnez pas la peine d'allonger davantage votre explication," dit Alice.

"Oh! ne parlez pas de ma peine," dit la Duchesse; "je vous fais cadeau de tout ce que j'ai dit jusqu'à présent."

"Voilà un cadeau qui n'est pas cher!" pensa Alice. "Je suis bien contente qu'on ne fasse pas de cadeau d'anniversaire comme cela!" Mais elle ne se hasarda pas à le dire tout haut.

"Encore à réfléchir?" demanda la Duchesse, avec un nouveau coup de son petit menton pointu.

"J'ai bien le droit de réfléchir," dit Alice sèchement, car elle commençait à se sentir un peu ennuyée.

"À peu près le même droit," dit la Duchesse, "que les cochons de voler, et la mo—"

Mais ici, au grand étonnement d'Alice, la voix de la Duchesse s'éteignit au milieu de son mot favori, morale, et le bras qui était passé sous le sien commença de trembler.

Alice leva les yeux et vit la Reine en face d'elle, les bras croisés, sombre et terrible comme un orage.

"Voilà un bien beau temps, Votre Majesté!" fit la Duchesse, d'une voix basse et tremblante.

"Je vous en préviens!" cria la Reine, trépignant tout le temps. "Hors d'ici, ou à bas la tête! et cela en moins de rien! Choisissez."

La Duchesse eut bientôt fait son choix: elle disparut en un clin d'œil.

"Continuons notre partie," dit la Reine à Alice; et Alice, trop effrayée pour souffler mot, la suivit lentement vers la pelouse.

Les autres invités, profitant de l'absence de la Reine, se reposaient à l'ombre, mais sitôt qu'ils la virent ils se hâtèrent de retourner au jeu, la Reine leur faisant simplement observer qu'un instant de retard leur coûterait la vie.

Tant que dura la partie, la Reine ne cessa de se quereller avec les autres joueurs et de crier: "Qu'on coupe la tête à celui-ci! Qu'on coupe la tête à celle-là!"

Ceux qu'elle condamnait étaient arrêtés par les soldats qui, bien entendu, avaient à cesser de servir d'arches, de sorte

to do this, so that by the end of half an hour or so there were no arches left, and all the players, except the King, the Queen, and Alice, were in custody and under sentence of execution.

Then the Queen left off, quite out of breath, and said to Alice: 'Have you seen the Mock Turtle yet?'

'No,' said Alice. 'I don't even know what a Mock Turtle is.'

'It's the thing Mock Turtle Soup is made from,' said the Queen.

I never saw one, or heard of one,' said Alice. 'Come on, then,' said the Queen: 'and he shall tell you his history,'

As they walked off together, Alice heard the King say in a low voice, to the company generally:

'You are all pardoned.' 'Come, that's a good thing!' she said to herself, for she had felt quite unhappy at the number of executions the Queen had ordered.

They very soon came upon a Gryphon, lying fast asleep in the sun. (If you don't know what a Gryphon is, look at the picture.)

'Up, lazy thing!' said the Queen: 'and take this young lady to see the Mock Turtle, and to hear his history. I must go back and see after some executions I have ordered'; and she walked off, leaving Alice alone with the Gryphon.

Alice did not quite like the look of the creature, but on the whole she thought it would be quite as safe to stay with it as to go after that savage Queen: so she waited.

The Gryphon sat up and rubbed its eyes: then it watched the Queen till she was out of sight: then it chuckled. 'What fun!' said the Gryphon, half to itself, half to Alice.

'What is the fun?' said Alice.

'Why, she,' said the Gryphon. 'It's all her fancy, that: they never executes nobody, you know. Come on!'

'Everybody says "come on!" here,' thought Alice, as she went slowly after it: 'I never was so ordered about in all my life, never!'

They had not gone far before they saw the Mock Turtle in the distance, sitting sad and lonely on a little ledge of rock,

qu'au bout d'une demi-heure environ, il ne restait plus d'arches, et tous les joueurs, à l'exception du Roi, de la Reine, et d'Alice, étaient arrêtés et condamnés à avoir la tête tranchée.

Alors la Reine cessa le jeu toute hors d'haleine, et dit à Alice: "Avez-vous vu la Fausse-Tortue?"

"Non," dit Alice; "je ne sais même pas ce que c'est qu'une Fausse-Tortue."

"C'est ce dont on fait la soupe à la Fausse-Tortue," dit la Reine.

"Je n'en ai jamais vu, et c'est la première fois que j'en entends parler," dit Alice. "Eh bien! venez," dit la Reine, "et elle vous contera son histoire."

Comme elles s'en allaient ensemble, Alice entendit le Roi dire à voix basse à toute la compagnie:

"Vous êtes tous graciés." "Allons, voilà qui est heureux!" se dit-elle en elle-même, car elle était toute chagrine du grand nombre d'exécutions que la Reine avait ordonnées.

Elles rencontrèrent bientôt un Griffon, étendu au soleil et dormant profondément. (Si vous ne savez pas ce que c'est qu'un Griffon, regardez l'image.)

"Debout! paresseux," dit la Reine, "et menez cette petite demoiselle voir la Fausse-Tortue, et l'entendre raconter son histoire. Il faut que je m'en retourne pour veiller à quelques exécutions que j'ai ordonnées;" et elle partit laissant Alice seule avec le Griffon.

La mine de cet animal ne plaisait pas trop à Alice, mais, tout bien considéré, elle pensa qu'elle ne courait pas plus de risques en restant auprès de lui, qu'en suivant cette Reine farouche.

Le Griffon se leva et se frotta les yeux, puis il guetta la Reine jusqu'à ce qu'elle fût disparue; et il se mit à ricaner. "Quelle farce!" dit le Griffon, moitié à part soi, moitié à Alice.

"Quelle est la farce?" demanda Alice.

"Elle!" dit le Griffon. "C'est une idée qu'elle se fait; jamais on n'exécute personne, vous comprenez. Venez donc!"

"Tout le monde ici dit: "Venez donc!"" pensa Alice, en suivant lentement le Griffon. "Jamais de ma vie on ne m'a fait aller comme cela; non, jamais!"

Ils ne firent pas beaucoup de chemin avant d'apercevoir dans l'éloignement la Fausse-Tortue assise, triste et solitaire, sur un petit récif, et, à mesure qu'ils approchaient, Alice pouvait

and, as they came nearer, Alice could hear him sighing as if his heart would break. She pitied him deeply.

'What is his sorrow?' she asked the Gryphon, and the Gryphon answered, very nearly in the same words as before: 'It's all his fancy, that: he hasn't got no sorrow, you know. Come on!'

So they went up to the Mock Turtle, who looked at them with large eyes full of tears, but said nothing.

This here young lady,' said the Gryphon: 'she wants for to know your history, she do.'

'I'll tell it her,' said the Mock Turtle in a deep, hollow tone: 'sit down, both of you, and don't speak a word till I've finished.'

So they sat down, and nobody spoke for some minutes. Alice thought to herself: 'I don't see how he can even finish, if he doesn't begin.' But she waited patiently.

Once,' said the Mock Turtle at last, with a deep sigh: 'I was a real Turtle.'

These words were followed by a very long silence, broken only by an occasional exclamation of 'Hjckrrh!' from the Gryphon, and the constant heavy sobbing of the Mock Turtle.

Alice was very nearly getting up and saying: 'Thank you, sir, for your interesting story,' but she could not help thinking there must be more to come, so she sat still and said nothing.

When we were little,' the Mock Turtle went on at last, more calmly, though still sobbing a little now and then: 'we went to school in the sea. The master was an old Turtle—we used to call him Tortoise—'

'Why did you call him Tortoise, if he wasn't one?' Alice asked. 'We called him Tortoise because he taught us,' said the Mock Turtle angrily: 'really you are very dull!'

You ought to be ashamed of yourself for asking such a simple question,' added the Gryphon; and then they both sat silent and looked at poor Alice, who felt ready to sink into the earth.

At last the Gryphon said to the Mock Turtle: 'Drive on, old fellow! Don't be all day about it!' and he went on in these words:

l'entendre qui soupirait comme si son cœur allait se briser; elle la plaignait sincèrement.

“Quel est donc son chagrin?” demanda-t-elle au Griffon; et le Griffon répondit, presque dans les mêmes termes qu'auparavant: “C'est une idée qu'elle se fait; elle n'a point de chagrin, vous comprenez. Venez donc!”

Ainsi ils s'approchèrent de la Fausse-Tortue, qui les regarda avec de grands yeux pleins de larmes, mais ne dit rien.

“Cette petite demoiselle,” dit le Griffon, “veut savoir votre histoire.”

“Je vais la lui raconter,” dit la Fausse-Tortue, d'un ton grave et sourd: “Asseyez-vous tous deux, et ne dites pas un mot avant que j'aie fini.”

Ils s'assirent donc, et pendant quelques minutes, personne ne dit mot. Alice pensait: “Je ne vois pas comment elle pourra jamais finir si elle ne commence pas.” Mais elle attendit patiemment.

“Autrefois,” dit enfin la Fausse-Tortue, “j'étais une vraie Tortue.”

Ces paroles furent suivies d'un long silence interrompu seulement de temps à autre par cette exclamation du Griffon: “Hjckrrh!” et les soupirs continuels de la Fausse-Tortue.

Alice était sur le point de se lever et de dire: “Merci de votre histoire intéressante,” mais elle ne pouvait s'empêcher de penser qu'il devait sûrement y en avoir encore à venir. Elle resta donc tranquille sans rien dire.

“Quand nous étions petits,” continua la Fausse Tortue d'un ton plus calme, quoiqu'elle laissât encore de temps à autre échapper un sanglot, “nous allions à l'école au fond de la mer. La maîtresse était une vieille tortue; nous l'appelions Chélonée.”

“Et pourquoi l'appeliez-vous Chélonée, si ce n'était pas son nom?” “Parce qu'on ne pouvait s'empêcher de s'écrier en la voyant: “Quel long nez!”“ dit la Fausse-Tortue d'un ton fâché; “vous êtes vraiment bien bornée!”

“Vous devriez avoir honte de faire une question si simple!” ajouta le Griffon; et puis tous deux gardèrent le silence, les yeux fixés sur la pauvre Alice, qui se sentait prête à rentrer sous terre.

Enfin le Griffon dit à la Fausse-Tortue, “En avant, camarade! Tâchez d'en finir aujourd'hui!” et elle continua en ces termes:

Yes, we went to school in the sea, though you mayn't believe it—'

"Oui, nous allions à l'école dans la mer, bien que cela vous étonne."

'I never said I didn't!' interrupted Alice.

"Je n'ai pas dit cela," interrompit Alice.

'You did,' said the Mock Turtle.

"Vous l'avez dit," répondit la Fausse-Tortue.

'Hold your tongue!' added the Gryphon, before Alice could speak again. The Mock Turtle went on.

"Taisez-vous donc," ajouta le Griffon, avant qu'Alice pût reprendre la parole. La Fausse-Tortue continua:

We had the best of educations—in fact, we went to school every day—'

"Nous recevions la meilleure éducation possible; au fait, nous allions tous les jours à l'école."

'I've been to a day-school, too,' said Alice; 'you needn't be so proud as all that.'

"Moi aussi, j'y ai été tous les jours," dit Alice; "il n'y a pas de quoi être si fière."

'With extras?' asked the Mock Turtle a little anxiously.

"Avec des "en sus,"" dit la Fausse-Tortue avec quelque inquiétude.

Yes,' said Alice: 'we learned French and music.'

"Oui," dit Alice, "nous apprenions l'italien et la musique en sus."

'And washing?' said the Mock Turtle.

"Et le blanchissage?" dit la Fausse-Tortue.

'Certainly not!' said Alice indignantly.

"Non, certainement!" dit Alice indignée.

Ah! then yours wasn't a really good school,' said the Mock Turtle in a tone of great relief. 'Now at ours they had at the end of the bill, "French, music, and washing—extra."'

"Ah! Alors votre pension n'était pas vraiment des bonnes," dit la Fausse-Tortue comme soulagée d'un grand poids. "Eh bien, à notre pension il y avait au bas du prospectus: "l'italien, la musique, et le blanchissage en sus.""

'You couldn't have wanted it much,' said Alice; 'living at the bottom of the sea.'

"Vous ne deviez pas en avoir grand besoin, puisque vous viviez au fond de la mer," dit Alice.

'I couldn't afford to learn it.' said the Mock Turtle with a sigh. 'I only took the regular course.'

"Je n'avais pas les moyens de l'apprendre," dit en soupirant la Fausse-Tortue; "je ne suivais que les cours ordinaires."

'What was that?' inquired Alice.

"Qu'est-ce que c'était?" demanda Alice.

Reeling and Writhing, of course, to begin with,' the Mock Turtle replied; 'and then the different branches of Arithmetic— Ambition, Distraction, Uglification, and Derision.'

"À Luire et à Médire, cela va sans dire," répondit la Fausse-Tortue; "et puis les différentes branches de l'Arithmétique: l'Ambition, la Distraction, l'Enjolification, et la Dérision."

'I never heard of "Uglification,"' Alice ventured to say. 'What is it?'

"Je n'ai jamais entendu parler d'enjolification," se hasarda de dire Alice. "Qu'est-ce que c'est?"

The Gryphon lifted up both its paws in surprise. 'What! Never heard of uglifying!' it exclaimed. 'You know what to beautify is, I suppose?'

Le Griffon leva les deux pattes en l'air en signe d'étonnement. "Vous n'avez jamais entendu parler d'enjolir!" s'écria-t-il. "Vous savez ce que c'est que "embellir," je suppose?"

Yes,' said Alice doubtfully: 'it means—to—make—anything—prettier.'

"Oui," dit Alice, en hésitant: "cela veut dire — rendre — une chose — plus belle."

'Well, then,' the Gryphon went on: 'if you don't know what to uglify is, you are a simpleton.'

Alice did not feel encouraged to ask any more questions about it, so she turned to the Mock Turtle, and said 'What else had you to learn?'

'Well, there was Mystery,' the Mock Turtle replied, counting off the subjects on his flappers: '—Mystery, ancient and modern, with Seaography: then Drawling—the Drawling-master was an old conger-eel, that used to come once a week: He taught us Drawling, Stretching, and Fainting in Coils.'

'What was that like?' said Alice.

'Well, I can't show it you myself,' the Mock Turtle said: 'I'm too stiff. And the Gryphon never learnt it.'

'Hadn't time,' said the Gryphon: 'I went to the Classics master, though. He was an old crab, he was.'

'I never went to him,' the Mock Turtle said with a sigh: 'he taught Laughing and Grief, they used to say.'

'So he did, so he did,' said the Gryphon, sighing in his turn; and both creatures hid their faces in their paws.

'And how many hours a day did you do lessons?' said Alice, in a hurry to change the subject.

'Ten hours the first day,' said the Mock Turtle: 'nine the next, and so on.'

'What a curious plan!' exclaimed Alice.

'That's the reason they're called lessons,' the Gryphon remarked: 'because they lessen from day to day.'

This was quite a new idea to Alice, and she thought it over a little before she made her next remark. 'Then the eleventh day must have been a holiday?'

'Of course it was,' said the Mock Turtle.

'And how did you manage on the twelfth?' Alice went on eagerly.

'That's enough about lessons,' the Gryphon interrupted in a very decided tone: 'tell her something about the games now.'

"Eh bien!" continua le Griffon, "si vous ne savez pas ce que c'est que "enjolir" vous êtes vraiment niaise."

Alice ne se sentit pas encouragée à faire de nouvelles questions là-dessus, elle se tourna donc vers la Fausse-Tortue, et lui dit, "Qu'appreniez-vous encore?"

"Eh bien, il y avait le Grimoire," répondit la Fausse-Tortue en comptant sur ses battoirs; "le Grimoire ancien et moderne, avec la Mérographie, et puis le Dédain; le maître de Dédain était un vieux congre qui venait une fois par semaine; il nous ēnseignait à Dédaigner, à Esquiver et à Feindre à l'huître."

"Qu'est-ce que cela?" dit Alice.

"Ah! je ne peux pas vous le montrer, moi," dit la Fausse-Tortue, "je suis trop gênée, et le Griffon ne l'a jamais appris."

"Je n'en avais pas le temps," dit le Griffon, "mais j'ai suivi les cours du professeur de langues mortes; c'était un vieux crabe, celui-là."

"Je n'ai jamais suivi ses cours," dit la Fausse-Tortue avec un soupir; "il enseignait le Larcin et la Grève."

"C'est ça, c'est ça," dit le Griffon, en soupirant à son tour; et ces deux créatures se cachèrent la figure dans leurs pattes.

"Combien d'heures de leçons aviez-vous par jour?" dit Alice vivement, pour changer la conversation.

"Dix heures, le premier jour," dit la Fausse-Tortue; "neuf heures, le second, et ainsi de suite."

"Quelle singulière méthode!" s'écria Alice.

"C'est pour cela qu'on les appelle leçons," dit le Griffon, "parce que nous les laissons là peu à peu."

C'était là pour Alice une idée toute nouvelle; elle y réfléchit un peu avant de faire une autre observation. "Alors le onzième jour devait être un jour de congé?"

"Assurément," répondit la Fausse-Tortue.

"Et comment vous arrangiez-vous le douzième jour?" s'empressa de demander Alice.

"En voilà assez sur les leçons," dit le Griffon intervenant d'un ton très-décidé; "parlez-lui des jeux maintenant."

10. The Lobster's Quadrille

10. Le Quadrille de Homards

The Mock Turtle sighed deeply, and drew the back of one flapper across his eyes. He looked at Alice, and tried to speak, but for a minute or two sobs choked his voice.

La Fausse-Tortue soupira profondément et passa le dos d'une de ses nageoires sur ses yeux. Elle regarda Alice et s'efforça de parler, mais les sanglots étouffèrent sa voix pendant une ou deux minutes.

Same as if he had a bone in his throat,' said the Gryphon: and it set to work shaking him and punching him in the back.

"On dirait qu'elle a un os dans le gosier," dit le Griffon, et il se mit à la secouer et à lui taper dans le dos.

At last the Mock Turtle recovered his voice, and, with tears running down his cheeks, he went on again:—

Enfin la Fausse-Tortue retrouva la voix, et, tandis que de grosses larmes coulaient le long de ses joues, elle continua:

You may not have lived much under the sea—' ('I haven't,' said Alice)— 'and perhaps you were never even introduced to a lobster—' (Alice began to say 'I once tasted—' but checked herself hastily, and said 'No, never')

"Peut-être n'avez-vous pas beaucoup vécu au fond de la mer?" — ("Non," dit Alice) — "et peut-être ne vous a-t-on jamais présentée à un homard?" (Alice allait dire: "J'en ai goûté une fois —" mais elle se reprit vivement, et dit: "Non, jamais.")

—so you can have no idea what a delightful thing a Lobster Quadrille is!'

"De sorte que vous ne pouvez pas du tout vous figurer quelle chose délicieuse c'est qu'un quadrille de homards."

'No, indeed,' said Alice. 'What sort of a dance is it?'

"Non, vraiment," dit Alice. "Qu'est-ce que c'est que cette danse-là?"

Why,' said the Gryphon: 'you first form into a line along the sea-shore—'

"D'abord," dit le Griffon, "on se met en rang le long des bords de la mer —"

Two lines!' cried the Mock Turtle. 'Seals, turtles, salmon, and so on; then, when you've cleared all the jelly-fish out of the way—'

"On forme deux rangs," cria la Fausse-Tortue: "des phoques, des tortues et des saumons, et ainsi de suite. Puis lorsqu'on a débarrassé la côte des gelées de mer —"

'That generally takes some time,' interrupted the Gryphon.

"Cela prend ordinairement longtemps," dit le Griffon.

—you advance twice—'

"— on avance deux fois —"

'Each with a lobster as a partner!' cried the Gryphon.

"Chacun ayant un homard pour danseur," cria le Griffon.

Of course,' the Mock Turtle said: 'advance twice, set to partners—' '—change lobsters, and retire in same order,' continued the Gryphon.

"Cela va sans dire," dit la Fausse-Tortue. "Avancez deux fois et balancez —" "Changez de homards, et revenez dans le même ordre," continua le Griffon.

Then, you know,' the Mock Turtle went on: 'you throw the—'

"Et puis, vous comprenez," continua la Fausse-Tortue, "vous jetez les —"

'The lobsters!' shouted the Gryphon, with a bound into the air.

"Les homards!" cria le Griffon, en faisant un bond en l'air.

—as far out to sea as you can—'

"— aussi loin à la mer que vous le pouvez —"

'Swim after them!' screamed the Gryphon.

'Turn a somersault in the sea!' cried the Mock Turtle, capering wildly about.

'Change lobster's again!' yelled the Gryphon at the top of its voice.

'Back to land again, and that's all the first figure,' said the Mock Turtle, suddenly dropping his voice; and the two creatures, who had been jumping about like mad things all this time, sat down again very sadly and quietly, and looked at Alice.

'It must be a very pretty dance,' said Alice timidly.

'Would you like to see a little of it?' said the Mock Turtle.

'Very much indeed,' said Alice.

'Come, let's try the first figure!' said the Mock Turtle to the Gryphon. 'We can do without lobsters, you know. Which shall sing?'

'Oh, you sing,' said the Gryphon. 'I've forgotten the words.'

So they began solemnly dancing round and round Alice, every now and then treading on her toes when they passed too close, and waving their forepaws to mark the time, while the Mock Turtle sang this, very slowly and sadly:

— '"Will you walk a little faster?" said a whiting to a snail. "There's a porpoise close behind us, and he's treading on my tail.

will you come and join the dance? Will you, won't you, will you, won't you, will you join the dance? Will you, won't you, will you, won't you, won't you join the dance? "You can really have no notion how delightful it will be When they take us up and throw us, with the lobsters, out to sea!"

But the snail replied "Too far, too far!" and gave a look askance— Said he thanked the whiting kindly, but he would not join the dance. Would not, could not, would not, could not, would not join the dance. Would not, could not, would not, could not, could not join the dance.

'Thank you, it's a very interesting dance to watch,' said Alice, feeling very glad that it was over at last: 'and I do so like that curious song about the whiting!'

"Vous nagez à leur poursuite!!" cria le Griffon.

"— vous faites une cabriole dans la mer!!!" cria la Fausse-Tortue, en cabriolant de tous côtés comme une folle.

"Changez encore de homards!!!!" hurla le Griffon de toutes ses forces.

"— revenez à terre; et — c'est là la première figure," dit la Fausse-Tortue, baissant tout à coup la voix; et ces deux êtres, qui pendant tout ce temps avaient bondi de tous côtés comme des fous, se rassirent bien tristement et bien posément, puis regardèrent Alice.

"Cela doit être une très-jolie danse," dit timidement Alice.

"Voudriez-vous voir un peu comment ça se danse?" dit la Fausse-Tortue.

"Cela me ferait grand plaisir," dit Alice.

"Allons, essayons la première figure," dit la Fausse-Tortue au Griffon; "nous pouvons la faire sans homards, vous comprenez. Qui va chanter?"

"Oh! chantez, vous," dit le Griffon; "moi j'ai oublié les paroles."

Ils se mirent donc à danser gravement tout autour d'Alice, lui marchant de temps à autre sur les pieds quand ils approchaient trop près, et remuant leurs pattes de devant pour marquer la mesure, tandis que la Fausse-Tortue chantait très-lentement et très-tristement:

"Nous n'irons plus à l'eau, Si tu n'avances tôt; Ce Marsouin trop pressé Va tous nous écraser. Colimaçon danse, Entre dans la danse; Sautons, dansons, Avant de faire un plongeon."

"Je ne veux pas danser, Je me f'rais fracasser." "Oh!" reprend le Merlan, "C'est pourtant bien plaisant." Colimaçon danse, Entre dans la danse; Sautons, dansons, Avant de faire un plongeon.

"Je ne veux pas plonger, Je ne sais pas nager." — "Le Homard et l'bateau D'sauv'tag' te tir'ont d'l'eau." Colimaçon danse, Entre dans la danse; Sautons, dansons, Avant de faire un plongeon.

"Merci; c'est une danse très-intéressante à voir danser," dit Alice, enchantée que ce fût enfin fini; "et je trouve cette curieuse chanson du merlan si agréable!"

Oh, as to the whiting,' said the Mock Turtle: 'they—you've seen them, of course?'

"Oh! quant aux merlans," dit la Fausse-Tortue, "ils — vous les avez vus, sans doute?"

Yes,' said Alice: 'I've often seen them at dinn—' she checked herself hastily.

"Oui," dit Alice, "je les ai souvent vus à dî—" elle s'arrêta tout court.

I don't know where Dinn may be,' said the Mock Turtle: 'but if you've seen them so often, of course you know what they're like.'

"Je ne sais pas où est Di," reprit la Fausse Tortue; "mais, puisque vous les avez vus si souvent, vous devez savoir l'air qu'ils ont?"

I believe so,' Alice replied thoughtfully. 'They have their tails in their mouths—and they're all over crumbs.'

"Je le crois," répliqua Alice, en se recueillant. "Ils ont la queue dans la bouche — et sont tout couverts de mie de pain."

You're wrong about the crumbs,' said the Mock Turtle: 'crumbs would all wash off in the sea. But they have their tails in their mouths; and the reason is—' here the Mock Turtle yawned and shut his eyes.—'Tell her about the reason and all that,' he said to the Gryphon.

"Vous vous trompez à l'endroit de la mie de pain," dit la Fausse-Tortue: "la mie serait enlevée dans la mer, mais ils ont bien la queue dans la bouche, et la raison en est que —" Ici la Fausse-Tortue bâilla et ferma les yeux. "Dites-lui-en la raison et tout ce qui s'ensuit," dit-elle au Griffon.

The reason is,' said the Gryphon: 'that they would go with the lobsters to the dance. So they got thrown out to sea. So they had to fall a long way. So they got their tails fast in their mouths. So they couldn't get them out again. That's all.'

"La raison, c'est que les merlans," dit le Griffon, "voulurent absolument aller à la danse avec les homards. Alors on les jeta à la mer. Alors ils eurent à tomber bien loin, bien loin. Alors ils s'entrèrent la queue fortement dans la bouche. Alors ils ne purent plus l'en retirer. Voilà tout."

Thank you,' said Alice: 'it's very interesting. I never knew so much about a whiting before.'

"Merci," dit Alice, "c'est très-intéressant; je n'en avais jamais tant appris sur le compte des merlans."

And the Gryphon added 'Come, let's hear some of your adventures.'

"Je propose donc," dit le Griffon, "que vous nous racontiez quelques-unes de vos aventures."

I could tell you my adventures—beginning from this morning,' said Alice a little timidly: 'but it's no use going back to yesterday, because I was a different person then.'

"Je pourrais vous conter mes aventures à partir de ce matin," dit Alice un peu timidement; "mais il est inutile de parler de la journée d'hier, car j'étais une personne tout à fait différente alors."

'Explain all that,' said the Mock Turtle.

"Expliquez-nous cela," dit la Fausse-Tortue.

'No, no! The adventures first,' said the Gryphon in an impatient tone: 'explanations take such a dreadful time.'

"Non, non, les aventures d'abord," dit le Griffon d'un ton d'impatience; "les explications prennent tant de temps."

So Alice began telling them her adventures from the time when she first saw the White Rabbit.

Alice commença donc à leur conter ses aventures depuis le moment où elle avait vu le Lapin Blanc pour la première fois.

She was a little nervous about it just at first, the two creatures got so close to her, one on each side, and opened their eyes and mouths so very wide, but she gained courage as she went on.

Elle fut d'abord un peu troublée dans le commencement; les deux créatures se tenaient si près d'elle, une de chaque côté, et ouvraient de si grands yeux et une si grande bouche! Mais elle reprenait courage à mesure qu'elle parlait.

Her listeners were perfectly quiet till she got to the part about her repeating 'You are old, Father William,' to the Caterpillar, and the words all coming different, and then the Mock Turtle drew a long breath, and said 'That's very curious.'

Les auditeurs restèrent fort tranquilles jusqu'à ce qu'elle arrivât au moment de son histoire où elle avait eu à répéter à la chenille: "Vous êtes vieux, Père Guillaume," et où les mots lui étaient venus tout de travers, et alors la Fausse-Tortue poussa un long soupir et dit: "C'est bien singulier."

'It's all about as curious as it can be,' said the Gryphon.

"Tout cela est on ne peut plus singulier," dit le Griffon.

'It all came different!' the Mock Turtle repeated thoughtfully. 'I should like to hear her try and repeat something now. Tell her to begin.' He looked at the Gryphon as if he thought it had some kind of authority over Alice.

"Tout de travers," répéta la Fausse-Tortue d'un air rêveur. "Je voudrais bien l'entendre réciter quelque chose à présent. Dites-lui de s'y mettre." Elle regardait le Griffon comme si elle lui croyait de l'autorité sur Alice.

'Stand up and repeat "'Tis the voice of the sluggard,"' said the Gryphon.

"Debout, et récitez: "C'est la voix du canon,"" dit le Griffon.

How the creatures order one about, and make one repeat lessons!' thought Alice; 'I might as well be at school at once.'

"Comme ces êtres-là vous commandent et vous font répéter des leçons!" pensa Alice; "autant vaudrait être à l'école."

However, she got up, and began to repeat it, but her head was so full of the Lobster Quadrille, that she hardly knew what she was saying, and the words came very queer indeed:—

Cependant elle se leva et se mit à réciter; mais elle avait la tête si pleine du Quadrille de Homards, qu'elle savait à peine ce qu'elle disait, et que les mots lui venaient tout drôlement: —

"'Tis the voice of the Lobster; I heard him declare,

"C'est la voix du homard grondant comme la foudre:

"You have baked me too brown, I must sugar my hair."

"On m'a trop fait bouillir, il faut que je me poudre!"

As a duck with its eyelids, so he with his nose Trims his belt and his buttons, and turns out his toes.'

Puis, les pieds en dehors, prenant la brosse en main, De se faire bien beau vite il se met en train."

'That's different from what I used to say when I was a child,' said the Gryphon.

"C'est tout différent de ce que je récitais quand j'étais petit, moi," dit le Griffon.

'Well, I never heard it before,' said the Mock Turtle; 'but it sounds uncommon nonsense.'

"Je ne l'avais pas encore entendu réciter," dit la Fausse-Tortue; "mais cela me fait l'effet d'un fameux galimatias."

Alice said nothing; she had sat down with her face in her hands, wondering if anything would ever happen in a natural way again.

Alice ne dit rien; elle s'était rassise, la figure dans ses mains, se demandant avec étonnement si jamais les choses reprendraient leur cours naturel.

'I should like to have it explained,' said the Mock Turtle.

"Je voudrais bien qu'on m'expliquât cela," dit la Fausse-Tortue.

'She can't explain it,' said the Gryphon hastily. 'Go on with the next verse.'

"Elle ne peut pas l'expliquer," dit le Griffon vivement. "Continuez, récitez les vers suivants."

'But about his toes?' the Mock Turtle persisted. 'How could he turn them out with his nose, you know?'

"Mais, les pieds en dehors," continua opiniâtrement la Fausse-Tortue. "Pourquoi dire qu'il avait les pieds en dehors?"

'It's the first position in dancing.' Alice said; but was dreadfully puzzled by the whole thing, and longed to change the subject.

"C'est la première position lorsqu'on apprend à danser," dit Alice; tout cela l'embarrassait fort, et il lui tardait de changer la conversation.

'Go on with the next verse,' the Gryphon repeated impatiently: 'it begins "I passed by his garden."'

"Récitez les vers suivants," répéta le Griffon avec impatience; "ça commence: "Passant près de chez lui —""

Alice did not dare to disobey, though she felt sure it would all come wrong, and she went on in a trembling voice:—

Alice n'osa pas désobéir, bien qu'elle fût sûre que les mots allaient lui venir tout de travers. Elle continua donc d'une voix tremblante:

I passed by his garden, and marked, with one eye, How the Owl and the Panther were sharing a pie—'

"Passant près de chez lui, j'ai vu, ne vous déplaise, Une huître et un hibou qui dînaient fort à l'aise."

What is the use of repeating all that stuff,' the Mock Turtle interrupted: 'if you don't explain it as you go on? It's by far the most confusing thing I ever heard!'

"À quoi bon répéter tout ce galimatias," interrompit la Fausse-Tortue, "si vous ne l'expliquez pas à mesure que vous le dites? C'est, de beaucoup, ce que j'ai entendu de plus embrouillant."

'Yes, I think you'd better leave off,' said the Gryphon: and Alice was only too glad to do so.

"Oui, je crois que vous feriez bien d'en rester là," dit le Griffon; et Alice ne demanda pas mieux.

'Shall we try another figure of the Lobster Quadrille?' the Gryphon went on. 'Or would you like the Mock Turtle to sing you a song?'

"Essaierons-nous une autre figure du Quadrille de Homards?" continua le Griffon. "Ou bien, préférez-vous que la Fausse-Tortue vous chante quelque chose?"

Oh, a song, please, if the Mock Turtle would be so kind,' Alice replied, so eagerly that the Gryphon said, in a rather offended tone: 'Hm! No accounting for tastes! Sing her "Turtle Soup," will you, old fellow?'

"Oh! une chanson, je vous prie; si la Fausse-Tortue veut bien avoir cette obligeance," répondit Alice, avec tant d'empressement que le Griffon dit d'un air un peu offensé: "Hum! Chacun son goût. Chantez-lui "La Soupe à la Tortue," hé! camarade!"

The Mock Turtle sighed deeply, and began, in a voice sometimes choked with sobs, to sing this:—

La Fausse-Tortue poussa un profond soupir et commença, d'une voix de temps en temps étouffée par les sanglots:

Beautiful Soup, so rich and green, Waiting in a hot tureen! Who for such dainties would not stoop? Soup of the evening, beautiful Soup! Soup of the evening, beautiful Soup! Beau—ootiful Soo—oop! Beau—ootiful Soo—oop! Soo—oop of the e—e—evening, Beautiful, beautiful Soup! 'Beautiful Soup! Who cares for fish, Game, or any other dish? Who would not give all else for two pennyworth only of beautiful Soup? Pennyworth only of beautiful Soup? Beau—ootiful Soo—oop! Beau—ootiful Soo—oop! Soo—oop of the e—e—evening, Beautiful, beauti—FUL SOUP!'

"Ô doux potage, Ô mets délicieux! Ah! pour partage, Quoi de plus précieux? Plonger dans ma soupière Cette vaste cuillère Est un bonheur Qui me réjouit le cœur. "Gibier, volaille, Lièvres, dindes, perdreaux, Rien qui te vaille, — Pas même les pruneaux! Plonger dans ma soupière Cette vaste cuillère Est un bonheur Qui me réjouit le cœur."

'Chorus again!' cried the Gryphon, and the Mock Turtle had just begun to repeat it, when a cry of 'The trial's beginning!' was heard in the distance.

"Bis au refrain!" cria le Griffon; et la Fausse-Tortue venait de le reprendre, quand un cri, "Le procès va commencer!" se fit entendre au loin.

'Come on!' cried the Gryphon, and, taking Alice by the hand, it hurried off, without waiting for the end of the song.

"Venez donc!" cria le Griffon; et, prenant Alice par la main, il se mit à courir sans attendre la fin de la chanson.

What trial is it?' Alice panted as she ran; but the Gryphon only answered 'Come on!' and ran the faster, while more and more faintly came, carried on the breeze that followed them, the melancholy words:—

"Qu'est-ce que c'est que ce procès?" demanda Alice hors d'haleine; mais le Griffon se contenta de répondre: "Venez donc!" en courant de plus belle, tandis que leur parvenaient, de plus en plus faibles, apportées par la brise qui les poursuivait, ces paroles pleines de mélancolie:

Soo—oop of the e—e—evening, Beautiful, beautiful Soup!'

"Plonger dans ma soupière Cette vaste cuillère Est un bonheur Qui me réjouit le cœur."

11. Who Stole the Tarts?

The King and Queen of Hearts were seated on their throne when they arrived, with a great crowd assembled about them—all sorts of little birds and beasts, as well as the whole pack of cards:

the Knave was standing before them, in chains, with a soldier on each side to guard him; and near the King was the White Rabbit, with a trumpet in one hand, and a scroll of parchment in the other.

In the very middle of the court was a table, with a large dish of tarts upon it: they looked so good, that it made Alice quite hungry to look at them—'I wish they'd get the trial done,' she thought: 'and hand round the refreshments!'

But there seemed to be no chance of this, so she began looking at everything about her, to pass away the time.

Alice had never been in a court of justice before, but she had read about them in books, and she was quite pleased to find that she knew the name of nearly everything there.

'That's the judge,' she said to herself: 'because of his great wig.'

The judge, by the way, was the King; and as he wore his crown over the wig, (look at the frontispiece if you want to see how he did it,) he did not look at all comfortable, and it was certainly not becoming.

And that's the jury-box,' thought Alice: 'and those twelve creatures,' (she was obliged to say 'creatures,' you see, because some of them were animals, and some were birds,) 'I suppose they are the jurors.'

She said this last word two or three times over to herself, being rather proud of it: for she thought, and rightly too, that very few little girls of her age knew the meaning of it at all. However: 'jury-men' would have done just as well.

The twelve jurors were all writing very busily on slates. 'What are they doing?' Alice whispered to the Gryphon. 'They can't have anything to put down yet, before the trial's begun.'

11. Qui a Volé les Tartes?

Le Roi et la Reine de Cœur étaient assis sur leur trône, entourés d'une nombreuse assemblée: toutes sortes de petits oiseaux et d'autres bêtes, ainsi que le paquet de cartes tout entier.

Le Valet, chargé de chaînes, gardé de chaque côté par un soldat, se tenait debout devant le trône, et près du roi se trouvait le Lapin Blanc, tenant d'une main une trompette et de l'autre un rouleau de parchemin.

Au beau milieu de la salle était une table sur laquelle on voyait un grand plat de tartes; ces tartes semblaient si bonnes que cela donna faim à Alice, rien que de les regarder. "Je voudrais bien qu'on se dépêchât de finir le procès," pensa-t-elle, "et qu'on fît passer les rafraîchissements,"

mais cela ne paraissait guère probable, aussi se mit-elle à regarder tout autour d'elle pour passer le temps.

C'était la première fois qu'Alice se trouvait dans une cour de justice, mais elle en avait lu des descriptions dans les livres, et elle fut toute contente de voir qu'elle savait le nom de presque tout ce qu'il y avait là.

"Ça, c'est le juge," se dit-elle; "je le reconnais à sa grande perruque."

Le juge, disons-le en passant, était le Roi, et, comme il portait sa couronne par-dessus sa perruque (regardez le frontispice, si vous voulez savoir comment il s'était arrangé) il n'avait pas du tout l'air d'être à son aise, et cela ne lui allait pas bien du tout.

"Et ça, c'est le banc du jury," pensa Alice; "et ces douze créatures" (elle était forcée de dire "créatures," vous comprenez, car quelques-uns étaient des bêtes et quelques autres des oiseaux), "je suppose que ce sont les jurés;"

elle se répéta ce dernier mot deux ou trois fois, car elle en était assez fière: pensant avec raison que bien peu de petites filles de son âge savent ce que cela veut dire.

Les douze jurés étaient tous très-occupés à écrire sur des ardoises. "Qu'est-ce qu'ils font là?" dit Alice à l'oreille du Griffon. "Ils ne peuvent rien avoir à écrire avant que le procès soit commencé."

They're putting down their names,' the Gryphon whispered in reply: 'for fear they should forget them before the end of the trial.'

"Ils inscrivent leur nom," répondit de même le Griffon, "de peur de l'oublier avant la fin du procès."

Stupid things!' Alice began in a loud, indignant voice, but she stopped hastily, for the White Rabbit cried out: 'Silence in the court!' and the King put on his spectacles and looked anxiously round, to make out who was talking.

"Les niais!" s'écria Alice d'un ton indigné, mais elle se retint bien vite, car le Lapin Blanc cria: "Silence dans l'auditoire!" Et le Roi, mettant ses lunettes, regarda vivement autour de lui pour voir qui parlait.

Alice could see, as well as if she were looking over their shoulders, that all the jurors were writing down 'stupid things!' on their slates, and she could even make out that one of them didn't know how to spell 'stupid,' and that he had to ask his neighbour to tell him.

Alice pouvait voir, aussi clairement que si elle eût regardé par-dessus leurs épaules, que tous les jurés étaient en train d'écrire "les niais" sur leurs ardoises, et elle pouvait même distinguer que l'un d'eux ne savait pas écrire "niais" et qu'il était obligé de le demander à son voisin.

'A nice muddle their slates'll be in before the trial's over!' thought Alice.

"Leurs ardoises seront dans un bel état avant la fin du procès!" pensa Alice.

One of the jurors had a pencil that squeaked. This of course, Alice could not stand, and she went round the court and got behind him, and very soon found an opportunity of taking it away.

Un des jurés avait un crayon qui grinçait; Alice, vous le pensez bien, ne pouvait pas souffrir cela; elle fit le tour de la salle, arriva derrière lui, et trouva bientôt l'occasion d'enlever le crayon.

She did it so quickly that the poor little juror (it was Bill, the Lizard) could not make out at all what had become of it; so, after hunting all about for it, he was obliged to write with one finger for the rest of the day; and this was of very little use, as it left no mark on the slate.

Ce fut si tôt fait que le pauvre petit juré (c'était Jacques, le lézard) ne pouvait pas s'imaginer ce qu'il était devenu. Après avoir cherché partout, il fut obligé d'écrire avec un doigt tout le reste du jour, et cela était fort inutile, puisque son doigt ne laissait aucune marque sur l'ardoise.

'Herald, read the accusation!' said the King.

"Héraut, lisez l'acte d'accusation!" dit le Roi.

On this the White Rabbit blew three blasts on the trumpet, and then unrolled the parchment scroll, and read as follows:—

Sur ce, le Lapin Blanc sonna trois fois de la trompette, et puis, déroulant le parchemin, lut ainsi qu'il suit:

'The Queen of Hearts, she made some tarts, All on a summer day: The Knave of Hearts, he stole those tarts, And took them quite away!'

"La Reine de Cœur fit des tartes, Un beau jour de printemps; Le Valet de Cœur prit les tartes, Et s'en fut tout content!"

'Consider your verdict,' the King said to the jury.

"Délibérez," dit le Roi aux jurés.

'Not yet, not yet!' the Rabbit hastily interrupted. 'There's a great deal to come before that!'

"Pas encore, pas encore," interrompit vivement le Lapin; "il y a bien des choses à faire auparavant!"

Call the first witness,' said the King; and the White Rabbit blew three blasts on the trumpet, and called out: 'First witness!'

"Appelez les témoins," dit le Roi; et le Lapin Blanc sonna trois fois de la trompette, et cria: "Le premier témoin!"

The first witness was the Hatter. He came in with a teacup in one hand and a piece of bread-and-butter in the other.

Le premier témoin était le Chapelier. Il entra, tenant d'une main une tasse de thé et de l'autre une tartine de beurre. "

'I beg pardon, your Majesty,' he began: 'for bringing these in: but I hadn't quite finished my tea when I was sent for.'

Pardon, Votre Majesté," dit il, "si j'apporte cela ici; je n'avais pas tout à fait fini de prendre mon thé lorsqu'on est venu me chercher."

'You ought to have finished,' said the King. 'When did you begin?'

"Vous auriez dû avoir fini," dit le Roi; "quand avez-vous commencé?"

The Hatter looked at the March Hare, who had followed him into the court, arm-in-arm with the Dormouse. 'Fourteenth of March, I think it was,' he said.

Le Chapelier regarda le Lièvre qui l'avait suivi dans la salle, bras dessus bras dessous avec le Loir. "Le Quatorze Mars, je crois bien," dit-il.

'Fifteenth,' said the March Hare.

"Le Quinze!" dit le Lièvre.

'Sixteenth,' added the Dormouse.

"Le Seize!" ajouta le Loir.

'Write that down,' the King said to the jury, and the jury eagerly wrote down all three dates on their slates, and then added them up, and reduced the answer to shillings and pence.

"Notez cela," dit le Roi aux jurés. Et les jurés s'empressèrent d'écrire les trois dates sur leurs ardoises; puis en firent l'addition, dont ils cherchèrent à réduire le total en francs et centimes.

'Take off your hat,' the King said to the Hatter.

"Ôtez votre chapeau," dit le Roi au Chapelier.

'It isn't mine,' said the Hatter.

"Il n'est pas à moi," dit le Chapelier.

'Stolen!' the King exclaimed, turning to the jury, who instantly made a memorandum of the fact.

"Volé!" s'écria le Roi en se tournant du côté des jurés, qui s'empressèrent de prendre note du fait.

'I keep them to sell,' the Hatter added as an explanation; 'I've none of my own. I'm a hatter.'

"Je les tiens en vente," ajouta le Chapelier, comme explication. "Je n'en ai pas à moi; je suis chapelier."

Here the Queen put on her spectacles, and began staring at the Hatter, who turned pale and fidgeted.

Ici la Reine mit ses lunettes, et se prit à regarder fixement le Chapelier, qui devint pâle et tremblant.

'Give your evidence,' said the King; 'and don't be nervous, or I'll have you executed on the spot.'

"Faites votre déposition," dit le Roi; "et ne soyez pas agité; sans cela je vous fais exécuter sur-le-champ."

This did not seem to encourage the witness at all: he kept shifting from one foot to the other, looking uneasily at the Queen, and in his confusion he bit a large piece out of his teacup instead of the bread-and-butter.

Cela ne parut pas du tout encourager le témoin; il ne cessait de passer d'un pied sur l'autre en regardant la Reine d'un air inquiet, et, dans son trouble, il mordit dans la tasse et en enleva un grand morceau, au lieu de mordre dans la tartine de beurre.

Just at this moment Alice felt a very curious sensation, which puzzled her a good deal until she made out what it was: she was beginning to grow larger again, and she thought at first she would get up and leave the court; but on second thoughts she decided to remain where she was as long as there was room for her.

Juste à ce moment-là, Alice éprouva une étrange sensation qui l'embarrassa beaucoup, jusqu'à ce qu'elle se fût rendu compte de ce que c'était. Elle recommençait à grandir, et elle pensa d'abord à se lever et à quitter la cour: mais, toute réflexion faite, elle se décida à rester où elle était, tant qu'il y aurait de la place pour elle.

'I wish you wouldn't squeeze so.' said the Dormouse, who was sitting next to her. 'I can hardly breathe.'

"Ne poussez donc pas comme ça," dit le Loir; "je puis à peine respirer."

'I can't help it,' said Alice very meekly: 'I'm growing.'

"Ce n'est pas de ma faute," dit Alice doucement; "je grandis."

'You've no right to grow here,' said the Dormouse.

"Vous n'avez pas le droit de grandir ici," dit le Loir.

'Don't talk nonsense,' said Alice more boldly: 'you know you're growing too.'

"Ne dites pas de sottises," répliqua Alice plus hardiment; "vous savez bien que vous aussi vous grandissez."

'Yes, but I grow at a reasonable pace,' said the Dormouse: 'not in that ridiculous fashion.' And he got up very sulkily and crossed over to the other side of the court.

All this time the Queen had never left off staring at the Hatter, and, just as the Dormouse crossed the court, she said to one of the officers of the court:

'Bring me the list of the singers in the last concert!' on which the wretched Hatter trembled so, that he shook both his shoes off.

Give your evidence,' the King repeated angrily: 'or I'll have you executed, whether you're nervous or not.'

I'm a poor man, your Majesty,' the Hatter began, in a trembling voice: '—and I hadn't begun my tea—not above a week or so—and what with the bread-and-butter getting so thin—and the twinkling of the tea—'

'The twinkling of the what?' said the King.

'It began with the tea,' the Hatter replied.

'Of course twinkling begins with a T!' said the King sharply. 'Do you take me for a dunce? Go on!'

I'm a poor man,' the Hatter went on: 'and most things twinkled after that—only the March Hare said—'

'I didn't!' the March Hare interrupted in a great hurry.

'You did!' said the Hatter.

'I deny it!' said the March Hare.

'He denies it,' said the King: 'leave out that part.'

Well, at any rate, the Dormouse said—' the Hatter went on, looking anxiously round to see if he would deny it too: but the Dormouse denied nothing, being fast asleep.

After that,' continued the Hatter: 'I cut some more bread-and-butter—'

'But what did the Dormouse say?' one of the jury asked.

'That I can't remember,' said the Hatter.

You must remember,' remarked the King: 'or I'll have you executed.'

The miserable Hatter dropped his teacup and bread-and-butter, and went down on one knee. 'I'm a poor man, your Majesty,' he began.

“Oui, mais je grandis raisonnablement, moi,” dit le Loir; “et non de cette façon ridicule.” Il se leva en faisant la mine, et passa de l’autre côté de la salle.

Pendant tout ce temps-là, la Reine n’avait pas cessé de fixer les yeux sur le Chapelier, et, comme le Loir traversait la salle, elle dit à un des officiers du tribunal:

“Apportez-moi la liste des chanteurs du dernier concert.” Sur quoi, le malheureux Chapelier se mit à trembler si fortement qu’il en perdit ses deux souliers.

“Faites votre déposition,” répéta le Roi en colère; “ou bien je vous fais exécuter, que vous soyez troublé ou non!”

“Je suis un pauvre homme, Votre Majesté,” fit le Chapelier d’une voix tremblante; “et il n’y avait guère qu’une semaine ou deux que j’avais commencé à prendre mon thé, et avec ça les tartines devenaient si minces et les dragées du thé —”

“Les dragées de quoi?” dit le Roi.

“Ça a commencé par le thé,” répondit le Chapelier.

“Je vous dis que dragée commence par un d!” cria le Roi vivement. “Me prenez-vous pour un âne? Continuez!”

“Je suis un pauvre homme,” continua le Chapelier; “et les dragées et les autres choses me firent perdre la tête. Mais le Lièvre dit —”

“C’est faux!” s’écria le Lièvre se dépêchant de l’interrompre.

“C’est vrai!” cria le Chapelier.

“Je le nie!” cria le Lièvre.

“Il le nie!” dit le Roi. “Passez là-dessus.”

“Eh bien! dans tous les cas, le Loir dit —” continua le Chapelier, regardant autour de lui pour voir s’il nierait aussi; mais le Loir ne nia rien, car il dormait profondément.

“Après cela,” continua le Chapelier, “je me coupai d’autres tartines de beurre.”

“Mais, que dit le Loir?” demanda un des jurés.

“C’est ce que je ne peux pas me rappeler,” dit le Chapelier.

“Il faut absolument que vous vous le rappeliez,” fit observer le Roi; “ou bien je vous fais exécuter.”

Le malheureux Chapelier laissa tomber sa tasse et sa tartine de beurre, et mit un genou en terre. “Je suis un pauvre homme, Votre Majesté!” commença-t-il.

'You're a very poor speaker,' said the King.

Here one of the guinea-pigs cheered, and was immediately suppressed by the officers of the court.

(As that is rather a hard word, I will just explain to you how it was done. They had a large canvas bag, which tied up at the mouth with strings: into this they slipped the guinea-pig, head first, and then sat upon it.)

I'm glad I've seen that done,' thought Alice. 'I've so often read in the newspapers, at the end of trials,

"There was some attempts at applause, which was immediately suppressed by the officers of the court," and I never understood what it meant till now.'

'If that's all you know about it, you may stand down,' continued the King.

'I can't go no lower,' said the Hatter: 'I'm on the floor, as it is.'

'Then you may sit down,' the King replied.

Here the other guinea-pig cheered, and was suppressed.

'Come, that finished the guinea-pigs!' thought Alice. 'Now we shall get on better.'

'I'd rather finish my tea,' said the Hatter, with an anxious look at the Queen, who was reading the list of singers.

'You may go,' said the King, and the Hatter hurriedly left the court, without even waiting to put his shoes on.

—and just take his head off outside,' the Queen added to one of the officers: but the Hatter was out of sight before the officer could get to the door.

'Call the next witness!' said the King.

The next witness was the Duchess's cook. She carried the pepper-box in her hand, and Alice guessed who it was, even before she got into the court, by the way the people near the door began sneezing all at once.

'Give your evidence,' said the King.

'Shan't,' said the cook.

The King looked anxiously at the White Rabbit, who said in a low voice: 'Your Majesty must cross-examine this witness.'

"Vous êtes un très-pauvre orateur," dit le Roi.

Ici un des cochons d'Inde applaudit, et fut immédiatement réprimé par un des huissiers.

(Comme ce mot est assez difficile, je vais vous expliquer comment cela se fit. Ils avaient un grand sac de toile qui se fermait à l'aide de deux ficelles attachées à l'ouverture; dans ce sac ils firent glisser le cochon d'Inde la tête la première, puis ils s'assirent dessus.)

"Je suis contente d'avoir vu cela," pensa Alice. "J'ai souvent lu dans les journaux, à la fin des procès:

"Il se fit quelques tentatives d'applaudissements qui furent bientôt réprimées par les huissiers," et je n'avais jamais compris jusqu'à présent ce que cela voulait dire."

"Si c'est là tout ce que vous savez de l'affaire, vous pouvez vous prosterner," continua le Roi.

"Je ne puis pas me prosterner plus bas que cela," dit le Chapelier; "je suis déjà par terre."

"Alors asseyez-vous," répondit le Roi.

Ici l'autre cochon d'Inde applaudit et fut réprimé.

"Bon, cela met fin aux cochons d'Inde!" pensa Alice. "Maintenant ça va mieux aller."

"J'aimerais bien aller finir de prendre mon thé," dit le Chapelier, en lançant un regard inquiet sur la Reine, qui lisait la liste des chanteurs.

"Vous pouvez vous retirer," dit le Roi; et le Chapelier se hâta de quitter la cour, sans même prendre le temps de mettre ses souliers.

"Et coupez-lui la tête dehors," ajouta la Reine, s'adressant à un des huissiers; mais le Chapelier était déjà bien loin avant que l'huissier arrivât à la porte.

"Appelez un autre témoin," dit le Roi.

L'autre témoin, c'était la cuisinière de la Duchesse; elle tenait la poivrière à la main, et Alice devina qui c'était, même avant qu'elle entrât dans la salle, en voyant éternuer, tout à coup et tous à la fois, les gens qui se trouvaient près de la porte.

"Faites votre déposition," dit le Roi.

"Non!" dit la cuisinière.

Le Roi regarda d'un air inquiet le Lapin Blanc, qui lui dit à voix basse: "Il faut que Votre Majesté interroge ce témoin-là contradictoirement."

'Well, if I must, I must,' the King said, with a melancholy air, and, after folding his arms and frowning at the cook till his eyes were nearly out of sight, he said in a deep voice,

'What are tarts made of?'

'Pepper, mostly,' said the cook.

'Treacle,' said a sleepy voice behind her.

'Collar that Dormouse,' the Queen shrieked out. 'Behead that Dormouse! Turn that Dormouse out of court! Suppress him! Pinch him! Off with his whiskers!'

For some minutes the whole court was in confusion, getting the Dormouse turned out, and, by the time they had settled down again, the cook had disappeared.

Never mind!' said the King, with an air of great relief. 'Call the next witness.' And he added in an undertone to the Queen: 'Really, my dear, you must cross-examine the next witness. It quite makes my forehead ache!'

Alice watched the White Rabbit as he fumbled over the list, feeling very curious to see what the next witness would be like: '—for they haven't got much evidence yet,' she said to herself. Imagine her surprise, when the White Rabbit read out, at the top of his shrill little voice, the name 'Alice!'

"Puisqu'il le faut, il le faut," dit le Roi, d'un air triste; et, après avoir croisé les bras et froncé les sourcils en regardant la cuisinière, au point que les yeux lui étaient presque complètement rentrés dans la tête, il dit d'une voix creuse:

"De quoi les tartes sont-elles faites?"

"De poivre principalement!" dit la cuisinière.

"De mélasse," dit une voix endormie derrière elle.

"Saisissez ce Loir au collet!" cria la Reine. "Coupez la tête à ce Loir! Mettez ce Loir à la porte! Réprimez-le, pincez-le, arrachez-lui ses moustaches!"

Pendant quelques instants, toute la cour fut sens dessus dessous pour mettre le Loir à la porte; et, quand le calme fut rétabli, la cuisinière avait disparu.

"Cela ne fait rien," dit le Roi, comme soulagé d'un grand poids. "Appelez le troisième témoin;" et il ajouta à voix basse en s'adressant à la Reine: "Vraiment, mon amie, il faut que vous interrogiez cet autre témoin; cela me fait trop mal au front!"

Alice regardait le Lapin Blanc tandis qu'il tournait la liste dans ses doigts, curieuse de savoir quel serait l'autre témoin. "Car les dépositions ne prouvent pas grand'chose jusqu'à présent," se dit-elle. Imaginez sa surprise quand le Lapin Blanc cria, du plus fort de sa petite voix criarde: "Alice!"

12. Alice's Evidence

'Here!' cried Alice, quite forgetting in the flurry of the moment how large she had grown in the last few minutes, and she jumped up in such a hurry that she tipped over the jury-box with the edge of her skirt, upsetting all the jurymen on to the heads of the crowd below, and there they lay sprawling about, reminding her very much of a globe of goldfish she had accidentally upset the week before.

'Oh, I beg your pardon!' she exclaimed in a tone of great dismay, and began picking them up again as quickly as she could, for the accident of the goldfish kept running in her head, and she had a vague sort of idea that they must be collected at once and put back into the jury-box, or they would die.

'The trial cannot proceed,' said the King in a very grave voice: 'until all the jurymen are back in their proper places— all,' he repeated with great emphasis, looking hard at Alice as he said do.

Alice looked at the jury-box, and saw that, in her haste, she had put the Lizard in head downwards, and the poor little thing was waving its tail about in a melancholy way, being quite unable to move.

She soon got it out again, and put it right; 'not that it signifies much,' she said to herself; 'I should think it would be quite as much use in the trial one way up as the other.'

As soon as the jury had a little recovered from the shock of being upset, and their slates and pencils had been found and handed back to them, they set to work very diligently to write out a history of the accident, all except the Lizard, who seemed too much overcome to do anything but sit with its mouth open, gazing up into the roof of the court.

'What do you know about this business?' the King said to Alice.

'Nothing,' said Alice.

'Nothing whatever?' persisted the King.

'Nothing whatever,' said Alice.

That's very important,' the King said, turning to the jury. They were just beginning to write this down on their slates, when the White Rabbit interrupted:

12. Déposition d'Alice

"Voilà!" cria Alice, oubliant tout à fait dans le trouble du moment combien elle avait grandi depuis quelques instants, et elle se leva si brusquement qu'elle accrocha le banc des jurés avec le bord de sa robe, et le renversa, avec tous ses occupants, sur la tête de la foule qui se trouvait au-dessous, et on les vit se débattant de tous côtés, comme les poissons rouges du vase qu'elle se rappelait avoir renversé par accident la semaine précédente.

"Oh! je vous demande bien pardon!" s'écria-t-elle toute confuse, et elle se mit à les ramasser bien vite, car l'accident arrivé aux poissons rouges lui trottait dans la tête, et elle avait une idée vague qu'il fallait les ramasser tout de suite et les remettre sur les bancs, sans quoi ils mourraient.

"Le procès ne peut continuer," dit le Roi d'une voix grave, "avant que les jurés soient tous à leurs places; tous!" répéta-t-il avec emphase en regardant fixement Alice.

Alice regarda le banc des jurés, et vit que dans son empressement elle y avait placé le Lézard la tête en bas, et le pauvre petit être remuait la queue d'une triste façon, dans l'impossibilité de se redresser.

Elle l'eut bientôt retourné et replacé convenablement. "Non que cela soit bien important," se dit-elle, "car je pense qu'il serait tout aussi utile au procès la tête en bas qu'autrement."

Sitôt que les jurés se furent un peu remis de la secousse, qu'on eut retrouvé et qu'on leur eut rendu leurs ardoises et leurs crayons, ils se mirent fort diligemment à écrire l'histoire de l'accident, à l'exception du Lézard, qui paraissait trop accablé pour faire autre chose que demeurer la bouche ouverte, les yeux fixés sur le plafond de la salle.

"Que savez-vous de cette affaire-là?" demanda le Roi à Alice.

"Rien," répondit-elle.

"Rien absolument?" insista le Roi.

"Rien absolument," dit Alice.

"Voilà qui est très-important," dit le Roi, se tournant vers les jurés. Ils allaient écrire cela sur leurs ardoises quand le Lapin Blanc interrompant:

'Unimportant, your Majesty means, of course,' he said in a very respectful tone, but frowning and making faces at him as he spoke.

Unimportant, of course, I meant,' the King hastily said, and went on to himself in an undertone:

'important—unimportant— unimportant—important—' as if he were trying which word sounded best.

Some of the jury wrote it down 'important,' and some 'unimportant.' Alice could see this, as she was near enough to look over their slates; 'but it doesn't matter a bit,' she thought to herself.

At this moment the King, who had been for some time busily writing in his note-book, cackled out 'Silence!' and read out from his book:

'Rule Forty-two. All persons more than a mile hight to leave the court.'

Everybody looked at Alice.

'I'm not a mile high,' said Alice.

'You are,' said the King. 'Nearly two miles high,' added the Queen.

'Well, I shan't go, at any rate,' said Alice: 'besides, that's not a regular rule: you invented it just now.'

'It's the oldest rule in the book,' said the King.

'Then it ought to be Number One,' said Alice.

The King turned pale, and shut his note-book hastily. 'Consider your verdict,' he said to the jury, in a low, trembling voice.

'There's more evidence to come yet, please your Majesty,' said the White Rabbit, jumping up in a great hurry; 'this paper has just been picked up.'

'What's in it?' said the Queen.

I haven't opened it yet,' said the White Rabbit: 'but it seems to be a letter, written by the prisoner to—to somebody.'

It must have been that,' said the King: 'unless it was written to nobody, which isn't usual, you know.'

"Peu important, veut dire Votre Majesté, sans doute," dit-il d'un ton très-respectueux, mais en fronçant les sourcils et en lui faisant des grimaces.

"Peu important, bien entendu, c'est ce que je voulais dire," répliqua le Roi avec empressement. Et il continua de répéter à demi-voix:

"Très-important, peu important, peu important, très-important;" comme pour essayer lequel des deux était le mieux sonnant.

Quelques-uns des jurés écrivirent "très-important," d'autres, "peu important." Alice voyait tout cela, car elle était assez près d'eux pour regarder sur leurs ardoises. "Mais cela ne fait absolument rien," pensa-t-elle.

À ce moment-là, le Roi, qui pendant quelque temps avait été fort occupé à écrire dans son carnet, cria: "Silence!" et lut sur son carnet:

"Règle Quarante-deux: Toute personne ayant une taille de plus d'un mille de haut devra quitter la cour."

Tout le monde regarda Alice.

"Je n'ai pas un mille de haut," dit-elle.

"Si fait," dit le Roi. "Près de deux milles," ajouta la Reine.

"Eh bien! je ne sortirai pas quand même; d'ailleurs cette règle n'est pas d'usage, vous venez de l'inventer."

"C'est la règle la plus ancienne qu'il y ait dans le livre," dit le Roi.

"Alors elle devrait porter le numéro Un."

Le Roi devint pâle et ferma vivement son carnet. "Délibérez," dit-il aux jurés d'une voix faible et tremblante.

"Il y a d'autres dépositions à recevoir, s'il plaît à Votre Majesté," dit le Lapin, se levant précipitamment; "on vient de ramasser ce papier."

"Qu'est-ce qu'il y a dedans?" dit la Reine.

"Je ne l'ai pas encore ouvert," dit le Lapin Blanc; "mais on dirait que c'est une lettre écrite par l'accusé à — à quelqu'un."

"Cela doit être ainsi," dit le Roi, "à moins qu'elle ne soit écrite à personne, ce qui n'est pas ordinaire, vous comprenez."

'Who is it directed to?' said one of the jurymen.

"À qui est-elle adressée?" dit un des jurés.

'It isn't directed at all,' said the White Rabbit; 'in fact, there's nothing written on the outside.' He unfolded the paper as he spoke, and added 'It isn't a letter, after all: it's a set of verses.'

"Elle n'est pas adressée du tout," dit le Lapin Blanc; "au fait, il n'y a rien d'écrit à l'extérieur." Il déplia le papier tout en parlant et ajouta: "Ce n'est pas une lettre, après tout; c'est une pièce de vers."

'Are they in the prisoner's handwriting?' asked another of they jurymen.

"Est-ce l'écriture de l'accusé?" demanda un autre juré.

No, they're not,' said the White Rabbit: 'and that's the queerest thing about it.' (The jury all looked puzzled.)

"Non," dit le Lapin Blanc, "et c'est ce qu'il y a de plus drôle." (Les jurés eurent tous l'air fort embarrassé.)

'He must have imitated somebody else's hand,' said the King. (The jury all brightened up again.)

"Il faut qu'il ait imité l'écriture d'un autre," dit le Roi. (Les jurés reprirent l'air serein.)

Please your Majesty,' said the Knave: 'I didn't write it, and they can't prove I did: there's no name signed at the end.'

"Pardon, Votre Majesté," dit le Valet, "ce n'est pas moi qui ai écrit cette lettre, et on ne peut pas prouver que ce soit moi; il n'y a pas de signature."

If you didn't sign it,' said the King: 'that only makes the matter worse. You must have meant some mischief, or else you'd have signed your name like an honest man.'

"Si vous n'avez pas signé," dit le Roi, "cela ne fait qu'empirer la chose; il faut absolument que vous ayez eu de mauvaises intentions, sans cela vous auriez signé, comme un honnête homme."

There was a general clapping of hands at this: it was the first really clever thing the King had said that day.

Là-dessus tout le monde battit des mains; c'était la première réflexion vraiment bonne que le Roi eût faite ce jour-là.

'That proves his guilt,' said the Queen.

"Cela prouve sa culpabilité," dit la Reine.

'It proves nothing of the sort!' said Alice. 'Why, you don't even know what they're about!'

"Cela ne prouve rien," dit Alice. "Vous ne savez même pas ce dont il s'agit."

'Read them,' said the King.

"Lisez ces vers," dit le Roi.

The White Rabbit put on his spectacles. 'Where shall I begin, please your Majesty?' he asked.

Le Lapin Blanc mit ses lunettes. "Par où commencerai-je, s'il plaît à Votre Majesté?" demanda-t-il. «

Begin at the beginning,' the King said gravely: 'and go on till you come to the end: then stop.'

Commencez par le commencement," dit gravement le Roi, "et continuez jusqu'à ce que vous arriviez à la fin; là, vous vous arrêterez."

These were the verses the White Rabbit read:—

Voici les vers que lut le Lapin Blanc:

'They told me you had been to her, And mentioned me to him: She gave me a good character, But said I could not swim.

"On m'a dit que tu fus chez elle Afin de lui pouvoir parler, Et qu'elle assura, la cruelle, Que je ne savais pas nager!

He sent them word I had not gone (We know it to be true): If she should push the matter on, What would become of you?

Bientôt il leur envoya dire (Nous savons fort bien que c'est vrai!) Qu'il ne faudrait pas en médire, Ou gare les coups de balai!

I gave her one, they gave him two, You gave us three or more; They all returned from him to you, Though they were mine before.

J'en donnai trois, elle en prit une; Combien donc en recevrons-nous? (Il y a là quelque lacune.) Toutes revinrent d'eux à vous.

If I or she should chance to be Involved in this affair, He trusts to you to set them free, Exactly as we were.

Si vous ou moi, dans cette affaire, Étions par trop embarrassés, Prions qu'il nous laisse, confrère, Tous deux comme il nous a trouvés.

My notion was that you had been (Before she had this fit) An obstacle that came between Him, and ourselves, and it.

Vous les avez, j'en suis certaine, (Avant que de ses nerfs l'accès Ne bouleversât l'inhumaine,) Trompés tous trois avec succès.

Don't let him know she liked them best, For this must ever be A secret, kept from all the rest, Between yourself and me.'

Cachez-lui qu'elle les préfère; Car ce doit être, par ma foi, (Et sera toujours, je l'espère) Un secret entre vous et moi."

That's the most important piece of evidence we've heard yet,' said the King, rubbing his hands; 'so now let the jury—'

"Voilà la pièce de conviction la plus importante que nous ayons eue jusqu'à présent,"dit le Roi en se frottant les mains; "ainsi, que le jury maintenant — —"

If any one of them can explain it,' said Alice, (she had grown so large in the last few minutes that she wasn't a bit afraid of interrupting him,)

"S'il y a un seul des jurés qui puisse l'expliquer,"dit Alice (elle était devenue si grande dans ces derniers instants qu'elle n'avait plus du tout peur de l'interrompre),

'I'll give him sixpence. _I_ don't believe there's an atom of meaning in it.'

"je lui donne une pièce de dix sous. Je ne crois pas qu'il y ait un atome de sens commun là-dedans."

The jury all wrote down on their slates: 'She doesn't believe there's an atom of meaning in it,' but none of them attempted to explain the paper.

Tous les jurés écrivirent sur leurs ardoises: "Elle ne croit pas qu'il y ait un atome de sens commun là-dedans,"mais aucun d'eux ne tenta d'expliquer la pièce de vers.

If there's no meaning in it,' said the King: 'that saves a world of trouble, you know, as we needn't try to find any. And yet I don't know,' he went on, spreading out the verses on his knee, and looking at them with one eye;

"Si elle ne signifie rien,"dit le Roi, "cela nous épargne un monde d'ennuis, vous comprenez; car il est inutile d'en chercher l'explication; et cependant je ne sais pas trop,"continua-t-il en étalant la pièce de vers sur ses genoux et les regardant d'un œil;

'I seem to see some meaning in them, after all. "-said I could not swim—" you can't swim, can you?' he added, turning to the Knave.

"il me semble que j'y vois quelque chose, après tout. "Que je ne savais pas nager! "Vous ne savez pas nager, n'est-ce pas? "ajouta-t-il en se tournant vers le Valet.

The Knave shook his head sadly. 'Do I look like it?' he said. (Which he certainly did not, being made entirely of cardboard.)

Le Valet secoua la tête tristement. "En ai-je l'air, "dit-il. (Non, certainement, il n'en avait pas l'air, étant fait tout entier de carton.)

All right, so far,' said the King, and he went on muttering over the verses to himself: '"We know it to be true—" that's the jury, of course— "I gave her one, they gave him two—" why, that must be what he did with the tarts, you know—'

"Jusqu'ici c'est bien, "dit le Roi; et il continua de marmotter tout bas, ""Nous savons fort bien que c'est vrai. "C'est le jury qui dit cela, bien sûr! "J'en donnai trois, elle en prit une; "justement, c'est là ce qu'il fit des tartes, vous comprenez. "

'But, it goes on "they all returned from him to you,"' said Alice.

"Mais vient ensuite: "Toutes revinrent d'eux à vous, """dit Alice.

Why, there they are!' said the King triumphantly, pointing to the tarts on the table. 'Nothing can be clearer than that. Then again—"before she had this fit—" you never had fits, my dear, I think?' he said to the Queen.

"Tiens, mais les voici! "dit le Roi d'un air de triomphe, montrant du doigt les tartes qui étaient sur la table. "Il n'y a rien de plus clair que cela; et encore: "Avant que de ses nerfs l'accès. "Vous n'avez jamais eu d'attaques de nerfs, je crois, mon épouse? "dit-il à la Reine.

Never!' said the Queen furiously, throwing an inkstand at the Lizard as she spoke.

(The unfortunate little Bill had left off writing on his slate with one finger, as he found it made no mark; but he now hastily began again, using the ink, that was trickling down his face, as long as it lasted.)

'Then the words don't fit you,' said the King, looking round the court with a smile. There was a dead silence.

It's a pun!' the King added in an offended tone, and everybody laughed: 'Let the jury consider their verdict,' the King said, for about the twentieth time that day.

No, no!' said the Queen. 'Sentence first—verdict afterwards.'

'Stuff and nonsense!' said Alice loudly. 'The idea of having the sentence first!'

'Hold your tongue!' said the Queen, turning purple. 'I won't!' said Alice.

'Off with her head!' the Queen shouted at the top of her voice. Nobody moved.

'Who cares for you?' said Alice, (she had grown to her full size by this time.) 'You're nothing but a pack of cards!'

At this the whole pack rose up into the air, and came flying down upon her: she gave a little scream, half of fright and half of anger, and tried to beat them off, and found herself lying on the bank, with her head in the lap of her sister, who was gently brushing away some dead leaves that had fluttered down from the trees upon her face.

Wake up, Alice dear!' said her sister; 'Why, what a long sleep you've had!'

It was a curious dream, dear, certainly: but now run in to your tea; it's getting late.'

So Alice got up and ran off, thinking while she ran, as well she might, what a wonderful dream it had been.

But her sister sat still just as she left her, leaning her head on her hand, watching the setting sun, and thinking of

"Jamais! "dit la Reine d'un air furieux en jetant un encrier à la tête du Lézard.

(Le malheureux Jacques avait cessé d'écrire sur son ardoise avec un doigt, car il s'était aperçu que cela ne faisait aucune marque; mais il se remit bien vite à l'ouvrage en se servant de l'encre qui lui découlait le long de la figure, aussi longtemps qu'il y en eut.)

"Non, mon épouse, vous avez trop bon air, "dit le Roi, promenant son regard tout autour de la salle et souriant. Il se fit un silence de mort.

"C'est un calembour, "ajouta le Roi d'un ton de colère; et tout le monde se mit à rire. "Que le jury délibère, "ajouta le Roi, pour à peu près la vingtième fois ce jour-là.

"Non, non, "dit la Reine, "l'arrêt d'abord, on délibérera après. "

"Cela n'a pas de bon sens! "dit tout haut Alice. "Quelle idée de vouloir prononcer l'arrêt d'abord! "

"Taisez-vous, "dit la Reine, devenant pourpre de colère. "Je ne me tairai pas, "dit Alice.

"Qu'on lui coupe la tête! "hurla la Reine de toutes ses forces. Personne ne bougea.

"On se moque bien de vous, "dit Alice (elle avait alors atteint toute sa grandeur naturelle). "Vous n'êtes qu'un paquet de cartes! "

Là-dessus tout le paquet sauta en l'air et retomba en tourbillonnant sur elle; Alice poussa un petit cri, moitié de peur, moitié de colère, et essaya de les repousser; elle se trouva étendue sur le gazon, la tête sur les genoux de sa sœur, qui écartait doucement de sa figure les feuilles mortes tombées en voltigeant du haut des arbres.

"Oh! j'ai fait un si drôle de rêve, "dit Alice; et elle raconta à sa sœur, autant qu'elle put s'en souvenir, toutes les étranges aventures que vous venez de lire; et, quand elle eut fini son récit, sa sœur lui dit en l'embrassant:

"Certes, c'est un bien drôle de rêve; mais maintenant courez à la maison prendre le thé; il se fait tard. "

Alice se leva donc et s'éloigna en courant, pensant le long du chemin, et avec raison, quel rêve merveilleux elle venait de faire.

Mais sa sœur demeura assise tranquillement, tout comme elle l'avait laissée, la tête appuyée sur la main, contemplant le coucher du soleil et pensant à la petite Alice et à ses

little Alice and all her wonderful Adventures, till she too began dreaming after a fashion, and this was her dream:

First, she dreamed of little Alice herself, and once again the tiny hands were clasped upon her knee, and the bright eager eyes were looking up into hers.

She could hear the very tones of her voice, and see that queer little toss of her head to keep back the wandering hair that would always get into her eyes. And still, as she listened, or seemed to listen, the whole place around her became alive the strange creatures of her little sister's dream.

The long grass rustled at her feet as the White Rabbit hurried by—the frightened Mouse splashed his way through the neighbouring pool—she could hear the rattle of the teacups as the March Hare and his friends shared their never-ending meal, and the shrill voice of the Queen ordering off her unfortunate guests to execution—once more the pig-baby was sneezing on the Duchess's knee, while plates and dishes crashed around it—once more the shriek of the Gryphon, the squeaking of the Lizard's slate-pencil, and the choking of the suppressed guinea-pigs, filled the air, mixed up with the distant sobs of the miserable Mock Turtle.

So she sat on, with closed eyes, and half believed herself in Wonderland, though she knew she had but to open them again, and all would change to dull reality—the grass would be only rustling in the wind, and the pool rippling to the waving of the reeds—the rattling teacups would change to tinkling sheep-bells, and the Queen's shrill cries to the voice of the shepherd boy—and the sneeze of the baby, the shriek of the Gryphon, and all the other queer noises, would change (she knew) to the confused clamour of the busy farm-yard—while the lowing of the cattle in the distance would take the place of the Mock Turtle's heavy sobs.

Lastly, she pictured to herself how this same little sister of hers would, in the after-time, be herself a grown woman; and how she would keep, through all her riper years, the simple and loving heart of her childhood: and how she would gather about her other little children, and make their eyes bright and eager with many a strange tale, perhaps even with the dream of Wonderland of long ago: and how she would feel with all their simple sorrows, and find a pleasure in all their simple joys, remembering her own child-life, and the happy summer days.

merveilleuses aventures; si bien qu'elle aussi se mit à rêver, en quelque sorte; et voici son rêve:

D'abord elle rêva de la petite Alice personnellement: — les petites mains de l'enfant étaient encore jointes sur ses genoux, et ses yeux vifs et brillants plongeaient leur regard dans les siens.

Elle entendait jusqu'au son de sa voix; elle voyait ce singulier petit mouvement de tête par lequel elle rejetait en arrière les cheveux vagabonds qui sans cesse lui revenaient dans les yeux; et, comme elle écoutait ou paraissait écouter, tout s'anima autour d'elle et se peupla des étranges créatures du rêve de sa jeune sœur.

Les longues herbes bruissaient à ses pieds sous les pas précipités du Lapin Blanc; la Souris effrayée faisait clapoter l'eau en traversant la mare voisine; elle entendait le bruit des tasses, tandis que le Lièvre et ses amis prenaient leur repas qui ne finissait jamais, et la voix perçante de la Reine envoyant à la mort ses malheureux invités. Une fois encore l'enfant-porc éternuait sur les genoux de la Duchesse, tandis que les assiettes et les plats se brisaient autour de lui; une fois encore la voix criarde du Griffon, le grincement du crayon d'ardoise du Lézard, et les cris étouffés des cochons d'Inde mis dans le sac par ordre de la cour, remplissaient les airs, en se mêlant aux sanglots que poussait au loin la malheureuse Fausse-Tortue.

C'est ainsi qu'elle demeura assise, les yeux fermés, et se croyant presque dans le Pays des Merveilles, bien qu'elle sût qu'elle n'avait qu'à rouvrir les yeux pour que tout fût changé en une triste réalité: les herbes ne bruiraient plus alors que sous le souffle du vent, et l'eau de la mare ne murmurerait plus qu'au balancement des roseaux; le bruit des tasses deviendrait le tintement des clochettes au cou des moutons, et elle reconnaîtrait les cris aigus de la Reine dans la voix perçante du petit berger; l'éternuement du bébé, le cri du Griffon et tous les autres bruits étranges ne seraient plus, elle le savait bien, que les clameurs confuses d'une cour de ferme, tandis que le beuglement des bestiaux dans le lointain remplacerait les lourds sanglots de la Fausse-Tortue.

Enfin elle se représenta cette même petite sœur, dans l'avenir, devenue elle aussi une grande personne; elle se la représenta conservant, jusque dans l'âge mûr, le cœur simple et aimant de son enfance, et réunissant autour d'elle d'autres petits enfants dont elle ferait briller les yeux vifs et curieux au récit de bien des aventures étranges, et peut-être même en leur contant le songe du Pays des Merveilles du temps jadis: elle la voyait partager leurs petits chagrins et trouver plaisir à leurs innocentes joies, se rappelant sa propre enfance et les heureux jours d'été.

How To Use This Dictionary

abbreviation	*abr*	phrase	*phr*
adjective	*adj*	prefix	*pfx*
adverb	*adv*	preposition	*prp*
article	*art*	pronoun	*prn*
auxiliary verb	*av*	suffix	*sfx*
conjunction	*con*	verb	*vb*
interjection	*int*	singular	*sg*
noun	*f(eminine), m(asculine)*	plural	*pl*
numeral	*num*		
particle	*part*		

Word Order

The most common translations are generally given first. This resets by every new respective part of speech. Different parts of speech are divided by ";".

Translations

We made the decision to give the most common translation(s) of a word, and respectively the most common part(s) of speech. It does, however, not mean that this is the only possible translations or the only part of speech the word can be used for.

Lemmatization

The words in this book have been lemmatized. All inflections of a word have been grouped together, and linked back to their lemma, or dictionary form.

International Phonetic Alphabet (IPA)

The pronunciation of foreign vocabulary can be tricky. To help you get it right, we added IPA entries for each entry. If you already have a base understanding of the pronunciation, you will find the IPA pronunciation straightforward. For more information, please visit www.internationalphoneticalphabet.org

French-English Frequency Dictionary

Rank	French-*Part of Speech*	Translation
1	**de**-*prp*	of, from
2	**le**-*art; prn*	the; it
3	**et**-*con*	and
4	**à**-*prp*	to
5	**elle**-*prn*	she, it
6	**un**-*art; adj; num; prn*	a; one; one; one
7	**dire**-*vb*	say, speak
8	**que**-*con; prn; prp; adj; adv*	that; that; than; which; how
9	**en**-*prp; adv*	in; thereof
10	**je**-*prn*	I
11	**vous**-*prn*	you (form, pl)
12	**il**-*prn*	he, it
13	**se**-*prn*	-self (reflexive marker)
14	**pas**-*adv; m*	not; step
15	**ne**-*adv*	not
16	**être**-*vb*	be, exist
17	**tout**-*adj; adv; m; prn*	all; all; all; all
18	**ce**-*prn; adj*	this; that
19	**bien**-*adv; m; adj*	well, very; good; right
20	**qui**-*prn*	which
21	**dans**-*prp; adv*	in; aboard
22	**mais**-*con; adv*	but; probably
23	**cela**-*prn*	it, that
24	**si**-*con; adv*	if; so
25	**pour**-*prp*	for
26	**lui**-*prn*	him
27	**avoir**-*vb; m*	have; asset
28	**par**-*prp; m*	by; par
29	**comme**-*con; prp; adj*	as; as; such as
30	**sur**-*prp*	on
31	**plus**-*adj; adv; m*	more; more; plus
32	**avec**-*prp*	with
33	**son**-*adj; m*	its; sound
34	**là**-*adv*	there
35	**on**-*prn*	we
36	**me**-*prn*	me, myself
37	**reine**-*f*	queen
38	**tête**-*f*	head, top
39	**faire**-*vb*	do
40	**même**-*adj; adv*	same; even
41	**deux**-*num*	two
42	**peu**-*adv; m; adj*	little; bit; few
43	**roi**-*m*	king
44	**donc**-*con; adv*	therefore; consequently
45	**tortue**-*f*	turtle
46	**autre**-*prn; adj; adv*	other; another; else
47	**chapelier**-*m*	milliner
48	**sans**-*prp*	without
49	**ou**-*con*	or
50	**rien**-*m; prn; adv*	nothing; anything; nix
51	**sourire**-*m; vb*	smile; smile
52	**nous**-*prn*	we, us
53	**voix**-*f*	voice
54	**fausser**-*vb*	distort, skew
55	**très**-*adv*	very
56	**puis**-*adv*	then
57	**quand**-*adv; con*	when; when
58	**lapin**-*m*	rabbit
59	**griffon**-*m*	griffon
60	**temps**-*m*	time
61	**petit**-*adj; m*	small, little; child
62	**moi**-*prn; m*	me; ego
63	**air**-*m*	air
64	**car**-*m*	car
65	**alors**-*adv*	then
66	**jamais**-*adv*	never, ever
67	**penser**-*vb*	think, reflect
68	**fois**-*f*	time
69	**continuer**-*vb*	continue
70	**duchesse**-*f*	duchess
71	**œil**-*m*	eye
72	**ici**-*adv*	here
73	**chose**-*f*	thing
74	**ton**-*adj; prn; m*	your; your; tone
75	**non**-*adv; part*	not; no
76	**votre**-*adj; prn*	your; your
77	**encore**-*adv*	still, again
78	**oh**-*i*	oh
79	**quelque**-*adj; adv*	some; about
80	**répondre**-*vb*	answer
81	**porte**-*f*	door, gate
82	**crier**-*vb*	shout, shriek
83	**loir**-*m*	dormouse
84	**près**-*adv*	near, by
85	**voir**-*vb*	see, view
86	**mettre**-*vb*	put, apply
87	**aussi**-*adv; con*	also, as; and
88	**comment**-*adv*	how
89	**chat**-*m*	cat
90	**pouvoir**-*m; vb; av*	power; can; might
91	**trop**-*adv*	too, too much
92	**grand**-*adj*	large, wide
93	**chenille**-*f*	caterpillar
94	**trois**-*num*	three
95	**lièvre**-*m; adj*	hare; hare's
96	**avant**-*adv; prp; adj; m*	before; before; front
97	**fort**-*adj; m; adv*	strong, loud; fort; highly
98	**mon**-*prn*	my
99	**côté**-*m*	side
100	**haut**-*adj; m; adv*	high; top; in heaven

101 **voilà**-*adv* here
102 **après**-*adv; prp* after, next; after
103 **trouver**-*vb* find, get
104 **abord**-*m* first, start
105 **bientôt**-*adv* soon, almost
106 **savoir**-*vb; m* know; knowledge
107 **pied**-*m* foot, leg
108 **falloir**-*vb* have to
109 **quoi**-*prn* what
110 **bon**-*adj; m; adv* good, well; voucher; then
111 **où**-*adv; prn; con* where; that; wherein
112 **vers**-*prp; adv; m* to, towards; about; verse
113 **monde**-*m* world
114 **bras**-*m* arm
115 **parler**-*vb* speak, tell
116 **assez**-*adv* enough, quite
117 **mot**-*m* word
118 **blanc**-*adj; m* white, albescent; white
119 **quel**-*adj; prn* what; what
120 **table**-*f* table
122 **dessus**-*adv* over
123 **autour**-*adv* around
124 **maintenant**-*adv* now
125 **jurer**-*vb* swear
126 **enfin**-*adv* finally, after all
127 **ainsi**-*adv; con* thus, thereby; as
128 **vite**-*adv* quickly, fast
129 **pauvre**-*adj; m* poor; poor person
130 **ajouter**-*vb* add
131 **demander**-*vb* request, seek
132 **eh**-*i* eh
133 **croire**-*vb* believe, think
134 **main**-*f* hand
135 **aller**-*vb* go, travel
136 **mieux**-*adv; adj* better; adj
137 **peiner**-*vb* labor, pain
138 **bout**-*m* end, toe
139 **instant**-*m; adj* moment, while; urgent
140 **prendre**-*vb* take, have
141 **coup**-*m* blow, shot
142 **enfant**-*m* child
143 **leur**-*prn* their
144 **moment**-*m* time, moment
145 **bas**-*adj; m* low, base; bottom
146 **pendant**-*adv* during
147 **sou**-*m* cent
148 **commencer**-*vb* start, begin
149 **vouloir**-*vb* want, wish
150 **salle**-*f* room
151 **silence**-*m* silence, pause
152 **histoire**-*f* history, story
153 **idée**-*f* idea
154 **tandis**-*adv* while
155 **thé**-*m* tea
156 **terre**-*f* earth, land
157 **beaucoup**-*prn; adj; adv* many; much; much
158 **long**-*adj* long
159 **bonne**-*f* housemaid
160 **premier**-*adj* first, prime
161 **maison**-*f* house, home
162 **nouveau**-*adj; m* new, further; incoming
163 **question**-*f* question, issue
164 **pourquoi**-*adv; con* why; wherefore
165 **laquais**-*m; adj* lackey; menial
166 **cœur**-*m* heart, core
167 **ah**-*i* ah
168 **personne**-*f; prn* person; nobody
169 **gens**-*npl* people
170 **comprendre**-*vb* understand, include
171 **regarder**-*vb* look, watch
172 **effet**-*m* effect
173 **colérer**-*vb* argue
174 **vivement**-*adv* deeply
175 **oui**-*part; m* yes; yea
176 **jour**-*m* day
177 **bébé**-*m* baby, kid
178 **apercevoir**-*vb* see, perceive
179 **cependant**-*con; adv* however, yet; though
180 **tant**-*adv* so such
181 **jardin**-*m* garden
182 **presque**-*adv; adj* almost; all but
183 **boucher**-*m; vb* butcher; plug
184 **entendre**-*vb* hear
185 **drôle**-*adj* funny
186 **loin**-*adv; adj* far; distant
187 **dodo**-*m* dodo, sleep
188 **toujours**-*adv* always, still
189 **heure**-*f* time
190 **mal**-*m; adv; adj* evil, wrong; amiss; untimely
191 **vraiment**-*adv* really, actually
192 **écrier**-*vb* cry
193 **contre**-*prp* against
194 **moitié**-*adv; f* half; half
195 **aussitôt**-*adv* immediately
196 **venir**-*vb* come
197 **passer**-*vb* pass, spend
198 **partie**-*f* part
199 **bruit**-*m* noise, sound
200 **place**-*f* square, spot
201 **mare**-*f* pond
202 **minute**-*f* minute
203 **mer**-*f* sea
204 **cuisinière**-*f* cook

205 **chapitre**-*m* chapter
206 **rester**-*vb* stay, keep
207 **peur**-*f* fear, scare
208 **majesté**-*f* majesty
209 **prier**-*vb* pray
210 **manière**-*f* way, form
211 **grandir**-*vb* grow, augment
212 **juste**-*adj; adv* just, fair; just
213 **pigeon**-*m* pigeon
214 **raison**-*f* reason, why
215 **douter**-*vb* doubt
216 **fin**-*f; adj* end; fine
217 **conversation**-*f* conversation, talk
218 **chien**-*m* dog
219 **moins**-*adv; m; prp* less; minus; wanting
220 **vieux**-*adj; m* old, ancient; old man
221 **présent**-*adj; m* present; present
222 **larme**-*f* tear, drop
223 **croquet**-*m* croquet
224 **leçon**-*f* lesson
225 **danser**-*vb* dance
226 **queue**-*f* tail, queue
227 **chemin**-*m* path, road
228 **suite**-*f* suite, sequence
229 **important**-*adj* important
230 **taire**-*vb* hush up
231 **beau**-*adj; m* beautiful, nice; beautiful
232 **longtemps**-*adv; adj* for a long time; longtime
233 **moindre**-*adj* lesser
234 **écrire**-*vb* write
235 **point**-*m* point, item
236 **procès**-*m* trial, process
237 **clef**-*f; adj* key; pivotal
238 **maître**-*m* master, teacher
239 **beurrer**-*vb* butter
240 **sorte**-*f* kind, manner
241 **pourtant**-*con; adv* yet, however; nevertheless
242 **soldat**-*m* soldier
243 **entre**-*adv; prp* between; between
244 **bouteille**-*f* bottle
245 **milieu**-*m* medium
246 **tourner**-*vb* turn, rotate
247 **gant**-*m* glove
248 **derrière**-*adv; m; prp* behind; behind; behind
249 **figurer**-*vb* figure
250 **éventail**-*m* range
251 **sœur**-*adj; f* sister; sister
252 **couper**-*vb* cut
253 **eau**-*f* water
254 **eux**-*prn* them
255 **jeu**-*m* game
256 **champignon**-*m* mushroom
257 **vivre**-*vb* live
258 **souvent**-*adv* often
259 **quatre**-*num* four
260 **soit**-*con* whether, either
261 **ni**-*con; adv* or; neither
262 **or**-*m* gold
263 **répliquer**-*vb* reply
264 **timidement**-*adv* timidly
265 **bois**-*m* wood, timber
266 **partir**-*vb* depart, leave
267 **tour**-*m; f* turn; tower
268 **serpent**-*m* snake
269 **valet**-*m* valet
270 **porc**-*m* pork, pig
271 **celui**-*prn* that
272 **chercher**-*vb* search, try
273 **tristement**-*adv* sadly
274 **déjà**-*adv* already
275 **asseoir**-*vb* sit
276 **témoin**-*m* witness
277 **puits**-*m* well
278 **paraître**-*vb* seem, appear
279 **doigt**-*m* finger
280 **vrai**-*adj; m* true, real; right
281 **courir**-*vb* run, race
282 **cas**-*m* case, event
283 **homard**-*m* lobster
284 **reprendre**-*vb* resume, retake
285 **sens**-*m* direction
286 **répéter**-*vb* repeat, rehearse
287 **fini**-*adj; m* finished, finite; finish
288 **remettre**-*vb* deliver, return
289 **fond**-*m* bottom
290 **tabler**-*vb* rely
291 **ci**-*adv* this
292 **parce que**-*adv* because
293 **auprès**-*adv* nearby
294 **morceau**-*m* piece, track
295 **lequel**-*prn* which
296 **morale**-*f* morals, ethics
297 **fenêtre**-*f* window
298 **chaque**-*adj; prn* each; either
299 **disparaître**-*vb* disappear
300 **chez**-*prp* in, by
301 **cinq**-*num* five
302 **longue**-*adj* long
303 **grandeur**-*f* size, magnitude
304 **travers**-*m* across
305 **droit**-*adj; m; adv* right; right; due
306 **finir**-*vb* end, finish
307 **attention**-*f* attention

308	**expliquer**-*vb*	explain
309	**inquiet**-*adj*	worried, concerned
310	**manger**-*vb*	eat, feed
311	**esprit**-*m*	mind, spirit
312	**dont**-*prn*	whose
313	**ardoise**-*f*	slate
314	**chacun**-*prn; adv*	each; apiece
315	**tarte**-*f*	pie
316	**dehors**-*adv; m*	outside, out; outside
317	**aventure**-*f*	adventure
318	**cou**-*m*	neck
319	**fou**-*adj; m*	crazy; fool
320	**tailler**-*vb*	cut, carve
321	**nez**-*m*	nose
322	**vie**-*f*	life
323	**sûr**-*adj*	sure, safe
324	**oiseau**-*m*	bird
325	**face**-*f*	face, front
326	**patte**-*f*	tab, leg
327	**attendre**-*vb*	expect, wait for
328	**te**-*prn*	you
329	**créature**-*f*	creature, being
330	**bourreau**-*m*	executioner
331	**tard**-*adv*	late
332	**arbre**-*m*	tree, shaft
333	**notre**-*prn*	our
334	**sembler**-*vb*	seem, sound
335	**arriver**-*vb*	arrive, happen
336	**ensuite**-*adv*	then, later
337	**empêcher**-*vb*	prevent, stop
338	**prix**-*m*	price, prize
339	**cour**-*f*	court
340	**pardon**-*m*	forgiveness
341	**combien**-*adv*	how many
342	**soupe**-*f*	soup
343	**doucement**-*adv*	gently, slowly
344	**observation**-*f*	observation, comment
345	**façon**-*f*	way, method
346	**grimace**-*f*	grimace
347	**plaire**-*vb*	please
348	**menton**-*m*	chin
349	**quant**-*adv*	about
350	**environ**-*adv; prp; adj*	about; around; all but
351	**depuis**-*adv; prp*	since; since
352	**flamant**-*m*	flamingo
353	**course**-*f*	race, running
354	**passant**-*adj; m*	elapsing; passer-by
355	**dos**-*m*	back, reverse
356	**certainement**-*adv*	definitely
357	**empressement**-*m*	willingness
358	**aimer**-*vb*	love, like
359	**aise**-*adj; f*	pleased; pleasure
360	**étranger**-*adj; m*	foreign, overseas; foreigner
361	**jardinier**-*m*	gardener
362	**espèce**-*f*	species, kind
363	**train**-*m*	train
364	**inquiétude**-*f*	concern
365	**mélasse**-*f*	treacle, molasses
366	**seul**-*adj; m; adv*	only; only one; very
367	**aucun**-*adj; prn*	no; none
368	**possible**-*adj; m*	possible; possible
369	**brou**-*m*	husk
370	**moyen**-*m; adj*	means, medium; medium
371	**plaisir**-*m*	pleasure
372	**frapper**-*vb*	hit, knock
373	**fleur**-*f*	flower
374	**pouce**-*m*	inch
375	**hérisson**-*m*	hedgehog
376	**affairer**-*vb*	attend, bustle about
377	**lézard**-*m*	lizard
378	**verre**-*m*	glass
379	**gros**-*adj; m*	large, fat; fat man
380	**tomber**-*vb*	fall, drop
381	**devant**-*adv; prp; m*	before, past; before; front
382	**simplement**-*adv*	simply
383	**fille**-*f*	daughter, girl
384	**dragée**-*m*	lozenge
385	**tombe**-*f*	grave, tomb
386	**sortir**-*vb*	exit, come out
387	**tremblant**-*adj; adv*	trembling; trembling
388	**parole**-*f*	word, speech
389	**hors**-*prp*	except
390	**tenir**-*vb*	hold, keep
391	**mine**-*f*	mine, lead
392	**tantôt**-*adv*	sometimes
393	**assurément**-*adv*	certainly
394	**observer**-*vb*	observe, watch
395	**voyant**-*m; adj*	seer; clairvoyant
396	**porter**-*vb*	wear, carry
397	**profond**-*adj; m*	deep, profound; deep
398	**changer**-*vb*	change, switch
399	**poliment**-*adv*	politely
400	**rapetisser**-*vb*	shrink
401	**mille**-*num*	thousand
402	**âge**-*m*	age
403	**Inde**-*f*	India
404	**livrer**-*vb*	deliver
405	**apprendre**-*vb*	learn, teach
406	**jeune**-*adj; m*	young; youth
407	**oreille**-*f*	ear
408	**dessous**-*adv; m; prp*	beneath; underside; under it
409	**impatience**-*f*	impatience

410	**dix**-*num*	ten
411	**étai**-*f*	strut
412	**passage**-*m*	passage, passing
413	**genou**-*m*	knee
414	**debout**-*adj*	standing
415	**chanson**-*f*	song
416	**poivre**-*m*	pepper
417	**absolument**-*adv*	absolutely
418	**ouvrir**-*vb*	open, start
419	**occasion**-*f*	opportunity, occasion
420	**sept**-*num*	seven
421	**œuf**-*m*	egg
422	**curieux**-*adj; m*	curious; onlooker
423	**montrer**-*vb*	show
424	**revenir**-*vb*	return, get back
425	**inutile**-*adj*	unnecessary, useless
426	**ordinaire**-*adj; m*	ordinary; ordinary
427	**guère**-*adv*	little
428	**tirer**-*vb*	take, draw
429	**sitôt**-*adv*	soon
430	**mesure**-*f*	measure, step
431	**bord**-*m*	edge, board
432	**réciter**-*vb*	recite
433	**pain**-*m*	bread
434	**chagrin**-*m*	grief, heartache
435	**trou**-*m*	hole
436	**arrêter**-*vb*	stop, quit
437	**tasse**-*f*	cup
438	**content**-*adj*	content, happy
439	**devoir**-*m; vb; av*	duty; have to; must
440	**secouer**-*vb*	shake, rock
441	**chut**-*i; nm*	hush!; shushing
442	**pleurer**-*vb*	cry, mourn
443	**perdre**-*vb*	lose, waste
444	**hasarder**-*vb*	hazard
445	**feuille**-*f*	sheet, leaf
446	**interrompre**-*vb*	interrupt, stop
447	**cocher**-*vb; m*	check; coachman
448	**exemple**-*m*	example, sample
449	**seulement**-*adv; con*	only, just; only
450	**chauve**-*adj*	bald
451	**plein**-*adj*	full, fraught
452	**plonger**-*vb*	dive, plunge
453	**écouter**-*vb*	listen, hear
454	**gauche**-*adj; f*	left; left
455	**paquet**-*m*	package, pack
456	**entrer**-*vb*	enter
457	**marquer**-*vb*	mark, tag
458	**héler**-*vb*	hail
459	**certes**-*adv*	certainly
460	**mort**-*adj; f*	dead; death
461	**tranquillement**-*adv*	quietly
462	**commencement**-*m*	beginning, start
463	**rêve**-*m*	dream
464	**quitter**-*vb*	leave, quit
465	**dedans**-*adv; prp; m*	in; in; inside
466	**rire**-*m; vb*	laugh; laugh
467	**pièce**-*f; adv*	piece, room; apiece
468	**cheveu**-*m*	hair
469	**importer**-*vb*	import
470	**puisque**-*con*	since
471	**toutefois**-*con; adv*	however; nevertheless
472	**cri**-*m*	cry, scream
473	**neuf**-*num*	nine
474	**feu**-*m*	fire
475	**carte**-*f*	map, card
476	**étonnement**-*m; adv*	astonishment; surprisingly
477	**sentir**-*vb*	feel
478	**curiosité**-*f*	curiosity
479	**merci**-*m; i*	thanks; thanks
480	**nom**-*m*	name
481	**soupir**-*m*	sigh
482	**jeter**-*vb*	throw
483	**large**-*adj*	wide, large
484	**surprendre**-*vb*	surprise, catch
485	**nager**-*vb*	swim
486	**triste**-*adj*	sad
487	**réponse**-*f*	response
488	**raconter**-*vb*	tell
489	**matin**-*m*	morning
490	**joie**-*f*	joy
491	**supposer**-*vb*	assume, suppose
492	**exécuter**-*vb*	execute
493	**simple**-*adj*	simple; singles
494	**malheureux**-*adj; m*	unfortunate, unhappy; unfortunate
495	**paire**-*f*	pair
496	**explication**-*f*	explanation, explication
497	**dé**-*pfx*	un-, in-
498	**tartine**-*f*	sandwich
499	**école**-*f*	school
500	**animal**-*adj; m*	animal; animal
501	**chuter**-*vb*	tumble
502	**envoyer**-*vb*	send, forward
503	**procession**-*f*	procession
504	**poche**-*f*	pocket
505	**extraordinaire**-*adj*	extraordinary
506	**couronne**-*f*	crown
507	**murmurer**-*vb*	murmur
508	**réfléchir**-*vb*	reflect, think
509	**déposition**-*f*	deposition
510	**autrefois**-*adv*	once, in the past
511	**connaître**-*vb*	know

512	**père**-*m*	father, dad
513	**Mademoiselle**-*abr; f*	Ms.; miss
514	**pays**-*m*	country
515	**télescope**-*m*	telescope
516	**hurler**-*vb*	scream, howl
517	**contenter**-*vb*	satisfy
518	**gravement**-*adv*	seriously, gravely
519	**rendre**-*vb*	render, restore
520	**impossible**-*adj*	impossible
521	**dernier**-*adj; m*	last, latter; last
522	**cher**-*adj; m*	expensive, dear; dear
523	**sanglot**-*m*	sob
524	**retourner**-*vb*	return
525	**difficile**-*adj*	difficult
526	**autant**-*con*	as far as
527	**coin**-*m*	corner, wedge
528	**rose**-*adj; f*	pink; rose
529	**auparavant**-*adv*	before
530	**arche**-*f*	ark
531	**quadrille**-*m*	quadrille
532	**grave**-*adj*	serious, grave
533	**camarade**-*m/f*	comrade, fellow
534	**calme**-*adj; m*	quiet, calm; calm
535	**courant**-*adj; m*	current, running; current
536	**appeler**-*vb*	call, appeal
537	**épaule**-*f*	shoulder
538	**singulier**-*adj; m*	singular, strange; singular
539	**chambre**-*f*	room
540	**justement**-*adv*	rightly, exactly
541	**ridicule**-*adj; m*	ridiculous; ridicule
542	**enchanter**-*vb*	enchant, rejoice
543	**cheminer**-*vb*	plod
544	**boire**-*vb*	drink
545	**étendre**-*vb*	extend, expand
546	**descendre**-*vb*	descend, get off
547	**profondément**-*adv*	deeply, heavily
548	**bête**-*f; adj*	beast, idiot; stupid
549	**oublier**-*vb*	forget
550	**cuisine**-*f*	kitchen, cuisine
551	**agréable**-*adj*	pleasant, nice
552	**glisser**-*vb*	slip, run
553	**garde**-*f; adj*	custody, guard; guarding
554	**espérer**-*vb*	hope, expect
555	**arrière**-*adj; m*	rear, back; back
556	**joueur**-*m*	player
557	**coude**-*m*	elbow, bend
558	**donner**-*vb*	give, yield
559	**rosier**-*m*	rosebush
560	**autrement**-*adv*	otherwise
561	**corbeau**-*m*	raven
562	**sujet**-*m; adj*	subject; prone
563	**pareil**-*adj; prn; m*	such, similar; the same; equal
564	**douze**-*num*	twelve
565	**portant**-*adj*	carrying
566	**règle**-*f*	rule
567	**former**-*vb*	form, train
568	**nombre**-*m*	number
569	**lentement**-*adv*	slowly, leisurely
570	**prêt**-*adj; m*	ready, willing; loan
571	**gâteau**-*m*	cake
572	**terrier**-*m*	terrier
573	**lever**-*vb; m*	lift, raise; rise
574	**plafond**-*m*	ceiling, plafond
575	**afin**-*adv*	in order
576	**homme**-*m*	man, person
577	**enlever**-*vb*	remove, take off
578	**pic**-*m*	peak, woodpecker
579	**retirer**-*vb*	withdraw, pull
580	**rappeler**-*vb*	remind, call back
581	**terrain**-*m*	field, ground
582	**sec**-*adj*	dry, dried
583	**chanter**-*vb*	sing
584	**regard**-*m*	look, gaze
585	**vilain**-*adj; m*	ugly; villein
586	**vue**-*m*	view
587	**tôt**-*adv*	early, soon
588	**étrange**-*adj*	strange
589	**chère**-*adj*	dear
590	**fortement**-*adv*	strongly
591	**grenouille**-*f*	frog
592	**échapper**-*vb*	escape
593	**jury**-*m*	jury
594	**mauvais**-*adj; m*	bad, ill; brute
595	**nageant**-*adj*	swimming
596	**banc**-*m*	bench, bank
597	**cadeau**-*m*	gift
598	**fâcher**-*vb*	upset
599	**trompeter**-*vb*	trumpet
600	**trembler**-*vb*	tremble, shake
601	**os**-*m*	bone
602	**demeurer**-*vb*	remain, dwell
603	**grogne**-*f*	discontent
604	**grogner**-*vb*	grumble
605	**endormir**-*vb*	put to sleep
606	**conter**-*vb*	tell
607	**jambe**-*f*	leg
608	**minuter**-*vb*	time
609	**pénétrer**-*vb*	enter, penetrate
610	**çà**-*prn*	it, that
611	**sévère**-*adj*	severe, strict
612	**parmi**-*prp*	among
613	**pousser**-*vb*	push, drive

614 **souvenir**-*m* memory, souvenir
615 **causer**-*vb* cause, chat
616 **huissier**-*m* bailiff
617 **poursuite**-*f* pursuit, prosecution
618 **absence**-*f* absence
619 **intéresser**-*vb* interest
620 **vingt**-*num* twenty
621 **vitre**-*f* window
622 **révérence**-*f* reverence, bow
623 **imaginer**-*vb* imagine
624 **craindre**-*vb* fear
625 **pâle**-*adj* pale
626 **naturel**-*adj; m* natural; nature
627 **grimoire**-*m* grimoire
628 **soupirer**-*vb* sigh
629 **gare**-*f* station, train station
630 **perçant**-*adj* piercing, shrill
631 **retenir**-*vb* retain, hold
632 **habitude**-*f* habit
633 **éternuer**-*vb* sneeze
634 **contempler**-*vb* contemplate
635 **crabe**-*m* crab
636 **terrible**-*adj* terrible
637 **saisir**-*vb* seize, grasp
638 **toit**-*m* roof
639 **ignorer**-*vb* ignore
640 **poisson**-*m* fish
641 **humeur**-*f* mood, spirit
642 **italien**-*adj; m* Italian; Italian
643 **dommage**-*m* damage, pity
644 **rencontrer**-*vb* meet, encounter
645 **levant**-*adj;* rising; east
646 **pipe**-*f* pipe
647 **endroit**-*m* place, spot
648 **plongeon**-*m* dive, plunge
649 **deviner**-*vb* guess, divine
650 **soupirant**-*m* suitor
651 **second**-*adj; m* second; second
652 **rond**-*adj; m* round; round
653 **goût**-*m* taste, flavor
654 **sécher**-*vb* dry, cure
655 **poil**-*m* hair
656 **capital**-*adj; m* capital; capital
657 **compter**-*vb* count, expect
658 **rapidement**-*adv* quickly, rapidly
659 **devenir**-*vb* become, be
660 **hâter**-*vb* hasten, accelerate
661 **appuyer**-*vb* support, press
662 **tâcher**-*vb* try
663 **vaste**-*adj* vast, wide
664 **cuillère**-*f* spoon
665 **colimaçon**-*adj* spiral
666 **rouge**-*adj; m* red; red
667 **lieu**-*m* place, venue
668 **position**-*f* position
669 **cesser**-*vb* stop, desist
670 **moutarde**-*f* mustard
671 **tressaillir**-*vb* flinch
672 **proposer**-*vb* propose, offer
673 **refrain**-*m* refrain
674 **star**-*f* star
675 **escalier**-*m* staircase, stairs
676 **dent**-*f* tooth
677 **meilleur**-*m; adj* best; better
678 **accident**-*m* accident
679 **courage**-*m* courage
680 **vivant**-*adj; m* living, alive; living
681 **hier**-*adv* yesterday; yesterday
682 **plat**-*adj; m* flat; flat, dish
683 **allier**-*vb* combine
684 **voici**-*prp* here is
685 **voler**-*vb* fly, steal
686 **fixé**-*adj* fixed, appointed
687 **visage**-*m* face
688 **fatiguer**-*vb* tire, stress
689 **demi**-*adj; m* half; half
690 **humblement**-*adv* humbly
691 **huître**-*f* oyster
692 **envie**-*f* desire
693 **avancer**-*vb* advance, forward
694 **lunettes**-*msf* glasses
695 **herbe**-*f* grass, herb
696 **doux**-*adj* soft, sweet
697 **éloigner**-*vb* drive away
698 **mouvement**-*m* movement, stir
699 **vent**-*m* wind
700 **invitation**-*f* invitation
701 **partout**-*adv* everywhere, throughout
702 **trancher**-*vb* settle, slice
703 **soupier**-*vb* worry about
704 **ranger**-*m; vb* ranger; put away
705 **mois**-*m* month
706 **vif**-*adj; m* bright, lively; quick
707 **image**-*f* image
708 **faute**-*f* fault
709 **probable**-*adj* likely
710 **corps**-*m* body
711 **laisser**-*vb* leave, let
712 **niais**-*m; adj* simpleton; simple
713 **suivre**-*vb* follow
714 **attraper**-*vb* catch, seize
715 **davantage**-*adv* further
716 **gazon**-*m* grass, lawn
717 **liste**-*f* list

718	**prosterner**-*vb*	bow down
719	**casser**-*vb*	break, crack
720	**demoiselle**-*f*	young lady
721	**compagnie**-*f*	company
722	**soulier**-*m*	shoe
723	**clairement**-*adv*	clearly
724	**intérieur**-*adj; m*	inside, interior; inside
725	**lorsque**-*prp*	during
726	**bâton**-*m*	stick, baton
727	**bah**-*i*	bah
728	**bis**-*m; adv; adj*	bis; twice; repeat
729	**baisser**-*vb*	lower, fall
730	**merlan**-*m*	whiting
731	**méprendre**-*vb*	misunderstand
732	**bonheur**-*m; adj*	happiness; welfare
733	**crayon**-*m*	pencil
734	**aiglon**-*m*	eaglet
735	**canard**-*m*	duck
736	**carnet**-*m*	book
737	**besoin**-*m*	need
738	**découvrir**-*vb*	discover
739	**ordre**-*m*	order
740	**foule**-*f*	crowd, host
741	**ramasser**-*vb*	pick up
742	**pointu**-*adj*	sharp
743	**entrée**-*f*	input, entry
744	**réjouir**-*vb*	rejoice
745	**lire**-*vb; f*	read; lira
746	**mie**-*f*	crumb
747	**poison**-*m*	poison
748	**indigner**-*vb*	outrage
749	**Madame**-*f*	madame, Mrs
750	**brancher**-*vb*	connect
751	**pot**-*m*	pot, jar
752	**semaine**-*f*	week
753	**reparaître**-*vb*	reappear
754	**inviter**-*vb*	invite, ask
755	**furieux**-*adj; m*	furious; madman
756	**lointain**-*adj*	distant, far
757	**haleine**-*m*	breath
758	**sac**-*m*	bag, sack
759	**adresser**-*vb*	address
760	**nerf**-*m*	nerve
761	**ami**-*m*	friend
762	**direction**-*f*	direction, management
763	**assemblée**-*f*	assembly
764	**nuire**-*vb*	harm, damage
765	**réflexion**-*f*	reflection, thinking
766	**merveille**-*f*	wonder, marvel
767	**ressembler**-*vb*	look like
768	**joli**-*adj*	pretty
769	**faim**-*f*	hunger
770	**raisonnement**-*m*	reasoning
771	**faible**-*adj; m*	low, weak; weakling
772	**justice**-*f*	justice, law
773	**traînant**-*adj*	shuffling
774	**croiser**-*vb*	cross, pass
775	**brusque**-*adj*	sudden, brusque
776	**papier**-*m*	paper
777	**archevêque**-*m*	Archbishop
778	**cercle**-*m*	circle, ring
779	**jouer**-*vb*	play, act
780	**juge**-*m*	judge, beak
781	**cocasse**-*adj*	funny
782	**battre**-*vb*	beat, fight
783	**étonner**-*vb*	surprise, wonder
784	**longitude**-*f*	longitude
785	**quinze**-*num*	fifteen
786	**mordre**-*vb*	bite, snap
787	**latitude**-*f*	latitude
788	**oignon**-*m*	onion
789	**approcher**-*vb*	hang over
790	**œuvre**-*f*	work
791	**pensif**-*adj*	thoughtful
792	**garnir**-*vb*	line
793	**mélange**-*m*	mixture
794	**superbe**-*adj*	superb; stunner
795	**couplet**-*m*	verse
796	**trône**-*m*	throne
797	**produire**-*vb*	produce
798	**parier**-*vb*	bet, gamble
799	**pari**-*m*	bet, betting
800	**différent**-*adj*	different
801	**pauser**-*vb*	pause
802	**assiette**-*f*	plate, dish
803	**amour**-*m*	love
804	**rentrer**-*vb*	return
805	**franchement**-*adv*	honestly, openly
806	**délibérer**-*vb*	deliberate
807	**emporter**-*vb*	take, take away
808	**obéir**-*vb*	obey
809	**enfance**-*f*	childhood
810	**atteindre**-*vb*	reach, achieve
811	**embarrasser**-*vb*	embarrass, bother
812	**chaudron**-*m*	cauldron
813	**épouser**-*vb*	marry
814	**retard**-*m*	delay
815	**bond**-*m*	leap, jump
816	**grignoter**-*vb*	nibble
817	**ordinairement**-*adv*	usually
818	**mourir**-*vb*	die, end
819	**suivant**-*adj; prp; adv*	following; according to; as follows
820	**savon**-*m*	soap

821	**existier**-*vb*	exist
822	**allonger**-*vb*	lengthen
823	**ensemble**-*adv; m; f*	together; ensemble; collection
824	**salut**-*m; i*	salvation; hi
825	**entier**-*adj*	whole, full
826	**poids**-*m*	weight
827	**aiguiller**-*vb*	switch
828	**pendre**-*vb*	hang
829	**habituer**-*vb*	accustom, get used to
830	**forcé**-*adj*	forced
831	**élever**-*vb*	raise, elevate
832	**condamner**-*vb*	condemn, convict
833	**obligé**-*adj*	obliged
834	**accuser**-*vb*	accuse, blame
835	**diminuer**-*vb*	decrease, reduce
836	**boudeur**-*adj*	mopey
837	**caressant**-*adj*	caressing
838	**saler**-*vb*	salt
839	**pelouse**-*f*	lawn
840	**langue**-*f*	language
841	**apporter**-*vb*	bring
842	**parvenir**-*vb*	get through
843	**affaire**-*f*	case, matter
844	**dresser**-*vb*	draw up, develop
845	**quantième**-*m*	date
846	**musique**-*f*	music
847	**taper**-*vb*	type, beat
848	**grommeler**-*vb*	grumble
849	**sauter**-*vb*	jump, skip
850	**débarrasser**-*vb*	rid
851	**verdure**-*f*	greenery, greenness
852	**affairé**-*adj*	busy
853	**couvert**-*adj; m*	covered; place
854	**humble**-*adj*	humble
855	**bouger**-*vb*	move, budge
856	**plutôt**-*adv*	rather, quite
857	**tranquille**-*adj*	quiet
858	**juger**-*vb*	judge, assess
859	**cabriole**-*f*	somersault
860	**accoutumer**-*vb*	accustom
861	**sourcil**-*m*	eyebrow
862	**commun**-*adj*	common, joint
863	**arrêt**-*m*	stop, stopping
864	**ailleurs**-*adv*	somewhere else
865	**fier**-*adj*	proud
866	**gousset**-*m*	gusset
867	**conclusion**-*f*	conclusion
868	**pension**-*f*	pension
869	**adresse**-*m*	address
870	**décider**-*vb*	decide, choose
871	**recommencer**-*vb*	restart, start again
872	**lait**-*m*	milk
873	**raisonnable**-*adj*	reasonable
874	**empresser**-*vb*	hasten
875	**exprimer**-*vb*	express, voice
876	**écriture**-*f*	writing
877	**poli**-*adj*	polished, polite
878	**poser**-*vb*	pose, rest
879	**satisfaire**-*vb*	satisfy, please
880	**chantant**-*adj*	singing
881	**rêver**-*vb*	dream
882	**éternuement**-*m*	sneeze
883	**représenter**-*vb*	represent
884	**frère**-*m*	brother
885	**propre**-*adj; m*	own, clean; proper
886	**offrir**-*vb*	offer, give
887	**clin**-*m*	wink
888	**année**-*f*	year
889	**sonner**-*vb*	ring, sound
890	**siffler**-*vb*	whistle, hiss
891	**amuser**-*vb*	amuse, entertain
892	**cheval**-*m*	horse
893	**complètement**-*adv*	completely, fully
894	**fermé**-*adj*	closed, sealed
895	**offenser**-*vb*	offend, insult
896	**route**-*f*	road, way
897	**idiot**-*m; adj*	idiot; silly
898	**rouet**-*m*	spinning wheel
899	**bâiller**-*vb*	yawn
900	**continuel**-*adj*	continuous
901	**demie**-*f*	half
902	**prouver**-*vb*	prove
903	**fermer**-*vb*	close
904	**haie**-*f*	hedge, hurdle
905	**sot**-*m*	fool
906	**décapiter**-*vb*	decapitate
907	**présenter**-*vb*	present, offer
908	**précipitamment**-*adv*	hastily, precipitately
909	**embarrassant**-*adj*	embarrassing
910	**courber**-*vb*	bend
911	**exécution**-*f*	execution, implementation
912	**perruque**-*f*	wig
913	**changement**-*m*	change, changing
914	**pailler**-*vb*	mulch
915	**sérieusement**-*adv*	seriously, gravely
916	**vaisselle**-*f*	dishes
917	**effrayer**-*vb*	scare, spook
918	**songer**-*vb*	reflect, wonder
919	**saluer**-*vb*	greet
920	**étroit**-*adj*	narrow, close
921	**front**-*m*	front, forehead
922	**restant**-*adj; m*	remaining; remnant

923	**criant**-*adj*	crying
924	**placer**-*vb*	place, put
925	**énorme**-*adj*	huge, enormous
926	**malade**-*adj; m*	sick, invalid; patient
927	**garçon**-*m*	boy, lad
928	**criard**-*adj; nm*	garish; screamer
929	**comte**-*m*	count
930	**plier**-*vb*	bend
931	**cause**-*f*	cause, case
932	**conseil**-*m*	board, council
933	**fable**-*f*	fable
934	**ennui**-*m*	boredom, trouble
935	**énigme**-*f*	enigma, puzzle
936	**dormant**-*adj*	dormant
937	**galimatias**-*m*	rigmarole
938	**hauteur**-*f*	height, pitch
939	**ferme**-*f; adj*	farm; firm
940	**boîte**-*f*	box, can
941	**chardon**-*m*	thistle
942	**mars**-*f*	March
943	**avance**-*f*	advance, lead
944	**traverser**-*vb*	cross, pass through
945	**servir**-*vb*	serve, help
946	**plancher**-*m; vb*	floor; floor
947	**apprêter**-*vb*	ready
948	**discussion**-*f*	discussion, debate
949	**troupe**-*f*	troop
950	**personnage**-*m*	character, figure
951	**utile**-*adj*	useful
952	**gagner**-*vb*	win, earn
953	**quelquefois**-*adv*	sometimes
954	**soulager**-*vb*	relieve, alleviate
955	**réprimer**-*vb*	repress
956	**valoir**-*vb*	be worth
957	**applaudir**-*vb*	applaud, cheer
958	**accepter**-*vb*	accept
959	**dormir**-*vb*	sleep
960	**cochon**-*m; adj*	pig, swine; dirty
961	**croisé**-*adj; m*	cross; crusader
962	**timide**-*adj*	shy
963	**farce**-*f*	farce, joke
964	**souffrir**-*vb*	suffer, experience
965	**confus**-*adj*	confused
966	**certain**-*adj*	certain
967	**terme**-*m*	term
968	**dialoguer**-*vb*	dialogue
969	**heureusement**-*adv*	fortunately, happily
970	**admirablement**-*adv*	admirably
971	**patiemment**-*adv*	patiently
972	**ordonner**-*vb*	order, direct
973	**patience**-*f*	patience
974	**emphase**-*f*	emphasis
975	**chandelle**-*f*	candle
976	**franc**-*adj; m*	frank; franc
977	**fontaine**-*f*	fountain, spring
978	**sombre**-*adj*	dark, gloomy
979	**concert**-*m*	concert
980	**examiner**-*vb*	examine
981	**dédain**-*m*	disdain
982	**subitement**-*adv*	suddenly
983	**rat**-*m*	rat
984	**indignation**-*f*	indignation
985	**chanteur**-*m*	singer
986	**court**-*adj; m*	short, brief; court
987	**succès**-*m*	success
988	**secousse**-*f*	shock, shake
989	**atome**-*m*	atom
990	**agiter**-*vb*	shake, wave
991	**appartenir**-*vb*	behove
992	**Monsieur**-*abr; m*	Mr.; sir
993	**moustache**-*f*	mustache, whiskers
994	**intéressant**-*adj*	interesting
995	**considérer**-*vb*	consider
996	**frais**-*npl; adj*	costs; fresh
997	**chœur**-*m*	choir
998	**embarras**-*m*	embarrassment
999	**manque**-*m*	lack
1000	**médire**-*vb*	speak ill
1001	**rive**-*f*	bank, shore
1002	**froncer**-*vb*	frown
1003	**solennel**-*adj*	solemn
1004	**briser**-*vb*	break, shatter
1005	**sommer**-*vb*	summon
1006	**sommet**-*m*	top, vertex
1007	**égal**-*adj; m*	equal, even; equal
1008	**sottise**-*f*	folly, silliness
1009	**accès**-*m*	access
1010	**robe**-*f*	dress, gown
1011	**vérité**-*f*	truth
1012	**dorloter**-*vb*	pamper, mother
1013	**sèche**-*f; adj*	fag; dry
1014	**tellement**-*adv*	so
1015	**exception**-*f*	exception
1016	**fer**-*m*	iron
1017	**foi**-*f*	faith
1018	**rauque**-*adj*	hoarse
1019	**précipiter**-*vb*	precipitate
1020	**plupart**-*f*	most
1021	**heureux**-*adj*	happy
1022	**hum**-*i*	hum
1023	**difficulté**-*f*	difficulty
1024	**inventer**-*vb*	invent, make up
1025	**ravissant**-*adj*	delightful
1026	**pointer**-*vb*	point

1027	**châssis**-*m*	chassis
1028	**foyer**-*m*	home, fireplace
1029	**profiter**-*vb*	benefit, avail
1030	**coussin**-*m*	cushion
1031	**parchemin**-*m*	parchment, diploma
1032	**agir**-*vb*	act
1033	**caillou**-*m*	pebble
1034	**honte**-*f*	shame
1035	**nid**-*m*	nest
1036	**nier**-*vb*	deny
1037	**bourru**-*adj*	gruff
1038	**brillant**-*adj; m*	brilliant, bright; gloss
1039	**oser**-*vb*	dare
1040	**blanchissage**-*m*	laundry
1041	**aisé**-*adj*	easy, fluent
1042	**pie**-*f*	magpie
1043	**six**-*num*	six
1044	**soi**-*m; prn*	self; self
1045	**lancer**-*vb*	launch
1046	**houka**-*m*	hookah
1047	**courtisan**-*m*	courtier
1048	**vin**-*m*	wine
1049	**profondeur**-*f*	depth, hollowness
1050	**désordre**-*m*	disorder
1051	**étiquette**-*f*	label, etiquette
1052	**réveiller**-*vb*	wake, awake
1053	**champ**-*m*	field
1054	**épouvante**-*f*	dread
1055	**retrouver**-*vb*	find, meet
1056	**détour**-*m*	detour, bend
1057	**signer**-*vb*	sign
1058	**livre**-*m*	book
1059	**chaud**-*adj*	hot, warm
1060	**furet**-*m*	ferret
1061	**avis**-*m*	opinion, notice
1062	**récit**-*m*	story, recital
1063	**embrouiller**-*vb*	confuse
1064	**gaspiller**-*vb*	waste, throw away
1065	**remarquer**-*vb*	notice, note
1066	**armoire**-*f*	cabinet
1067	**fracas**-*m*	crash, smash
1068	**soleil**-*m*	sun
1069	**aboiement**-*m*	bark
1070	**signifier**-*vb*	mean, imply
1071	**trouble**-*m; adj*	disorder, trouble; dim
1072	**pomme**-*f*	apple
1073	**pourpre**-*adj*	purple
1074	**soir**-*m*	evening
1075	**soin**-*m*	care, carefulness
1076	**tarder**-*vb*	delay
1077	**frisé**-*adj*	curly
1078	**enseigner**-*vb*	teach, educate
1079	**fixement**-*adv*	fixedly
1080	**parfaitement**-*adv*	perfectly, thoroughly
1081	**indiquer**-*vb*	indicate, show
1082	**avaler**-*vb*	swallow
1083	**ennuyer**-*vb*	bore, annoy
1084	**noyer**-*m; vb*	walnut; drown
1085	**corinthe**-*f*	Corinth
1086	**remplacer**-*vb*	replace, change
1087	**magique**-*adj*	magic
1088	**mouton**-*m*	sheep
1089	**bain**-*m*	bath
1090	**fourrer**-*vb*	stick
1091	**étourdir**-*vb*	stun, surprise
1092	**éventer**-*vb*	fan
1093	**tracer**-*vb*	draw, mark
1094	**perpendiculairement**-*adv*	perpendicularly
1095	**boucler**-*vb*	buckle, fasten
1096	**occuper**-*vb*	occupy, hold
1097	**conserver**-*vb*	maintain
1098	**confusément**-*adv*	confusedly
1099	**cuiller**-*f*	spoon
1100	**soutenir**-*vb*	support, back
1101	**fagot**-*m*	bundle, faggot
1102	**éclat**-*m*	eclat, brightness
1103	**grelotter**-*vb*	shivering
1104	**addition**-*f*	addition, sum
1105	**maillet**-*m*	mallet
1106	**serrure**-*f*	lock
1107	**hé**-*i*	Hey
1108	**brasser**-*vb*	stir
1109	**culpabilité**-*f*	guilt
1110	**choix**-*m*	choice, selection
1111	**mesurer**-*vb*	measure
1112	**injustice**-*f*	injustice, unfairness
1113	**vinaigrer**-*vb*	souse
1114	**résoudre**-*vb*	solve, resolve
1115	**roseau**-*m*	reed
1116	**coucher**-*vb; m*	sleep, lay down; sunset
1117	**reposer**-*vb*	rest
1118	**gronder**-*vb*	scold, rumble
1119	**concombre**-*m*	cucumber
1120	**jointure**-*f*	joint
1121	**fournir**-*vb*	provide, afford
1122	**indifféremment**-*adv*	interchangeably
1123	**grandissant**-*adj*	growing
1124	**tortueux**-*adj*	tortuous
1125	**seize**-*num*	sixteen
1126	**chérubin**-*m*	cherub
1127	**calembour**-*m*	pun
1128	**tricher**-*vb*	cheat
1129	**évanouir**-*vb*	pass out

1130	**repas**-*m*	meal
1131	**garder**-*vb*	keep, maintain
1132	**confrère**-*m*	colleague
1133	**prétexte**-*m*	pretext, excuse
1134	**terminer**-*vb*	finish, conclude
1135	**ouvert**-*adj*	open
1136	**pensée**-*f*	thought
1137	**précieux**-*adj*	precious, valuable
1138	**fatigue**-*f*	fatigue, exhaustion
1139	**obligeance**-*f*	helpfulness
1140	**trépigner**-*vb*	sitting there all
1141	**assister**-*vb*	assist
1142	**câlinerie**-*f*	caress
1143	**ressortir**-*vb*	stand out
1144	**délicieux**-*adj*	delicious
1145	**douleur**-*f*	pain
1146	**merveilleux**-*adj*	wonderful
1147	**lâcher**-*vb*	release, drop
1148	**réunir**-*vb*	gather, reunite
1149	**fumer**-*vb*	smoke
1150	**sabler**-*vb*	sand
1151	**tremper**-*vb*	soak, dip
1152	**aider**-*vb*	help, support
1153	**méchant**-*adj; m*	wicked, bad; naughty child
1154	**avantageux**-*adj*	advantageous
1155	**larcin**-*m*	petty theft
1156	**biler**-*vb*	muse
1157	**faculté**-*f*	faculty, ability
1158	**monter**-*vb*	mount, climb
1159	**impossibilité**-*f*	impossibility
1160	**serein**-*adj; m*	serene; collection
1161	**ramener**-*vb*	bring back
1162	**sèchement**-*adv*	curtly
1163	**personnellement**-*adv*	personally
1164	**sommeil**-*m*	sleep, rest
1165	**congre**-*m*	conger
1166	**guetter**-*vb*	await
1167	**londre**-	London
1168	**refuser**-*vb*	refuse
1169	**arrivant**-*adj; m*	incoming; arrival
1170	**ignorant**-*adj; m*	ignorant; ignoramus
1171	**piétinement**-*m*	trampling
1172	**bercer**-*vb*	rock
1173	**inhumain**-*adj*	inhuman
1174	**écraser**-*vb*	crush, overwrite
1175	**moquer**-*vb*	mock
1176	**revue**-*m*	review
1177	**entourer**-*vb*	surround, enclose
1178	**rompre**-*vb*	break, break up
1179	**clarté**-*f*	clarity, lightness
1180	**écarter**-*vb*	exclude
1181	**orge**-*f*	barley
1182	**manquer**-*vb*	miss
1183	**parer**-*vb*	parry, ward off
1184	**pincer**-*vb*	pinch, pluck
1185	**rendormir**-*vb*	go back to sleep
1186	**ficelle**-*m*	twine
1187	**croyant**-*m; adj*	believer; god-fearing
1188	**aigu**-*adj*	acute, shrill
1189	**nommer**-*vb*	appoint, name
1190	**soufflet**-*m*	bellow
1191	**serrer**-*vb*	tighten, clamp
1192	**vil**-*adj*	vile, base
1193	**série**-*f*	series, set
1194	**embrasser**-*vb*	embrace, kiss
1195	**payer**-*vb*	pay
1196	**lampe**-*f*	lamp
1197	**server**-*m*	server
1198	**désirer**-*vb*	desire, wish
1199	**aigre**-*adj*	sour
1200	**rouvrir**-*vb*	reopen
1201	**perdreau**-*m*	partridge
1202	**berger**-*m*	shepherd
1203	**vraisemblable**-*adj*	similar
1204	**baigneur**-*m*	bather
1205	**brosse**-*f*	brush
1206	**nouvellement**-*adv*	newly
1207	**affection**-*f*	affection, ailment
1208	**brouiller**-*vb*	blur, scramble
1209	**tenter**-*vb*	try, attempt
1210	**trotter**-*vb*	trot
1211	**poudrer**-*vb*	powder
1212	**embrasure**-*f*	doorway
1213	**ménager**-*adj; vb*	household; spare
1214	**coûter**-*vb*	cost
1215	**rang**-*m*	rank, row
1216	**poêler**-*vb*	fry
1217	**plume**-*f*	feather
1218	**enfoncer**-*vb*	push, sink
1219	**permettre**-*vb*	allow, enable
1220	**aile**-*f*	wing, blade
1221	**sûrement**-*adv*	surely
1222	**boule**-*f*	ball
1223	**anglais**-*adj; m/npl*	English; English
1224	**mélancolie**-*f*	melancholy
1225	**creux**-*adj; m*	hollow, sunken; hollow
1226	**bref**-*adj; adv*	short, brief; in short
1227	**promener**-*vb*	promenade
1228	**ananas**-*m*	pineapple
1229	**familiarité**-*f*	Familiarity
1230	**sévèrement**-*adv*	severely
1231	**débarbouiller**-*vb*	wash up
1232	**auditoire**-*m*	audience

1233	**noter**-*vb*	note
1234	**braver**-*vb*	brave
1235	**couler**-*vb*	flow, cast
1236	**saigner**-*vb*	bleed
1237	**aveuglette**-*f*	blind
1238	**flamme**-*f*	flame
1239	**voisin**-*m; adj*	neighbor; neighboring
1240	**arithmétique**-*adj; f*	arithmetic; arithmetic
1241	**immédiat**-*adj*	immediate
1242	**pique**-*m; f*	spade; pike
1243	**guillotiner**-*vb*	guillotine
1244	**chevreau**-*m*	goat
1245	**étoile**-*f*	star
1246	**illustration**-*f*	illustration
1247	**renoncer**-*vb*	renounce, give up
1248	**abandonner**-*vb*	abandon, give up
1249	**tige**-*f*	stem, spindle
1250	**assoupir**-*vb*	dull
1251	**ricaner**-*vb*	sneer
1252	**sillon**-*m*	groove
1253	**patriote**-*m*	patriot
1254	**peigner**-*vb*	comb
1255	**convenir**-*vb*	admit, agree with
1256	**apaiser**-*vb*	appease, soothe
1257	**dessin**-*m*	drawing, design
1258	**chaleur**-*f*	heat
1259	**gratter**-*vb*	scratch, strum
1260	**aisance**-*f*	ease
1261	**friser**-*vb*	curl
1262	**tulipe**-*f*	tulip
1263	**intriguer**-*vb*	intrigue
1264	**consulter**-*vb*	consult, search
1265	**phrase**-*f*	phrase
1266	**fusée**-*m*	rocket, fuse
1267	**mériter**-*vb*	deserve, earn
1268	**attacher**-*vb*	attach, fasten
1269	**piquer**-*vb*	prick, sting
1270	**zigzag**-*m*	zigzag
1271	**promesse**-*f*	promise
1272	**imbécile**-*m/f; adj*	imbecile; stupid
1273	**dîner**-*m; vb*	dinner; dine
1274	**frayeur**-*f*	fear
1275	**trébuchant**-*adj*	stumbling
1276	**cligner**-*vb*	wink, blink
1277	**auquel**-*prn*	which
1278	**étaler**-*vb*	spread out, display
1279	**végétal**-*adj*	plant
1280	**joyeusement**-*adv*	merrily
1281	**paix**-*f*	peace
1282	**pape**-*m*	pope
1283	**papa**-*m*	papa
1284	**grotesque**-*adj; m*	grotesque; grotesque
1285	**adoption**-*f*	adoption, passage
1286	**haletant**-*adj*	panting
1287	**talus**-*m*	slope
1288	**sûreté**-*f*	safety
1289	**prince**-*m*	prince
1290	**discourir**-*vb*	discourse
1291	**rayon**-*m*	radius, ray
1292	**polir**-*vb*	polish, buff
1293	**brusquement**-*adv*	suddenly, sharply
1294	**cerise**-*adj; f*	cherry; cherry
1295	**intenter**-*vb*	bring
1296	**tape**-*f*	slap
1297	**dégringoler**-*vb*	plummet
1298	**tort**-*m*	wrong, harm
1299	**charrette**-*f*	cart
1300	**gênant**-*adj*	embarrassing
1301	**tentative**-*f*	attempt, bid
1302	**sauver**-*vb*	save
1303	**brin**-*m*	strand, sprig
1304	**errer**-*vb*	wander
1305	**vente**-*f*	sale
1306	**malice**-*f*	malice, mischief
1307	**bouleverser**-*vb*	upset, shake
1308	**conduire**-*vb*	lead, drive
1309	**préférer**-*vb; av*	prefer; would rather
1310	**poudre**-*f*	powder
1311	**chapeau**-*m*	hat
1312	**rejoindre**-*vb*	rejoin
1313	**réussir**-*vb*	succeed, pass
1314	**joindre**-*vb*	join, attach
1315	**révolution**-*f*	revolution
1316	**haleter**-*vb*	gasp
1317	**tourbillonner**-*vb*	swirl
1318	**esquiver**-*vb*	dodge, avoid
1319	**éteindre**-*vb*	turn off, put out
1320	**marmelade**-*f*	marmelade
1321	**traiter**-*vb*	treat, deal
1322	**antipathie**-*f*	antipathy
1323	**intervalle**-*m*	interval
1324	**étonnant**-*adj*	surprising, astonishing
1325	**dinde**-*f*	turkey
1326	**plaisant**-*adj*	pleasant
1327	**éclabousser**-*vb*	splash
1328	**tapir**-*m*	tapir
1329	**recevoir**-*vb*	receive, take
1330	**essayer**-*vb*	try, attempt
1331	**recueillir**-*vb*	collect, gather
1332	**vague**-*f; adj*	wave; vague
1333	**intervenant**-*m*	speaker, intervener
1334	**parterre**-*m*	flower bed
1335	**commettre**-*vb*	commit
1336	**adoucir**-*vb*	soften

1337	**frontispice**-*m*	frontispiece
1338	**usage**-*m*	use, usage
1339	**grondant**-*adj*	growling
1340	**facile**-*adj*	easy, simple
1341	**coupure**-*f; adj*	cut; clipping
1342	**disputer**-*vb*	compete, fight
1343	**âtre**-*m*	hearth
1344	**tuer**-*vb*	kill, murder
1345	**encourager**-*vb*	encourage
1346	**plainte**-*f*	complaint
1347	**peinturer**-*vb*	paint
1348	**fourrure**-*f*	fur
1349	**gosier**-*m*	throat, gullet
1350	**foudre**-*f*	lightning
1351	**protection**-*f*	protection
1352	**brûler**-*vb*	burn, burn off
1353	**vain**-*adj*	vain
1354	**goûter**-*vb*	taste
1355	**exercice**-*m*	exercise, fiscal year
1356	**anima**-*f*	anima
1357	**envelopper**-*vb*	envelop, wrap up
1358	**encourageant**-*adj*	encouraging
1359	**secret**-*adj; m*	secret, covert; secret
1360	**désagréable**-*adj*	unpleasant
1361	**fréquenter**-*vb*	patronize, frequent
1362	**ceci**-*prn; adj*	this; following
1363	**instruction**-*f*	instruction, education
1364	**errant**-*adj; m*	wandering; wanderer
1365	**camomille**-*f*	chamomile
1366	**projet**-*m*	project
1367	**troisième**-*num*	third
1368	**marmotter**-*vb*	mutter
1369	**ténébreux**-*adj*	gloomy
1370	**sensation**-*f*	sensation, feeling
1371	**plan**-*m; adj*	plan; plane
1372	**tournure**-*f*	twist, turning
1373	**autorité**-*f*	authority
1374	**éprouver**-*vb*	experience, test
1375	**formalité**-*f*	formality
1376	**charger**-*vb*	load, charge
1377	**clochette**-*f*	bell
1378	**rattraper**-*vb*	catch up, make up
1379	**débattre**-*vb*	discuss, debate
1380	**bottine**-*f*	bootie
1381	**visite**-*f*	visit
1382	**brun**-*adj; m*	brown; brown
1383	**citer**-*vb*	quote, mention
1384	**enrouer**-*vb*	to go hoarse
1385	**fromage**-*m*	cheese
1386	**féroce**-*adj*	fierce, savage
1387	**babiller**-*vb*	prattle on
1388	**roman**-*m; adj*	novel; Romance
1389	**ciel**-*m*	sky, heaven
1390	**massif**-*adj; m*	massive; massif
1391	**respect**-*m*	respect
1392	**pouf**-*m*	ottoman, beanbag
1393	**onzième**-*num*	eleventh
1394	**percher**-*vb*	perch, hang
1395	**sangloter**-*vb*	sob
1396	**impoli**-*adj*	impolite
1397	**supplier**-*vb*	beg, entreat
1398	**confiture**-*f*	jam
1399	**promis**-*adj*	promised
1400	**habilement**-*adv*	skilfully, cleverly
1401	**dénouer**-*vb*	resolve
1402	**accrocher**-*vb*	hang
1403	**plusieurs**-*adj*	several, divers
1404	**lécher**-*vb*	lick
1405	**partager**-*vb*	share, divide
1406	**propos**-*m*	talk
1407	**défier**-*vb*	challenge, defy
1408	**employer**-*vb*	use, employ
1409	**chauffer**-*vb*	heat
1410	**détester**-*vb*	hate
1411	**éclater**-*vb*	burst, erupt
1412	**côte**-*f*	coast
1413	**engageant**-*adj*	engaging
1414	**importance**-*f*	importance, significance
1415	**risque**-*m*	risk, hazard
1416	**grincement**-*m*	grinding, squeak
1417	**grâce**-*f*	grace, favor
1418	**hippopotame**-*m*	hippopotamus
1419	**replier**-*vb*	replicate, fold up
1420	**nageoire**-*f*	fin
1421	**imprimer**-*vb*	print, print out
1422	**convive**-*m*	guest
1423	**ôter**-*vb*	remove
1424	**reconnaître**-*vb*	recognize, admit
1425	**officier**-*m*	officer
1426	**somme**-*f*	sum
1427	**degré**-*m*	degree
1428	**imager**-*vb*	image
1429	**hourra**-*m*	cheer
1430	**lacune**-*f*	gap
1431	**enfuir**-*vb*	run away
1432	**arranger**-*vb*	arrange
1433	**domestique**-*adj; m/f*	domestic; domestic
1434	**océan**-*m*	ocean
1435	**effort**-*m*	effort, stress
1436	**fendre**-*vb*	split, slit
1437	**famille**-*f*	family
1438	**conquête**-*f*	conquest
1439	**paresseux**-*adj; m*	lazy; sloth
1440	**approuver**-*vb*	approve, endorse

1441	**déclarer**-*vb*	declare
1442	**grammaire**-*f*	grammar
1443	**luire**-*vb*	gleam, glisten
1444	**souffle**-*m*	breath, blast
1445	**souffler**-*vb*	breathe, whisper
1446	**prospectus**-*m*	prospectus
1447	**loisir**-*m*	leisure
1448	**toile**-*f*	web
1449	**roue**-*f*	wheel
1450	**baguette**-*f*	baguette, stick
1451	**éloignement**-*m*	remoteness
1452	**aspect**-*m*	aspect, appearance
1453	**ressourcer**-*vb*	rejuvenate
1454	**pinceau**-*m*	brush
1455	**grève**-*f*	strike
1456	**poivrière**-*f*	pepper shaker
1457	**désespérer**-*vb*	despair
1458	**ouverture**-*f*	opening
1459	**frotter**-*vb*	rub, scrub
1460	**grouper**-*vb*	group
1461	**conséquent**-*adj*	consequent
1462	**terriblement**-*adv*	terribly
1463	**cru**-*adj; m*	vintage, raw; vineyard
1464	**rafraîchissement**-*m*	refreshment
1465	**balai**-*m*	broom
1466	**irriter**-*vb*	irritate
1467	**chance**-*f*	chance, luck
1468	**bruisser**-*vb*	rustle
1469	**fureter**-*vb*	browse
1470	**choisir**-*vb*	choose
1471	**haïr**-*vb*	hate
1472	**accompagner**-*vb*	accompany, follow
1473	**hibou**-*m*	owl
1474	**membre**-*f*	member
1475	**dérouler**-*vb*	unwind, roll
1476	**mouiller**-*vb*	wet, anchor
1477	**immodérément**-*adv*	Immoderately
1478	**rapprocher**-*vb*	bring closer
1479	**trottiner**-*vb*	scurrying
1480	**saumon**-*m*	salmon
1481	**remuer**-*vb*	stir, move
1482	**combiner**-*vb*	combine, compound
1483	**grain**-*m*	grain
1484	**éducation**-*f*	education, upbringing
1485	**revoir**-*vb*	revise
1486	**grêle**-*f; adj*	hail; thin
1487	**lors**-*adv*	then, while
1488	**couvrir**-*vb*	cover, coat
1489	**empirer**-*vb*	worse
1490	**ébranler**-*vb*	shake, undermine
1491	**alarmer**-*vb*	alarm
1492	**dépêcher**-*vb*	dispatch
1493	**incontestable**-*adj*	indisputable
1494	**douzième**-*num*	twelfth
1495	**accusation**-*f*	charge, accusation
1496	**questionner**-*vb*	question
1497	**racine**-*f*	root
1498	**amicalement**-*adv*	friendly
1499	**mien**-*adj*	mine
1500	**imiter**-*vb*	imitate
1501	**encre**-*f*	ink
1502	**grincer**-*vb*	squeak, grind
1503	**suppliant**-*adj; m*	begging; suppliant
1504	**hein**-*i*	right
1505	**sourd**-*adj*	deaf, dull
1506	**susceptible**-*adj*	susceptible
1507	**résulter**-*vb*	result
1508	**dépit**-*m*	spite
1509	**vainement**-*adv*	in vain
1510	**prononcer**-*vb*	pronounce
1511	**marcher**-*vb*	walk, work
1512	**immédiatement**-*adv*	immediately
1513	**prévenir**-*vb*	warn, inform
1514	**dimension**-*f*	dimension, size
1515	**distinguer**-*vb*	distinguish
1516	**transformer**-*vb*	transform, change
1517	**fouler**-*vb*	tread
1518	**métamorphoser**-*vb*	metamorphose
1519	**maîtresse**-*f*	mistress
1520	**commodément**-*adv*	conveniently
1521	**entraîner**-*vb*	train, drive
1522	**berceau**-*m*	cradle, bed
1523	**théière**-*f*	teapot
1524	**efforcer**-*vb*	strive
1525	**touffu**-*adj*	furry
1526	**coureur**-*m; adj*	runner; racing
1527	**accourir**-*vb*	come running
1528	**chiffre**-*m*	figure, number
1529	**réduire**-*vb*	reduce, decrease
1530	**retomber**-*vb*	drop, relapse
1531	**canon**-*m*	gun
1532	**total**-*adj; m*	total, overall; total
1533	**événement**-*m*	event
1534	**redemander**-*vb*	ask again
1535	**mince**-*adj*	thin, slim
1536	**rideau**-*m*	curtain
1537	**rasseoir**-*vb*	sit down
1538	**énergique**-*adj*	energetic
1539	**miroir**-*m*	mirror
1540	**balancer**-*vb*	swing
1541	**désagréablement**-*adv*	unpleasantly
1542	**agripper**-*vb*	grip
1543	**violent**-*adj*	violent, severe
1544	**baiser**-*m; vb*	kiss; fuck

1545	**décrire**-*vb*	describe, depict
1546	**fixer**-*vb*	set, fix
1547	**bâillant**-*adj*	gaping
1548	**orateur**-*m*	speaker, orator
1549	**phoque**-*m*	seal
1550	**commander**-*vb*	order, command
1551	**convenable**-*adj*	suitable, appropriate
1552	**messager**-*m*	messenger
1553	**pair**-*adj; m*	even; peer
1554	**supporter**-*vb; m*	support, bear; supporter
1555	**alternativement**-*adv*	alternately
1556	**familièrement**-*adv*	colloquially
1557	**volte-face**-*f*	turnabout
1558	**femme**-*f*	woman
1559	**paroi**-*f*	wall
1560	**ténèbre**-*f*	darkness
1561	**versant**-*m*	hillslope
1562	**faiblement**-*adv*	low
1563	**dérision**-*f*	derision, mockery
1564	**féerie**-*f*	fairytale
1565	**dame**-*f*	dame
1566	**amer**-*adj; m*	bitter; bitter
1567	**cacher**-*vb*	hide, conceal
1568	**circonstance**-*f*	circumstance
1569	**rêveur**-*m; adj*	dreamer; dreamy
1570	**potage**-*m*	soup
1571	**opiniâtrement**-*adv*	stubbornly
1572	**groin**-*m*	snout
1573	**poursuivre**-*vb*	continue, pursue
1574	**remplir**-*vb*	fill, fill in
1575	**replacer**-*vb*	replace
1576	**embellir**-*vb*	embellish
1577	**découverte**-*f*	discovery
1578	**variant**-*m*	variant
1579	**innocent**-*adj; m*	innocent; innocent
1580	**déposer**-*vb*	deposit, file
1581	**découler**-*vb*	arise from
1582	**impatientant**-*adj*	impatient
1583	**journal**-*m*	newspaper, journal
1584	**promenade**-*f*	walk
1585	**solennellement**-*adv*	solemnly
1586	**erreur**-*f*	error, mistake
1587	**propice**-*adj*	suitable
1588	**gris**-*adj; m*	gray; gray
1589	**vapeur**-*m*	steam
1590	**amical**-*adj*	friendly
1591	**mentir**-*vb*	lie
1592	**relever**-*vb*	raise, pick up
1593	**défendre**-*vb*	defend, uphold
1594	**croquer**-*vb*	crunch, eat
1595	**velours**-*m*	velvet
1596	**hurlement**-*m*	howl, yell
1597	**rôtir**-*vb*	roast
1598	**renard**-*m*	fox
1599	**ennuyeux**-*adj*	boring, annoying
1600	**pelle**-*f*	shovel
1601	**mère**-*f*	mother
1602	**tapinois**-*adv*	stealthily
1603	**date**-*f*	date
1604	**assurer**-*vb*	ensure, insure
1605	**borner**-*vb*	restrict
1606	**tabouret**-*m*	stool
1607	**hardiment**-*adv*	boldly
1608	**manier**-*vb*	handle, use
1609	**réalité**-*f*	reality
1610	**indifférent**-*adj*	indifferent
1611	**politique**-*f; adj*	policy; political
1612	**mignon**-*adj*	cute, sweet
1613	**nœud**-*m*	node, knot
1614	**renverser**-*vb*	reverse, turn
1615	**renversé**-*adj*	reversed
1616	**agenouiller**-*vb*	kneel
1617	**hiver**-*m*	winter
1618	**instrument**-*m*	instrument, implement
1619	**interroger**-*vb*	question, examine
1620	**genre**-*m*	kind, gender
1621	**héraut**-*m*	herald
1622	**contenu**-*nm; adj*	content; content
1623	**distraction**-*f*	distraction, entertainment
1624	**contredire**-*vb*	contradict
1625	**campagne**-*f*	campaign
1626	**triomphant**-*adj*	triumphant
1627	**bondir**-*vb*	pounce
1628	**compère**-*m*	accomplice
1629	**tromper**-*vb*	deceive, mislead
1630	**aventurer**-*vb*	venture
1631	**moral**-*adj; m*	moral; morale
1632	**toucher**-*m; vb*	touch; touch
1633	**secourir**-*vb*	rescue
1634	**épuiser**-*vb*	exhaust, drain
1635	**tonnerre**-*m*	thunder
1636	**épargner**-*vb*	save
1637	**journée**-*f*	day
1638	**magnifique**-*adj*	magnificent
1639	**numéro**-*m*	number
1640	**mets**-*m*	dish
1641	**pincette**-*f*	pincette
1642	**quereller**-*vb*	quarrel
1643	**orange**-*adj*	orange
1644	**grimacer**-*vb*	wince
1645	**échelle**-*f*	scale, ladder
1646	**charge**-*f*	load, charge
1647	**ouvrier**-*m*	worker
1648	**centime**-*m*	centime

1649	**étouffer**-*vb*	stifle, smother
1650	**origine**-*f*	origin
1651	**vase**-*f*	vase
1652	**hasard**-*m*	chance, accident
1653	**insister**-*vb*	insist
1654	**collet**-*m*	collar, neck
1655	**carreau**-*m*	tile
1656	**latin**-*adj*	Latin
1657	**presser**-*vb*	press, squeeze
1658	**jouet**-*adj; m*	toy; toy
1659	**revenu**-*m*	income
1660	**clairière**-*f*	clearing
1661	**promptement**-*adv*	promptly
1662	**cinquième**-*adj*	fifth
1663	**désireux**-*adj*	eager
1664	**pluie**-*f*	rain
1665	**chiche**-*adj; i*	stingy; I dare you
1666	**outre**-*prp; f*	besides; skin
1667	**libre**-*adj*	free, open
1668	**bonté**-*f*	goodness
1669	**faillir**-*vb*	fail
1670	**peupler**-*vb*	populate
1671	**posément**-*adv*	calmly
1672	**coller**-*vb*	stick, glue
1673	**attaque**-*f*	attack
1674	**conseiller**-*m; vb*	advisor, counselor; advise
1675	**proposition**-*f*	proposal, proposition
1676	**vexer**-*vb*	vex, upset
1677	**insolence**-*f*	insolence
1678	**extérieur**-*adj; m*	outside, exterior; outside
1679	**contradictoirement**-*adv*	contradictorily
1680	**tribunal**-*m*	court, courthouse
1681	**veiller**-*vb*	watch
1682	**impertinent**-*adj*	impertinent
1683	**éclairer**-*vb*	light, enlighten
1684	**poivrer**-*vb*	pepper
1685	**solitaire**-*adj; m/f*	solitary; loner
1686	**congé**-*m*	leave
1687	**botter**-*vb*	kick
1688	**ligne**-*f*	line, design
1689	**clameur**-*f*	clamor, shouting
1690	**déplier**-*vb*	unfold
1691	**vide**-*adj; m*	empty; empty
1692	**meurtre**-*m*	murder
1693	**favori**-*adj; nm*	favorite; favorite
1694	**durer**-*vb*	last
1695	**reconnaissant**-*adj*	grateful
1696	**parade**-*f*	parade
1697	**ombre**-*m*	shadow
1698	**hérisser**-*vb*	bristle
1699	**grimper**-*vb*	climb, soar
1700	**fauve**-*nf; adj*	beast; tawny
1701	**sucrerie**-*f*	suger refinery
1702	**commission**-*f*	commission, board
1703	**pupitre**-*m*	desk
1704	**caractère**-*m*	character, nature
1705	**dédaigner**-*vb*	scorn
1706	**corde**-*f*	rope
1707	**précaution**-*f*	precaution
1708	**couver**-*vb*	smolder, brood
1709	**cabine**-*f*	cabin, cab
1710	**torrent**-*m*	torrent
1711	**éclair**-*m*	lightning
1712	**onguent**-*m*	ointment
1713	**apparition**-*f*	appearance
1714	**mener**-*vb*	lead, carry on
1715	**chuchotement**-*m*	whisper
1716	**disposer**-*vb*	dispose, arrange
1717	**premièrement**-*adv*	firstly
1718	**fondant**-*m; adj*	fondant; melting
1719	**sucre**-*m*	sugar
1720	**géographique**-*adj*	geographical
1721	**cervelle**-*f*	brain, brains
1722	**étagère**-*f*	shelf
1723	**plaindre**-*vb*	complain, pity
1724	**geler**-*vb*	freeze
1725	**coupé**-*adj*	disconnected
1726	**pruneau**-*m*	prune
1727	**circonspection**-*f*	caution, circumspection
1728	**essai**-*m*	test, testing
1729	**avantage**-*m*	advantage
1730	**cueillir**-*vb*	pick, collect
1731	**habitation**-*f*	home, habitation
1732	**jadis**-*adv*	once
1733	**sifflement**-*m*	whistling, hiss
1734	**abondance**-*f*	abundance
1735	**retrousser**-*vb*	roll up
1736	**rejeter**-*vb*	reject, dismiss
1737	**balancement**-*m*	swing
1738	**ramper**-*vb*	crawl, trail
1739	**marguerite**-*f*	daisy
1740	**hésiter**-*vb*	hesitate
1741	**encrier**-*m*	inkwell
1742	**rarement**-*adv*	rarely, hardly
1743	**évertuer**-*vb*	strive
1744	**sonore**-*f; adj*	sound; acoustic
1745	**anniversaire**-*adj; m*	anniversary; anniversary
1746	**fracasser**-*vb*	smash
1747	**repousser**-*vb*	repel, fend off
1748	**flamboyant**-*adj*	flamboyant
1749	**demain**-*adv; m*	tomorrow; tomorrow
1750	**triompher**-*vb*	triumph
1751	**véracité**-*f*	veracity
1752	**déboucher**-*vb*	unblock, cork off

1753	**peindre**-*vb*	paint
1754	**chérir**-*vb*	cherish
1755	**gibier**-*m*	game, prey
1756	**interruption**-*f*	interruption
1757	**ronfler**-*vb*	snore
1758	**accabler**-*vb*	overwhelm
1759	**casserole**-*f*	pan
1760	**tunnel**-*m*	tunnel
1761	**âgé**-*adj*	old
1762	**âne**-*m*	donkey
1763	**dévorer**-*vb*	devour, eat up
1764	**pendule**-*f*	pendulum
1765	**vingtième**-*num*	twentieth
1766	**suffire**-*vb*	suffice
1767	**centre**-*m*	center, focus
1768	**ébahir**-*vb*	astonish
1769	**vôtre**-*prn*	yours
1770	**professeur**-*m*	professor, teacher
1771	**muet**-*adj; m*	silent; mute
1772	**exclamation**-*f*	exclamation
1773	**général**-*adj; m*	general; general
1774	**normand**-*adj*	Norman
1775	**entortiller**-*vb*	wind, tangle
1776	**parcelle**-*f*	parcel, plot
1777	**établir**-*vb*	establish
1778	**tuile**-*f*	tile
1779	**piteux**-*adj*	sorry
1780	**fermier**-*m*	farmer
1781	**ouvrage**-*m*	handiwork
1782	**extrême**-*adj; m*	extreme; extreme
1783	**taquiner**-*vb*	tease
1784	**gambader**-*vb*	frolic
1785	**ancien**-*adj; m; pfx*	former, ancient; former; ex-
1786	**prison**-*f*	prison
1787	**souhaiter**-*vb*	wish, hope
1788	**blâme**-*m*	blame, reprimand
1789	**caresser**-*vb*	caress, stroke
1790	**français**-*adj; m/npl*	French; French
1791	**hésitant**-*adj*	hesitant
1792	**redresser**-*vb*	straighten, redress
1793	**machine**-*f*	machine
1794	**respectueux**-*adj*	respectful
1795	**danseur**-*m*	dancer
1796	**description**-*f*	description, depiction
1797	**anguille**-*f; adj*	eel; anguine
1798	**redevenir**-*vb*	become again
1799	**élancer**-*vb*	leap
1800	**émouvoir**-*vb*	move, stir
1801	**entamer**-*vb*	start, launch
1802	**papillon**-*m*	butterfly
1803	**principalement**-*adv*	mainly, mostly
1804	**orage**-*m*	storm
1805	**chrysalide**-*f*	chrysalis
1806	**enfantillage**-*m*	childishness
1807	**apparemment**-*adv*	apparently
1808	**partage**-*m*	sharing, division
1809	**abattre**-*vb*	down, slaughter
1810	**quatorze**-*num*	fourteen
1811	**désobéir**-*vb*	disobey
1812	**vert**-*adj; m*	green, young; putting green
1813	**repli**-*m*	withdrawal, fold
1814	**chaîne**-*f*	chain, string
1815	**inquisiteur**-*m; adj*	inquisitor; inquisitive
1816	**quarante**-*num*	forty
1817	**correct**-*adj; adv*	correct; alright
1818	**reculer**-*vb*	back, retreat
1819	**grimaçant**-*adj*	grimacing
1820	**précisément**-*adv*	precisely
1821	**conciliant**-*adj*	conciliatory
1822	**rhume**-*m*	cold
1823	**puissant**-*adj*	powerful, strong
1824	**nombreux**-*adj*	numerous
1825	**canari**-*m*	canary
1826	**heurter**-*vb*	hit, offend
1827	**volaille**-*f*	poultry, fowl
1828	**étrangler**-*vb*	strangle, choke
1829	**terreur**-*f*	terror
1830	**nonchalamment**-*adv*	casually
1831	**gêner**-*vb*	hinder
1832	**briller**-*vb*	shine, sparkle
1833	**recherche**-*f*	research, search
1834	**volontiers**-*adv*	willingly
1835	**respirer**-*vb*	breathe
1836	**hésitation**-*f*	hesitation
1837	**diamant**-*m*	diamond
1838	**mêler**-*vb*	mix, mingle
1839	**regret**-*m*	regret
1840	**raisonnablement**-*adv*	reasonably
1841	**ambition**-*f*	ambition
1842	**tordant**-*adj*	hilarious
1843	**conquérir**-*vb*	conquer
1844	**crainte**-*f*	fear
1845	**ému**-*adj*	affected
1846	**interpeller**-*vb*	question
1847	**jatte**-*f*	bowl
1848	**dès**-*prp*	from, since
1849	**vagabond**-*adj; m*	vagabond; vagabond
1850	**bataille**-*f*	battle
1851	**fauteuil**-*m*	armchair
1852	**lettre**-*f*	letter
1853	**stupide**-*adj; m*	stupid; stupid
1854	**préciser**-*vb*	specify, point out

1855	**cruel**-*adj*	cruel
1856	**intention**-*f*	intention, mind
1857	**flûte**-*f*	flute
1858	**entremêler**-*vb*	entangle
1859	**excellent**-*adj*	excellent
1860	**acte**-*m*	act, certificate
1861	**distance**-*f*	distance, range
1862	**farouche**-*adj*	fierce
1863	**prudemment**-*adv*	carefully
1864	**soumettre**-*vb*	submit, refer
1865	**évidemment**-*adv*	obviously
1866	**grossièreté**-*f*	rudeness
1867	**forêt**-*f*	forest
1868	**gentiment**-*adv*	kindly, gently
1869	**laid**-*adj*	ugly
1870	**forcer**-*vb*	force, compel
1871	**parfaire**-*vb*	perfect
1872	**essuyer**-*vb*	wipe, dry
1873	**espérance**-*f*	hope, expectation
1874	**tisonnier**-*m*	poker
1875	**demande**-*f*	request
1876	**bouton**-*m*	button
1877	**loi**-*f*	law
1878	**ajournement**-*m*	adjournment
1879	**turque**-*adj; nf*	Turkish; Turk
1880	**diriger**-*vb*	direct, run
1881	**bleu**-*adj; m*	blue; blue
1882	**diligemment**-*adv*	diligently
1883	**auditeur**-*m; adj*	auditor; auditorial
1884	**fumant**-*adj*	smoking
1885	**gorger**-*vb*	gorge
1886	**signature**-*f*	signature
1887	**cuivre**-*m*	copper
1888	**niaiser**-*vb*	run around
1889	**net**-*adj; adv*	net, sharp; outright
1890	**état**-*m*	state, condition
1891	**patauger**-*vb*	wade
1892	**déplaire**-*vb*	displease
1893	**causerie**-*f*	talk
1894	**ramage**-*f*	song
1895	**refermer**-*vb*	close
1896	**clair**-*adj*	clear, bright
1897	**aide**-*f*	aid, relief
1898	**noir**-*adj; m*	black; black
1899	**note**-*f*	note
1900	**moderne**-*adj*	modern
1901	**printemps**-*m*	spring
1902	**service**-*m*	service, serving
1903	**pis**-*m*	worse, udder
1904	**veille**-*f*	eve, day before
1905	**beuglement**-*m*	holler
1906	**aboyant**-*adj*	barking
1907	**fermement**-*adv*	firmly
1908	**plante**-*f*	plant
1909	**jean**-*m*	jeans
1910	**mûr**-*adj*	mature, grown
1911	**repasser**-*vb*	iron, replay
1912	**plaquer**-*vb*	stick, tackle
1913	**orner**-*vb*	adorn
1914	**vassal**-*m*	vassal
1915	**plaque**-*m*	plate
1916	**bateau**-*m*	boat
1917	**niaisement**-*adv*	foolishly
1918	**formé**-*adj*	formed, trained
1919	**mécontentement**-*m*	discontent
1920	**bouillir**-*vb*	boil
1921	**deuxièmement**-*num*	secondly
1922	**sol**-*m*	soil
1923	**Noël**-*m*	Christmas
1924	**rapporter**-*vb*	report, relate
1925	**inscrire**-*vb*	enroll, list
1926	**tas**-*m*	pile
1927	**tel**-*adj*	such
1928	**tir**-*m*	shot
1929	**toi**-*prn*	you
1930	**nougat**-*m*	nougat
1931	**clapoter**-*vb*	lap
1932	**marsouin**-*m*	porpoise
1933	**cruauté**-*f*	cruelty
1934	**dépendre**-*vb*	depend
1935	**raisin**-*m*	grape
1936	**conviction**-*f*	conviction, belief
1937	**lourd**-*adj*	heavy
1938	**lourder**-*vb*	kicked out
1939	**strident**-*adj*	shrill
1940	**troubler**-*vb*	disturb, trouble
1941	**truffer**-*vb*	fill
1942	**ver**-*m*	worm
1943	**courroucer**-*vb*	incur
1944	**lèvre**-*f*	lip
1945	**grognement**-*m*	grunt
1946	**griffe**-*f*	claw
1947	**occupant**-*m; adj*	occupant; occupying
1948	**sautant**-*adj*	jumping
1949	**laver**-*vb*	wash, launder
1950	**tourmenter**-*vb*	torment, plague
1951	**gracier**-*vb*	pardon
1952	**manche**-*m; f*	handle; sleeve
1953	**toilette**-*f*	toilet
1954	**proie**-*f*	prey, decoy
1955	**discuter**-*vb*	discuss
1956	**avenir**-*m*	future
1957	**départ**-*m*	departure, starting
1958	**ressemblance**-*f*	resemblance, likeness

1959	**grossier**-*adj*	coarse, rude
1960	**bestiaux**-*npl; adj*	livestock; beastly
1961	**sien**-*prn*	one's own
1962	**sérieux**-*adj; m*	serious; seriousness
1963	**assembler**-*vb*	assemble
1964	**fée**-*f; adj*	fairy; pixy
1965	**marin**-*adj; m*	marine; marine
1966	**usurpation**-*f*	usurpation
1967	**violemment**-*adv*	violently
1968	**joyeux**-*adj*	happy
1969	**légèrement**-*adv*	slightly, lightly
1970	**indiscrétion**-*f*	indiscretion
1971	**jusque**-*adv*	until
1972	**honnête**-*adj*	honest
1973	**faveur**-*f*	favor
1974	**faux**-*adj*	false, fake
1975	**voltigeant**-	flitting
1976	**drôlement**-*adv*	funnily
1977	**convenablement**-*adv*	properly
1978	**clou**-*m*	nail
1979	**tristesse**-*f*	sadness
1980	**servant**-*adj; nm*	useful; servant
1981	**échauffer**-*vb*	warm
1982	**parent**-*m; adj*	relative; kin
1983	**maxillaire**-*m*	jaw
1984	**chevelure**-*f*	hair
1985	**multiplication**-*f*	multiplication
1986	**chef**-*m*	chief, leader
1987	**frémir**-*vb*	tremble, shudder
1988	**inscription**-*f*	registration, entry
1989	**précédent**-*adj; m*	previous; precedent
1990	**insulter**-*vb*	insult, offend
1991	**récif**-*m*	reef
1992	**soigneusement**-*adv*	carefully
1993	**applaudissement**-*m*	cheering
1994	**gracieux**-*adj*	gracious, graceful
1995	**géographie**-*f*	geography
1996	**embrouillé**-*adj*	confused, muddled
1997	**battoir**-*m*	beater
1998	**arracher**-*vb*	snatch, extract
1999	**méthode**-*f*	method
2000	**minette**-*f*	kitty
2001	**aigrir**-*vb*	turn bitter
2002	**logis**-*m*	dwelling
2003	**miette**-*f*	crumb
2004	**perte**-*f*	loss, waste
2005	**raccourcir**-*vb*	shorten
2006	**sincèrement**-*adv*	truly, sincerely
2007	**gentil**-*adj; m*	nice, kind; gentile
2008	**treize**-*num*	thirteen
2009	**souriant**-*adj*	smiling
2010	**couteau**-*m*	knife
2011	**carton**-*m*	carton
2012	**minéral**-*adj; m*	mineral; mineral
2013	**correctement**-*adv*	correctly
2014	**sinon**-*con; adv*	otherwise; or else
2015	**joue**-*f*	cheek
2016	**trait**-*m*	trait
2017	**butte**-*f*	mound, butt
2018	**fils**-*m*	son
2019	**adieu**-*m*	farewell
2020	**nabot**-*m; adj*	runt; dwarfish
2021	**pencher**-*vb*	lean
2022	**favorite**-*adj*	favored
2023	**rassembler**-*vb*	gather, collect
2024	**serré**-*adj*	tight
2025	**feindre**-*vb*	pretend, put on
2026	**effleurer**-*vb*	touch
2027	**portraire**-*adj*	port

2028 **trace**-*f* trace, track
2029 **débarquer**-*vb* land, disembark
2030 **tintement**-*m* ringing
2031 **fameux**-*adj* famous
2032 **rouleau**-*m* roller, roll

French-English Dictionary

French-*Part of Speech*	Translation	IPA pronunciation
à-*prp*	to	[a]
abandonner-*vb*	abandon, give up	[abɑ̃dɔne]
abattre-*vb*	down, slaughter	[abatʁ]
aboiement-*m*	bark	[abwamɑ̃]
abondance-*f*	abundance	[abɔ̃dɑ̃s]
abord-*m*	first, start	[abɔʁ]
aboyant-*adj*	barking	[abwajɑ̃]
absence-*f*	absence	[apsɑ̃s]
absolument-*adv*	absolutely	[apsɔlymɑ̃]
accabler-*vb*	overwhelm	[akable]
accepter-*vb*	accept	[aksɛpte]
accès-*m*	access	[aksɛ]
accident-*m*	accident	[aksidɑ̃]
accompagner-*vb*	accompany, follow	[akɔ̃paɲe]
accourir-*vb*	come running	[akuʁiʁ]
accoutumer-*vb*	accustom	[akutyme]
accrocher-*vb*	hang	[akʁɔʃe]
accusation-*f*	charge, accusation	[akyzasjɔ̃]
accuser-*vb*	accuse, blame	[akyze]
acte-*m*	act, certificate	[akt]
addition-*f*	addition, sum	[adisjɔ̃]
adieu-*m*	farewell	[adjø]
admirablement-*adv*	admirably	[admiʁabləmɑ̃]
adoption-*f*	adoption, passage	[adɔpsjɔ̃]
adoucir-*vb*	soften	[adusiʁ]
adresse-*m*	address	[adʁɛs]
adresser-*vb*	address	[adʁese]
affaire-*f*	case, matter	[afɛʁ]
affairé-*adj*	busy	[afeʁe]
affairer-*vb*	attend, bustle about	[afeʁe]
affection-*f*	affection, ailment	[afɛksjɔ̃]
afin-*adv*	in order	[afɛ̃]
âge-*m*	age	[aʒ]
âgé-*adj*	old	[aʒe]
agenouiller-*vb*	kneel	[aʒnuje]
agir-*vb*	act	[aʒiʁ]
agiter-*vb*	shake, wave	[aʒite]
agréable-*adj*	pleasant, nice	[agʁeabl]
agripper-*vb*	grip	[agʁipe]
ah-*i*	ah	[a]
aide-*f*	aid, relief	[ɛd]
aider-*vb*	help, support	[ede]
aiglon-*m*	eaglet	[ɛglɔ̃]
aigre-*adj*	sour	[ɛgʁ]
aigrir-*vb*	turn bitter	[ɛgʁiʁ]
aigu-*adj*	acute, shrill	[egy]
aiguiller-*vb*	switch	[egɥije]
aile-*f*	wing, blade	[ɛl]
ailleurs-*adv*	somewhere else	[ajœʁ]
aimer-*vb*	love, like	[eme]
ainsi-*adv; con*	thus, thereby; as	[ɛ̃si]
air-*m*	air	[ɛʁ]
aisance-*f*	ease	[ɛzɑ̃s]
aise-*adj; f*	pleased; pleasure	[ɛz]
aisé-*adj*	easy, fluent	[eze]
ajournement-*m*	adjournment	[aʒuʁnəmɑ̃]
ajouter-*vb*	add	[aʒute]
alarmer-*vb*	alarm	[alaʁme]
aller-*vb*	go, travel	[ale]
allier-*vb*	combine	[alje]
allonger-*vb*	lengthen	[alɔ̃ʒe]
alors-*adv*	then	[alɔʁ]
alternativement-*adv*	alternately	[altɛʁnativmɑ̃]
ambition-*f*	ambition	[ɑ̃bisjɔ̃]
amer-*adj; m*	bitter; bitter	[amɛʁ]
ami-*m*	friend	[ami]
amical-*adj*	friendly	[amikal]
amicalement-*adv*	friendly	[amikalmɑ̃]
amour-*m*	love	[amuʁ]
amuser-*vb*	amuse, entertain	[amyze]
ananas-*m*	pineapple	[anana]
ancien-*adj; m; pfx*	former, ancient; former; ex-	[ɑ̃sjɛ̃]
âne-*m*	donkey	[an]
anglais-*adj; m/npl*	English; English	[ɑ̃glɛ]
anguille-*f; adj*	eel; anguine	[ɑ̃gij]
anima-*f*	anima	[anima]
animal-*adj; m*	animal; animal	[animal]
année-*f*	year	[ane]
anniversaire-*adj; m*	anniversary; anniversary	[anivɛʁsɛʁ]
antipathie-*f*	antipathy	[ɑ̃tipati]

apaiser-*vb*	appease, soothe	[apeze]
apercevoir-*vb*	see, perceive	[apɛʁsəvwaʁ]
apparemment-*adv*	apparently	[apaʁamɑ̃]
apparition-*f*	appearance	[apaʁisjɔ̃]
appartenir-*vb*	behove	[apaʁtəniʁ]
appeler-*vb*	call, appeal	[aple]
applaudir-*vb*	applaud, cheer	[aplodiʁ]
applaudissement-*m*	cheering	[aplodismɑ̃]
apporter-*vb*	bring	[apɔʁte]
apprendre-*vb*	learn, teach	[apʁɑ̃dʁ]
apprêter-*vb*	ready	[apʁete]
approcher-*vb*	hang over	[apʁɔʃe]
approuver-*vb*	approve, endorse	[apʁuve]
appuyer-*vb*	support, press	[apɥije]
après-*adv; prp*	after, next; after	[apʁɛ]
arbre-*m*	tree, shaft	[aʁbʁ]
arche-*f*	ark	[aʁʃ]
archevêque-*m*	Archbishop	[aʁʃəvɛk]
ardoise-*f*	slate	[aʁdwaz]
arithmétique-*adj; f*	arithmetic; arithmetic	[aʁitmetik]
armoire-*f*	cabinet	[aʁmwaʁ]
arracher-*vb*	snatch, extract	[aʁaʃe]
arranger-*vb*	arrange	[aʁɑ̃ʒe]
arrêt-*m*	stop, stopping	[aʁɛ]
arrêter-*vb*	stop, quit	[aʁete]
arrière-*adj; m*	rear, back; back	[aʁjɛʁ]
arrivant-*adj; m*	incoming; arrival	[aʁivɑ̃]
arriver-*vb*	arrive, happen	[aʁive]
aspect-*m*	aspect, appearance	[aspɛ]
assemblée-*f*	assembly	[asɑ̃ble]
assembler-*vb*	assemble	[asɑ̃ble]
asseoir-*vb*	sit	[aswaʁ]
assez-*adv*	enough, quite	[ase]
assiette-*f*	plate, dish	[asjɛt]
assister-*vb*	assist	[asiste]
assoupir-*vb*	dull	[asupiʁ]
assurément-*adv*	certainly	[asyʁemɑ̃]
assurer-*vb*	ensure, insure	[asyʁe]
atome-*m*	atom	[atom]
âtre-*m*	hearth	[atʁ]
attacher-*vb*	attach, fasten	[ataʃe]
attaque-*f*	attack	[atak]
atteindre-*vb*	reach, achieve	[atɛ̃dʁ]
attendre-*vb*	expect, wait for	[atɑ̃dʁ]
attention-*f*	attention	[atɑ̃sjɔ̃]
attraper-*vb*	catch, seize	[atʁape]
aucun-*adj; prn*	no; none	[okɛ̃]
auditeur-*m; adj*	auditor; auditorial	[oditœʁ]
auditoire-*m*	audience	[oditwaʁ]
auparavant-*adv*	before	[opaʁavɑ̃]
auprès-*adv*	nearby	[opʁɛ]
auquel-*prn*	which	[okɛl]
aussi-*adv; con*	also, as; and	[osi]
aussitôt-*adv*	immediately	[osito]
autant-*con*	as far as	[otɑ̃]
autorité-*f*	authority	[ɔtɔʁite]
autour-*adv*	around	[otuʁ]
autre-*prn; adj; adv*	other; another; else	[otʁ]
autrefois-*adv*	once, in the past	[otʁəfwa]
autrement-*adv*	otherwise	[otʁəmɑ̃]
avaler-*vb*	swallow	[avale]
avance-*f*	advance, lead	[avɑ̃s]
avancer-*vb*	advance, forward	[avɑ̃se]
avant-*adv; prp; adj; m*	before; before; front	[avɑ̃]
avantage-*m*	advantage	[avɑ̃taʒ]
avantageux-*adj*	advantageous	[avɑ̃taʒø]
avec-*prp*	with	[avɛk]
avenir-*m*	future	[avniʁ]
aventure-*f*	adventure	[avɑ̃tyʁ]
aventurer-*vb*	venture	[avɑ̃tyʁe]
aveuglette-*f*	blind	[avœglɛt]
avis-*m*	opinion, notice	[avi]
avoir-*vb; m*	have; asset	[avwaʁ]

B

babiller-*vb*	prattle on	[babije]
baguette-*f*	baguette, stick	[bagɛt]
bah-*i*	bah	[ba]
baigneur-*m*	bather	[bɛɲœʁ]
bâillant-*adj*	gaping	[bajɑ̃]
bâiller-*vb*	yawn	[baje]
bain-*m*	bath	[bɛ̃]
baiser-*m; vb*	kiss; fuck	[beze]
baisser-*vb*	lower, fall	[bese]
balai-*m*	broom	[balɛ]
balancement-*m*	swing	[balɑ̃smɑ̃]
balancer-*vb*	swing	[balɑ̃se]
banc-*m*	bench, bank	[bɑ̃]
bas-*adj; m*	low, base; bottom	[ba]
bataille-*f*	battle	[bataj]
bateau-*m*	boat	[bato]

bâton-*m*	stick, baton	[batɔ̃]
battoir-*m*	beater	[batwaʁ]
battre-*vb*	beat, fight	[batʁ]
beau-*adj; m*	beautiful, nice; beautiful	[bo]
beaucoup-*prn; adj; adv*	many; much; much	[boku]
bébé-*m*	baby, kid	[bebe]
berceau-*m*	cradle, bed	[bɛʁso]
bercer-*vb*	rock	[bɛʁse]
berger-*m*	shepherd	[bɛʁʒe]
besoin-*m*	need	[bəzwɛ̃]
bestiaux-*npl; adj*	livestock; beastly	[bɛstjo]
bête-*f; adj*	beast, idiot; stupid	[bɛt]
beuglement-*m*	holler	[bœgləmɑ̃]
beurrer-*vb*	butter	[bœʁe]
bien-*adv; m; adj*	well, very; good; right	[bjɛ̃]
bientôt-*adv*	soon, almost	[bjɛ̃to]
biler-*vb*	muse	[bile]
bis-*m; adv; adj*	bis; twice; repeat	[bis]
blâme-*m*	blame, reprimand	[blam]
blanc-*adj; m*	white, albescent; white	[blɑ̃]
blanchissage-*m*	laundry	[blɑ̃ʃisaʒ]
bleu-*adj; m*	blue; blue	[blø]
boire-*vb*	drink	[bwaʁ]
bois-*m*	wood, timber	[bwa]
boîte-*f*	box, can	[bwat]
bon-*adj; m; adv*	good, well; voucher; then	[bɔ̃]
bond-*m*	leap, jump	[bɔ̃]
bondir-*vb*	pounce	[bɔ̃diʁ]
bonheur-*m; adj*	happiness; welfare	[bɔnœʁ]
bonne-*f*	housemaid	[bɔn]
bonté-*f*	goodness	[bɔ̃te]
bord-*m*	edge, board	[bɔʁ]
borner-*vb*	restrict	[bɔʁne]
botter-*vb*	kick	[bɔte]
bottine-*f*	bootie	[bɔtin]
boucher-*m; vb*	butcher; plug	[buʃe]
boucler-*vb*	buckle, fasten	[bukle]
boudeur-*adj*	mopey	[budœʁ]
bouger-*vb*	move, budge	[buʒe]
bouillir-*vb*	boil	[bujiʁ]
boule-*f*	ball	[bul]
bouleverser-*vb*	upset, shake	[bulvɛʁse]
bourreau-*m*	executioner	[buʁo]
bourru-*adj*	gruff	[buʁy]
bout-*m*	end, toe	[bu]
bouteille-*f*	bottle	[butɛj]
bouton-*m*	button	[butɔ̃]
brancher-*vb*	connect	[bʁɑ̃ʃe]
bras-*m*	arm	[bʁa]
brasser-*vb*	stir	[bʁase]
braver-*vb*	brave	[bʁave]
bref-*adj; adv*	short, brief; in short	[bʁɛf]
brillant-*adj; m*	brilliant, bright; gloss	[bʁijɑ̃]
briller-*vb*	shine, sparkle	[bʁije]
brin-*m*	strand, sprig	[bʁɛ̃]
briser-*vb*	break, shatter	[bʁize]
brosse-*f*	brush	[bʁɔs]
brou-*m*	husk	[bʁu]
brouiller-*vb*	blur, scramble	[bʁuje]
bruisser-*vb*	rustle	[bʁɥise]
bruit-*m*	noise, sound	[bʁɥi]
brûler-*vb*	burn, burn off	[bʁyle]
brun-*adj; m*	brown; brown	[bʁɛ̃]
brusque-*adj*	sudden, brusque	[bʁysk]
brusquement-*adv*	suddenly, sharply	[bʁyskəmɑ̃]
butte-*f*	mound, butt	[byt]

C

çà-*prn*	it, that	[sa]
cabine-*f*	cabin, cab	[kabin]
cabriole-*f*	somersault	[kabʁijɔl]
cacher-*vb*	hide, conceal	[kaʃe]
cadeau-*m*	gift	[kado]
caillou-*m*	pebble	[kaju]
calembour-*m*	pun	[kalɑ̃buʁ]
câlinerie-*f*	caress	[kalinʁi]
calme-*adj; m*	quiet, calm; calm	[kalm]
camarade-*m/f*	comrade, fellow	[kamaʁad]
camomille-*f*	chamomile	[kamɔmij]
campagne-*f*	campaign	[kɑ̃paɲ]
canard-*m*	duck	[kanaʁ]
canari-*m*	canary	[kanaʁi]
canon-*m*	gun	[kanɔ̃]
capital-*adj; m*	capital; capital	[kapital]
car-*m*	car	[kaʁ]

caractère-*m*	character, nature	[kaʁaktɛʁ]
caressant-*adj*	caressing	[kaʁesɑ̃]
caresser-*vb*	caress, stroke	[kaʁese]
carnet-*m*	book	[kaʁnɛ]
carreau-*m*	tile	[kaʁo]
carte-*f*	map, card	[kaʁt]
carton-*m*	carton	[kaʁtɔ̃]
cas-*m*	case, event	[ka]
casser-*vb*	break, crack	[kase]
casserole-*f*	pan	[kasʁɔl]
cause-*f*	cause, case	[koz]
causer-*vb*	cause, chat	[koze]
causerie-*f*	talk	[kozʁi]
ce-*prn; adj*	this; that	[sə]
ceci-*prn; adj*	this; following	[səsi]
cela-*prn*	it, that	[səla]
celui-*prn*	that	[səlɥi]
centime-*m*	centime	[sɑ̃tim]
centre-*m*	center, focus	[sɑ̃tʁ]
cependant-*con; adv*	however, yet; though	[səpɑ̃dɑ̃]
cercle-*m*	circle, ring	[sɛʁkl]
cerise-*adj; f*	cherry; cherry	[səʁiz]
certain-*adj*	certain	[sɛʁtɛ̃]
certainement-*adv*	definitely	[sɛʁtɛnmɑ̃]
certes-*adv*	certainly	[sɛʁt]
cervelle-*f*	brain, brains	[sɛʁvɛl]
cesser-*vb*	stop, desist	[sese]
chacun-*prn; adv*	each; apiece	[ʃakɛ̃]
chagrin-*m*	grief, heartache	[ʃagʁɛ̃]
chaîne-*f*	chain, string	[ʃɛn]
chaleur-*f*	heat	[ʃalœʁ]
chambre-*f*	room	[ʃɑ̃bʁ]
champ-*m*	field	[ʃɑ̃]
champignon-*m*	mushroom	[ʃɑ̃piɲɔ̃]
chance-*f*	chance, luck	[ʃɑ̃s]
chandelle-*f*	candle	[ʃɑ̃dɛl]
changement-*m*	change, changing	[ʃɑ̃ʒmɑ̃]
changer-*vb*	change, switch	[ʃɑ̃ʒe]
chanson-*f*	song	[ʃɑ̃sɔ̃]
chantant-*adj*	singing	[ʃɑ̃tɑ̃]
chanter-*vb*	sing	[ʃɑ̃te]
chanteur-*m*	singer	[ʃɑ̃tœʁ]
chapeau-*m*	hat	[ʃapo]
chapelier-*m*	milliner	[ʃapəlje]
chapitre-*m*	chapter	[ʃapitʁ]
chaque-*adj; prn*	each; either	[ʃak]
chardon-*m*	thistle	[ʃaʁdɔ̃]
charge-*f*	load, charge	[ʃaʁʒ]
charger-*vb*	load, charge	[ʃaʁʒe]
charrette-*f*	cart	[ʃaʁɛt]
châssis-*m*	chassis	[ʃasi]
chat-*m*	cat	[ʃa]
chaud-*adj*	hot, warm	[ʃo]
chaudron-*m*	cauldron	[ʃodʁɔ̃]
chauffer-*vb*	heat	[ʃofe]
chauve-*adj*	bald	[ʃov]
chef-*m*	chief, leader	[ʃɛf]
chemin-*m*	path, road	[ʃəmɛ̃]
cheminer-*vb*	plod	[ʃəmine]
chenille-*f*	caterpillar	[ʃənij]
cher-*adj; m*	expensive, dear; dear	[ʃɛʁ]
chercher-*vb*	search, try	[ʃɛʁʃe]
chère-*adj*	dear	[ʃɛʁ]
chérir-*vb*	cherish	[ʃeʁiʁ]
chérubin-*m*	cherub	[ʃeʁybɛ̃]
cheval-*m*	horse	[ʃəval]
chevelure-*f*	hair	[ʃəvlyʁ]
cheveu-*m*	hair	[ʃəvø]
chevreau-*m*	goat	[ʃəvʁo]
chez-*prp*	in, by	[ʃe]
chiche-*adj; i*	stingy; I dare you	[ʃiʃ]
chien-*m*	dog	[ʃjɛ̃]
chiffre-*m*	figure, number	[ʃifʁ]
chœur-*m*	choir	[kœʁ]
choisir-*vb*	choose	[ʃwaziʁ]
choix-*m*	choice, selection	[ʃwa]
chose-*f*	thing	[ʃoz]
chrysalide-*f*	chrysalis	[kʁizalid]
chuchotement-*m*	whisper	[ʃyʃɔtmɑ̃]
chut-*i; nm*	hush!; shushing	[ʃy]
chuter-*vb*	tumble	[ʃyte]
ci-*adv*	this	[si]
ciel-*m*	sky, heaven	[sjɛl]
cinq-*num*	five	[sɛ̃k]
cinquième-*adj*	fifth	[sɛ̃kjɛm]
circonspection-*f*	caution, circumspection	[siʁkɔ̃spɛksjɔ̃]
circonstance-*f*	circumstance	[siʁkɔ̃stɑ̃s]
citer-*vb*	quote, mention	[site]
clair-*adj*	clear, bright	[klɛʁ]
clairement-*adv*	clearly	[klɛʁmɑ̃]
clairière-*f*	clearing	[klɛʁjɛʁ]
clameur-*f*	clamor, shouting	[klamœʁ]
clapoter-*vb*	lap	[klapɔte]
clarté-*f*	clarity, lightness	[klaʁte]
clef-*f; adj*	key; pivotal	[kle]

cligner-*vb*	wink, blink	[kliɲe]
clin-*m*	wink	[klɛ̃]
clochette-*f*	bell	[klɔʃɛt]
clou-*m*	nail	[klu]
cocasse-*adj*	funny	[kɔkas]
cocher-*vb; m*	check; coachman	[kɔʃe]
cochon-*m; adj*	pig, swine; dirty	[kɔʃɔ̃]
cœur-*m*	heart, core	[kœʁ]
coin-*m*	corner, wedge	[kwɛ̃]
colérer-*vb*	argue	[kɔleʁe]
colimaçon-*adj*	spiral	[kɔlimasɔ̃]
coller-*vb*	stick, glue	[kɔle]
collet-*m*	collar, neck	[kɔlɛ]
combien-*adv*	how many	[kɔ̃bjɛ̃]
combiner-*vb*	combine, compound	[kɔ̃bine]
commander-*vb*	order, command	[kɔmɑ̃de]
comme-*con; prp; adj*	as; as; such as	[kɔm]
commencement-*m*	beginning, start	[kɔmɑ̃smɑ̃]
commencer-*vb*	start, begin	[kɔmɑ̃se]
comment-*adv*	how	[kɔmɑ̃]
commettre-*vb*	commit	[kɔmɛtʁ]
commission-*f*	commission, board	[kɔmisjɔ̃]
commodément-*adv*	conveniently	[kɔmɔdemɑ̃]
commun-*adj*	common, joint	[kɔmɛ̃]
compagnie-*f*	company	[kɔ̃paɲi]
compère-*m*	accomplice	[kɔ̃pɛʁ]
complètement-*adv*	completely, fully	[kɔ̃plɛtmɑ̃]
comprendre-*vb*	understand, include	[kɔ̃pʁɑ̃dʁ]
compter-*vb*	count, expect	[kɔ̃te]
comte-*m*	count	[kɔ̃t]
concert-*m*	concert	[kɔ̃sɛʁ]
conciliant-*adj*	conciliatory	[kɔ̃siljɑ̃]
conclusion-*f*	conclusion	[kɔ̃klyzjɔ̃]
concombre-*m*	cucumber	[kɔ̃kɔ̃bʁ]
condamner-*vb*	condemn, convict	[kɔ̃dane]
conduire-*vb*	lead, drive	[kɔ̃dɥiʁ]
confiture-*f*	jam	[kɔ̃fityʁ]
confrère-*m*	colleague	[kɔ̃fʁɛʁ]
confus-*adj*	confused	[kɔ̃fy]
confusément-*adv*	confusedly	[kɔ̃fyzemɑ̃]
congé-*m*	leave	[kɔ̃ʒe]
congre-*m*	conger	[kɔ̃gʁ]
connaître-*vb*	know	[kɔnɛtʁ]
conquérir-*vb*	conquer	[kɔ̃keʁiʁ]
conquête-*f*	conquest	[kɔ̃kɛt]
conseil-*m*	board, council	[kɔ̃sɛj]
conseiller-*m; vb*	advisor, counselor; advise	[kɔ̃seje]
conséquent-*adj*	consequent	[kɔ̃sekɑ̃]
conserver-*vb*	maintain	[kɔ̃sɛʁve]
considérer-*vb*	consider	[kɔ̃sideʁe]
consulter-*vb*	consult, search	[kɔ̃sylte]
contempler-*vb*	contemplate	[kɔ̃tɑ̃ple]
content-*adj*	content, happy	[kɔ̃tɑ̃]
contenter-*vb*	satisfy	[kɔ̃tɑ̃te]
contenu-*nm; adj*	content; content	[kɔ̃tny]
conter-*vb*	tell	[kɔ̃te]
continuel-*adj*	continuous	[kɔ̃tinɥɛl]
continuer-*vb*	continue	[kɔ̃tinɥe]
contradictoirement-*adv*	contradictorily	[kɔ̃tʁadiktwaʁmɑ̃]
contre-*prp*	against	[kɔ̃tʁ]
contredire-*vb*	contradict	[kɔ̃tʁədiʁ]
convenable-*adj*	suitable, appropriate	[kɔ̃vənabl]
convenablement-*adv*	properly	[kɔ̃vənabləmɑ̃]
convenir-*vb*	admit, agree with	[kɔ̃vəniʁ]
conversation-*f*	conversation, talk	[kɔ̃vɛʁsasjɔ̃]
conviction-*f*	conviction, belief	[kɔ̃viksjɔ̃]
convive-*m*	guest	[kɔ̃viv]
corbeau-*m*	raven	[kɔʁbo]
corde-*f*	rope	[kɔʁd]
corinthe-*f*	Corinth	[kɔʁɛ̃t]
corps-*m*	body	[kɔʁ]
correct-*adj; adv*	correct; alright	[kɔʁɛkt]
correctement-*adv*	correctly	[kɔʁɛktəmɑ̃]
côte-*f*	coast	[kot]
côté-*m*	side	[kote]
cou-*m*	neck	[ku]
coucher-*vb; m*	sleep, lay down; sunset	[kuʃe]
coude-*m*	elbow, bend	[kud]
couler-*vb*	flow, cast	[kule]
coup-*m*	blow, shot	[ku]
coupé-*adj*	disconnected	[kupe]
couper-*vb*	cut	[kupe]
couplet-*m*	verse	[kuplɛ]
coupure-*f; adj*	cut; clipping	[kupyʁ]
cour-*f*	court	[kuʁ]
courage-*m*	courage	[kuʁaʒ]

courant-*adj; m*	current, running; current	[kuʁɑ̃]
courber-*vb*	bend	[kuʁbe]
coureur-*m; adj*	runner; racing	[kuʁœʁ]
courir-*vb*	run, race	[kuʁiʁ]
couronne-*f*	crown	[kuʁɔn]
courroucer-*vb*	incur	[kuʁuse]
course-*f*	race, running	[kuʁs]
court-*adj; m*	short, brief; court	[kuʁ]
courtisan-*m*	courtier	[kuʁtizɑ̃]
coussin-*m*	cushion	[kusɛ̃]
couteau-*m*	knife	[kuto]
coûter-*vb*	cost	[kute]
couver-*vb*	smolder, brood	[kuve]
couvert-*adj; m*	covered; place	[kuvɛʁ]
couvrir-*vb*	cover, coat	[kuvʁiʁ]
crabe-*m*	crab	[kʁab]
craindre-*vb*	fear	[kʁɛ̃dʁ]
crainte-*f*	fear	[kʁɛ̃t]
crayon-*m*	pencil	[kʁɛjɔ̃]
créature-*f*	creature, being	[kʁeatyʁ]
creux-*adj; m*	hollow, sunken; hollow	[kʁø]
cri-*m*	cry, scream	[kʁi]
criant-*adj*	crying	[kʁijɑ̃]
criard-*adj; nm*	garish; screamer	[kʁijaʁ]
crier-*vb*	shout, shriek	[kʁije]
croire-*vb*	believe, think	[kʁwaʁ]
croisé-*adj; m*	cross; crusader	[kʁwaze]
croiser-*vb*	cross, pass	[kʁwaze]
croquer-*vb*	crunch, eat	[kʁɔke]
croquet-*m*	croquet	[kʁɔkɛ]
croyant-*m; adj*	believer; god-fearing	[kʁwajɑ̃]
cru-*adj; m*	vintage, raw; vineyard	[kʁy]
cruauté-*f*	cruelty	[kʁyote]
cruel-*adj*	cruel	[kʁyɛl]
cueillir-*vb*	pick, collect	[kœjiʁ]
cuiller-*f*	spoon	[kyje]
cuillère-*f*	spoon	[kɥijɛʁ]
cuisine-*f*	kitchen, cuisine	[kɥizin]
cuisinière-*f*	cook	[kɥizinjɛʁ]
cuivre-*m*	copper	[kɥivʁ]
culpabilité-*f*	guilt	[kylpabilite]
curieux-*adj; m*	curious; onlooker	[kyʁjø]
curiosité-*f*	curiosity	[kyʁjozite]

D

dame-*f*	dame	[dame]
dans-*prp; adv*	in; aboard	[dɑ̃]
danser-*vb*	dance	[dɑ̃se]
danseur-*m*	dancer	[dɑ̃sœʁ]
date-*f*	date	[dat]
davantage-*adv*	further	[davɑ̃taʒ]
de-*prp*	of, from	[də]
dé-*pfx*	un-, in-	[de]
débarbouiller-*vb*	wash up	[debaʁbuje]
débarquer-*vb*	land, disembark	[debaʁke]
débarrasser-*vb*	rid	[debaʁase]
débattre-*vb*	discuss, debate	[debatʁ]
déboucher-*vb*	unblock, cork off	[debuʃe]
debout-*adj*	standing	[dəbu]
décapiter-*vb*	decapitate	[dekapite]
décider-*vb*	decide, choose	[deside]
déclarer-*vb*	declare	[deklaʁe]
découler-*vb*	arise from	[dekule]
découverte-*f*	discovery	[dekuvɛʁt]
découvrir-*vb*	discover	[dekuvʁiʁ]
décrire-*vb*	describe, depict	[dekʁiʁ]
dédaigner-*vb*	scorn	[dedeɲe]
dédain-*m*	disdain	[dedɛ̃]
dedans-*adv; prp; m*	in; in; inside	[dədɑ̃]
défendre-*vb*	defend, uphold	[defɑ̃dʁ]
défier-*vb*	challenge, defy	[defje]
degré-*m*	degree	[dəgʁe]
dégringoler-*vb*	plummet	[degʁɛ̃gɔle]
dehors-*adv; m*	outside, out; outside	[dəɔʁ]
déjà-*adv*	already	[deʒa]
délibérer-*vb*	deliberate	[delibeʁe]
délicieux-*adj*	delicious	[delisjø]
demain-*adv; m*	tomorrow; tomorrow	[dəmɛ̃]
demande-*f*	request	[dəmɑ̃d]
demander-*vb*	request, seek	[dəmɑ̃de]
demeurer-*vb*	remain, dwell	[dəmœʁe]
demi-*adj; m*	half; half	[dəmi]
demie-*f*	half	[dəmi]
demoiselle-*f*	young lady	[dəmwazɛl]
dénouer-*vb*	resolve	[denwe]
dent-*f*	tooth	[dɑ̃]
départ-*m*	departure, starting	[depaʁ]
dépêcher-*vb*	dispatch	[depeʃe]
dépendre-*vb*	depend	[depɑ̃dʁ]
dépit-*m*	spite	[depi]

déplaire-*vb*	displease	[deplɛʁ]
déplier-*vb*	unfold	[deplije]
déposer-*vb*	deposit, file	[depoze]
déposition-*f*	deposition	[depozisjɔ̃]
depuis-*adv; prp*	since; since	[dəpɥi]
dérision-*f*	derision, mockery	[deʁizjɔ̃]
dernier-*adj; m*	last, latter; last	[dɛʁnje]
dérouler-*vb*	unwind, roll	[deʁule]
derrière-*adv; m; prp*	behind; behind; behind	[dɛʁjɛʁ]
dès-*prp*	from, since	[dɛ]
désagréable-*adj*	unpleasant	[dezagʁeabl]
désagréablement-*adv*	unpleasantly	[dezagʁeabləmɑ̃]
descendre-*vb*	descend, get off	[desɑ̃dʁ]
description-*f*	description, depiction	[dɛskʁipsjɔ̃]
désespérer-*vb*	despair	[dezɛspeʁe]
désirer-*vb*	desire, wish	[deziʁe]
désireux-*adj*	eager	[deziʁø]
désobéir-*vb*	disobey	[dezɔbeiʁ]
désordre-*m*	disorder	[dezɔʁdʁ]
dessin-*m*	drawing, design	[desɛ̃]
dessous-*adv; m; prp*	beneath; underside; under it	[dəsu]
dessus-*adv*	over	[dəsy]
détester-*vb*	hate	[detɛste]
détour-*m*	detour, bend	[detuʁ]
deux-*num*	two	[dø]
deuxièmement-*num*	secondly	[døzjɛmmɑ̃]
devant-*adv; prp; m*	before, past; before; front	[dəvɑ̃]
devenir-*vb*	become, be	[dəvəniʁ]
deviner-*vb*	guess, divine	[dəvine]
devoir-*m; vb; av*	duty; have to; must	[dəvwaʁ]
dévorer-*vb*	devour, eat up	[devɔʁe]
dialoguer-*vb*	dialogue	[djalɔge]
diamant-*m*	diamond	[djamɑ̃]
différent-*adj*	different	[difeʁɑ̃]
difficile-*adj*	difficult	[difisil]
difficulté-*f*	difficulty	[difikylte]
diligemment-*adv*	diligently	[diliʒamɑ̃]
dimension-*f*	dimension, size	[dimɑ̃sjɔ̃]
diminuer-*vb*	decrease, reduce	[diminɥe]
dinde-*f*	turkey	[dɛ̃d]
dîner-*m; vb*	dinner; dine	[dine]
dire-*vb*	say, speak	[diʁ]
direction-*f*	direction, management	[diʁɛksjɔ̃]
diriger-*vb*	direct, run	[diʁiʒe]
discourir-*vb*	discourse	[diskuʁiʁ]
discussion-*f*	discussion, debate	[diskysjɔ̃]
discuter-*vb*	discuss	[diskyte]
disparaître-*vb*	disappear	[dispaʁɛtʁ]
disposer-*vb*	dispose, arrange	[dispoze]
disputer-*vb*	compete, fight	[dispyte]
distance-*f*	distance, range	[distɑ̃s]
distinguer-*vb*	distinguish	[distɛ̃ge]
distraction-*f*	distraction, entertainment	[distʁaksjɔ̃]
dix-*num*	ten	[dis]
dodo-*m*	dodo, sleep	[dodo]
doigt-*m*	finger	[dwa]
domestique-*adj; m/f*	domestic; domestic	[dɔmɛstik]
dommage-*m*	damage, pity	[dɔmaʒ]
donc-*con; adv*	therefore; consequently	[dɔ̃k]
donner-*vb*	give, yield	[dɔne]
dont-*prn*	whose	[dɔ̃]
dorloter-*vb*	pamper, mother	[dɔʁlɔte]
dormant-*adj*	dormant	[dɔʁmɑ̃]
dormir-*vb*	sleep	[dɔʁmiʁ]
dos-*m*	back, reverse	[do]
doucement-*adv*	gently, slowly	[dusmɑ̃]
douleur-*f*	pain	[dulœʁ]
douter-*vb*	doubt	[dute]
doux-*adj*	soft, sweet	[du]
douze-*num*	twelve	[duz]
douzième-*num*	twelfth	[duzjɛm]
dragée-*m*	lozenge	[dʁaʒe]
dresser-*vb*	draw up, develop	[dʁese]
droit-*adj; m; adv*	right; right; due	[dʁwa]
drôle-*adj*	funny	[dʁol]
drôlement-*adv*	funnily	[dʁolmɑ̃]
duchesse-*f*	duchess	[dyʃɛs]
durer-*vb*	last	[dyʁe]

E

eau-*f*	water	[o]
ébahir-*vb*	astonish	[ebaiʁ]
ébranler-*vb*	shake, undermine	[ebʁɑ̃le]
écarter-*vb*	exclude	[ekaʁte]

échapper-*vb*	escape	[eʃape]
échauffer-*vb*	warm	[eʃofe]
échelle-*f*	scale, ladder	[eʃɛl]
éclabousser-*vb*	splash	[eklabuse]
éclair-*m*	lightning	[eklɛʁ]
éclairer-*vb*	light, enlighten	[ekleʁe]
éclat-*m*	eclat, brightness	[ekla]
éclater-*vb*	burst, erupt	[eklate]
école-*f*	school	[ekɔl]
écouter-*vb*	listen, hear	[ekute]
écraser-*vb*	crush, overwrite	[ekʁaze]
écrier-*vb*	cry	[ekʁije]
écrire-*vb*	write	[ekʁiʁ]
écriture-*f*	writing	[ekʁityʁ]
éducation-*f*	education, upbringing	[edykasjɔ̃]
effet-*m*	effect	[efɛ]
effleurer-*vb*	touch	[eflœʁe]
efforcer-*vb*	strive	[efɔʁse]
effort-*m*	effort, stress	[efɔʁ]
effrayer-*vb*	scare, spook	[efʁeje]
égal-*adj; m*	equal, even; equal	[egal]
eh-*i*	eh	[e]
élancer-*vb*	leap	[elɑ̃se]
élever-*vb*	raise, elevate	[elve]
elle-*prn*	she, it	[ɛl]
éloignement-*m*	remoteness	[elwaɲmɑ̃]
éloigner-*vb*	drive away	[elwaɲe]
embarras-*m*	embarrassment	[ɑ̃baʁa]
embarrassant-*adj*	embarrassing	[ɑ̃baʁasɑ̃]
embarrasser-*vb*	embarrass, bother	[ɑ̃baʁase]
embellir-*vb*	embellish	[ɑ̃beliʁ]
embrasser-*vb*	embrace, kiss	[ɑ̃bʁase]
embrasure-*f*	doorway	[ɑ̃bʁazyʁ]
embrouillé-*adj*	confused, muddled	[ɑ̃bʁuje]
embrouiller-*vb*	confuse	[ɑ̃bʁuje]
émouvoir-*vb*	move, stir	[emuvwaʁ]
empêcher-*vb*	prevent, stop	[ɑ̃peʃe]
emphase-*f*	emphasis	[ɑ̃faz]
empirer-*vb*	worse	[ɑ̃piʁe]
employer-*vb*	use, employ	[ɑ̃plwaje]
emporter-*vb*	take, take away	[ɑ̃pɔʁte]
empressement-*m*	willingness	[ɑ̃pʁɛsmɑ̃]
empresser-*vb*	hasten	[ɑ̃pʁese]
ému-*adj*	affected	[emy]
en-*prp; adv*	in; thereof	[ɑ̃]
enchanter-*vb*	enchant, rejoice	[ɑ̃ʃɑ̃te]
encore-*adv*	still, again	[ɑ̃kɔʁ]
encourageant-*adj*	encouraging	[ɑ̃kuʁaʒɑ̃]
encourager-*vb*	encourage	[ɑ̃kuʁaʒe]
encre-*f*	ink	[ɑ̃kʁ]
encrier-*m*	inkwell	[ɑ̃kʁije]
endormir-*vb*	put to sleep	[ɑ̃dɔʁmiʁ]
endroit-*m*	place, spot	[ɑ̃dʁwa]
énergique-*adj*	energetic	[enɛʁʒik]
enfance-*f*	childhood	[ɑ̃fɑ̃s]
enfant-*m*	child	[ɑ̃fɑ̃]
enfantillage-*m*	childishness	[ɑ̃fɑ̃tijaʒ]
enfin-*adv*	finally, after all	[ɑ̃fɛ̃]
enfoncer-*vb*	push, sink	[ɑ̃fɔ̃se]
enfuir-*vb*	run away	[ɑ̃fɥiʁ]
engageant-*adj*	engaging	[ɑ̃gaʒɑ̃]
énigme-*f*	enigma, puzzle	[enigm]
enlever-*vb*	remove, take off	[ɑ̃lve]
ennui-*m*	boredom, trouble	[ɑ̃nɥi]
ennuyer-*vb*	bore, annoy	[ɑ̃nɥije]
ennuyeux-*adj*	boring, annoying	[ɑ̃nɥijø]
énorme-*adj*	huge, enormous	[enɔʁm]
enrouer-*vb*	to go hoarse	[ɑ̃ʁwe]
enseigner-*vb*	teach, educate	[ɑ̃seɲe]
ensemble-*adv; m; f*	together; ensemble; collection	[ɑ̃sɑ̃bl]
ensuite-*adv*	then, later	[ɑ̃sɥit]
entamer-*vb*	start, launch	[ɑ̃tame]
entendre-*vb*	hear	[ɑ̃tɑ̃dʁ]
entier-*adj*	whole, full	[ɑ̃tje]
entortiller-*vb*	wind, tangle	[ɑ̃tɔʁtije]
entourer-*vb*	surround, enclose	[ɑ̃tuʁe]
entraîner-*vb*	train, drive	[ɑ̃tʁene]
entre-*adv; prp*	between; between	[ɑ̃tʁ]
entrée-*f*	input, entry	[ɑ̃tʁe]
entremêler-*vb*	entangle	[ɑ̃tʁəmele]
entrer-*vb*	enter	[ɑ̃tʁe]
envelopper-*vb*	envelop, wrap up	[ɑ̃vlɔpe]
envie-*f*	desire	[ɑ̃vi]
environ-*adv; prp; adj*	about; around; all but	[ɑ̃viʁɔ̃]
envoyer-*vb*	send, forward	[ɑ̃vwaje]
épargner-*vb*	save	[epaʁɲe]

épaule-*f*	shoulder	[epol]
épouser-*vb*	marry	[epuze]
épouvante-*f*	dread	[epuvɑ̃t]
éprouver-*vb*	experience, test	[epʁuve]
épuiser-*vb*	exhaust, drain	[epɥize]
errant-*adj; m*	wandering; wanderer	[eʁɑ̃]
errer-*vb*	wander	[eʁe]
erreur-*f*	error, mistake	[eʁœʁ]
escalier-*m*	staircase, stairs	[ɛskalje]
espèce-*f*	species, kind	[ɛspɛs]
espérance-*f*	hope, expectation	[ɛspeʁɑ̃s]
espérer-*vb*	hope, expect	[ɛspeʁe]
esprit-*m*	mind, spirit	[ɛspʁi]
esquiver-*vb*	dodge, avoid	[ɛskive]
essai-*m*	test, testing	[esɛ]
essayer-*vb*	try, attempt	[eseje]
essuyer-*vb*	wipe, dry	[esɥije]
et-*con*	and	[e]
établir-*vb*	establish	[etabliʁ]
étagère-*f*	shelf	[etaʒɛʁ]
étai-*f*	strut	[etɛ]
étaler-*vb*	spread out, display	[etale]
état-*m*	state, condition	[eta]
éteindre-*vb*	turn off, put out	[etɛ̃dʁ]
étendre-*vb*	extend, expand	[etɑ̃dʁ]
éternuement-*m*	sneeze	[etɛʁnymɑ̃]
éternuer-*vb*	sneeze	[etɛʁnɥe]
étiquette-*f*	label, etiquette	[etikɛt]
étoile-*f*	star	[etwal]
étonnant-*adj*	surprising, astonishing	[etɔnɑ̃]
étonnement-*m; adv*	astonishment; surprisingly	[etɔnmɑ̃]
étonner-*vb*	surprise, wonder	[etɔne]
étouffer-*vb*	stifle, smother	[etufe]
étourdir-*vb*	stun, surprise	[etuʁdiʁ]
étrange-*adj*	strange	[etʁɑ̃ʒ]
étranger-*adj; m*	foreign, overseas; foreigner	[etʁɑ̃ʒe]
étrangler-*vb*	strangle, choke	[etʁɑ̃gle]
être-*vb*	be, exist	[ɛtʁ]
étroit-*adj*	narrow, close	[etʁwa]
eux-*prn*	them	[ø]
évanouir-*vb*	pass out	[evanwiʁ]
événement-*m*	event	[evɛnmɑ̃]
éventail-*m*	range	[evɑ̃taj]
éventer-*vb*	fan	[evɑ̃te]
évertuer-*vb*	strive	[evɛʁtɥe]
évidemment-*adv*	obviously	[evidamɑ̃]
examiner-*vb*	examine	[ɛgzamine]
excellent-*adj*	excellent	[ɛksɛlɑ̃]
exception-*f*	exception	[ɛksɛpsjɔ̃]
exclamation-*f*	exclamation	[ɛksklamasjɔ̃]
exécuter-*vb*	execute	[ɛgzekyte]
exécution-*f*	execution, implementation	[ɛgzekysjɔ̃]
exemple-*m*	example, sample	[ɛgzɑ̃pl]
exercice-*m*	exercise, fiscal year	[ɛgzɛʁsis]
exister-*vb*	exist	[ɛgziste]
explication-*f*	explanation, explication	[ɛksplikasjɔ̃]
expliquer-*vb*	explain	[ɛksplike]
exprimer-*vb*	express, voice	[ɛkspʁime]
extérieur-*adj; m*	outside, exterior; outside	[ɛksteʁjœʁ]
extraordinaire-*adj*	extraordinary	[ɛkstʁaɔʁdinɛʁ]
extrême-*adj; m*	extreme; extreme	[ɛkstʁɛm]

F

fable-*f*	fable	[fabl]
face-*f*	face, front	[fas]
fâcher-*vb*	upset	[faʃe]
facile-*adj*	easy, simple	[fasil]
façon-*f*	way, method	[fasɔ̃]
faculté-*f*	faculty, ability	[fakylte]
fagot-*m*	bundle, faggot	[fago]
faible-*adj; m*	low, weak; weakling	[fɛbl]
faiblement-*adv*	low	[fɛbləmɑ̃]
faillir-*vb*	fail	[fajiʁ]
faim-*f*	hunger	[fɛ̃]
faire-*vb*	do	[fɛʁ]
falloir-*vb*	have to	[falwaʁ]
fameux-*adj*	famous	[famø]
familiarité-*f*	Familiarity	[familjaʁite]
familièrement-*adv*	colloquially	[familjɛʁmɑ̃]
famille-*f*	family	[famij]
farce-*f*	farce, joke	[faʁs]
farouche-*adj*	fierce	[faʁuʃ]
fatigue-*f*	fatigue, exhaustion	[fatig]

fatiguer-*vb*	tire, stress	[fatige]
fausser-*vb*	distort, skew	[fose]
faute-*f*	fault	[fot]
fauteuil-*m*	armchair	[fotœj]
fauve-*nf; adj*	beast; tawny	[fov]
faux-*adj*	false, fake	[fo]
faveur-*f*	favor	[favœʁ]
favori-*adj; nm*	favorite; favorite	[favɔʁi]
favorite-*adj*	favored	[favɔʁit]
fée-*f; adj*	fairy; pixy	[fe]
féerie-*f*	fairytale	[feeʁi]
feindre-*vb*	pretend, put on	[fɛ̃dʁ]
femme-*f*	woman	[fam]
fendre-*vb*	split, slit	[fɑ̃dʁ]
fenêtre-*f*	window	[fənɛtʁ]
fer-*m*	iron	[fɛʁ]
ferme-*f; adj*	farm; firm	[fɛʁm]
fermé-*adj*	closed, sealed	[fɛʁme]
fermement-*adv*	firmly	[fɛʁməmɑ̃]
fermer-*vb*	close	[fɛʁme]
fermier-*m*	farmer	[fɛʁmje]
féroce-*adj*	fierce, savage	[feʁɔs]
feu-*m*	fire	[fø]
feuille-*f*	sheet, leaf	[fœj]
ficelle-*m*	twine	[fisɛl]
fier-*adj*	proud	[fjɛʁ]
figurer-*vb*	figure	[figyʁe]
fille-*f*	daughter, girl	[fij]
fils-*m*	son	[fis]
fin-*f; adj*	end; fine	[fɛ̃]
fini-*adj; m*	finished, finite; finish	[fini]
finir-*vb*	end, finish	[finiʁ]
fixé-*adj*	fixed, appointed	[fikse]
fixement-*adv*	fixedly	[fiksəmɑ̃]
fixer-*vb*	set, fix	[fikse]
flamant-*m*	flamingo	[flamɑ̃]
flamboyant-*adj*	flamboyant	[flɑ̃bwajɑ̃]
flamme-*f*	flame	[flam]
fleur-*f*	flower	[flœʁ]
flûte-*f*	flute	[flyte]
foi-*f*	faith	[fwa]
fois-*f*	time	[fwa]
fond-*m*	bottom	[fɔ̃]
fondant-*m; adj*	fondant; melting	[fɔ̃dɑ̃]
fontaine-*f*	fountain, spring	[fɔ̃tɛn]
forcé-*adj*	forced	[fɔʁse]
forcer-*vb*	force, compel	[fɔʁse]
forêt-*f*	forest	[fɔʁɛ]
formalité-*f*	formality	[fɔʁmalite]
formé-*adj*	formed, trained	[fɔʁme]
former-*vb*	form, train	[fɔʁme]
fort-*adj; m; adv*	strong, loud; fort; highly	[fɔʁ]
fortement-*adv*	strongly	[fɔʁtəmɑ̃]
fou-*adj; m*	crazy; fool	[fu]
foudre-*f*	lightning	[fudʁ]
foule-*f*	crowd, host	[ful]
fouler-*vb*	tread	[fule]
fournir-*vb*	provide, afford	[fuʁniʁ]
fourrer-*vb*	stick	[fuʁe]
fourrure-*f*	fur	[fuʁyʁ]
foyer-*m*	home, fireplace	[fwaje]
fracas-*m*	crash, smash	[fʁaka]
fracasser-*vb*	smash	[fʁakase]
frais-*npl; adj*	costs; fresh	[fʁɛ]
franc-*adj; m*	frank; franc	[fʁɑ̃]
français-*adj; m/npl*	French; French	[fʁɑ̃sɛ]
franchement-*adv*	honestly, openly	[fʁɑ̃ʃmɑ̃]
frapper-*vb*	hit, knock	[fʁape]
frayeur-*f*	fear	[fʁɛjœʁ]
frémir-*vb*	tremble, shudder	[fʁemiʁ]
fréquenter-*vb*	patronize, frequent	[fʁekɑ̃te]
frère-*m*	brother	[fʁɛʁ]
frisé-*adj*	curly	[fʁize]
friser-*vb*	curl	[fʁize]
fromage-*m*	cheese	[fʁɔmaʒ]
froncer-*vb*	frown	[fʁɔ̃se]
front-*m*	front, forehead	[fʁɔ̃]
frontispice-*m*	frontispiece	[fʁɔ̃tispis]
frotter-*vb*	rub, scrub	[fʁɔte]
fumant-*adj*	smoking	[fymɑ̃]
fumer-*vb*	smoke	[fyme]
furet-*m*	ferret	[fyʁɛ]
fureter-*vb*	browse	[fyʁte]
furieux-*adj; m*	furious; madman	[fyʁjø]
fusée-*m*	rocket, fuse	[fyze]

G

gagner-*vb*	win, earn	[gaɲe]
galimatias-*m*	rigmarole	[galimatja]
gambader-*vb*	frolic	[gɑ̃bade]
gant-*m*	glove	[gɑ̃]
garçon-*m*	boy, lad	[gaʁsɔ̃]
garde-*f; adj*	custody, guard; guarding	[gaʁd]

garder-*vb*	keep, maintain	[gaʁde]
gare-*f*	station, train station	[gaʁ]
garnir-*vb*	line	[gaʁniʁ]
gaspiller-*vb*	waste, throw away	[gaspije]
gâteau-*m*	cake	[gato]
gauche-*adj; f*	left; left	[goʃ]
gazon-*m*	grass, lawn	[gazɔ̃]
geler-*vb*	freeze	[ʒəle]
gênant-*adj*	embarrassing	[ʒɛnɑ̃]
gêner-*vb*	hinder	[ʒene]
général-*adj; m*	general; general	[ʒeneʁal]
genou-*m*	knee	[ʒənu]
genre-*m*	kind, gender	[ʒɑ̃ʁ]
gens-*npl*	people	[ʒɑ̃]
gentil-*adj; m*	nice, kind; gentile	[ʒɑ̃ti]
gentiment-*adv*	kindly, gently	[ʒɑ̃timɑ̃]
géographie-*f*	geography	[ʒeɔgʁafi]
géographique-*adj*	geographical	[ʒeɔgʁafik]
gibier-*m*	game, prey	[ʒibje]
glisser-*vb*	slip, run	[glise]
gorger-*vb*	gorge	[gɔʁʒe]
gosier-*m*	throat, gullet	[gozje]
gousset-*m*	gusset	[gusɛ]
goût-*m*	taste, flavor	[gu]
goûter-*vb*	taste	[gute]
grâce-*f*	grace, favor	[gʁas]
gracier-*vb*	pardon	[gʁasje]
gracieux-*adj*	gracious, graceful	[gʁasjø]
grain-*m*	grain	[gʁɛ̃]
grammaire-*f*	grammar	[gʁamɛʁ]
grand-*adj*	large, wide	[gʁɑ̃]
grandeur-*f*	size, magnitude	[gʁɑ̃dœʁ]
grandir-*vb*	grow, augment	[gʁɑ̃diʁ]
grandissant-*adj*	growing	[gʁɑ̃disɑ̃]
gratter-*vb*	scratch, strum	[gʁate]
grave-*adj*	serious, grave	[gʁav]
gravement-*adv*	seriously, gravely	[gʁavmɑ̃]
grêle-*f; adj*	hail; thin	[gʁɛl]
grelotter-*vb*	shivering	[gʁəlɔte]
grenouille-*f*	frog	[gʁənuj]
grève-*f*	strike	[gʁɛv]
griffe-*f*	claw	[gʁif]
griffon-*m*	griffon	[gʁifɔ̃]
grignoter-*vb*	nibble	[gʁiɲɔte]
grimaçant-*adj*	grimacing	[gʁimasɑ̃]
grimace-*f*	grimace	[gʁimas]
grimacer-*vb*	wince	[gʁimase]
grimoire-*m*	grimoire	[gʁimwaʁ]
grimper-*vb*	climb, soar	[gʁɛ̃pe]
grincement-*m*	grinding, squeak	[gʁɛ̃smɑ̃]
grincer-*vb*	squeak, grind	[gʁɛ̃se]
gris-*adj; m*	gray; gray	[gʁi]
grogne-*f*	discontent	[gʁɔɲ]
grognement-*m*	grunt	[gʁɔɲmɑ̃]
grogner-*vb*	grumble	[gʁɔɲe]
groin-*m*	snout	[gʁwɛ̃]
grommeler-*vb*	grumble	[gʁɔmle]
grondant-*adj*	growling	[gʁɔ̃dɑ̃]
gronder-*vb*	scold, rumble	[gʁɔ̃de]
gros-*adj; m*	large, fat; fat man	[gʁo]
grossier-*adj*	coarse, rude	[gʁosje]
grossièreté-*f*	rudeness	[gʁosjɛʁte]
grotesque-*adj; m*	grotesque; grotesque	[gʁɔtɛsk]
grouper-*vb*	group	[gʁupe]
guère-*adv*	little	[gɛʁ]
guetter-*vb*	await	[gete]
guillotiner-*vb*	guillotine	[gijɔtine]

H

habilement-*adv*	skilfully, cleverly	[abilmɑ̃]
habitation-*f*	home, habitation	[abitasjɔ̃]
habitude-*f*	habit	[abityd]
habituer-*vb*	accustom, get used to	[abitɥe]
haie-*f*	hedge, hurdle	[ɛ]
haïr-*vb*	hate	[aiʁ]
haleine-*m*	breath	[alɛn]
haletant-*adj*	panting	[altɑ̃]
haleter-*vb*	gasp	[alte]
hardiment-*adv*	boldly	[aʁdimɑ̃]
hasard-*m*	chance, accident	[azaʁ]
hasarder-*vb*	hazard	[azaʁde]
hâter-*vb*	hasten, accelerate	[ate]
haut-*adj; m; adv*	high; top; in heaven	[o]
hauteur-*f*	height, pitch	[otœʁ]
hé-*i*	Hey	[e]
hein-*i*	right	[ɛ̃]
héler-*vb*	hail	[ele]
héraut-*m*	herald	[eʁo]

herbe-*f*	grass, herb	[ɛʁb]
hérisser-*vb*	bristle	[eʁise]
hérisson-*m*	hedgehog	[eʁisɔ̃]
hésitant-*adj*	hesitant	[ezitɑ̃]
hésitation-*f*	hesitation	[ezitasjɔ̃]
hésiter-*vb*	hesitate	[ezite]
heure-*f*	time	[œʁ]
heureusement-*adv*	fortunately, happily	[øʁøzmɑ̃]
heureux-*adj*	happy	[øʁø]
heurter-*vb*	hit, offend	[œʁte]
hibou-*m*	owl	[ibu]
hier-*adv*	yesterday; yesterday	[ijɛʁ]
hippopotame-*m*	hippopotamus	[ipɔpɔtam]
histoire-*f*	history, story	[istwaʁ]
hiver-*m*	winter	[ivɛʁ]
homard-*m*	lobster	[ɔmaʁ]
homme-*m*	man, person	[ɔm]
honnête-*adj*	honest	[ɔnɛt]
honte-*f*	shame	[ɔ̃t]
hors-*prp*	except	[ɔʁ]
houka-*m*	hookah	[uka]
hourra-*m*	cheer	[uʁa]
huissier-*m*	bailiff	[ɥisje]
huître-*f*	oyster	[ɥitʁ]
hum-*i*	hum	[œm]
humble-*adj*	humble	[ɛ̃bl]
humblement-*adv*	humbly	[ɛ̃bləmɑ̃]
humeur-*f*	mood, spirit	[ymœʁ]
hurlement-*m*	howl, yell	[yʁləmɑ̃]
hurler-*vb*	scream, howl	[yʁle]

I

ici-*adv*	here	[isi]
idée-*f*	idea	[ide]
idiot-*m; adj*	idiot; silly	[idjo]
ignorant-*adj; m*	ignorant; ignoramus	[iɲɔʁɑ̃]
ignorer-*vb*	ignore	[iɲɔʁe]
il-*prn*	he, it	[il]
illustration-*f*	illustration	[ilystʁasjɔ̃]
image-*f*	image	[imaʒ]
imager-*vb*	image	[imaʒe]
imaginer-*vb*	imagine	[imaʒine]
imbécile-*m/f; adj*	imbecile; stupid	[ɛ̃besil]
imiter-*vb*	imitate	[imite]
immédiat-*adj*	immediate	[imedja]
immédiatement-*adv*	immediately	[imedjatmɑ̃]
immodérément-*adv*	Immoderately	[imɔdeʁemɑ̃]
impatience-*f*	impatience	[ɛ̃pasjɑ̃s]
impatientant-*adj*	impatient	[ɛ̃pasjɑ̃tɑ̃]
impertinent-*adj*	impertinent	[ɛ̃pɛʁtinɑ̃]
impoli-*adj*	impolite	[ɛ̃pɔli]
importance-*f*	importance, significance	[ɛ̃pɔʁtɑ̃s]
important-*adj*	important	[ɛ̃pɔʁtɑ̃]
importer-*vb*	import	[ɛ̃pɔʁte]
impossibilité-*f*	impossibility	[ɛ̃pɔsibilite]
impossible-*adj*	impossible	[ɛ̃pɔsibl]
imprimer-*vb*	print, print out	[ɛ̃pʁime]
incontestable-*adj*	indisputable	[ɛ̃kɔ̃tɛstabl]
Inde-*f*	India	[ɛ̃d]
indifféremment-*adv*	interchangeabl y	[ɛ̃difeʁamɑ̃]
indifférent-*adj*	indifferent	[ɛ̃difeʁɑ̃]
indignation-*f*	indignation	[ɛ̃diɲasjɔ̃]
indigner-*vb*	outrage	[ɛ̃diɲe]
indiquer-*vb*	indicate, show	[ɛ̃dike]
indiscrétion-*f*	indiscretion	[ɛ̃diskʁesjɔ̃]
inhumain-*adj*	inhuman	[inymɛ̃]
injustice-*f*	injustice, unfairness	[ɛ̃ʒystis]
innocent-*adj; m*	innocent; innocent	[inɔsɑ̃]
inquiet-*adj*	worried, concerned	[ɛ̃kjɛ]
inquiétude-*f*	concern	[ɛ̃kjetyd]
inquisiteur-*m; adj*	inquisitor; inquisitive	[ɛ̃kizitœʁ]
inscription-*f*	registration, entry	[ɛ̃skʁipsjɔ̃]
inscrire-*vb*	enroll, list	[ɛ̃skʁiʁ]
insister-*vb*	insist	[ɛ̃siste]
insolence-*f*	insolence	[ɛ̃sɔlɑ̃s]
instant-*m; adj*	moment, while; urgent	[ɛ̃stɑ̃]
instruction-*f*	instruction, education	[ɛ̃stʁyksjɔ̃]
instrument-*m*	instrument, implement	[ɛ̃stʁymɑ̃]
insulter-*vb*	insult, offend	[ɛ̃sylte]
intenter-*vb*	bring	[ɛ̃tɑ̃te]
intention-*f*	intention, mind	[ɛ̃tɑ̃sjɔ̃]
intéressant-*adj*	interesting	[ɛ̃teʁesɑ̃]
intéresser-*vb*	interest	[ɛ̃teʁese]
intérieur-*adj; m*	inside, interior; inside	[ɛ̃teʁjœʁ]
interpeller-*vb*	question	[ɛ̃tɛʁpəle]
interroger-*vb*	question, examine	[ɛ̃tɛʁɔʒe]
interrompre-*vb*	interrupt, stop	[ɛ̃tɛʁɔ̃pʁ]
interruption-*f*	interruption	[ɛ̃tɛʁypsjɔ̃]

intervalle-*m*	interval	[ɛ̃tɛʁval]
intervenant-*m*	speaker, intervener	[ɛ̃tɛʁvənɑ̃]
intriguer-*vb*	intrigue	[ɛ̃tʁige]
inutile-*adj*	unnecessary, useless	[inytil]
inventer-*vb*	invent, make up	[ɛ̃vɑ̃te]
invitation-*f*	invitation	[ɛ̃vitasjɔ̃]
inviter-*vb*	invite, ask	[ɛ̃vite]
irriter-*vb*	irritate	[iʁite]
italien-*adj; m*	Italian; Italian	[italjɛ̃]

J

jadis-*adv*	once	[ʒadis]
jamais-*adv*	never, ever	[ʒamɛ]
jambe-*f*	leg	[ʒɑ̃b]
jardin-*m*	garden	[ʒaʁdɛ̃]
jardinier-*m*	gardener	[ʒaʁdinje]
jatte-*f*	bowl	[ʒat]
je-*prn*	I	[ʒə]
jean-*m*	jeans	[dʒin]
jeter-*vb*	throw	[ʒəte]
jeu-*m*	game	[ʒø]
jeune-*adj; m*	young; youth	[ʒœn]
joie-*f*	joy	[ʒwa]
joindre-*vb*	join, attach	[ʒwɛ̃dʁ]
jointure-*f*	joint	[ʒwɛ̃tyʁ]
joli-*adj*	pretty	[ʒɔli]
joue-*f*	cheek	[ʒu]
jouer-*vb*	play, act	[ʒwe]
jouet-*adj; m*	toy; toy	[ʒwɛ]
joueur-*m*	player	[ʒwœʁ]
jour-*m*	day	[ʒuʁ]
journal-*m*	newspaper, journal	[ʒuʁnal]
journée-*f*	day	[ʒuʁne]
joyeusement-*adv*	merrily	[ʒwajøzmɑ̃]
joyeux-*adj*	happy	[ʒwajø]
juge-*m*	judge, beak	[ʒyʒ]
juger-*vb*	judge, assess	[ʒyʒe]
jurer-*vb*	swear	[ʒyʁe]
jury-*m*	jury	[ʒyʁi]
jusque-*adv*	until	[ʒysk]
juste-*adj; adv*	just, fair; just	[ʒyst]
justement-*adv*	rightly, exactly	[ʒystəmɑ̃]
justice-*f*	justice, law	[ʒystis]

L

là-*adv*	there	[la]
lâcher-*vb*	release, drop	[laʃe]
lacune-*f*	gap	[lakyn]
laid-*adj*	ugly	[lɛ]
laisser-*vb*	leave, let	[lese]
lait-*m*	milk	[lɛ]
lampe-*f*	lamp	[lɑ̃p]
lancer-*vb*	launch	[lɑ̃se]
langue-*f*	language	[lɑ̃g]
lapin-*m*	rabbit	[lapɛ̃]
laquais-*m; adj*	lackey; menial	[lakɛ]
larcin-*m*	petty theft	[laʁsɛ̃]
large-*adj*	wide, large	[laʁʒ]
larme-*f*	tear, drop	[laʁm]
latin-*adj*	Latin	[latɛ̃]
latitude-*f*	latitude	[latityd]
laver-*vb*	wash, launder	[lave]
le-*art; prn*	the; it	[lə]
lécher-*vb*	lick	[leʃe]
leçon-*f*	lesson	[ləsɔ̃]
légèrement-*adv*	slightly, lightly	[leʒɛʁmɑ̃]
lentement-*adv*	slowly, leisurely	[lɑ̃tmɑ̃]
lequel-*prn*	which	[ləkɛl]
lettre-*f*	letter	[lɛtʁ]
leur-*prn*	their	[lœʁ]
levant-*adj;*	rising; east	[ləvɑ̃]
lever-*vb; m*	lift, raise; rise	[ləve]
lèvre-*f*	lip	[lɛvʁ]
lézard-*m*	lizard	[lezaʁ]
libre-*adj*	free, open	[libʁ]
lieu-*m*	place, venue	[ljø]
lièvre-*m; adj*	hare; hare's	[ljɛvʁ]
ligne-*f*	line, design	[liɲ]
lire-*vb; f*	read; lira	[liʁ]
liste-*f*	list	[list]
livre-*m*	book	[livʁ]
livrer-*vb*	deliver	[livʁe]
logis-*m*	dwelling	[lɔʒi]
loi-*f*	law	[lwa]
loin-*adv; adj*	far; distant	[lwɛ̃]
lointain-*adj*	distant, far	[lwɛ̃tɛ̃]
loir-*m*	dormouse	[lwaʁ]
loisir-*m*	leisure	[lwaziʁ]
londre-	London	[lɔ̃dʁ]
long-*adj*	long	[lɔ̃]
longitude-*f*	longitude	[lɔ̃ʒityd]
longtemps-*adv; adj*	for a long time; longtime	[lɔ̃tɑ̃]
longue-*adj*	long	[lɔ̃g]
lors-*adv*	then, while	[lɔʁ]
lorsque-*prp*	during	[lɔʁsk]
lourd-*adj*	heavy	[luʁ]
lourder-*vb*	kicked out	[luʁde]

lui-*prn*	him	[lɥi]
luire-*vb*	gleam, glisten	[lɥiʁ]
lunettes-*npl*	glasses	[lynɛt]

M

machine-*f*	machine	[maʃin]
Madame-*f*	madame, Mrs	[madam]
Mademoiselle-*abr; f*	Ms.; miss	[madmwazɛl]
magique-*adj*	magic	[maʒik]
magnifique-*adj*	magnificent	[maɲifik]
maillet-*m*	mallet	[majɛ]
main-*f*	hand	[mɛ̃]
maintenant-*adv*	now	[mɛ̃tnɑ̃]
mais-*con; adv*	but; probably	[mɛ]
maison-*f*	house, home	[mɛzɔ̃]
maître-*m*	master, teacher	[mɛtʁ]
maîtresse-*f*	mistress	[mɛtʁɛs]
majesté-*f*	majesty	[maʒɛste]
mal-*m; adv; adj*	evil, wrong; amiss; untimely	[mal]
malade-*adj; m*	sick, invalid; patient	[malad]
malheureux-*adj; m*	unfortunate, unhappy; unfortunate	[maløʁø]
malice-*f*	malice, mischief	[malis]
manche-*m; f*	handle; sleeve	[mɑ̃ʃ]
manger-*vb*	eat, feed	[mɑ̃ʒe]
manier-*vb*	handle, use	[manje]
manière-*f*	way, form	[manjɛʁ]
manque-*m*	lack	[mɑ̃k]
manquer-*vb*	miss	[mɑ̃ke]
marcher-*vb*	walk, work	[maʁʃe]
mare-*f*	pond	[maʁ]
marguerite-*f*	daisy	[maʁgəʁit]
marin-*adj; m*	marine; marine	[maʁɛ̃]
marmelade-*f*	marmelade	[maʁməlad]
marmotter-*vb*	mutter	[maʁmɔte]
marquer-*vb*	mark, tag	[maʁke]
mars-*f*	March	[maʁs]
marsouin-*m*	porpoise	[maʁswɛ̃]
massif-*adj; m*	massive; massif	[masif]
matin-*m*	morning	[matɛ̃]
mauvais-*adj; m*	bad, ill; brute	[movɛ]
maxillaire-*m*	jaw	[maksilɛʁ]
me-*prn*	me, myself	[mə]
méchant-*adj; m*	wicked, bad; naughty child	[meʃɑ̃]
mécontentement-*m*	discontent	[mekɔ̃tɑ̃tmɑ̃]
médire-*vb*	speak ill	[mediʁ]
meilleur-*m; adj*	best; better	[mɛjœʁ]
mélancolie-*f*	melancholy	[melɑ̃kɔli]
mélange-*m*	mixture	[melɑ̃ʒ]
mélasse-*f*	treacle, molasses	[melas]
mêler-*vb*	mix, mingle	[mele]
membre-*f*	member	[mɑ̃bʁ]
même-*adj; adv*	same; even	[mɛm]
ménager-*adj; vb*	household; spare	[menaʒe]
mener-*vb*	lead, carry on	[məne]
mentir-*vb*	lie	[mɑ̃tiʁ]
menton-*m*	chin	[mɑ̃tɔ̃]
méprendre-*vb*	misunderstand	[mepʁɑ̃dʁ]
mer-*f*	sea	[mɛʁ]
merci-*m; i*	thanks; thanks	[mɛʁsi]
mère-*f*	mother	[mɛʁ]
mériter-*vb*	deserve, earn	[meʁite]
merlan-*m*	whiting	[mɛʁlɑ̃]
merveille-*f*	wonder, marvel	[mɛʁvɛj]
merveilleux-*adj*	wonderful	[mɛʁvɛjø]
messager-*m*	messenger	[mesaʒe]
mesure-*f*	measure, step	[məzyʁ]
mesurer-*vb*	measure	[məzyʁe]
métamorphoser-*vb*	metamorphose	[metamɔʁfoze]
méthode-*f*	method	[metɔd]
mets-*m*	dish	[mɛ]
mettre-*vb*	put, apply	[mɛtʁ]
meurtre-*m*	murder	[mœʁtʁ]
mie-*f*	crumb	[mi]
mien-*adj*	mine	[mjɛ̃]
miette-*f*	crumb	[mjɛt]
mieux-*adv; adj*	better; adj	[mjø]
mignon-*adj*	cute, sweet	[miɲɔ̃]
milieu-*m*	medium	[miljø]
mille-*num*	thousand	[mil]
mince-*adj*	thin, slim	[mɛ̃s]
mine-*f*	mine, lead	[min]
minéral-*adj; m*	mineral; mineral	[mineʁal]
minette-*f*	kitty	[minɛt]
minute-*f*	minute	[minyt]
minuter-*vb*	time	[minyte]
miroir-*m*	mirror	[miʁwaʁ]
moderne-*adj*	modern	[mɔdɛʁn]
moi-*prn; m*	me; ego	[mwa]
moindre-*adj*	lesser	[mwɛ̃dʁ]
moins-*adv; m; prp*	less; minus; wanting	[mwɛ̃]
mois-*m*	month	[mwa]
moitié-*adv; f*	half; half	[mwatje]
moment-*m*	time, moment	[mɔmɑ̃]

mon-*prn*	my	[mɔ̃]
monde-*m*	world	[mɔ̃d]
Monsieur-*abr; m*	Mr.; sir	[məsjø]
monter-*vb*	mount, climb	[mɔ̃te]
montrer-*vb*	show	[mɔ̃tʁe]
moquer-*vb*	mock	[mɔke]
moral-*adj; m*	moral; morale	[mɔʁal]
morale-*f*	morals, ethics	[mɔʁal]
morceau-*m*	piece, track	[mɔʁso]
mordre-*vb*	bite, snap	[mɔʁdʁ]
mort-*adj; f*	dead; death	[mɔʁ]
mot-*m*	word	[mo]
mouiller-*vb*	wet, anchor	[muje]
mourir-*vb*	die, end	[muʁiʁ]
moustache-*f*	mustache, whiskers	[mustaʃ]
moutarde-*f*	mustard	[mutaʁd]
mouton-*m*	sheep	[mutɔ̃]
mouvement-*m*	movement, stir	[muvmɑ̃]
moyen-*m; adj*	means, medium; medium	[mwajɛ̃]
muet-*adj; m*	silent; mute	[mɥɛ]
multiplication-*f*	multiplication	[myltiplikasjɔ̃]
mûr-*adj*	mature, grown	[myʁ]
murmurer-*vb*	murmur	[myʁmyʁe]
musique-*f*	music	[myzik]

N

nabot-*m; adj*	runt; dwarfish	[nabo]
nageant-*adj*	swimming	[naʒɑ̃]
nageoire-*f*	fin	[naʒwaʁ]
nager-*vb*	swim	[naʒe]
naturel-*adj; m*	natural; nature	[natyʁɛl]
ne-*adv*	not	[nə]
nerf-*m*	nerve	[nɛʁ]
net-*adj; adv*	net, sharp; outright	[nɛt]
neuf-*num*	nine	[nœf]
nez-*m*	nose	[ne]
ni-*con; adv*	or; neither	[ni]
niais-*m; adj*	simpleton; simple	[njɛ]
niaisement-*adv*	foolishly	[njɛzmɑ̃]
niaiser-*vb*	run around	[njeze]
nid-*m*	nest	[ni]
nier-*vb*	deny	[nje]
Noël-*m*	Christmas	[nɔɛl]
nœud-*m*	node, knot	[nø]
noir-*adj; m*	black; black	[nwaʁ]
nom-*m*	name	[nɔ̃]
nombre-*m*	number	[nɔ̃bʁ]
nombreux-*adj*	numerous	[nɔ̃bʁø]
nommer-*vb*	appoint, name	[nɔme]
non-*adv; part*	not; no	[nɔ̃]
nonchalamment-*adv*	casually	[nɔ̃ʃalamɑ̃]
normand-*adj*	Norman	[nɔʁmɑ̃]
note-*f*	note	[nɔt]
noter-*vb*	note	[nɔte]
notre-*prn*	our	[nɔtʁ]
nougat-*m*	nougat	[nuga]
nous-*prn*	we, us	[nu]
nouveau-*adj; m*	new, further; incoming	[nuvo]
nouvellement-*adv*	newly	[nuvɛlmɑ̃]
noyer-*m; vb*	walnut; drown	[nwaje]
nuire-*vb*	harm, damage	[nɥiʁ]
numéro-*m*	number	[nymeʁo]

O

obéir-*vb*	obey	[ɔbeiʁ]
obligé-*adj*	obliged	[ɔbliʒe]
obligeance-*f*	helpfulness	[ɔbliʒɑ̃s]
observation-*f*	observation, comment	[ɔpsɛʁvasjɔ̃]
observer-*vb*	observe, watch	[ɔpsɛʁve]
occasion-*f*	opportunity, occasion	[ɔkazjɔ̃]
occupant-*m; adj*	occupant; occupying	[ɔkypɑ̃]
occuper-*vb*	occupy, hold	[ɔkype]
océan-*m*	ocean	[ɔseɑ̃]
œil-*m*	eye	[œj]
œuf-*m*	egg	[œf]
œuvre-*f*	work	[œvʁ]
offenser-*vb*	offend, insult	[ɔfɑ̃se]
officier-*m*	officer	[ɔfisje]
offrir-*vb*	offer, give	[ɔfʁiʁ]
oh-*i*	oh	[o]
oignon-*m*	onion	[ɔɲɔ̃]
oiseau-*m*	bird	[wazo]
ombre-*m*	shadow	[ɔ̃bʁ]
on-*prn*	we	[ɔ̃]
onguent-*m*	ointment	[ɔ̃gɑ̃]
onzième-*num*	eleventh	[ɔ̃zjɛm]
opiniâtrement-*adv*	stubbornly	[ɔpinjatʁəmɑ̃]
or-*m*	gold	[ɔʁ]
orage-*m*	storm	[ɔʁaʒ]
orange-*adj*	orange	[ɔʁɑ̃ʒ]
orateur-*m*	speaker, orator	[ɔʁatœʁ]
ordinaire-*adj; m*	ordinary; ordinary	[ɔʁdinɛʁ]

ordinairement-*adv*	usually	[ɔʁdinɛʁmɑ̃]
ordonner-*vb*	order, direct	[ɔʁdɔne]
ordre-*m*	order	[ɔʁdʁ]
oreille-*f*	ear	[ɔʁɛj]
orge-*f*	barley	[ɔʁʒ]
origine-*f*	origin	[ɔʁiʒin]
orner-*vb*	adorn	[ɔʁne]
os-*m*	bone	[ɔs]
oser-*vb*	dare	[oze]
ôter-*vb*	remove	[ote]
ou-*con*	or	[u]
où-*adv; prn; con*	where; that; wherein	[u]
oublier-*vb*	forget	[ublije]
oui-*part; m*	yes; yea	[wi]
outre-*prp; f*	besides; skin	[utʁ]
ouvert-*adj*	open	[uvɛʁ]
ouverture-*f*	opening	[uvɛʁtyʁ]
ouvrage-*m*	handiwork	[uvʁaʒ]
ouvrier-*m*	worker	[uvʁije]
ouvrir-*vb*	open, start	[uvʁiʁ]

P

pailler-*vb*	mulch	[paje]
pain-*m*	bread	[pɛ̃]
pair-*adj; m*	even; peer	[pɛʁ]
paire-*f*	pair	[pɛʁ]
paix-*f*	peace	[pɛ]
pâle-*adj*	pale	[pal]
papa-*m*	papa	[papa]
pape-*m*	pope	[pap]
papier-*m*	paper	[papje]
papillon-*m*	butterfly	[papijɔ̃]
paquet-*m*	package, pack	[pakɛ]
par-*prp; m*	by; par	[paʁ]
parade-*f*	parade	[paʁad]
paraître-*vb*	seem, appear	[paʁɛtʁ]
parce que-*adv*	because	[paʁsə kə]
parcelle-*f*	parcel, plot	[paʁsɛl]
parchemin-*m*	parchment, diploma	[paʁʃəmɛ̃]
pardon-*m*	forgiveness	[paʁdɔ̃]
pareil-*adj; prn; m*	such, similar; the same; equal	[paʁɛj]
parent-*m; adj*	relative; kin	[paʁɑ̃]
parer-*vb*	parry, ward off	[paʁe]
paresseux-*adj; m*	lazy; sloth	[paʁesø]
parfaire-*vb*	perfect	[paʁfɛʁ]
parfaitement-*adv*	perfectly, thoroughly	[paʁfɛtmɑ̃]
pari-*m*	bet, betting	[paʁi]
parier-*vb*	bet, gamble	[paʁje]
parler-*vb*	speak, tell	[paʁle]
parmi-*prp*	among	[paʁmi]
paroi-*f*	wall	[paʁwa]
parole-*f*	word, speech	[paʁɔl]
partage-*m*	sharing, division	[paʁtaʒ]
partager-*vb*	share, divide	[paʁtaʒe]
parterre-*m*	flower bed	[paʁtɛʁ]
partie-*f*	part	[paʁti]
partir-*vb*	depart, leave	[paʁtiʁ]
partout-*adv*	everywhere, throughout	[paʁtu]
parvenir-*vb*	get through	[paʁvəniʁ]
pas-*adv; m*	not; step	[pa]
passage-*m*	passage, passing	[pasaʒ]
passant-*adj; m*	elapsing; passer-by	[pasɑ̃]
passer-*vb*	pass, spend	[pase]
patauger-*vb*	wade	[patoʒe]
patiemment-*adv*	patiently	[pasjamɑ̃]
patience-*f*	patience	[pasjɑ̃s]
patriote-*m*	patriot	[patʁijɔt]
patte-*f*	tab, leg	[pat]
pauser-*vb*	pause	[poze]
pauvre-*adj; m*	poor; poor person	[povʁ]
payer-*vb*	pay	[peje]
pays-*m*	country	[pei]
peigner-*vb*	comb	[peɲe]
peindre-*vb*	paint	[pɛ̃dʁ]
peiner-*vb*	labor, pain	[pene]
peinturer-*vb*	paint	[pɛ̃tyʁe]
pelle-*f*	shovel	[pɛl]
pelouse-*f*	lawn	[pəluz]
pencher-*vb*	lean	[pɑ̃ʃe]
pendant-*adv*	during	[pɑ̃dɑ̃]
pendre-*vb*	hang	[pɑ̃dʁ]
pendule-*f*	pendulum	[pɑ̃dyl]
pénétrer-*vb*	enter, penetrate	[penetʁe]
pensée-*f*	thought	[pɑ̃se]
penser-*vb*	think, reflect	[pɑ̃se]
pensif-*adj*	thoughtful	[pɑ̃sif]
pension-*f*	pension	[pɑ̃sjɔ̃]
perçant-*adj*	piercing, shrill	[pɛʁsɑ̃]
percher-*vb*	perch, hang	[pɛʁʃe]
perdre-*vb*	lose, waste	[pɛʁdʁ]
perdreau-*m*	partridge	[pɛʁdʁo]
père-*m*	father, dad	[pɛʁ]

permettre-*vb*	allow, enable	[pɛʁmɛtʁ]
perpendiculairement -*adv*	perpendicularly	[pɛʁpɑ̃dikylɛʁmɑ̃]
perruque-*f*	wig	[peʁyk]
personnage-*m*	character, figure	[pɛʁsɔnaʒ]
personne-*f; prn*	person; nobody	[pɛʁsɔn]
personnellement-*adv*	personally	[pɛʁsɔnɛlmɑ̃]
perte-*f*	loss, waste	[pɛʁt]
petit-*adj; m*	small, little; child	[pəti]
peu-*adv; m; adj*	little; bit; few	[pø]
peupler-*vb*	populate	[pœple]
peur-*f*	fear, scare	[pœʁ]
phoque-*m*	seal	[fɔk]
phrase-*f*	phrase	[fʁaz]
pic-*m*	peak, woodpecker	[pik]
pie-*f*	magpie	[pi]
pièce-*f; adv*	piece, room; apiece	[pjɛs]
pied-*m*	foot, leg	[pje]
piétinement-*m*	trampling	[pjetinmɑ̃]
pigeon-*m*	pigeon	[piʒɔ̃]
pinceau-*m*	brush	[pɛ̃so]
pincer-*vb*	pinch, pluck	[pɛ̃se]
pincette-*f*	pincette	[pɛ̃sɛt]
pipe-*f*	pipe	[pip]
pique-*m; f*	spade; pike	[pik]
piquer-*vb*	prick, sting	[pike]
pis-*m*	worse, udder	[pi]
piteux-*adj*	sorry	[pitø]
place-*f*	square, spot	[plas]
placer-*vb*	place, put	[plase]
plafond-*m*	ceiling, plafond	[plafɔ̃]
plaindre-*vb*	complain, pity	[plɛ̃dʁ]
plainte-*f*	complaint	[plɛ̃t]
plaire-*vb*	please	[plɛʁ]
plaisant-*adj*	pleasant	[plɛzɑ̃]
plaisir-*m*	pleasure	[pleziʁ]
plan-*m; adj*	plan; plane	[plɑ̃]
plancher-*m; vb*	floor; floor	[plɑ̃ʃe]
plante-*f*	plant	[plɑ̃t]
plaque-*m*	plate	[plak]
plaquer-*vb*	stick, tackle	[plake]
plat-*adj; m*	flat; flat, dish	[pla]
plein-*adj*	full, fraught	[plɛ̃]
pleurer-*vb*	cry, mourn	[plœʁe]
plier-*vb*	bend	[plije]
plongeon-*m*	dive, plunge	[plɔ̃ʒɔ̃]
plonger-*vb*	dive, plunge	[plɔ̃ʒe]
pluie-*f*	rain	[plɥi]

plume-*f*	feather	[plym]
plupart-*f*	most	[plypaʁ]
plus-*adj; adv; m*	more; more; plus	[ply]
plusieurs-*adj*	several, divers	[plyzjœʁ]
plutôt-*adv*	rather, quite	[plyto]
poche-*f*	pocket	[pɔʃ]
poêler-*vb*	fry	[pwale]
poids-*m*	weight	[pwa]
poil-*m*	hair	[pwal]
point-*m*	point, item	[pwɛ̃]
pointer-*vb*	point	[pwɛ̃te]
pointu-*adj*	sharp	[pwɛ̃ty]
poison-*m*	poison	[pwazɔ̃]
poisson-*m*	fish	[pwasɔ̃]
poivre-*m*	pepper	[pwavʁ]
poivrer-*vb*	pepper	[pwavʁe]
poivrière-*f*	pepper shaker	[pwavʁijɛʁ]
poli-*adj*	polished, polite	[pɔli]
poliment-*adv*	politely	[pɔlimɑ̃]
polir-*vb*	polish, buff	[pɔliʁ]
politique-*f; adj*	policy; political	[pɔlitik]
pomme-*f*	apple	[pɔm]
porc-*m*	pork, pig	[pɔʁ]
portant-*adj*	carrying	[pɔʁtɑ̃]
porte-*f*	door, gate	[pɔʁt]
porter-*vb*	wear, carry	[pɔʁte]
portraire-*adj*	port	[pɔʁtʁɛʁ]
posément-*adv*	calmly	[pozemɑ̃]
poser-*vb*	pose, rest	[poze]
position-*f*	position	[pozisjɔ̃]
possible-*adj; m*	possible; possible	[pɔsibl]
pot-*m*	pot, jar	[po]
potage-*m*	soup	[pɔtaʒ]
pouce-*m*	inch	[pus]
poudre-*f*	powder	[pudʁ]
poudrer-*vb*	powder	[pudʁe]
pouf-*m*	ottoman, beanbag	[puf]
pour-*prp*	for	[puʁ]
pourpre-*adj*	purple	[puʁpʁ]
pourquoi-*adv; con*	why; wherefore	[puʁkwa]
poursuite-*f*	pursuit, prosecution	[puʁsɥit]
poursuivre-*vb*	continue, pursue	[puʁsɥivʁ]
pourtant-*con; adv*	yet, however; nevertheless	[puʁtɑ̃]
pousser-*vb*	push, drive	[puse]
pouvoir-*m; vb; av*	power; can; might	[puvwaʁ]

précaution-*f*	precaution	[pʁekosjɔ̃]
précédent-*adj; m*	previous; precedent	[pʁesedɑ̃]
précieux-*adj*	precious, valuable	[pʁesjø]
précipitamment-*adv*	hastily, precipitately	[pʁesipitamɑ̃]
précipiter-*vb*	precipitate	[pʁesipite]
précisément-*adv*	precisely	[pʁesizemɑ̃]
préciser-*vb*	specify, point out	[pʁesize]
préférer-*vb; av*	prefer; would rather	[pʁefeʁe]
premier-*adj*	first, prime	[pʁəmje]
premièrement-*adv*	firstly	[pʁəmjɛʁmɑ̃]
prendre-*vb*	take, have	[pʁɑ̃dʁ]
près-*adv*	near, by	[pʁɛ]
présent-*adj; m*	present; present	[pʁezɑ̃]
présenter-*vb*	present, offer	[pʁezɑ̃te]
presque-*adv; adj*	almost; all but	[pʁɛsk]
presser-*vb*	press, squeeze	[pʁese]
prêt-*adj; m*	ready, willing; loan	[pʁɛ]
prétexte-*m*	pretext, excuse	[pʁetɛkst]
prévenir-*vb*	warn, inform	[pʁevəniʁ]
prier-*vb*	pray	[pʁije]
prince-*m*	prince	[pʁɛ̃s]
principalement-*adv*	mainly, mostly	[pʁɛ̃sipalmɑ̃]
printemps-*m*	spring	[pʁɛ̃tɑ̃]
prison-*f*	prison	[pʁizɔ̃]
prix-*m*	price, prize	[pʁi]
probable-*adj*	likely	[pʁɔbabl]
procès-*m*	trial, process	[pʁɔsɛ]
procession-*f*	procession	[pʁɔsesjɔ̃]
produire-*vb*	produce	[pʁɔdɥiʁ]
professeur-*m*	professor, teacher	[pʁɔfesœʁ]
profiter-*vb*	benefit, avail	[pʁɔfite]
profond-*adj; m*	deep, profound; deep	[pʁɔfɔ̃]
profondément-*adv*	deeply, heavily	[pʁɔfɔ̃demɑ̃]
profondeur-*f*	depth, hollowness	[pʁɔfɔ̃dœʁ]
proie-*f*	prey, decoy	[pʁwa]
projet-*m*	project	[pʁɔʒɛ]
promenade-*f*	walk	[pʁɔmnad]
promener-*vb*	promenade	[pʁɔmne]
promesse-*f*	promise	[pʁɔmɛs]
promis-*adj*	promised	[pʁɔmi]
promptement-*adv*	promptly	[pʁɔ̃ptəmɑ̃]
prononcer-*vb*	pronounce	[pʁɔnɔ̃se]
propice-*adj*	suitable	[pʁɔpis]
propos-*m*	talk	[pʁɔpo]
proposer-*vb*	propose, offer	[pʁɔpoze]
proposition-*f*	proposal, proposition	[pʁɔpozisjɔ̃]
propre-*adj; m*	own, clean; proper	[pʁɔpʁ]
prospectus-*m*	prospectus	[pʁɔspɛktys]
prosterner-*vb*	bow down	[]
protection-*f*	protection	[pʁɔtɛksjɔ̃]
prouver-*vb*	prove	[pʁuve]
prudemment-*adv*	carefully	[pʁydamɑ̃]
pruneau-*m*	prune	[pʁyno]
puis-*adv*	then	[pɥi]
puisque-*con*	since	[pɥisk]
puissant-*adj*	powerful, strong	[pɥisɑ̃]
puits-*m*	well	[pɥi]
pupitre-*m*	desk	[pypitʁ]

Q

quadrille-*m*	quadrille	[kadʁij]
quand-*adv; con*	when; when	[kɑ̃]
quant-*adv*	about	[kɑ̃]
quantième-*m*	date	[kɑ̃tjɛm]
quarante-*num*	forty	[kaʁɑ̃t]
quatorze-*num*	fourteen	[katɔʁz]
quatre-*num*	four	[katʁ]
que-*con; prn; prp; adj; adv*	that; that; than; which; how	[kə]
quel-*adj; prn*	what; what	[kɛl]
quelque-*adj; adv*	some; about	[kɛlk]
quelquefois-*adv*	sometimes	[kɛlkəfwa]
quereller-*vb*	quarrel	[kəʁele]
question-*f*	question, issue	[kɛstjɔ̃]
questionner-*vb*	question	[kɛstjɔne]
queue-*f*	tail, queue	[kø]
qui-*prn*	which	[ki]
quinze-*num*	fifteen	[kɛ̃z]
quitter-*vb*	leave, quit	[kite]
quoi-*prn*	what	[kwa]

R

raccourcir-*vb*	shorten	[ʁakuʁsiʁ]
racine-*f*	root	[ʁasin]
raconter-*vb*	tell	[ʁakɔ̃te]
rafraîchissement-*m*	refreshment	[ʁafʁeʃismɑ̃]
raisin-*m*	grape	[ʁezɛ̃]
raison-*f*	reason, why	[ʁɛzɔ̃]

raisonnable-*adj*	reasonable	[ʁɛzɔnabl]
raisonnablement-*adv*	reasonably	[ʁɛzɔnabləmɑ̃]
raisonnement-*m*	reasoning	[ʁɛzɔnmɑ̃]
ramage-*f*	song	[ʁamaʒ]
ramasser-*vb*	pick up	[ʁamase]
ramener-*vb*	bring back	[ʁamne]
ramper-*vb*	crawl, trail	[ʁɑ̃pe]
rang-*m*	rank, row	[ʁɑ̃]
ranger-*m; vb*	ranger; put away	[ʁɑ̃ʒe]
rapetisser-*vb*	shrink	[ʁaptise]
rapidement-*adv*	quickly, rapidly	[ʁapidmɑ̃]
rappeler-*vb*	remind, call back	[ʁaple]
rapporter-*vb*	report, relate	[ʁapɔʁte]
rapprocher-*vb*	bring closer	[ʁapʁɔʃe]
rarement-*adv*	rarely, hardly	[ʁaʁmɑ̃]
rassembler-*vb*	gather, collect	[ʁasɑ̃ble]
rasseoir-*vb*	sit down	[ʁaswaʁ]
rat-*m*	rat	[ʁa]
rattraper-*vb*	catch up, make up	[ʁatʁape]
rauque-*adj*	hoarse	[ʁok]
ravissant-*adj*	delightful	[ʁavisɑ̃]
rayon-*m*	radius, ray	[ʁɛjɔ̃]
réalité-*f*	reality	[ʁealite]
recevoir-*vb*	receive, take	[ʁəsəvwaʁ]
recherche-*f*	research, search	[ʁəʃɛʁʃ]
récif-*m*	reef	[ʁesif]
récit-*m*	story, recital	[ʁesi]
réciter-*vb*	recite	[ʁesite]
recommencer-*vb*	restart, start again	[ʁəkɔmɑ̃se]
reconnaissant-*adj*	grateful	[ʁəkɔnɛsɑ̃]
reconnaître-*vb*	recognize, admit	[ʁəkɔnɛtʁ]
recueillir-*vb*	collect, gather	[ʁəkœjiʁ]
reculer-*vb*	back, retreat	[ʁəkyle]
redemander-*vb*	ask again	[ʁədəmɑ̃de]
redevenir-*vb*	become again	[ʁədəvəniʁ]
redresser-*vb*	straighten, redress	[ʁədʁese]
réduire-*vb*	reduce, decrease	[ʁedɥiʁ]
refermer-*vb*	close	[ʁəfɛʁme]
réfléchir-*vb*	reflect, think	[ʁefleʃiʁ]
réflexion-*f*	reflection, thinking	[ʁeflɛksjɔ̃]
refrain-*m*	refrain	[ʁəfʁɛ̃]
refuser-*vb*	refuse	[ʁəfyze]
regard-*m*	look, gaze	[ʁəgaʁ]
regarder-*vb*	look, watch	[ʁəgaʁde]
règle-*f*	rule	[ʁɛgl]
regret-*m*	regret	[ʁəgʁɛ]
reine-*f*	queen	[ʁɛn]
rejeter-*vb*	reject, dismiss	[ʁəʒəte]
rejoindre-*vb*	rejoin	[ʁəʒwɛ̃dʁ]
réjouir-*vb*	rejoice	[ʁeʒwiʁ]
relever-*vb*	raise, pick up	[ʁələve]
remarquer-*vb*	notice, note	[ʁəmaʁke]
remettre-*vb*	deliver, return	[ʁəmɛtʁ]
remplacer-*vb*	replace, change	[ʁɑ̃plase]
remplir-*vb*	fill, fill in	[ʁɑ̃pliʁ]
remuer-*vb*	stir, move	[ʁəmɥe]
renard-*m*	fox	[ʁənaʁ]
rencontrer-*vb*	meet, encounter	[ʁɑ̃kɔ̃tʁe]
rendormir-*vb*	go back to sleep	[ʁɑ̃dɔʁmiʁ]
rendre-*vb*	render, restore	[ʁɑ̃dʁ]
renoncer-*vb*	renounce, give up	[ʁənɔ̃se]
rentrer-*vb*	return	[ʁɑ̃tʁe]
renversé-*adj*	reversed	[ʁɑ̃vɛʁse]
renverser-*vb*	reverse, turn	[ʁɑ̃vɛʁse]
reparaître-*vb*	reappear	[ʁəpaʁɛtʁ]
repas-*m*	meal	[ʁəpa]
repasser-*vb*	iron, replay	[ʁəpase]
répéter-*vb*	repeat, rehearse	[ʁepete]
replacer-*vb*	replace	[ʁəplase]
repli-*m*	withdrawal, fold	[ʁəpli]
replier-*vb*	replicate, fold up	[ʁəplije]
répliquer-*vb*	reply	[ʁeplike]
répondre-*vb*	answer	[ʁepɔ̃dʁ]
réponse-*f*	response	[ʁepɔ̃s]
reposer-*vb*	rest	[ʁəpoze]
repousser-*vb*	repel, fend off	[ʁəpuse]
reprendre-*vb*	resume, retake	[ʁəpʁɑ̃dʁ]
représenter-*vb*	represent	[ʁəpʁezɑ̃te]
réprimer-*vb*	repress	[ʁepʁime]
résoudre-*vb*	solve, resolve	[ʁezudʁ]
respect-*m*	respect	[ʁɛspɛ]
respectueux-*adj*	respectful	[ʁɛspɛktɥø]
respirer-*vb*	breathe	[ʁɛspiʁe]
ressemblance-*f*	resemblance, likeness	[ʁəsɑ̃blɑ̃s]
ressembler-*vb*	look like	[ʁəsɑ̃ble]
ressortir-*vb*	stand out	[ʁəsɔʁtiʁ]
ressourcer-*vb*	rejuvenate	[ʁəsuʁse]

estant-*adj; m*	remaining; remnant	[ʁɛstɑ̃]
ester-*vb*	stay, keep	[ʁɛste]
ésulter-*vb*	result	[ʁezylte]
etard-*m*	delay	[ʁətaʁ]
etenir-*vb*	retain, hold	[ʁətəniʁ]
etirer-*vb*	withdraw, pull	[ʁətiʁe]
etomber-*vb*	drop, relapse	[ʁətɔ̃be]
etourner-*vb*	return	[ʁətuʁne]
etrousser-*vb*	roll up	[ʁətʁuse]
etrouver-*vb*	find, meet	[ʁətʁuve]
éunir-*vb*	gather, reunite	[ʁeyniʁ]
éussir-*vb*	succeed, pass	[ʁeysiʁ]
êve-*m*	dream	[ʁɛv]
réveiller-*vb*	wake, awake	[ʁeveje]
revenir-*vb*	return, get back	[ʁəvəniʁ]
revenu-*m*	income	[ʁəvəny]
rêver-*vb*	dream	[ʁeve]
révérence-*f*	reverence, bow	[ʁeveʁɑ̃s]
rêveur-*m; adj*	dreamer; dreamy	[ʁɛvœʁ]
revoir-*vb*	revise	[ʁəvwaʁ]
révolution-*f*	revolution	[ʁevɔlysjɔ̃]
revue-*m*	review	[ʁəvy]
rhume-*m*	cold	[ʁym]
ricaner-*vb*	sneer	[ʁikane]
rideau-*m*	curtain	[ʁido]
ridicule-*adj; m*	ridiculous; ridicule	[ʁidikyl]
rien-*m; prn; adv*	nothing; anything; nix	[ʁjɛ̃]
rire-*m; vb*	laugh; laugh	[ʁiʁ]
risque-*m*	risk, hazard	[ʁisk]
rive-*f*	bank, shore	[ʁiv]
robe-*f*	dress, gown	[ʁɔb]
roi-*m*	king	[ʁwa]
roman-*m; adj*	novel; Romance	[ʁɔmɑ̃]
rompre-*vb*	break, break up	[ʁɔ̃pʁ]
rond-*adj; m*	round; round	[ʁɔ̃]
ronfler-*vb*	snore	[ʁɔ̃fle]
rose-*adj; f*	pink; rose	[ʁoz]
roseau-*m*	reed	[ʁozo]
rosier-*m*	rosebush	[ʁozje]
rôtir-*vb*	roast	[ʁotiʁ]
roue-*f*	wheel	[ʁu]
rouet-*m*	spinning wheel	[ʁwɛ]
rouge-*adj; m*	red; red	[ʁuʒ]
rouleau-*m*	roller, roll	[ʁulo]
route-*f*	road, way	[ʁut]
rouvrir-*vb*	reopen	[ʁuvʁiʁ]

S

sabler-*vb*	sand	[sable]
sac-*m*	bag, sack	[sak]
saigner-*vb*	bleed	[seɲe]
saisir-*vb*	seize, grasp	[seziʁ]
saler-*vb*	salt	[sale]
salle-*f*	room	[sal]
saluer-*vb*	greet	[salɥe]
salut-*m; i*	salvation; hi	[saly]
sanglot-*m*	sob	[sɑ̃glo]
sangloter-*vb*	sob	[sɑ̃glɔte]
sans-*prp*	without	[sɑ̃]
satisfaire-*vb*	satisfy, please	[satisfɛʁ]
saumon-*m*	salmon	[somɔ̃]
sautant-*adj*	jumping	[sotɑ̃]
sauter-*vb*	jump, skip	[sote]
sauver-*vb*	save	[sove]
savoir-*vb; m*	know; knowledge	[savwaʁ]
savon-*m*	soap	[savɔ̃]
se-*prn*	-self (reflexive marker)	[sə]
sec-*adj*	dry, dried	[sɛk]
sèche-*f; adj*	fag; dry	[sɛʃ]
sèchement-*adv*	curtly	[sɛʃmɑ̃]
sécher-*vb*	dry, cure	[seʃe]
second-*adj; m*	second; second	[səgɔ̃]
secouer-*vb*	shake, rock	[səkwe]
secourir-*vb*	rescue	[səkuʁiʁ]
secousse-*f*	shock, shake	[səkus]
secret-*adj; m*	secret, covert; secret	[səkʁɛ]
seize-*num*	sixteen	[sɛz]
semaine-*f*	week	[səmɛn]
sembler-*vb*	seem, sound	[sɑ̃ble]
sens-*m*	direction	[sɑ̃s]
sensation-*f*	sensation, feeling	[sɑ̃sasjɔ̃]
sentir-*vb*	feel	[sɑ̃tiʁ]
sept-*num*	seven	[sɛt]
serein-*adj; m*	serene; collection	[səʁɛ̃]
série-*f*	series, set	[seʁi]
sérieusement-*adv*	seriously, gravely	[seʁjøzmɑ̃]
sérieux-*adj; m*	serious; seriousness	[seʁjø]
serpent-*m*	snake	[sɛʁpɑ̃]
serré-*adj*	tight	[seʁe]
serrer-*vb*	tighten, clamp	[seʁe]

serrure-*f*	lock	[seʁyʁ]
servant-*adj; nm*	useful; servant	[sɛʁvɑ̃]
server-*m*	server	[sɛʁve]
service-*m*	service, serving	[sɛʁvis]
servir-*vb*	serve, help	[sɛʁviʁ]
seul-*adj; m; adv*	only; only one; very	[sœl]
seulement-*adv; con*	only, just; only	[sœlmɑ̃]
sévère-*adj*	severe, strict	[sevɛʁ]
sévèrement-*adv*	severely	[sevɛʁmɑ̃]
si-*con; adv*	if; so	[si]
sien-*prn*	one's own	[sjɛ̃]
sifflement-*m*	whistling, hiss	[sifləmɑ̃]
siffler-*vb*	whistle, hiss	[sifle]
signature-*f*	signature	[siɲatyʁ]
signer-*vb*	sign	[siɲe]
signifier-*vb*	mean, imply	[siɲifje]
silence-*m*	silence, pause	[silɑ̃s]
sillon-*m*	groove	[sijɔ̃]
simple-*adj*	simple; singles	[sɛ̃pl]
simplement-*adv*	simply	[sɛ̃pləmɑ̃]
sincèrement-*adv*	truly, sincerely	[sɛ̃sɛʁmɑ̃]
singulier-*adj; m*	singular, strange; singular	[sɛ̃gylje]
sinon-*con; adv*	otherwise; or else	[sinɔ̃]
sitôt-*adv*	soon	[sito]
six-*num*	six	[sis]
sœur-*adj; f*	sister; sister	[sœʁ]
soi-*m; prn*	self; self	[swa]
soigneusement-*adv*	carefully	[swaɲøzmɑ̃]
soin-*m*	care, carefulness	[swɛ̃]
soir-*m*	evening	[swaʁ]
soit-*con*	whether, either	[swa]
sol-*m*	soil	[sɔl]
soldat-*m*	soldier	[sɔlda]
soleil-*m*	sun	[sɔlɛj]
solennel-*adj*	solemn	[sɔlanɛl]
solennellement-*adv*	solemnly	[sɔlanɛlmɑ̃]
solitaire-*adj; m/f*	solitary; loner	[sɔlitɛʁ]
sombre-*adj*	dark, gloomy	[sɔ̃bʁ]
somme-*f*	sum	[sɔm]
sommeil-*m*	sleep, rest	[sɔmɛj]
sommer-*vb*	summon	[sɔme]
sommet-*m*	top, vertex	[sɔmɛ]
son-*adj; m*	its; sound	[sɔ̃]
songer-*vb*	reflect, wonder	[sɔ̃ʒe]
sonner-*vb*	ring, sound	[sɔne]
sonore-*f; adj*	sound; acoustic	[sɔnɔʁ]
sorte-*f*	kind, manner	[sɔʁt]

sortir-*vb*	exit, come out	[sɔʁtiʁ]
sot-*m*	fool	[so]
sottise-*f*	folly, silliness	[sɔtiz]
sou-*m*	cent	[su]
souffle-*m*	breath, blast	[sufl]
souffler-*vb*	breathe, whisper	[sufle]
soufflet-*m*	bellow	[suflɛ]
souffrir-*vb*	suffer, experience	[sufʁiʁ]
souhaiter-*vb*	wish, hope	[swete]
soulager-*vb*	relieve, alleviate	[sulaʒe]
soulier-*m*	shoe	[sulje]
soumettre-*vb*	submit, refer	[sumɛtʁ]
soupe-*f*	soup	[sup]
soupier-*vb*	worry about	[supje]
soupir-*m*	sigh	[supiʁ]
soupirant-*m*	suitor	[supiʁɑ̃]
soupirer-*vb*	sigh	[supiʁe]
sourcil-*m*	eyebrow	[suʁsil]
sourd-*adj*	deaf, dull	[suʁ]
souriant-*adj*	smiling	[suʁjɑ̃]
sourire-*m; vb*	smile; smile	[suʁiʁ]
soutenir-*vb*	support, back	[sutniʁ]
souvenir-*m*	memory, souvenir	[suvəniʁ]
souvent-*adv*	often	[suvɑ̃]
star-*f*	star	[staʁ]
strident-*adj*	shrill	[stʁidɑ̃]
stupide-*adj; m*	stupid; stupid	[stypid]
subitement-*adv*	suddenly	[sybitmɑ̃]
succès-*m*	success	[syksɛ]
sucre-*m*	sugar	[sykʁ]
sucrerie-*f*	suger refinery	[sykʁəʁi]
suffire-*vb*	suffice	[syfiʁ]
suite-*f*	suite, sequence	[sɥit]
suivant-*adj; prp; adv*	following; according to; as follows	[sɥivɑ̃]
suivre-*vb*	follow	[sɥivʁ]
sujet-*m; adj*	subject; prone	[syʒɛ]
superbe-*adj*	superb; stunner	[sypɛʁb]
suppliant-*adj; m*	begging; suppliant	[syplijɑ̃]
supplier-*vb*	beg, entreat	[syplije]
supporter-*vb; m*	support, bear; supporter	[sypɔʁte]
supposer-*vb*	assume, suppose	[sypoze]
sur-*prp*	on	[syʁ]
sûr-*adj*	sure, safe	[syʁ]

sûrement-*adv*	surely	[syʁmɑ̃]
sûreté-*f*	safety	[syʁte]
surprendre-*vb*	surprise, catch	[syʁpʁɑ̃dʁ]
susceptible-*adj*	susceptible	[sysɛptibl]

T

table-*f*	table	[tabl]
tabler-*vb*	rely	[table]
tabouret-*m*	stool	[tabuʁɛ]
tâcher-*vb*	try	[taʃe]
tailler-*vb*	cut, carve	[taje]
taire-*vb*	hush up	[tɛʁ]
talus-*m*	slope	[taly]
tandis-*adv*	while	[tɑ̃di]
tant-*adv*	so such	[tɑ̃]
tantôt-*adv*	sometimes	[tɑ̃to]
tape-*f*	slap	[tap]
taper-*vb*	type, beat	[tape]
tapinois-*adv*	stealthily	[tapinwa]
tapir-*m*	tapir	[tapiʁ]
taquiner-*vb*	tease	[takine]
tard-*adv*	late	[taʁ]
tarder-*vb*	delay	[taʁde]
tarte-*f*	pie	[taʁt]
tartine-*f*	sandwich	[taʁtin]
tas-*m*	pile	[ta]
tasse-*f*	cup	[tas]
te-*prn*	you	[tə]
tel-*adj*	such	[tɛl]
télescope-*m*	telescope	[telɛskɔp]
tellement-*adv*	so	[tɛlmɑ̃]
témoin-*m*	witness	[temwɛ̃]
temps-*m*	time	[tɑ̃]
ténèbre-*f*	darkness	[tenɛbʁ]
ténébreux-*adj*	gloomy	[tenebʁø]
tenir-*vb*	hold, keep	[təniʁ]
tentative-*f*	attempt, bid	[tɑ̃tativ]
tenter-*vb*	try, attempt	[tɑ̃te]
terme-*m*	term	[tɛʁm]
terminer-*vb*	finish, conclude	[tɛʁmine]
terrain-*m*	field, ground	[teʁɛ̃]
terre-*f*	earth, land	[tɛʁ]
terreur-*f*	terror	[teʁœʁ]
terrible-*adj*	terrible	[teʁibl]
terriblement-*adv*	terribly	[teʁibləmɑ̃]
terrier-*m*	terrier	[teʁje]
tête-*f*	head, top	[tɛt]
thé-*m*	tea	[te]
théière-*f*	teapot	[tejɛʁ]
tige-*f*	stem, spindle	[tiʒ]
timide-*adj*	shy	[timid]
timidement-*adv*	timidly	[timidmɑ̃]
tintement-*m*	ringing	[tɛ̃tmɑ̃]
tir-*m*	shot	[tiʁ]
tirer-*vb*	take, draw	[tiʁe]
tisonnier-*m*	poker	[tizɔnje]
toi-*prn*	you	[twa]
toile-*f*	web	[twal]
toilette-*f*	toilet	[twalɛt]
toit-*m*	roof	[twa]
tombe-*f*	grave, tomb	[tɔ̃b]
tomber-*vb*	fall, drop	[tɔ̃be]
ton-*adj; prn; m*	your; your; tone	[tɔ̃]
tonnerre-*m*	thunder	[tɔnɛʁ]
tordant-*adj*	hilarious	[tɔʁdɑ̃]
torrent-*m*	torrent	[tɔʁɑ̃]
tort-*m*	wrong, harm	[tɔʁ]
tortue-*f*	turtle	[tɔʁty]
tortueux-*adj*	tortuous	[tɔʁtɥø]
tôt-*adv*	early, soon	[to]
total-*adj; m*	total, overall; total	[tɔtal]
toucher-*m; vb*	touch; touch	[tuʃe]
touffu-*adj*	furry	[tufy]
toujours-*adv*	always, still	[tuʒuʁ]
tour-*m; f*	turn; tower	[tuʁ]
tourbillonner-*vb*	swirl	[tuʁbijɔne]
tourmenter-*vb*	torment, plague	[tuʁmɑ̃te]
tourner-*vb*	turn, rotate	[tuʁne]
tournure-*f*	twist, turning	[tuʁnyʁ]
tout-*adj; adv; m; prn*	all; all; all; all	[tu]
toutefois-*con; adv*	however; nevertheless	[tutfwa]
trace-*f*	trace, track	[tʁas]
tracer-*vb*	draw, mark	[tʁase]
train-*m*	train	[tʁɛ̃]
traînant-*adj*	shuffling	[tʁɛnɑ̃]
trait-*m*	trait	[tʁɛ]
traiter-*vb*	treat, deal	[tʁete]
trancher-*vb*	settle, slice	[tʁɑ̃ʃe]
tranquille-*adj*	quiet	[tʁɑ̃kil]
tranquillement-*adv*	quietly	[tʁɑ̃kilmɑ̃]
transformer-*vb*	transform, change	[tʁɑ̃sfɔʁme]
travers-*m*	across	[tʁavɛʁ]
traverser-*vb*	cross, pass through	[tʁavɛʁse]
trébuchant-*adj*	stumbling	[tʁebyʃɑ̃]
treize-*num*	thirteen	[tʁɛz]
tremblant-*adj; adv*	trembling; trembling	[tʁɑ̃blɑ̃]

trembler-*vb*	tremble, shake	[tʁɑ̃ble]
tremper-*vb*	soak, dip	[tʁɑ̃pe]
trépigner-*vb*	sitting there all	[tʁepiɲe]
très-*adv*	very	[tʁɛ]
tressaillir-*vb*	flinch	[tʁesajiʁ]
tribunal-*m*	court, courthouse	[tʁibynal]
tricher-*vb*	cheat	[tʁiʃe]
triomphant-*adj*	triumphant	[tʁijɔ̃fɑ̃]
triompher-*vb*	triumph	[tʁijɔ̃fe]
triste-*adj*	sad	[tʁist]
tristement-*adv*	sadly	[tʁistəmɑ̃]
tristesse-*f*	sadness	[tʁistɛs]
trois-*num*	three	[tʁwa]
troisième-*num*	third	[tʁwazjɛm]
tromper-*vb*	deceive, mislead	[tʁɔ̃pe]
trompeter-*vb*	trumpet	[tʁɔ̃pte]
trône-*m*	throne	[tʁon]
trop-*adv*	too, too much	[tʁo]
trotter-*vb*	trot	[tʁɔte]
trottiner-*vb*	scurrying	[tʁɔtine]
trou-*m*	hole	[tʁu]
trouble-*m; adj*	disorder, trouble; dim	[tʁubl]
troubler-*vb*	disturb, trouble	[tʁuble]
troupe-*f*	troop	[tʁup]
trouver-*vb*	find, get	[tʁuve]
truffer-*vb*	fill	[tʁyfe]
tuer-*vb*	kill, murder	[tɥe]
tuile-*f*	tile	[tɥil]
tulipe-*f*	tulip	[tylip]
tunnel-*m*	tunnel	[tynɛl]
turque-*adj; nf*	Turkish; Turk	[tyʁk]

U

un-*art; adj; num; prn*	a; one; one; one	[ɛ̃]
usage-*m*	use, usage	[yzaʒ]
usurpation-*f*	usurpation	[yzyʁpasjɔ̃]
utile-*adj*	useful	[ytil]

V

vagabond-*adj; m*	vagabond; vagabond	[vagabɔ̃]
vague-*f; adj*	wave; vague	[vag]
vain-*adj*	vain	[vɛ̃]
vainement-*adv*	in vain	[vɛnmɑ̃]
vaisselle-*f*	dishes	[vɛsɛl]
valet-*m*	valet	[valɛ]
valoir-*vb*	be worth	[valwaʁ]
vapeur-*m*	steam	[vapœʁ]
variant-*m*	variant	[vaʁjɑ̃]
vassal-*m*	vassal	[vasal]
vaste-*adj*	vast, wide	[vast]
végétal-*adj*	plant	[veʒetal]
veille-*f*	eve, day before	[vɛj]
veiller-*vb*	watch	[veje]
velours-*m*	velvet	[vəluʁ]
venir-*vb*	come	[vəniʁ]
vent-*m*	wind	[vɑ̃]
vente-*f*	sale	[vɑ̃t]
ver-*m*	worm	[vɛʁ]
véracité-*f*	veracity	[veʁasite]
verdure-*f*	greenery, greenness	[vɛʁdyʁ]
vérité-*f*	truth	[veʁite]
verre-*m*	glass	[vɛʁ]
vers-*prp; adv; m*	to, towards; about; verse	[vɛʁ]
versant-*m*	hillslope	[vɛʁsɑ̃]
vert-*adj; m*	green, young; putting green	[vɛʁ]
vexer-*vb*	vex, upset	[vɛkse]
vide-*adj; m*	empty; empty	[vid]
vie-*f*	life	[vi]
vieux-*adj; m*	old, ancient; old man	[vjø]
vif-*adj; m*	bright, lively; quick	[vif]
vil-*adj*	vile, base	[vil]
vilain-*adj; m*	ugly; villein	[vilɛ̃]
vin-*m*	wine	[vɛ̃]
vinaigrer-*vb*	souse	[vinegʁe]
vingt-*num*	twenty	[vɛ̃]
vingtième-*num*	twentieth	[vɛ̃tjɛm]
violemment-*adv*	violently	[vjɔlamɑ̃]
violent-*adj*	violent, severe	[vjɔlɑ̃]
visage-*m*	face	[vizaʒ]
visite-*f*	visit	[vizit]
vite-*adv*	quickly, fast	[vit]
vitre-*f*	window	[vitʁ]
vivant-*adj; m*	living, alive; living	[vivɑ̃]
vivement-*adv*	deeply	[vivmɑ̃]
vivre-*vb*	live	[vivʁ]
voici-*prp*	here is	[vwasi]
voilà-*adv*	here	[vwala]
voir-*vb*	see, view	[vwaʁ]
voisin-*m; adj*	neighbor; neighboring	[vwazɛ̃]
voix-*f*	voice	[vwa]

volaille-*f*	poultry, fowl	[vɔlaj]
voler-*vb*	fly, steal	[vɔle]
volontiers-*adv*	willingly	[vɔlɔ̃tje]
volte-face-*f*	turnabout	[vɔltəfas]
voltigeant-*adj*	flitting	[vɔltiʒɑ̃]
voyant-*m; adj*	seer; clairvoyant	[vwajɑ̃]
vrai-*adj; m*	true, real; right	[vʁɛ]
vraiment-*adv*	really, actually	[vʁɛmɑ̃]
vraisemblable-*adj*	similar	[vʁɛsɑ̃blabl]
vue-*m*	view	[vy]

Z

zigzag-*m*	zigzag	[zigzag]

votre-*adj; prn*	your; your	[vɔtʁ]
vôtre-*prn*	yours	[votʁ]
vouloir-*vb*	want, wish	[vulwaʁ]
vous-*prn*	you (form, pl)	[vu]

Contact, Further Reading & Resources

For more tools, tips & tricks visit our site www.mostusedwords.com. We publish various language learning resources.

We hope that you will find this bilingual book a truly handy tool. If you like it, please let others know about it, so they can enjoy it too. Or leave a review/comment online, e.g. on social media, blogs or on forums.

Frequency Dictionaries

The most common 2.500 words in any language account for roughly 90% of all spoken language and 80% of all written texts.

We listed all these essential words and more for you in our Frequency Dictionaries. The books range from the most common 2.500 words to the most common 10.000 words.

In addition, we give you word usage through dual language example sentences and phonetic spelling of foreign words by help of the International Phonetic Alphabet (IPA).

We are always working hard to add more languages to our selection. Currently we have frequency dictionaries available for the following languages: French, Italian, Swedish, Spanish, German, Dutch, Romanian, Finnish, Russian, Portuguese and more. Please visit https://store.mostusedwords.com/frequency-dictionaries for more information

Bilingual books

We're creating a selection of dual language books. Our selection is ever expanding.

Current bilingual books available are in English, Spanish, Portuguese, Italian, French, and German.

For more information, check https://store.mostusedwords.com/bilingual-books. Check back regularly for new books and languages.

Other language learning methods

You'll find reviews of other 3rd party language learning applications, software, audio courses, and apps. There are so many available, and some are (much) better than others.

Check out our reviews at www.mostusedwords.com/reviews.

Contact

If you have any questions, you can contact us through e-mail info@mostusedwords.com.

Made in the USA
Las Vegas, NV
08 May 2023

71776723R00077